What Reviewers Say Abo

"Fast-paced action scenes, intriguing character revelations, and a refreshing approach to the romance thriller genre all make for an enjoyable reading experience in the Big Easy…an engrossing reading experience, a noticeably more literate effort than the first in the Casey Clan series. It is always satisfying to see an author grow as Vali has displayed in this novel. The structural details in the plot, the adept handling of action and suspense, and the more delineated major characters produce a coherent and stylish technique. *The Devil Unleashed* is definitely a novel not to be missed." – *Midwest Book Review*

"*The Devil Inside* by Ali Vali is an unusual, unpredictable, and thought-provoking love story that will have the reader questioning the definition of right and wrong long after she finishes the book…unlike most romance novels. Nothing about the story and its characters is conventional." – *Just About Write*

"*The Devil Inside* is that rarity: a fascinating crime novel which includes a tender love story and leaves the reader with a cliffhanger ending. Look for this excellent read at your favorite gay and lesbian bookstore." – *MegaScene*

"Vali's fluid writing style quickly puts the reader at ease, which makes the story and its characters equally easy to get to know and care about. When you find yourself talking out loud to the characters in a book, you know the work is polished and professional, as well as entertaining." – *Family & Friends Magazine*

"Not only is *The Devil Inside* a ripping mystery, it's also an intimate character study, especially in terms of Cain Casey. As ruthless as she is, Cain is also fiercely loyal and will go to great lengths to protect what she holds dear. The overall plot moves along at just the right pace; nothing feels rushed and nothing lags." – *L-word.com Literature*

"It's no surprise that passion is indeed possible a second time around…" – *Q Syndicate*

"Set in the drama of Hurricanes Katrina and Rita, *Second Season*…is a rich, enjoyable read that's not to be missed." – *Just About Write*

Visit us at www.boldstrokesbooks.com

DEAL
WITH THE
DEVIL

by

Ali Vali

2008

DEAL WITH THE DEVIL
© 2008 By Ali Vali. All Rights Reserved.

ISBN10: 1-60282-012-0
ISBN13: 978-1-60282-012-8

This Trade Paperback Is Published By
Bold Strokes Books, Inc.
New York, USA

First Edition, April, 2008

Credits
Editors: Shelley Thrasher and J. B. Greystone
Production Design: J. B. Greystone
Cover Graphic: Sheri (graphicartist2020@hotmail.com)

By the Author

The Devil Inside

Carly's Sound

The Devil Unleashed

Second Season

Acknowledgments

I've said before that no book comes together alone, so there are many people to thank for this one.

The first thank you goes to Radclyffe for your continuous belief in my writing, and for your encouragement to bring Deal to life. Thank you also for your vision and your tireless efforts to make it grow and prosper. Bold Strokes Books is a team I'm proud to be a part of.

Shelley Thrasher has been my editor from the first page of the very first book, and that has been one of the best things to happen to me as a writer. There is no better teacher, gentle critic, friend, and editor. Thank you Shelley for your invaluable help and for your patience as we make our way through these stories.

Thank you to my copyeditor Julia Greystone for making it so easy to cross the finish line on this one. It was a pleasure working with you. And thanks to Sheri who always puts the final touch on every book with an incredible cover.

To my gold team of beta readers Connie Ward, Kathi Isserman, Lenore and Beth, I can't say thank you enough. You guys are the first people to see the stories in their infancy and you do a fabulous job of keeping me on track. I thank you for your time, effort, and dedication.

A big thank you to the readers. Without your acceptance of Cain, Emma, and the gang, they would be retired by now. It was your encouragement and your thirst for more that has been essential to their continued story.

And lastly, thank you to my partner. You believe in me enough to put up with me when I'm trying to find the next sentence when I'm stuck, take care of me when I'm hurting, and love me enough to do all of it with a beautiful smile. You've taught me all I know about romance, friendship, fun, and what it is to love and be loved in return. Each day with you is a gift.

DEDICATION

For C
A lifetime is not enough

CHAPTER ONE

St. Louis Cathedral in New Orleans, Louisiana

F orgive me, Father, for I have sinned." Derby Cain Casey knelt in a confessional in St. Louis Cathedral. She was the last one for the early morning session and smiled as she uttered the lines her mother had patiently taught her. So much had happened to her, those lessons seemed like they had occurred in another lifetime.

She'd lost Emma, her partner, to a misunderstanding. But after a four-year separation she had not only gotten her back, but gained a daughter. This time around, they had understood each other completely when she had methodically killed every single male member of the Bracato family as revenge for the deaths of her parents, brother Billy, and sister Marie. Emma was no longer blind to who Cain was and what the family business was. This time around she'd gladly made a deal with the devil in exchange for a life with Cain and their children, Hayden and Hannah.

Even in the shadows of the confessional Cain could see her old friend Bishop Andrew Goodman press his fingers to his chin.

"Do you know it's a sin to say things you don't mean to a priest?"

"It's a sin to ask for forgiveness?"

"Not at all. It's just the sins yet to come that make me worry about you, especially if I believe everything I read in the papers." He was referring to the series of articles about what had happened to Giovanni Bracato and his four sons. With no bodies for evidence, the police could only speculate.

"I'd argue with you, but what'd be the point?" Cain laughed when she saw him smile. "Since there's a good chance I'm going to sin again, how about you let me up and we'll go for a walk. We'll save my laundry list of wrongdoings for next time."

She genuflected more out of habit than deep faith before they left the confines of the safe zone the listeners in her life had ignored.

In the vestibule, Andrew went through the ritual of getting down to his unpretentious black pants and shirt and white collar. Though he'd been the bishop of St. Louis for over a decade, people who didn't know him still mistook him for just a parish priest. Andrew had grown up without the trappings of wealth, making his vows easy to abide by.

From the day Cain had accepted his invitation to come by for a talk, they had met regularly. While they would never be friends like Andrew and Cain's father Dalton had been, they were growing closer. Not having to hide any part of herself in Andrew's office and in his company comforted Cain. That rare luxury had made her look forward to their talks, especially today.

"If you aren't sinning then what have you been up to?"

Andrew dropped into his favorite chair. His hair had turned white and had thinned some, but he still moved like a man in his twenties.

"I've actually been building bridges." Cain accepted the cup of tea he offered her.

"That was one of your father's strongest traits. 'Never give up what you believe, Andy, but it's good to have friends when it counts,'" he said, trying to imitate Dalton's deep, booming voice. "He'd tell me that all the time."

"Da was right about that. Sometimes we seek alliances to help build our business, and sometimes to achieve our goals."

"And others are for survival," Andrew finished for her. "At the foot of what bridge do you find yourself, Derby?"

Cain liked Andrew to call her by her first name. He was the only one left who even remembered it, and it made her feel connected to the past and to her family.

"I'm beginning to think I'm a dinosaur in the modern world." She laughed because, even if she did do things the old-fashioned way, she didn't care. "Vices are a little different these days."

"Sometimes evolution isn't all it's cracked up to be."

Cain nodded once in agreement. "But if I don't evolve, I'll become obsolete, like the horse and buggy."

"But if you were Amish, you wouldn't need anything but a horse and buggy. You can expand into things that will make you untouchable, but my job is to save your soul."

"Conquest doesn't inspire my soul, you know that, but, for the safety of my family, it's time to expand. With Ramon and his family I can achieve that goal without having to sacrifice who I am."

Andrew put his cup down and bit into a peanut butter cookie his assistant had brought in. "So you do plan to sin again."

"I plan to try a couple of new things, and if there's sin involved I promise not to venture too much farther off the path than I have already."

They both laughed at her version of confession.

"Why Ramon and not Vincent? Vincent is who your father picked."

"My family is different than the family I grew up in. Da set an example that I like to think I'm living up to. Ramon is a better fit for what I want to leave Hayden and Hannah."

"That goal's appropriate for today. It's good to celebrate his life by marking the day of his death. But to live the honorable life he taught you truly validates what Dalton stood for." Andrew stood and waved her up. "Let's go for that walk you promised me."

Outside, Lou and two more men waited by Cain's car, and he lifted his hand in greeting when he spotted Andrew. They headed uptown, and Cain glanced back once and laughed when she saw the new paneled van with the black-tinted windows two cars behind them.

"Your friends are being rather conspicuous these days. Isn't that stressful?"

Cain ran her hand along her upper thigh before bringing it to her lips as a request for Andrew to stop talking. He was right, but with the stepped-up surveillance after she and Emma had returned from Wisconsin with their children, every conversation out in the open could potentially be used against her, no matter how many countermeasures she put in place. The suspicion that someone had destroyed Giovanni and his sons had swarmed the feds like someone stomping on a mound of fire ants.

The car stopped across the street from the famous Commander's Palace restaurant, and Lou jumped from the front seat to grab the door for them. For years the Brennan family had served culinary masterpieces on one side of the street, while on the other a ten-foot brick fence stood sentry around the Lafitte Cemetery where the Casey family had been laid to rest.

"It's been years but I still miss the sound of Dalton's voice," Andrew said. "Are you bringing the family out today?"

"Later on, when Hayden gets out of school. He never knew my father, but he likes bringing flowers for Marie." Cain unlocked the door of the crypt and stepped in. Slowly she ran her hand along Dalton's name on his grave marker. The date was in early March exactly fourteen years ago, but the pain of losing him was etched into her soul as it was in the stone.

"Derby, you have to let go of your guilt."

"We all have our crosses to bear, don't we, Father? This is mine, and I've done some things to ease the hurt of loss. But I'm afraid the guilt is eternal. There really isn't any rest for the wicked."

"Do you think that's what Dalton would've wanted for you? To live half a life by holding back from your partner and your children?"

"I've learned my lessons about holding back, don't worry. My family is the most important thing in my life, but I haven't forgotten the family I've lost."

She pressed her hand harder into the stone and he stood back. "You still blame yourself for all the names in here, don't you?"

"Why wouldn't I? Giovanni isn't that good," she said, carefully emphasizing the present tense. Little slipups like that could sink her.

"Do you think you were just negligent?"

"My father was a surprise, but the others…" She moved her fingers over her mother's name, then her brother's, and made a fist when she got to Marie's. "They were my responsibility. My father expected me to keep them safe." It had taken some time, but Cain had enlarged the crypt to make room for Marie's body, and even though she still hurt from her loss, that she was back among those who loved her most in life brought Cain comfort. And it'd been easier for Hayden this time around with Emma and Hannah there as they interred Marie again.

Andrew moved closer and placed one of his hands over her head. "May the Lord bring you peace then, because now they are His responsibility. Take care of your family, Derby, and the rest will take care of itself. Your father was like a brother to me, and I'd bet my eternal soul he doesn't blame you for any of it. The one to blame isn't of consequence anymore, so pay attention to the people who love you. I'm sure you'll keep them whole."

"Thank you." From her breast pocket she pulled a flask full of Dalton's favorite whiskey. She passed it to Andrew first, took a sip after him, then poured the rest over Dalton's grave stone. "To you, Da. Rest, knowing that I'm almost done."

"God bless you then," Andrew said as he moved his hand to her back.

"Be careful with your blessings, Father Andy. I've warned you before of my intentions to sin again."

"I'm also smart enough to know my flock, and like God, I have infinite patience to wait for you to find your way. The Lord loves even black sheep, Derby."

"The devil has a liking for us as well," she said as the prepaid cell phone in her pocket chirped.

It signaled an incoming text message of only one word that normally could hold a multitude of meaning, but for Cain it meant the Bracatos were that much closer to being a memory only a few would bother with. The word "DONE" meant another batch of Giovanni's henchmen on the street had shared his fate.

Some of Giovanni's foremen had tried to start their own businesses after his disappearance and had moved in on some of the storeowners Cain did business with. Cain had been willing to ignore them, but a couple of the storeowners had been attacked and one had been killed for their non-cooperation with the new entrepreneurs.

Once they'd gone after the people who depended on her for protection, she'd started taking the trash off the streets. All the kills weren't hers, but after she'd retaliated, no one had invaded her territory. With that situation resolved, she could plan something that would give the feds a show they wouldn't soon forget.

"I'm sure my wife and my beloved mother hope you're right when it comes to heaven and black sheep." She put the cell back in her pocket and pointed to the gate. "But for now you'll have to keep praying for the sinner I am."

CHAPTER TWO

Key West, Florida

The dragon soared to the top of the hill again, sending a stream of fire down on the dark knight's shield and igniting the wheat fields around him to a roaring blaze. The head encased within the armor was drenched in sweat, making the beast harder to see, but he wasn't ready to surrender and take cover. With sword upraised he spied his opening to vanquish the evil serpent when—

Beep. Beep. Beep.

Remington Jatibon reached out and quieted the Blackberry sitting on the cooler, then read the message on the screen.

Time to go, great knight. Your kingdom awaits and there are dragons to slay.

"Damn, and I just got to the part where they actually used the word 'vanquish.'"

The curse shattered the peaceful atmosphere created by the waves gently lapping on the shoreline. Remi punched in a phone number, and reality invaded her haven under the umbrella. "How far out are you, Simon? Your timing absolutely sucks, by the way."

Simon Jimenez, the Cuban-born middle-aged woman who served as Remi's main bodyguard, spoke. "The day you tell me one of the flying lizards actually wins, I'll leave you alone. We're five minutes out, so start walking to the landing pad. Juno's waiting at the airport in Key West with your itinerary for the next couple of days, and it's not looking pretty."

From her seat on the private island, Remi trained her eyes to the east, trying to spot the approaching helicopter. The island, just a patch of sand and some palm trees a few miles south of Key West, was one of her favorite spots.

Instead of getting ready, Remi sat back in the chair, pulled another beer from the cooler, and gazed out over the blue-green water. She wanted a final respite before the itinerary her assistant Juno had put together kicked in.

"I thought I told you to start walking?" Simon asked fifteen minutes later.

"And I thought you worked for me, Simon?"

"That would explain your signature on my paycheck. Just remember to tell Juno who delayed us, because I'm not taking the blame again. Why can't you go to Palm Springs like everybody else? The travel arrangements would be easier," Simon stepped close to Remi's chair, holding her hand up to shield her face from the sun.

"If I was like everybody else, your life would be infinitely boring. Besides, we aren't late. The reception isn't until tonight, so relax and have a beer."

"Your brother called and wants to review the casino contract again before the meeting. He called Cain, your father, and even Muriel Casey for a sit-down this afternoon."

"Once this thing is done I'll treat you to a bottle of champagne." Remi took a sip of beer and slowly faced her. "Come on, old girl, let's see what else hell can dredge up for us today."

Simon's smile faltered and she pointed at Remi. "Watch it. Don't tempt the fates."

"It's what I live for, Simon. It's what I live for."

New Orleans, Louisiana

"Are you sure?"

"Today, baby," Emma said after she drank a little of her juice. Her usual cup of coffee was absent.

Emma and Cain had been back in New Orleans for two months, living with Jarvis and Muriel Casey again while the contractor finished repairing their house. As Cain had promised, their life had returned to normal after they'd returned from Wisconsin, or as normal as life with Cain ever got.

The one thing hard to miss was the FBI surveillance that had been stepped up from the moment Cain had hit their radar again. The invasion of privacy aggravated Emma, but the authorities were still wondering what had happened to the Bracato family, so Cain had warned her in advance what to expect.

"Today?" Cain asked again as she pushed away from the table.

"If you've got something else planned, then I suggest you reschedule." Emma leaned back in her chair and tried to sound menacing. When Cain chuckled she realized she'd failed.

"Would you think less of me if I told you I'm scared?"

Emma laughed along with her. "I'm sure you're quaking in your shorts."

"Are you questioning your ability to make me quake in my shorts, lass?" Cain put her hand on her chest and widened her eyes.

"I just don't want to waste the opportunity, love."

Before Emma finished her statement, Cain had risen from her seat and dropped to her knees next to her. "You can't think I'm not going with you. I've been waiting for this day from the second we talked about it. I love you and I'm ready."

"I was just teasing you, honey. If anything, I'm enjoying my final days of you letting me lift my own glass." Emma put her hands on Cain's cheeks, then kissed her. "So are you free at ten?"

"Since my buddy, Dr. Casey, gave me a call and told me not to be late, I'll be there."

"Want to go upstairs and do everything we can to relax before our appointment?" Emma kissed her again. "Mook just left with the kids."

"Then come with me, Mrs. Casey." Cain stood and offered her hands. "Relaxation is my specialty."

"Cain?" Katlin Patrick, Cain's cousin and guard, stopped at the door of the dining room. "Sorry to interrupt."

"What's up?"

"Ramon called to remind you about today's meeting."

Cain glanced down at Emma before turning to Katlin. "Call him back and tell him today is out. Muriel can handle our end of things."

Emma rested a hand on Cain's chest and exercised her new partnership with Cain. "Katlin, please tell him if the meeting is after one this afternoon, Cain will be happy to be there." She patted Cain's chest when she felt her take a breath to start speaking. "We'll be done by then, and I'll be happy to nap while you're out."

"Call him then, and don't bother us unless the house is on fire."

"True, honey, you have other fires to start," Emma said as she slipped her hand into the front of Cain's pants to lead her upstairs.

CHAPTER THREE

Key West, Florida

"Dallas, why pick this fucking place? This dump is like a furnace." The sweaty, red-faced Bob Bennett ranted while he walked through the Key West airport. He kept a firm grip on Dallas Montgomery, who was trailing him. "At least the plane should be here soon, and we can get the hell out of here."

"No one asked you to come. It was my vacation, remember?" Dallas said. "Besides," she jerked out of his grasp, "I thought you said it was a studio plane. It's not like you can miss that." She tried to reason with Bob because once the irritating man got going, her life became that much more difficult.

"How about you shut the hell up. You've been nothing but a screw-up all your life, and it's time you start asking me before you plan these little excursions. You better resign yourself to the realities of your life because, believe me, whatever you're doing, it's going to be with me."

Dallas stayed quiet but mentally added another entry to her list of "ways to kill Bob"—*5614—setting him afloat one hundred miles offshore with nothing but a bloody rump roast around his neck.*

He was right, though. He wasn't going anywhere, and instead of enjoying her budding career, she had to deal with the leech who could take it all away. He knew a lifetime of secrets that could break her in ways she wasn't willing to think about.

In the air above the landing strip, the Jatibons' private jet was receiving its clearance to set down when Doug Price, the pilot, saw the helicopter cruising in from the east. "Might be the boss, so prepare for a quick turn-around," he told his copilot and navigator. They had flown the Jatibon family for years, shuttling the family around for business and pleasure, and had over the years become trusted employees. Their greatest asset was their short-term memory. Once the flight was over, no matter who they were escorting, they forgot the name and face as soon as the wheels hit the tarmac. No one could talk or testify about something he had no memory of.

The wheels of the jet touched down and the crew taxied away from the commercial side of the airport toward the section with a multitude of private planes sitting idle. Once the two men had shut down everything, they stepped from the cockpit to let Rosa, the attractive attendant, know they should be on the ground no longer than an hour.

They headed out into the ninety-degree heat in their pressed chino shorts and white polo shirts with the Jatibon name and snake-eyes logo stitched on the breast pockets. The same image of the hooded and slitted eyes of the king cobra was painted on the tail of the plane.

They were there to pick up not only Remi, but her two business partners, Dwayne and Steve, and their wives, Molly and Lisa. Remi's father, Ramon, affectionately referred to them and Remi as "the crew." The guys had attended school with her, and when it was time to conquer the world, Dwayne and Steve had signed on willingly with the ambitious Jatibon family. They had two kids each, with Remi the only holdout. She was still single, but the group meshed as well now as when they were prowling the campus at Louisiana State University, then later in law school.

Remi had met Dwayne in their freshman year at LSU and built an instant rapport with him. Steve joined the tight-knit group in their junior year after befriending Remi. Wanting to keep them together, Remi asked Ramon to invest in their future.

He had paid for all of them to attend law school, and the three graduated at the top of their class. They were by far the best negotiators Ramon had seen in corporate America. And after Remi took over the firm that protected Ramon's company from the sharks constantly circling the waters he chose to swim in, she had won every litigation.

"Steve, is that Rosa?" Lisa, his pretty brunette wife sitting on his lap in the overcrowded terminal, asked.

"Yep, that's her, which means our ride's here. Let me get up and start loading all this stuff. Remi should be back soon, and our schedule just got tighter."

In a few minutes, Steve and Dwayne were joking their way over to the plane, fighting to see who was going to sit next to Rosa, when they noticed the commotion at the bottom of the steps.

Doug was standing by the plane, blocking the entrance and trying to prevent the irate man who was confronting him from boarding.

"Troubles?" Steve asked. Not that he was the spokesman for the group, but at six-feet-five inches, two hundred and eighty-five pounds, he was by far the most intimidating in the bunch. The only thing taking away from his tough-guy image was the hat shaped like a parrot he was sporting. Even with that, he cast a shadow over the two men arguing by the door.

"I was trying to explain to this guy that this is the Jatibon jet, not his charter flight home from Gemini Studio."

Steve listened, then held out his right hand to the fuming man. "I'm Steve Palma, and you would be?"

"Bob Bennett," he said, and ignored the offered hand. "My girlfriend and I were waiting for this plane, so step aside, asshole, and I won't have to get you fired." Bob glared at Steve and his companions. The sound of the landing helicopter drowned out any further comments.

After they were on the ground, Simon stepped down as soon as the blades slowed. She motioned for Remi to stay put.

"While you're busy guarding me, I'm going to run in and get something for my mother," Remi told her.

Simon looked over at the standoff by the jet to see if a walkover was necessary. But when Steve made eye contact with her and waved her off, Remi stepped down from the helicopter.

Simon removed the Glock she kept in a shoulder holster and checked the clip. "If you can help it, try to stay out of trouble. And see if you can find Juno and the other girls. We've got to get going."

"Try not to shoot anyone, Simon. Just think of the paperwork involved, not to mention ruining Steve's great hat if there's any spray."

Getting to the main building, Remi headed toward the only gift shop in the Key West Airport. After she spotted a wall full of gorillas carved out of coconuts, she was removing the tackiest one from the rack when she heard the screaming.

Stepping out of the store, Remi looked at Simon, who was in the middle of the melee, because of the guy who was at the moment pitted against Steve, Dwayne, and Doug. Standing next to the screamer, though, was Dallas Montgomery, costar of the latest Gemini Studio's action adventure movie, *The Lady-Killers*.

"Bob, cool it before we become front-page news for the tabloids," Dallas said as Remi neared. "If you don't stop, that's what's going to happen, and I can't afford the publicity right now."

Remi ignored the angry tableau for the moment and extended her hand. "Ms. Montgomery, what a pleasant surprise. I'm pleased to meet you. I'm—"

Bob pushed between them. "Back off, dyke. My girlfriend may be the wet-dream fantasy of a lifetime, but she ain't gay. She just plays a lesbian on the big screen, or so people like you want to think," Bob said, glaring at Remi. The group behind Bob stiffened.

In her thirty-four years Remi had grown accustomed to the bigotry of others but not to stupidity, and this guy was no doubt an idiot of biblical proportions. At an even six feet, Remi had to look down at him, finding pleasure when he took a step back as she clenched her fists. A lifetime of training and pushing herself to the limit had given her the confidence to know she could do some serious damage to his looks without any help. The thought had never seemed so appealing.

"We can—" Doug stopped when Remi raised her hand.

"What's the problem?" Remi asked, never taking her eyes off Bob.

"Mr. Bennett thinks we're his ride this morning. I tried explaining that he was wrong, and he threatened to report me to my superior."

"That does sound like something that would end up in your personnel file," she said as she curled her lips into more of a snarl than a smile. "Why would you assume the plane is yours?" Remi asked Bob.

"You're telling me you're not with the studio?" Bob shot back. "If you're new at this, don't start your job fucking with someone like me as your first move."

"Sage advice indeed," Remi said, then turned to Doug. "Why not avoid the chance of us both getting written up and give him what he wants? I'm sure your superior won't mind, don't you agree?" Remi pinned everyone in her group with a look that almost dared anyone to speak.

"You bet. We should be ready in about fifteen minutes."

Bob first looked at Remi, then at Doug, holding his hands out as if waiting for someone to start explaining. When no one said anything, he asked, "Who are you, anyway?"

Remi decided to liven up the upcoming flight to New Orleans by having a little fun. "That isn't of importance now, Mr. Bennett. Is everyone ready to go?"

As Remi headed out of the terminal, Dallas fell in step with her, almost skipping to keep up with the much longer strides. "I want to apologize for Bob's comments, Ms?"

"Did you ask him to act that way?"

"Ah, no."

"Then you have nothing to apologize for, ma'am," Remi said, feeling more relaxed now. "As I tried to say before I was interrupted, I enjoyed your last picture with Jenny Tibbs. I seldom see such strong female characters in action films. You gave a great performance."

"It was a great role."

"You made it a great role. In most action films, the women are there to fill out the bikinis, not really act. That's not to say that you didn't look good in the bikini scene. Keep up the good work." Remi kept smiling down at Dallas, enjoying the blush creeping up her neck.

"Thank you," Dallas replied softly.

Once the group was outside, Remi walked ahead and got onto the plane. She stepped into the cockpit and watched for a moment as the pilots finished their preparations. Doug smiled. "What can I do for you, boss?"

"Please, call me the big dyke. It's all the rage." She smiled through the exchange, wanting them to know it would take much more on Bob's part to rattle her cage. "Could you call New Orleans and arrange for a car for our guests. I'd offer, but I have a meeting at Papi's as soon as we land."

"Belt up, everyone. We're ready for takeoff," Remi said, returning to the plush office on the plane.

"Aren't you going to go over the safety features and exit locations, good-looking?" Steve asked.

"If an air mask drops in front of you anytime during this flight, Lisa has my permission to strangle you with it. Now come on, let's get to work."

Remi sat at the table with her partners and handed out parts of the contract Mano had sent down with the staff. "Well, boys, vacation's over. Are we ready to go on Monday?"

"Yes, now that our hand's on the light switch, the cockroaches are starting to get nervous. Did you know the mob is taking over at Gemini?" Dwayne asked.

"Really, now, boys, it's not just the mob. It's Papi's version of the mob." The three laughed.

Ramon had always been a powerful force, but all three of them sitting at the table loved and admired him. They freely gave him their loyalty, and not because of what they owed him.

Remi exchanged her sunglasses for reading glasses, preparing to dissect the contract, but her thoughts turned to her family's history and what it had taken to get where they were today.

❖

The Jatibon family had always had money until Castro had come down from the Sierra Madres and destroyed generations of work and wealth in one short week. Arriving in the United States with nothing but the clothes on his back, his wife Marianna, and six-year-old twins Remi and Mano, Ramon set out to rebuild his empire for his children.

He settled in New Orleans and quickly learned that the city loved vices. The top three on the list were gambling, drinking, and women, but not always in that order.

With the backing and friendship of Dalton Casey and Vincent Carlotti, Ramon started with a small club, offering all three to upper-crust patrons who quickly helped to fund expansion. The Pescador clubs, named for his family's plantation home in Cuba, offered complimentary Cuban rum and Russian vodka, which were impossible to get at the time because of the embargo. A patron could gamble with a fine Cuban cigar in one hand and a beautiful woman on his arm, comfortable that the police wouldn't interrupt his fun. Dalton's connections made sure of that.

For a price, the women would do anything a customer desired for the evening, but Ramon didn't make his living off the ladies. He gave them a place to work and made the real money on the gaming tables, not from the lay afterward. The girls soothed the pain of losing, guaranteeing the gentlemen, and women, would be back.

Ramon's business thrived, and he now had clubs in New Orleans and along the Gulf Coast into Texas. With guidance from his children he had diversified over the years and now owned a multitude of legitimate businesses, including fifty-one percent of Gemini Studio.

He had brought his children into the business early, educating them as to where the luxuries in their lives came from. It brought him great pleasure when people told him how much like him they were, and not just in their looks. Both tall with midnight black curly hair, olive skin, broad shoulders, and chiseled features, Remi and Mano were too good-looking for their own good at times. But their father pushed them relentlessly, not wanting them to lose the fire that had built the Jatibon empire.

Their mother, Marianna, had taught them manners and style. Ramon had taught them leadership, strength, and killer instincts. Both Remi and Mano had inherited one green eye from Marianna and one blue from Ramon, though they were opposite. So when Mano stood at Remi's right, the two middle eyes were the ice blue of Ramon's.

While Ramon loved his children equally, his daughter was most like him. His son Ramon was very like his mother in most things. Remi, though, would rip an enemy's heart out and let him watch it stop beating in her hand. Ramon knew that Remi would expand and surpass what he'd built, and she would never leave her family behind. His first-born, though by only twenty-five minutes, Remi carried the responsibility of not only the family business but also insuring that her brother Ramon and his family never came to harm.

Ramon also realized that while Remi would probably never give him grandchildren, she would break even his record in bedding women. He had some difficulty with her lifestyle, considering his Catholic upbringing, but he had decided it was just one more thing that made his daughter unique.

On the streets and in the world Ramon controlled, his children were known as Snake Eyes. When the two showed up first without warning, as in the game of craps, their opponent knew lady luck had taken a holiday. To the feds that constantly hounded Ramon, Snake Eyes was a myth to scare the weak, but to him they were the heads of his businesses and made them thrive. They fought good-naturedly with one another, but needed each other for balance.

They ran different sections of the family business but shared the major decisions with him. Only Ramon was privy to some jobs they had done, and he would carry his knowledge of them to his grave. He was sure that both his children commanded respect, not only because of their last name, but because of their hard work.

❖

Remi let her reading glasses slide down her nose and stared out the window. Thinking of her parents always made her smile because each visit began with the same conversation. Her mother wanted to know if she had met a nice girl to settle down with, and her father told her to live the carefree life as long as she could.

Ramon Jr., or Mano, as everyone knew him, had acquiesced and given their mother what she had always wanted —grandchildren. Two more Jatibons with black curly hair running around Marianna's house bringing children's laughter back into the big place.

The buzzing in the office brought Remi out of her musings, and she rose to answer Doug's call. "Just wanted to let you know your brother took care of everything, including accommodations, if they're going to the reception tonight."

"Thanks, I'll pass the information along."

Walking toward the large living area of the jet, Remi noticed the girls were pumping Dallas for gossip. "I hate to break up this obviously important meeting, but I wanted to inform you, Ms. Montgomery, the studio will have a car waiting and hotel arrangements have been made," Remi said, looking only at Dallas.

"It's about time you made it back here." Bob said. "Do all Jatibon employees slack this much?"

"I'm sorry, did you need something, Dick?" Remi responded with an even tone.

"The name is Mr. Bennett, and yes, a beer would be great."

"Coming right up, Dick. I'll see what's available on board." Remi loitered nearby for a minute so she could overhear Bob and Dallas's conversation.

"Bob," Dallas said in a heated whisper.

"Relax. You have to show these types of people that they need to take their interests elsewhere."

Dallas smiled to the others as if in apology for Bob's behavior, then her eyes turned to Remi.

Remi headed into the galley before she gave in to the overwhelming feeling of wanting to strangle Bob. She came back quickly with a bottle of beer in one hand and a pitcher of Mojitos in the other.

"Here you go, Dick. In my bartending days I took great pride in my ability to match a beer to a person's personality, so drink up." Remi handed him the bottle, then started refilling the ladies' drinks.

"Again, shit for brains, the name's Bennett, not Dick. And what in the hell does a Dos XX have to do with my personality?" Bob held up the bottle she'd handed him.

"Well, the way I look at it, you're just a strike three waiting to happen." Molly and Lisa started laughing. "Enjoy your drinks. We should be landing in about forty-five minutes."

Remi left the pitcher and walked toward the private room at the rear of the plane to change.

"Bob Bennett, you fucking idiot, and fuck you!" Bob screamed to the retreating back.

He turned his attention to Molly and Lisa, who were still laughing. Using his best smile, he decided to do a bit of fishing, since Dallas was in contract negotiations for her sequel and any information on the new management couldn't hurt.

"Do you ladies know Remington Jatibon?" he asked in as smooth a voice as he could conjure up.

Lisa looked at Molly and smiled before opening her mouth. "Why yes, we do. What would you like to know?"

Bob thought again just how stupid women could be. At times they made it too easy. "What's he like?"

The two friends asked in unison, "*He*?"

"Is that a hard question or would you like for me to go a little slower? There isn't a lot of information out there about him, just a lot of gossip around the studio, but no pictures to back up the talk."

"Depends on who you ask," Lisa muttered. "There are so many facets to Remi it's hard to know where to begin."

Bob looked at them, wondering if they'd downed one drink too many.

"Well, what are his plans for the studio?" Bob started with what he assumed was an easy question.

Molly spoke up next. "Remi plans to turn the studio into a more lucrative venture by putting out a better product. For the past four years only about half of the films have made a substantial profit, while cost overruns bleed the winners like Dallas and Jenny's picture. Then I imagine it'll be back to the family business. That's where Remi's true heart lies."

"Is he the lady's man everyone says he is, or is he a legend in his own mind?" As he waited for the answer, Bob considered which outfit Dallas should wear that evening. The laughing women brought him back to the conversation, making him think again they were intoxicated.

Wiping tears from her eyes Lisa turned to Molly and asked, "If I gave him a hundred bucks, could he buy a clue?"

Dallas leaned forward, obviously wanting to hear the answer to his question.

"Remi has a unique way with the ladies. They find the looks combined with the devastating smile, style, charm, and lots and lots of money hard to resist. The money's only secondary, though, because Remi's a good listener who'll move mountains just to see someone smile." Molly finished, with Lisa nodding in agreement.

"Does that happen often?" Dallas joined the discussion for the first time.

"No, sweetie." Lisa smiled at her. "The woman who captures that heart is in for a lifetime of bliss. Remi has a huge capacity for love. We see it all the time. It's just that the right one hasn't come along yet."

"What are Remi's hobbies?" Dallas asked, and Bob snorted over the stupid question.

Molly glared at him, then answered. "Everyone would say work and winning, just because they don't know the real Remi. But the Remi we know loves to read adventure stories. You know, the ones with a damsel in distress, a dragon flying around somewhere wreaking havoc, and a knight who saves the day. The only requirement is that the word 'vanquish' appear somewhere in the text." Molly paused.

Lisa took up where Molly had left off. "Remi loves to work, don't get us wrong, but when the clock strikes quitting time, you've never spent time with a more fun-loving person. And we all know there's a romantic hidden in that big heart somewhere. It'll just take the right girl to bring it out. We know this because the idiots we're married to get all their romantic hints from Remi." Lisa patted Dallas's hand.

"Sounds like someone who'll be easy to work for," Dallas said.

"Please return your seats to the upright position and down your drinks, people. We're almost there," Remi said in her low voice, walking back into the room to sit by Steve and Dwayne.

"It's true Remi's easy to work for, and I'm sure you'll find out soon enough," Lisa said, smiling at Dallas.

The suit Remi now wore fit her tall, muscular body perfectly, accentuating the tanned skin, and the black cowboy boots added over an inch to her height, making even Bob take another look.

CHAPTER FOUR

New Orleans, Louisiana

"Good God, Casey, you look like shit," Cain told Dr. Sam Casey when she stepped into the exam room.

"Wait until you're only getting an hour of sleep a night. Then we'll see how great you look."

"Don't listen to this comedian." Emma squeezed Cain's fingers as a sign for her to behave. "I'm sorry we weren't here for the blessed event, but we wanted to pass along our congratulations." She handed Sam a gift for the birth of Sam and Ellie Eschete's baby. "How are Ellie and the baby doing?"

"Thanks, Emma, they're wonderful. I'd give up sleep for the rest of my life in exchange for holding that little angel when I get home." Sam put the gift down and rubbed her hands together. "Let's see what we can do about you losing some sleep," she teased Cain.

Emma smiled and said, "Today's the day, from the chart I've been keeping, so whenever you're ready, Sam."

Sam excused herself, and Cain helped Emma undress. "What are you thinking about, lass?" Cain rubbed her thumb just above Emma's nose.

"How much better my ring will look when we add a stone to it." She lifted her arms so Cain could slip the gown on for her and tie it. "If you're having any second thoughts, it's now or never, because I think I've proven how fertile we are."

"I haven't had many second thoughts from the day you came into my life. You, lass, and moments like this, balance out the bad I've done. You're my salvation."

Emma heard the rawness in Cain's voice, and her perception of herself pained Emma. She placed her hand over Cain's heart and pressed hard against her chest. "Do you think I'm a bad person?" Cain shook her head. "You love me enough to forgive me my mistakes—you love your children, and you're the most honorable person I've ever known. Don't say that about yourself again. I realize evil people exist. You, my love, are far from evil."

"Aren't you a wee bit biased?"

"You bet, but you'll never convince me you've got a bad side. A mischievous streak as wide and long as the Mississippi, but not bad." Emma kissed her and scratched the back of her head. "So tell me, mobster, are you feeling lucky?"

"Lucky enough to try for another girl, only blond this time, like her mama."

"I'm not sure how specific an order we can place, but I'll give it a shot." She kept her arms around Cain's neck as Cain lifted her up on the exam table. "I love you."

"When you say that, you make me think I've done something right in my life." Cain pressed her forehead against Emma's and kissed her.

When Sam came in, their lips were still locked together. "Should I come back?" she asked.

Cain sat at the head of the exam table to get out of the way while Sam set up. After a quick exam, she handed Cain a syringe so she could push the plunger. Then she left them in peace.

Cain wiped away Emma's tears. "You okay?"

"Just happy. These past months with you have been even more than I wished for when I was stuck in Wisconsin alone. Now I realize what an idiot I am."

"You're not an idiot."

Emma put her hand on the side of Cain's face. "I am, and I'm not just talking about the time apart I forced on us."

Cain kissed her palm before kissing her lips, knowing how much Emma loved the sensation. "I'm sorry you feel that way." She had moved back enough to see Emma's face and outlined her lips with her finger. "Since I'm not really sure what you're talking about."

"I've been with you for so long because I love you," Emma said, pausing as if to gather her thoughts. "But I never wanted to mess up the perfect picture of you in my head."

"Oh, lass, I'm far from perfect."

"My head might know that, but my heart doesn't. I could've tried harder and a lot sooner for the kind of relationship we have now. You and our children are the most important people in my life, and I'm looking forward to bringing this little guy home in nine months."

"Just remember what Sam said about having to try more than once."

"Just once is all it'll take." Emma accepted Cain's hand and sat up.

"How do you know?" Cain dressed Emma and glanced up from putting her shoes on when she didn't answer. "Well?"

Still no answer as Emma took her hand and led her out of the office to the waiting car. No one on the house staff bothered them when they got home and headed for their room. When the door closed and Cain locked it, Emma stripped for her.

The way Emma walked toward her made any curiosity about her answer fly from her thoughts. When Emma pushed her forward, the bed bounced under her as she gave in to her wishes and sat down. She was rewarded by a naked Emma straddling her lap.

"Tell me you remember the last step in this process," Emma said.

"Maybe."

Emma lifted Cain's hand to her mouth. "Then perhaps you need a refresher course." She took Cain's middle and index fingers into her mouth to the knuckle and sucked on them softly. Even though Cain closed her eyes and her breathing deepened, Emma had her full attention.

Emma opened her mouth and licked the length of her fingers, then just as quickly took them in again. "Is it coming back to you at all?" she asked before biting just the tips.

"Vaguely." Cain opened her eyes and wanted to keep them on Emma's face, but when she leaned back and spread her legs she couldn't help but admire the length of her.

"Need more hints, huh?"

"Just a couple."

Emma grasped Cain's wrist and dragged her hand down her stomach, then back up to her left nipple. "Pinch," Emma ordered, and Cain happily complied. She got only a brief touch before Emma moved her hand to her other nipple.

"With me now?" Emma asked.

"Just one more clue and I'll be good."

Emma laughed deeply, sounding sexy as hell. "Then I should make this one count." She took Cain's hand and put it between her legs.

The way Cain's fingers slid easily along Emma's sex proved just how turned on she was.

This little tradition had started when they were trying to conceive Hayden. They'd go to the doctor, then come home and make love. Even though Hannah had been a surprise to Cain, Emma had talked Cain into an afternoon in bed. She wanted to create lives based on the love she and Cain shared.

"Please tell me you can take it from here," Emma said. She moaned as Cain's fingers teased her opening and her thumb stroked her clitoris.

"I love you," Cain whispered in her ear. "So very much." She pushed her fingers in all the way.

Emma's muscles clamped down on Cain's fingers, but she didn't move, not wanting to come right away. That was difficult when Cain pulled out, then just as quickly pushed all the way in. "So good," Emma said.

"Then come for me," Cain said before kissing her.

Emma did just that as she brought her hips down to meet Cain's touch and moaned into her mouth. As the orgasm started, she pressed her legs into Cain's sides and let her head drop onto Cain's shoulder. Emma shuddered from the intensity as Cain rubbed her thumb over her clitoris one more time, and she grabbed Cain by the wrist again to stop any other movement.

"You're criminally good at that." She held Cain's hand in place, enjoying the way her sex was still pulsating around her fingers.

"You get an automatic head start when you're an actual criminal."

"Tsk." Emma clucked her tongue and pulled the hair at the base of Cain's neck. "When I get to spend time with you like this, you make me feel absolutely adored."

"That's a given, Mrs. Casey, so how about cluing me in as to why today's the day we made a baby."

"That's easy." Emma finally released Cain's hand so she could pull out. "I've been to the cemetery with you every year. A new baby can't make up for the loss of Dalton, but it's a good way to celebrate your father's life. I know how important family is to you, and you learned how to be a wonderful parent by following his example. He's not here, but he's still watching over you."

"I'd like to think he's watching over all of us."

"Then I'm sure he'll give us what we most want. After all, what's impossible for a Casey?"

"Depends on which one you ask."

"I'm asking this one." Emma placed her hands on the sides of Cain's face and kissed her, moaning when Cain's mouth opened and accepted her tongue.

"Then I'll do what I have to in order to make it happen. All I want is you, our family, a new baby, and peace. We've started on the baby part, and later on I'm going to lay the groundwork for the kind of peace that'll let us relax and enjoy the life we've built."

Emma had learned that, sometimes, happiness came at a price. She closed her eyes and prayed that this time the beast called fate would simply give them what they wanted and not demand the heavy tolls it had in the past. Emma fully agreed with Cain's wish list, but a sense of foreboding made her shiver and pull Cain forward in an effort to chase away the demons that fear sprouted.

She sensed that this time they'd have to walk a gauntlet before they received the peace and happiness they both wanted. So Emma added just one more prayer, one that Casey wives before her had recited—for the strength and perseverance to keep her partner and children free from harm, no matter the sacrifice.

Cain buttoned her jacket as she walked downstairs and ignored the smirk on Katlin's face. Merrick Runyon, Cain's longtime guard who was now assigned to Emma, was sitting close to Katlin on the antique settee in Jarvis's foyer. Katlin and Merrick's relationship was still new, and Cain had been holding off expressing her opinion about it until now.

"Ready to roll?" Katlin asked.

"In a minute. I need to talk with Merrick first." Cain passed them, continuing to the sunroom and expecting Merrick to follow.

"Problem?" Merrick asked.

Cain pointed to the chair across from hers and studied Merrick as she strolled across the room. Merrick was still fit and beautiful, but something in her appearance had softened. Her clothes were different—

more stylish with a hint of femininity, and her hair was longer. All these subtle signs that she was trying to keep Katlin's attention bothered Cain.

"You look nice today," Cain said, trying to keep her voice even.

Merrick blinked and opened and closed her mouth several times before answering. "Not our usual conversation, but thanks."

"I've noticed a few things these past months."

The disjointed tapping of Cain's fingers filled the room for a long minute. From the way Merrick's eyes shifted from her hand to her face, Cain knew she was searching for the right words.

"Like I asked, is there a problem?"

"I'm not going to tell you how to live your life outside your job, but I'm concerned."

Merrick took a deep, explosive breath. "I've proved my loyalty. What's changed to make you doubt me now?"

"I didn't say doubt—I said concern." Cain stopped tapping and let loose some of her own temper. "Don't put words in my mouth."

"Sorry. What are you concerned about?"

"When I changed your responsibilities you weren't pleased. I'm concerned that your unhappiness, coupled with your new social life, isn't in Emma's best interests."

Merrick gripped the armrests as if to keep from punching her. "First off, I know Emma didn't tell you she had a problem, and next time talk to me before you assume anything about me."

Their time together gave Merrick some latitude to talk like this, and Cain laughed. "Why do you think Emma didn't say anything?"

"Because we've come to a truce, Emma and I. I know my job and I'm happy to do it. As for Katlin, you can approve or not, that's up to you. I'm sorry for not bringing it up earlier, but I'd like your blessing."

Cain stood and put her hand up to keep Merrick in her seat. "You don't need my blessing, Merrick, but if you do, I'm happy you found someone you can confide in and be happy with."

"Thank you."

"Emma and I have started trying for another baby, though, and I'm trusting you to keep her safe. Don't let me down."

"You're going to worry no matter what I say." Merrick stood up and took Cain's hand. "But you have my word. Emma's fine with me."

"Good, and as to Katlin, congratulations. My father always said love drives our fierceness, and Emma and our children make me realize just how right he was." She let Merrick's hand go and took a few steps toward the door before turning around. "I'll have no mercy on whoever thinks to bring them harm," Cain said, sure that Merrick didn't need any further explanation. The statement encompassed everyone, including her, but Merrick nodded anyway.

Muriel was talking to Katlin when Cain came out. Even though they were all living in the same house, Cain hadn't seen much of Muriel since she'd returned from Mexico. She needed to find out why and had ignored that conversation until now. She walked with Muriel and the others to the waiting car.

"Another late night?" Cain asked as soon as the car door closed and the surveillance jamming equipment was activated.

Muriel glanced up at her from the file she was reading and chuckled. "I have a parent, thank you."

"Is it smart-off-to-Cain day and I didn't get the announcement? It's a simple question."

Muriel closed the file and faced Cain. "Sorry, that was rude."

"I'm just curious as to how things are going."

Muriel laughed. "Don't you mean you're *worried* about how things are going?"

"I trust you." Cain stared out the window. "So how's it going?" She didn't have to look to know that Muriel's new social interest wasn't too far behind them. Agent Shelby Philips was beautiful, smart, and outgoing—all the desirable characteristics in a woman. But Shelby's employer, the FBI, wasn't exactly a friend of the Casey family.

"We're just friends." Muriel put her hands up. "Before you give me any shit, I *have* been out late, but I've been working with Mano to get this contract done." She waved the file at Cain. "We had to make sure your name and the Jatibon name don't appear anywhere on this, but it still protects your interests."

"Fucking feds."

"True, but the Mississippi Gaming Authority won't push this through with the name Casey or Jatibon on the deed. Not that you've been convicted, but...hell, you don't need me to elaborate."

"No, you don't." Cain did turn around then, curling her fingers into a fist when the ever-present van came into view. "These guys need to either shit or get off the pot. This constant sitting on top of us is getting old."

"I'd get used to it, for awhile at least. They aren't going anywhere after you caught them with their pants down again."

If anyone but Muriel had said those exact words, Cain would've missed the meeting they were headed to and opted for a more private place to finish the talk. Of course the one-sided, short conversation would've ended badly for the person who sounded like they knew a little too much about the feds and their operations. But this was her cousin Muriel, and Cain trusted her wholeheartedly.

"Just a hunch or pillow talk?" Cain asked as they turned onto Ramon's property.

"More like observation." Muriel put her hand on the door to prevent Lou from opening it once they stopped. "This is no time to start questioning my place in your life and in this family. You do and they'll win." She tilted her head in the direction of the van parked on the street.

"I've just got a lot on my mind, so maybe that didn't come out right. But you have to admit things are different now. The people I count on have new priorities it seems."

Muriel nodded. "You can't blame us for wanting what you have, but just because that's true, we haven't forgotten what's important." She let go of the door and placed her hand on Cain's knee. "I'm a Casey. Don't think anything or anyone's blinded me to that fact and what it means."

CHAPTER FIVE

The plane taxied to a stop at the lakefront airport near New Orleans under a hangar belonging to the Jatibon family. After their bags were in the limo, Remi shook hands with Dallas.

"It was a pleasure meeting you, and I'm sure we'll see each other soon. I understand you have an apartment in the city, but I thought you'd enjoy a few nights at the Piquant."

"Thank you. It'll be convenient since that's where the reception is tonight. I didn't think there'd be an available room, with all the studio brass in town."

Remi laughed and bent her head to whisper something to Dallas, fully aware that Bob's eyes were trying to bore a hole in her skull. "I wouldn't want to give you the impression that all Gemini employees are slackers," she teased.

"I'm sorry again," Dallas said. "I know you said not to apologize, but the name-calling and Bob in general got out of hand. I don't want you to think I agree with him."

"I'm sure Dick will learn the error of his ways sooner than you think, Ms. Montgomery. That's an oath I'll personally keep in the near future," Remi said while still holding her hand.

Dallas stared at her, obviously just noticing the unique color combination of her eyes. "Will I really see you again? I'd like to treat you to dinner to make it up to you. Please call me Dallas, and thank you…"

Remi ignored the way Dallas had dragged out the word *you*, as if hoping for her to fill in the blank of her name. "You will and thank you. It really has been a pleasure, but if you'll excuse me, I have people waiting."

Remi let Dallas go, heading for the three waiting Suburbans and getting into the lead vehicle. She could figure out the mystery that was

Dallas Montgomery and her traveling companion later. There was definitely a story there, and she was dying to hear it.

❖

"Mano," Remi called from the open window. Ramon, Remi's twin brother, stood in front of their parents' home waiting for the vehicles to roll to a stop. From the time they had started talking, Remi had called him Mano, an abbreviation of *hermano*, meaning *brother* in Spanish.

"Remi, you're looking good. Vacation agrees with you."

After getting out of the truck Remi hugged and kissed Mano hello, then turned to the rest of the group exiting the remaining vehicles and pointed to the house in a silent request for time alone with Mano.

Remi was involved in, and usually responsible for, the daily operations of the family business not mentioned in their annual reports. She also controlled the muscle that kept those operations running smoothly. She did the job well, and Mano readily followed her lead, but that side of the business was seldom discussed outside the family.

Mano put his arm around Remi's shoulders and led her into the house. Their mother would have to wait for her kiss hello.

As they entered the large study reminiscent of an old Cuban plantation with its muted and tasteful mahogany furniture, Remi was reminded of the tradition that had been an important part of her upbringing. The tall, imposing man behind the desk, who stood when his children entered, embodied the lessons of who she was and what her family stood for.

"*Papi, como estas?* Papi, how are you?"

"*Muy bien, hija.* Very well, daughter. You look good. Dwayne and Steve aren't with you?" Ramon asked while wrapping her in a hug.

"In a minute. I have a favor to ask before we turn our attention to the Biloxi business."

The three took a seat, and Remi described the trip home and the unexpected guests. "Mano, dig until you find something, but I know Dallas Montgomery doesn't stay with that dickhead out of love and devotion. There's a reason, and I want to know what it is."

After she finished, Ramon and Mano glanced at each other. "This is new. Why do you care?" Mano asked.

"I just want to know." She didn't often get upset with her family, but this was no time for Mano's teasing. "In case you forgot, she hasn't signed on for the sequel that starts production in two months. Call that my motivating factor."

"Mano, I'll help you with this one. Consider it done," Ramon said, which stopped the discussion. "It'll be good to get out again before your mother finds something else for me to do. Speaking of which, go tell her hello."

"I'd appreciate it, Papi."

The three walked out to the large balcony that overlooked the pool and immaculate gardens. "Mami, the good-looking one has returned," Remi said as she picked Marianna up off the ground and kissed her.

Marianna held Remi for a moment before squeezing her face between her hands. "Any luck on your trip? I'm not getting any younger and I want more grandchildren."

"You could ask how I am first, you know."

"I can see by looking at you that you're fine, but I can't so easily detect if there's a woman in your heart. Now answer me." Marianna tapped her foot and waited.

"I'm still in the sampling phase, but don't worry. I'm ticking them off as fast as I can."

"If I didn't know better, I'd say your father carried you for nine months, you're so much like him," Marianna said, dripping sarcasm. Behind her, Steve, Dwayne, and their wives were laughing at the expression on Marianna's face.

"Hopefully that's true." Remi kissed her mother's forehead. "After all, he kept at it until he got it right, didn't he?" She knew what was coming, but didn't duck the cuff to the head her mother delivered.

"One day you won't have your poor mother's arm to pull, Remi. Then what will you do?"

"That'll be a sad day indeed, but remember one thing. It's leg, Mami, leg." This time Remi did dodge the little hand flying toward her head, seeing Marianna had swung with more intent.

The Jatibons' maid escorted Cain and Muriel out to the balcony while they were still laughing. "Still giving your mother a hard time?" Cain asked.

"You're crazy if you think you're immune, so watch your step,"

Remi said as she embraced Cain and kissed both her cheeks. "You look content, my friend."

"Thanks, and you should take your mother's advice. Children and a beautiful wife would look good on you."

"You tell her, Cain," Marianna said before Cain bent and kissed her hello.

"How about business first, then all of you can work on my love life?" Remi pointed in the direction of her father's study.

Steve and Dwayne followed and closed the doors. Ramon's man Emil had just swept the room for listening devices, and Remi felt comfortable discussing business even though the watchers weren't that far away.

"Muriel, you want to start?" Remi asked as she sat close to her father's desk.

"Katlin, along with some of our men, spent some time in Luca's casino, the Capri, last month. Only a few days, but enough to see that Stephano Bracato's network is still in place. She didn't want to dig too much and arouse attention, but she's guessing the dealers have either found a new patron, or they're working directly for Rodolfo and Juan Luis, since they were Stephano's main suppliers." She glanced at Cain, who nodded. "We've made Rodolfo's business difficult here recently, so he seems to have doubled his efforts on the Gulf Coast."

"Rodolfo made money here, though, so it's only a matter of time before he finds a willing partner," Ramon said. He opened the humidor on his desk and offered everyone a Cuban cigar. He and Remi were the only two who went through the ritual of preparing the Cohibas to smoke. "We all know drugs are part of our reality. We may choose to make our living elsewhere, but we can't keep them completely away from our businesses."

"That's why Remi and I agreed to give Vinny Carlotti our protection. We might not be able to keep drugs out, but we can try to control them," Cain said. "If he does business with the Luis family, though, I will no longer honor that understanding. I don't need to remind you all that Juan approached Emma twice the last time he and his uncle were in town. The idiot either has a high opinion of himself, or he doesn't respect women."

"We'll back you on that, Cain. Rodolfo is powerful but he's a pig, and his nephew isn't any better," Remi said. "But even if Vinny thinks about doing business with them, Vincent will most likely interfere much sooner than we will. Making a quick buck isn't worth breaking the friendship with both our families. With this deal we're about to close, and what we've done already, we'll have the capital to keep the peace, if it comes to that, or crush anyone who decides to break it."

"I agree," Cain said as she accepted the glass of Anejo dark rum Ramon had poured. "So before we move forward, do we agree with the recommendations Katlin and the others made?"

"We agree. Dwayne and Steve will represent us at the sale, and Ross Verde will sign for you," Ramon said, then held up his glass. He offered the toast that had christened all the good fortunes in his life. "To love, family, health, happiness, and money. And the time to enjoy them."

"Salud," the rest of them answered.

CHAPTER SIX

Cozumel, Mexico

W e lost another five kilos this week," Santos Esvillar said. He was in charge of the Luis family's Louisiana distribution chain, and so far it had been three months since he'd had good news. "Someone gunned down another six street vendors, so now no one wants to touch our business."

"What happened to the product?" Rodolfo Luis asked. He and his nephew Juan had returned to his estate in the hills right outside of Cozumel after Cain had declared war on Giovanni Bracato. It was a battle he'd wanted no part of, since he had no loyalties to Giovanni.

"The police arrived at the scene before we had a chance to retrieve anything, señor. After the last couple of hits, I had some backup at each location, but it was like somebody called the cops before it all went down."

"It's that fucking bitch," Juan said, almost spitting the words out. He stroked his chest, his fingers gliding with the help of the tanning oil one of the house girls had slathered on him when he'd come down to the pool. He had yet to grow one hair on his chest, but he figured that wasn't what made a man. However, he seldom let anyone outside his family see him with his shirt off. "It's always that fucking bitch trying to be a man."

"We tried to make the connection to Cain Casey, but we haven't had any luck," Santos said.

"It's her, and this has to fucking stop."

Rodolfo stood and moved his chair farther under the shade of the large umbrella close to the water. "Is this business or something else?" he asked Juan.

Juan's back came off the chaise lounge, but that's as much as he was willing to physically challenge his uncle. "Business before anything else, Papa. You know Cain's behind this. Let it go unpunished and it'll get worse."

"Word on the street is that Nunzio Luca has the Capri up for sale," Santos said, sounding like a man covering his ass.

Juan came fully erect at the news, leaving the sun for a seat in the shade next to Rodolfo. Most of their southeastern product arrived and was shipped out for distribution at the Biloxi casino. With the help of the New York-based Luca family, they were building a network that would stretch through the gaming industry from Mississippi to Nevada.

The plan was perfect, since the drop-off points were so close to major distribution areas in Florida and California. While the DEA was busy trying to bust mules coming over the border full of balloons of cocaine, no one bothered to check the fresh fish and beef being flown into the casinos for their cheap buffets. All it had taken was chump change to the customs' agent in both locations. If the new owner of the Capri was uncooperative, its sale would seriously hurt the operation Juan had worked hard to put into place.

"What do you know?" Juan asked.

"I don't know the particulars yet, but that's the rumor running through the casino."

"Then find out, moron. What in the hell are we paying you for?" Juan lifted his drink, ready to throw it at Santos, but just as quickly put it down. Giving in to the satisfaction wouldn't be a good way to prove to Rodolfo that he was fit to handle the situation. "The son of a bitch Nunzio hasn't told us anything about it."

"We're working on it, since if it's true, we'll need some cooperation to continue our business."

"Fly back to Biloxi and do some more digging, and we'll be there in a week," Rodolfo said. He took a sip of his lemonade and wiped the edges of his mustache. "If you find something before then, let me know." He lifted his glass again but waited for Santos to leave. "That's all," he said when Santos didn't get the message.

"If you want—" Juan said as soon as Santos was out of earshot.

"Don't ask for something I'm not going to give you."

"Why? I'm ready and you know it." This time Juan picked up his glass and threw it into the pool. "I put that fucking operation together, and I should get the chance to protect it."

"Remember two things." Rodolfo stood and buttoned his jacket. "When you use language like that, no one will respect you. Act like a common thug and that's all you'll ever be."

He started toward the house, but before he walked ten paces he heard a splash. When he turned around, the pitcher of lemonade had joined the glass in the pool.

"That was one thing. You said to remember two," Juan said, his chest heaving from what Rodolfo assumed was rage.

"Keep acting like a child and I'll send you back to your mother. I don't have time for theatrics and the mistakes that spring from men who act without thinking."

"I am a man, Papa, and I want you to let me prove it. If you do, I swear you won't be disappointed in me."

The sun was beating down, and not even the breeze was helping Rodolfo stay dry. All his life the sun had motivated him to grow his business. No way in hell was he going to spend his time sweating and working in someone else's yard like his father.

"A week, Juan, *we* leave in a week. That'll give you time to think, and once we get there we'll see."

As he strolled back to the house he heard another splash. He wasn't interested enough to turn around, but he figured one of the house servants would have to fish out the glass he'd been using, along with the rest of the service. Juan hadn't been the same since they'd returned from the States, but no matter how many times he'd asked, the boy had refused to tell him.

"Whatever it is, *hijo*, it's time to let it go," he said as he climbed the stairs to the house. His eyes landed on Juan, who'd gone back to his lounge chair and his sun worshipping. "Now's the time for cool heads who can strike back at anyone who dares mess with our livelihood. If I can't count on you for that, then I can't count on you for anything."

❖

Annabel Hicks, lead FBI agent in the New Orleans office, entered the conference room and threw a thick file onto the table before she sat at its head. Shelby Philips didn't need a rundown on what was in it, since her team had compiled most of the information. It contained a mixture of good and bad, but mostly it consisted of page after page of Cain's brilliance at avoiding being caught doing anything wrong. There was a lot of speculation about what she'd done, but prosecutors couldn't get convictions from theory.

"In case you missed it." Annabel opened the folder, pulled out the pictures on top, and handed them to her assistant to pin to the board behind her. "The New Orleans police added these to the unsolved pile today." Six photos were tacked up in the section marked "Bracato." "These men were found dead, along with the biggest cache of drugs since this housecleaning began."

"No leads?" Joe Simmons asked.

"Of course there's a ton of leads," Anthony Curtis whispered. "That's why we're in here wasting time."

"Do you have something you'd like to share with the rest of us, Agent Curtis?" Annabel asked.

"Not officially, ma'am."

"Then, unofficially, let's hear it."

"We have these meetings, ma'am, and while they're insightful we don't really get anywhere. We all know that the left side of the board," he pointed to the Bracato side, "is a dead subject. And we all know who brought that about." He pointed to the right where the top picture showed a smiling Cain Casey. "Sitting here is a waste of time."

"Gosh, Tony, if you've solved the case I'll be happy to buy you a drink," Shelby said, aggravated with the surly Anthony. "What's a waste of my time is your more-than-hashed-out grudges, but not one shred of anything that'll help us. Are you sitting on a mountain of evidence I don't know about?"

"If anyone's holding out, it's you. Aren't you screwing her—"

Annabel slammed her hand on the table. "Curtis, in my office now. Shelby, finish this up, then I'd like to talk to you," she said, and promptly left the room.

"Take a seat, Agent Curtis."

"You know I'm right about Casey, and I know you're aware of who Shelby is seeing socially."

"Shut up and sit down. If I have to repeat myself, I'll have you escorted from the building and have to send out one of those irritating official letters in lieu of this meeting." In no way did she mean for her tone to convey humor. "No one in that conference room is an idiot. They're professionals who are more than aware of what and who is responsible for our recent crime wave."

"Thank you for that, at least."

"I meant what I said about shutting up." She pulled a file from a desk drawer and opened it. "We still live in the United States, Agent, and we have to abide by those pesky little things called laws. We cannot hound and hang a person on speculation."

"What we're doing isn't working. You have to admit that too."

"You've got a real problem with authority, don't you?" She looked at him directly, daring him to open his mouth. "When you asked for a spot on Barney Kyle's team you showed tremendous promise, but somewhere along the line you've let your personal feelings about Casey cloud your judgment. You have a month to realign your priorities, starting now. I suggest you use this paid leave to delve deep and find that idealistic young agent who was an asset to his team. The agent who helped bring down his mentor Kyle, who wasn't afforded this opportunity, so use it wisely."

"You think I'm going to turn out like Kyle?" He came close to springing out of his chair but stopped as soon as his butt came off the seat.

"Only you can answer that, Anthony, but as your supervisor I can't take the chance. For now, I'm stating in your file that you're taking voluntary leave." She slid the papers across the desk for him to see.

"What if I wouldn't like to take voluntary leave?" He closed it and pushed it back at her.

"Then I'll replace that page with this one." She held up a page but didn't offer to show it to him. "Take the gamble if you want, but others have lost careers for less."

"Even if they can counter with the fact that their supervisor hasn't handled the situation in a professional manner?"

"Then I guess I have my answer." She ripped the top sheet out of the file and was about to tear it when Anthony did come out of his seat.

"All right, I'll take leave."

"During your time off you can pick where you'd like to be transferred. That would be your smartest next career move."

"If that's it," he spat at her.

When Anthony walked out, Shelby was talking to Annabel's secretary. He opened his mouth but closed it so violently Shelby heard his teeth click together. Then she noticed Annabel standing in the doorway of her office.

"Shelby." She waved her in. "Pick someone to take Curtis's place on your team."

"Yes, ma'am, but can I ask why?"

"He'll be on leave so you need to fill the slot. Do you have anything new on all this?"

Shelby referred to her notes. "We talked to the two lead detectives the police commissioner put on this case. Twenty gang-style slayings in such a short time makes this situation eligible for federal help, but this is the NOPD we're dealing with. They're not inviting us in without a court order, and even if we had one, they still wouldn't be highly motivated to work with us."

"What was their take?"

"Detective Oscar and his partner are busy slapping each other on the back for all the drugs they've gotten off the streets, along with a laundry list of bad guys whose combined rap sheets could circle the globe a couple of times over." She shook her head and sighed. "These guys being taken out aren't exactly high priority."

"Nothing that ties them to Casey?"

"You've been chasing her longer than I have. What do you think?" Shelby said and laughed, making Annabel join her. "Nothing on that, nothing on the Bracatos—nothing on top of nothing doesn't add up to much."

Annabel nodded and rested her elbows on her desk. "We have to talk about Muriel Casey."

"We're friends, ma'am, nothing more, and this isn't the armed services."

"I don't care that it's a woman, Shelby," Annabel said, sounding like she found the conversation distasteful. "But I have to care that she's the closest advisor and family member of your main investigation's target."

"Trust me. I'm fully aware of who Muriel is, and who'll fall out if I shake her family tree. But sometimes fate chooses for us, doesn't it?"

"Just be careful I don't want to have to make your personal business my official business. We understand each other?"

Shelby stood up and gathered her things. "Yes, ma'am, we do, and thanks for your latitude on this."

"Your team members are aware of this situation, and while I don't think they concur with Curtis, they *are* aware. I'm not the only one who can make this difficult for you."

"I'll keep you updated on the investigation," Shelby said, hoping Annabel accepted that the rest was off-limits. "And please feel free to join our regular meetings. We can use all the insight we can get."

"Have fun tonight then."

Shelby whipped around as she started to leave. "Thanks," she said hesitantly, not knowing how Annabel had found out about her plans for the evening.

"Remember that while I shuffle a lot of papers all day, I'm still an FBI agent."

CHAPTER SEVEN

"Can I have one more cookie, Mom? It'll make me not miss you later." Hannah Casey stood on Cain's feet in the kitchen and hung on to her pant legs, trying not to smile. "Please?"

"Let me know if that works for you, Hannah, because I'd love to borrow the car this afternoon," Hayden Casey said. "I doubt I can pull off that face, though. So I'd better go back to that hot-wiring how-to page I found on the Internet."

Emma took the open cookie container out of Cain's hands. "Before you complain about anything our son says, remember that your mother told me you were much worse than this. Hannah, you've already had two, and that face rarely works on me." She looked at Cain while she spoke to their daughter. "Hayden, did you decide what you want to do for your birthday?"

"Wet T-shirt contest and beer bash are high on my wish list."

"Ha," Cain let out, and Emma glared at her. "See, we're nothing alike," she teased.

"I bet that was on your wish list growing up."

"I didn't say it wasn't, lass, but I was a good fifteen before I started asking."

Hayden laughed and Emma shook her head.

"Last year's plans will be good enough, Mama," Hayden said. He picked up the sandwich he'd made and started out of the room.

When he heard Emma take a deep breath he stopped. The joking atmosphere bled from the room, and her trembling lip made him put his plate down. Emma and Hannah hadn't been here for his birthday last year. "I just had dinner with Mom then, but this year it'll be better with you and Hannah here."

"That sounds great," Emma said, her voice cracking on the last word.

"You're coming, right?" Hayden asked Emma.

"I wouldn't miss it."

"Then stop feeling bad." He moved closer to her and put his arms around her. "Of course the wet T-shirt contest and beer bash would go a long way to cure my bruised emotions."

"Go do your homework, and I'll think about getting you a pony for your past trauma." Emma held him tighter before letting go. "Thanks," she whispered into his ear, her voice still sounding raw with emotion.

"You're my mom, and I love you," he said before kissing her cheek. Hayden took his snack and books and left to go upstairs.

Emma stared at the door he'd walked out of, wiping her face before she turned back to Cain and Hannah. When she did, Hannah was nestled in Cain's arms eating her third cookie of the afternoon. It was useless to fuss since she didn't have a chance in hell of changing Cain's attitude toward their children. After Emma and Hannah had moved in, it didn't take her long to see that, as ruthless as Cain was on the streets, she was equally wrapped around Hannah's little finger at home. Hannah always went to Cain first when she wanted something.

"I'd tell you something about spoiling your kids, mobster. But you did such a great job the first time around, I don't think I could pull it off," she told Cain.

Carmen, their housekeeper who'd moved with them to Jarvis's, came in and took Hannah, shaking her head when she saw the cookie.

Since the kids were gone, Emma fell against Cain and enjoyed the way Cain was running her fingers through her hair. "Maybe I'm pregnant already, since I'm an emotional wreck."

"You just need a nap before tonight."

"I spent most of the day napping, thanks to you."

Cain scooped her off her feet. "And thanks to me that's what you'll be doing this afternoon as well." She started for their room. "I'm done with meetings for today, we've been to the cemetery, and all we have left is a party tonight. Let's enjoy the quiet while we still can, before things heat up again."

"Bite your tongue, baby. No more hot times for you for a long time to come."

"I'd rather suck on something than bite, and please tell me there's more than my share of hot times in my future."

"That's a given, as long as they center around me."

When they closed the door to the bedroom, Emma pointed Cain to the chair near the window instead of the bed. She was in the mood to be held. "How'd it go today?"

"Good. This casino deal is a great opportunity for us and gives us a better advantage in the future."

Emma nestled herself into Cain's lap and rested her head on her shoulder. "How so?" These talks were becoming more common as she tried to understand Cain's world better. After all, it would be her son's future, and she was through being sheltered.

"To be strong takes more than just good leadership—it takes money. The more money we make, the bigger the wall I can erect around us when it comes to scum like Bracato," Cain said as her hand rested on Emma's abdomen.

"Big Gino's not our concern anymore, baby."

"There's always someone just like him ready to fill the void."

Cain stopped when she heard Hannah's laughter as she ran down the hall. Carmen had obviously caught her before she reached their door.

"I plan to beef up our muscle so we become the eight-hundred pound gorilla in the room. Our enemies can still pick a fight if they want to, but they'll have to live with the consequences."

Emma ran her hand up Cain's arm and paused behind her neck. She was almost through asking questions and wanted to begin more pleasurable business ventures. They kissed until her nipples tightened at the way Cain's tongue pushed into her mouth. "And you trust Remi and Ramon enough to get this done?"

"It won't be long before Ramon takes a more advisory role in their business. He's earned it, and like me, he knows Remi's ready. I trust her since we want mostly the same things." Emma started to unbutton Cain's shirt and slipped her hand inside.

"What things?" Emma asked.

"To take care of our families and exterminate the vermin when necessary. Remi and I may come from different places, but we're alike in our thinking and in our positions. I grew up with her, Mano, and Vinny, so it's not exactly a new friendship, but our main alliance will be with Remi.

"What about tonight?"

"Tonight she'll introduce the world to the new owners of Gemini Studios. The main studio production will stay in California, but the management offices will be here. With the incentives the state's offering to film in New Orleans, we've become Hollywood South. It's the perfect vehicle for us to launder money so it's a good investment."

Emma could tell their talk was almost over, because Cain was breathing differently under her wandering hand. "Has anyone figured out who owns the other forty-nine percent?"

"Not yet." Cain laughed. "When they do they'll just think your father's finally decided to spend some of that milk money he's been hoarding."

"You're a riot, mobster," Emma said as she pinched Cain's nipple. "Anything else we need to talk about?"

"I see a long discussion about how many orgasms you'll have before we need to dress for tonight."

"What are the odds it's more than one?"

"Let's just say that's the safest bet you'll ever lay," Cain said as her hand went down the front of Emma's jeans. Emma stiffened when Cain stroked her clitoris firmly. "See, there's one already." Cain chuckled.

❖

"Mano, cut the third degree. I met the woman on the way back from Florida and that's it. I don't have time for anyone in my life right now, thanks to all we have going on." She finished pouring the last drink and handed it to him. "I'm giving this venture a year or two. That's how long it'll take to turn Gemini around and hand it off to someone we trust, or sell it."

"In life anything's possible, Remi. You just have to want it bad enough."

Remi puffed her cigar and for some reason thought of Dallas Montgomery and how impossibly blue her eyes were. "Maybe, but I'm not looking for anything here. I'm just curious."

She picked up the tray and headed out to her parents' patio to join the rest of the group. When she saw Molly, Lisa, and Mano's wife Sylvia sitting together with an empty space for her, she almost turned around.

"Come sit by us, lover," Lisa said.

"I don't know, who'll protect my virtue?" Remi asked. Her brother as well as her partners knew their women were safe from Remi's considerable charm, but the girls liked to exercise her wit when they had the chance.

Molly picked up one of Remi's hands and asked, "How are you going to win the hand of the fair Dallas?"

Remi squeezed Molly's hand and said, "Back off, I mean it. You all leave that poor woman alone. Dealing with Dick must be a full-time job, and we won't add to her load."

"Remi, starting tonight you'll be in the limelight more. It'll affect your reputation with the ladies if you show up at places alone. You don't want people to think you've lost your touch, do you?" Sylvia wheedled.

"Who said I'm going anywhere alone? Thanks for your concern, though."

As if on cue all the wives said, "Well, who is it?"

Loving the game and being a master of patience, Remi smiled, then got up and walked to her open briefcase. After she pulled out a local magazine, an issue dealing with a new line of swimwear, she held it up.

Dwayne's voice rose to a scary octave when he looked at the woman on the cover. "Get the fuck out of here. You're taking Susan Wilkins to this thing tonight?"

"I met her a month ago on one of my visits to the new studio offices. The magazine was using the pool on the roof to shoot the December cover. Juno, Simon, and I were taking a little tour and stopped to watch. During one of the breaks she came over and introduced herself. She's really a nice girl, so I called and asked if she wanted to go with me tonight." Remi smiled at the open-mouthed men and took a sip of her beer.

"Did she mention any friends?" Steve asked, looking at the beautiful African-American model on the cover. He stopped asking any further stupid questions when Lisa delivered a blow to his head.

"What's Dallas going to think when you show up with bikini girl?" Molly asked.

"I'm not seeing Dallas, so why does it matter?" Remi dropped the magazine and took her seat. "I'm not kidding—no matchmaking from you three."

"Of course not," Lisa said.

"We wouldn't dream of it," Molly followed.

"You have our word," Sylvia finished.

"I've seen cobras look more sincere," Remi said. "I'd think you'd have your hands full dealing with these fools." She pointed at the guys and laughed as all three raised their middle fingers in salute. "Come on, let's get this over with, and remember, no comments or interviews for the press. We don't need to become front-page news and give the feds an unfair advantage."

CHAPTER EIGHT

"Y ou need to wear the green Vera Wang tonight. You know, the one with the low-cut back," Bob said, rummaging through Dallas's closet. She'd passed on the room at the Piquant for the night, just wanting to go home. "We need the upper hand with this lowlife, and from the way those bitches waxed poetic about him, he seems like the type who thinks with his dick."

Hearing *dick* reminded Dallas of their flight home, and she wondered when she would see her new friend again. She wasn't looking forward to the party tonight to honor the new studio head, but future contract negotiations guaranteed her attendance. "I don't really care what I'm wearing. Get out of here so I can get ready."

"Watch your tone."

She closed the door to the bathroom and locked it, to avoid another argument. The hot water felt good as she took her time, wanting to relax before the command performance. When she put on her robe, she remembered that not so long ago an existence like this, even with Bob in it, was well beyond her reach.

Small bit parts had paid off eventually and landed her the role costarring with Jenny in a movie about two female detectives who uncover a ring of cops who hire themselves out as killers. The sequel was in the works, but in this business nothing was certain, and the public soon forgot you if you didn't work steadily.

The only weight dragging Dallas down was Bob, but the opportunist wasn't going anywhere, considering the information he constantly held over her. Her career gave her the kind of attention she needed to be successful, but it also kept her under his thumb, and she had no one to turn to. It didn't matter, though; she wasn't about to walk away and lose the best way she had to take care of her responsibilities. To keep her secrets buried, Dallas would suffer whatever Bob wanted to dish out.

Katie Lynn and Sue Lee Moores from Sparta, Tennessee were long dead, and Dallas had no desire to dredge them up. She wasn't ashamed of what she'd had to do for herself and her sister Sue Lee to survive. But having her brief porn career and the rest of what Bob had on her come out now would make her radioactive to Gemini Studios. And if it all surfaced, she faced another kind of spotlight that could have vastly different consequences.

Walking away from Bob was just wishful thinking. As much as she hated him, she wasn't willing to give up the lucrative career that kept Sue Lee, now Kristen Montgomery, a sophomore at the private school up North that Dallas had enrolled her in, safe. Their father's perversions would never touch Kristen's life the way they had tormented Dallas's.

After their mother had died, Dallas had done her best to shelter Kristen from the sick appetites of Johnny Moores and his equally sick circle of friends. One night after he'd finished with her and headed down the hill drinking with his friends, Dallas had packed a small bag, the coffee can of cash Johnny kept on the refrigerator, and taken off with a then fourteen-year-old Sue Lee. It's what had happened when they ran into their father's friend Timothy Pritchard that created the black cloud that would follow her forever.

They hitchhiked to California, and when the money for food had long run out, Katie Lynn Moores started her film career as Sweet China. The whole process had disgusted her, but it was no worse than what her father had done to her.

On the set of her first film, a fire had started in her to try for something better than what her father and his friends had used her for. No matter what it took, Dallas didn't want to spend the rest of her life on her back letting others take what they wanted whether she wanted to give it to them or not. Dallas and Kristen Montgomery were born that day, and they started running from a past that Bob could reveal with one phone call. He was a fellow Tennessean and had started his porn-film career as a cameraman who often bragged he could do wonders for your career if you would spend some time alone with him "rehearsing" for the next shoot.

Dallas put the morose memories back in their cage for the night and set her mind to what came next. After drying her hair and putting on a little makeup, she slipped into a different dress from the one lying on the bed. "God, I wish they'd make these things so that every so often you could actually put on underwear." Dallas checked the fit in the closet-door mirror, finding it satisfactory. She slipped on a pair of black pumps, and with one last glance in the mirror she was ready to face the evening.

❖

"You're early," Shelby Philips said, making her remark sound like an accusation.

"From where I'm standing I'd have to say I'm late," Muriel said.

"How do you figure?"

"Two minutes earlier and I would've caught you in the shower. The robe and wet hair mean I'm late." She took a step back and nodded in the direction of the car. "I can come back if you want."

"That doesn't sound like the cocky Muriel Casey I know. Running away doesn't suit you."

"True, but I've never dated a girl who carries handcuffs as part of her job description," Muriel said, taking another step back. The space gave her the opportunity to really admire Shelby.

"Just my luck." The door creaked as Shelby leaned against it. "I finally decide to take a walk on the dark side and date the bad girl, and she turns out to be a Girl Scout."

Muriel surged forward and grabbed Shelby by the waist, lifted her off her feet, and slammed the door closed with her hip. She made Shelby stop laughing by kissing her with so much passion that she moaned and pulled Muriel's hair. "Girl Scout, huh?"

"Let's say you're making a good comeback."

"Are you encouraging me to be bad?" She laughed when Shelby bit down on her neck. "I'll take that as a yes." Their next kiss was slower, and Muriel walked to the sofa and sat down with Shelby still in her arms. "This is going to look bad on your performance review at work."

"My fallback is that you aren't a criminal. You aren't, are you?"

"Like you said before, I'm a regular Girl Scout."

"Uh-huh." Shelby caught Muriel's hand inside her robe. "I don't think there's a badge for this."

"Sure there is. You weren't looking in the right manuals. A

little more research and you'd have found all the interesting badge requirements." Muriel moved her hand up and cupped Shelby's right breast.

"I think you just found something interesting."

"Nah, just checking for bugs," Muriel teased as she moved her other hand under the robe so Shelby's left breast wouldn't feel neglected. "Is that a pair of listening devices or are you just happy to see me?" Muriel asked as she pinched Shelby's nipples.

"If you don't stop trying to be funny, I'm going to make you drive around the block until it's time to go." Shelby put her knees on the sofa and pulled herself up until she could strip the robe off. "Want to prove to me that you missed me, since I haven't seen you in days."

"I did miss you, but it feels like you're never very far away," Muriel said, referring to the constant surveillance.

"No business, not now." Shelby pulled Muriel's bow tie off and worked her way down the studs of her pleated shirt until she reached the cummerbund. "Right now it's just you and me." She threw the long piece of silk behind her and unfastened the pants. "Take your own advice."

When Shelby pinched her clitoris between her fingers and tugged, Muriel let out a stream of air. "What…ah." Shelby tugged again. "What advice?"

"For a little while let's forget the three letters that represent my job, and let's forget your last name. All I want to think about is you lying over me making love to me."

Muriel's pants pooled around her ankles when she stood up, and she laughed when Shelby took the time to fold them over a chair before leading her to the bedroom. Coots, Shelby's cat, stretched before jumping off the bed and pranced down the hall after weaving through Muriel's legs.

"Did you really miss me?" Shelby asked.

"I did," Muriel said, letting Shelby take the lead for the moment and lying on her back so Shelby could sit on her. Shelby was so turned on, Muriel felt her stomach getting wet. "How about you?"

"Can't you tell?"

"I'd rather you showed me," Muriel said.

Shelby never lost eye contact as she positioned herself, then reached down and spread herself open. She brought her hand up and offered Muriel her wet fingers before reaching down again and repeating the action with Muriel. She started slowly pumping her hips, and Muriel jerked whenever Shelby's hard clitoris passed over hers.

She was squeezing Shelby's ass so hard she was sure she would leave fingerprints when they were done, but she wanted to hold out and let Shelby set their pace.

"Now, baby, give me what I want," Shelby said.

Muriel rolled her over and lifted herself up a little so she could move her hips more freely. When she felt Shelby's nails dig into her shoulders, she pumped harder and watched her breasts bounce from the force of her thrusts. All the stimulation brought her to the brink where she couldn't stop, but Shelby begged for more.

The headboard was starting to thump against the wall, and Shelby spread her legs farther apart in encouragement. Somewhere in the house a cell phone started ringing but went unanswered as Muriel felt her orgasm wash through her. She held on long enough to feel Shelby meet her thrust for thrust before she arched her back and said her name. Once she heard it, Muriel slumped down, pinning Shelby to the bed with the length of her body.

"My boss warned me about you today," Shelby said, the tips of her fingers skimming over Muriel's skin from her neck to her butt in a way that soothed rather than excited.

"Funny, my cousin warned me about you too." Muriel rolled off so they could change positions. "What'd you tell the esteemed Agent Annabel?"

"The woman is an accomplished and decorated agent, but why is it every time you say her name you make her sound like a hick?" In their new position Shelby found new territory to trace and moved to Muriel's forehead.

"The name Annabel opens you up to a certain amount of witty sarcasm, unless you're the mascot for a milk company. Then it's perfectly acceptable." Muriel had to move quickly to capture Shelby's hands when she reached down and pinched her.

"Behave and answer my question."

"I told her what I'm sure you told Cain—we're just friends."

"You mean you didn't say friends with benefits?" Muriel joked, then hissed when Shelby pinched her with a lot more force. "You're going to bruise me."

"I'm going to beat the crap out of you if you're paying out benefits to anyone else."

Muriel laughed and rolled over again so she could kiss her. "As if," she said when their lips parted. "I'm sleeping with an FBI agent who follows me around all day. Pretty stupid of me to break the rules, don't you think?"

"You're a Casey, honey. You're programmed to break the rules."

"Touché, but being a Casey means I'm as loyal as they come."

Shelby reached up and ran her fingers through her hair. "That's the only reason you got into my skirt. My problem now is that I happen to really like having you there."

"You see that as a problem?" Muriel kissed her again and rolled off so she could sit up.

"I didn't say it to make you mad," Shelby said, draping herself on Muriel's back.

"I'm not mad at you, just at fate."

"How do you mean?"

Muriel smiled when she felt Shelby's lips on the back of her neck. "Nothing important, just something Cain once told me about safe havens." Fate was indeed a cruel bitch, thought Muriel. She'd finally found the woman who stirred her in every possible way, but was also the one person in the world in whom she could never confide—not without life-changing consequences.

"You think this won't work, don't you?" Shelby asked.

"For once I don't have all the answers, but I do know what I want. The real question is, can I have it without one of us turning our backs on something we hold dear?"

Shelby sat next to her and took her hand. "Don't you mean someone? I'm not asking you to betray Cain. All I'm asking for is what you can give me. It's enough."

For now, thought Muriel, but didn't voice the words. She only nodded and followed Shelby to the bathroom for another shower. The impossible had happened, she thought as she watched the sway of Shelby's hips; she'd fallen in love with a woman who'd taken an oath to destroy her family. She'd never voice the words "I love you," either, and that was the cruelest fate of all.

CHAPTER NINE

Five black limousines turned into the Piquant, and Cain frowned as the pack of paparazzi got their cameras ready. They were almost as bad as the feds.

She and Emma emerged from the first car, both laughing when the wall of guards ruined any good shots. Muriel and Shelby, in the second car, nodded to them as they arrived and stood beside them, waiting for the others. The only person the photographers truly recognized got out next on Remi's arm, and they started shouting Susan's name. Ramon, Marianna, Mano, and Sylvia followed them, and in the last car were Dwayne, Steve, and their wives.

"Emma, you look stunning," Remi said as they walked in together. "And that's a beautiful dress you have on, Susan."

"What dress? You mean the strings hanging over her tits and ass. That's a dress?" someone said.

"Thank you. You're looking dapper yourself tonight. Maybe once this is over we could go somewhere more intimate?" Susan asked as she hung from her arm.

"Let's see what the night has to offer, shall we?" Remi said as they entered the packed ballroom a floor up. "Good turnout, but maybe it's just the crab puffs."

"The drinks are on me, so shall we?" Cain said, guiding Emma to their reserved table.

"Let's give ourselves thirty minutes, then we'll get this over with since I know you love big crowds as much as I do," Remi said to Cain. "Guys, meet me at the bar in twenty," she told Dwayne and Steve.

The purchase of Gemini was a joint venture, but Remi and the guys would be the front men on the project, which was how Cain had wanted it set up. With the acquisition of the studio, she'd found the perfect business to account for all the money she made, since moviemaking had a lot of accounting loopholes. Most important, she trusted Remi to keep her investment safe.

"I'll gladly dance with my wife while you do all the heavy lifting on this one," Cain said, taking Emma's hand. "Ramon, Marianna, join us?"

Remi left her date talking to a director and couldn't believe her luck as she neared the bar. She took in the vision in the black dress who sat nursing a drink and appearing bored with the whole process, and her curiosity grew. "Hello, stranger, come here often?" she whispered into Dallas's ear.

The low voice made Dallas visibly shiver. "My, but black is definitely your color," Dallas said. "Love the tux."

"Flatterer. I must agree on one thing though, Ms. Montgomery. Black is definitely my color," Remi said, looking from the top of Dallas's head down to the black pumps. "You're a vision. I can see why the movie was named *Lady-killers*. Are you here alone or is that just wishful thinking?"

"No, Bob's around here somewhere pumping the flesh."

"Not a flesh pumper yourself?"

"Actually, I'd much rather be people watching in the French Quarter, but these gatherings are necessary in the industry if you don't want to be passed over. Hopefully this guy won't be too long-winded and we can slip out of here early."

Remi had opened her mouth to tell Dallas to go home and do just that, when the voice she remembered from the plane boomed in her ear. "I thought I told you to stay away from her, pervert. You could ruin her image just by standing next to her," Bob said as he wrapped a proprietary arm around Dallas's waist. "Get lost."

Remi was about to comment he needed to have the jacket and the pants of his tuxedo let out some, but decided not to waste her time.

"Dallas, it was nice seeing you again. I'll do what I can about any long speeches." With that Remi turned and disappeared into the crowd.

"Bob, that was rude and unnecessary." Dallas pulled his arm away and wondered what her new friend meant by her long-speech comment.

"Looking after my property, babe. Can't have people thinking ill of you, can we? Look, the program's starting. Let's move where we'll be noticed." Bob pulled her off the barstool and started pushing people out of the way to get closer to the stage.

"Good evening, ladies and gentlemen and distinguished guests. I'm Robin Burrus of Gemini Studios, and I'd like to welcome you to our simple gathering tonight to welcome our new CEO.

"I've known Remington Jatibon for quite some time and am glad to see a Jatibon finally take the reins of the main offices of Gemini. This is a family who'll work tirelessly until we dominate the moviemaking industry. Remi, I know you'll do your parents Ramon and Marianna proud. Please help me in welcoming Remington Jatibon." He turned and hugged Remi when she stepped on stage, patting her back several times before letting go.

When Remi turned to face the gathering Bob hissed, "What in the hell is she doing up there?"

Dallas felt weak for a moment and uttered, "Oh, dear God, I'm screwed."

Lisa, standing behind them, answered Bob's question first. "She's up there because, Dickey, that's Remi Jatibon." Then turning to Dallas she said, "Not yet, sweetie, but we're working on it."

"Thank you, everyone, for coming out tonight. I won't keep you long since someone just reminded me how people feel about long speeches." Her eyes cut to the right of the stage and met Dallas's. Remi shrugged and smiled. Dallas crossed her arms and frowned slightly in return obviously not happy with her lie of omission as to who she was.

"Starting Monday, a new era will begin at Gemini. My team and I intend to build upon the great work you in this room have already done since the inception of the studio. Together we'll succeed in making Gemini better and more progressive than anyone else in the business.

"Through your craft you'll be present at many of our audience's first dates and first kisses. You'll touch people in ways you might not even realize. Our job is to help you continue to make the magic that has brought us to this point. My door is always open if any of you ever need my assistance." Remi looked back toward Dallas and smiled again.

"In closing, I'd like to introduce the new management team for Gemini Studio, Dwayne St. Germaine and Steve Palma." Remi waited for them to join her. "Thank you all for coming and good night. Please stay and enjoy the food and drink, and we look forward to Monday."

The inevitable press to the stage came, swallowing them as they stepped off of it. When they emerged, Dallas saw a striking woman take Remi's hand and figured she was Remi's date for the evening. "I'll be lucky to get cast as a stand-in extra now."

"Okay, babe, we've got some major damage control to do, starting now," Bob said from behind her. "But this isn't anything we can't fix."

"We? Who is *we*, Dickey? I'd get used to the name because, believe me, she isn't going to forget it anytime soon. I am so screwed. Do you think she'll forget, let's see," Dallas started counting off on her fingers, "'Dyke,' 'shit for brains,' 'moron,' and 'pervert'? Oh, yeah, she'll be in a big-ass hurry to forgive us both."

❖

The furor in the room died away when the doors the Caseys and Jatibons had departed through closed. Some people returned to the dance floor and most went back to the bar, but Muriel and Shelby kept their seats.

"Are Cain and Remi Jatibon going into business together?"

"This is a date, Shelby, not a fishing expedition." Muriel took a sip of her whiskey and thought about how quiet Cain had been around them in the short time she was there. It wasn't anger in her face, more like disappointment.

"Just a simple question."

"Tell me truthfully that the simple answer won't end up in some official report." She drained the glass and along with it went any good feelings left from the beginning of their evening.

"I can't do that."

"Then it's not really a simple question, is it?" She stood and held out her hand. "Let's call it a night."

"Cut me some slack here. I'm sorry."

"No need to be sorry, I'm just ready to go." There was no commotion when they left and no conversation in the limo on the way to Shelby's small house uptown.

"Thanks for coming," Muriel finally said when they stopped and she walked Shelby to the door. "I'll call you."

As Muriel turned, she thought she heard Shelby say "I bet you don't," but she couldn't be sure.

❖

"We have one thing going for us," Merrick said as she and Katlin got ready for bed. Katlin had moved out of Jarvis's pool house and in with her.

"We have plenty going for us, but what are you talking about?"

"Cain might not be thrilled we're together, but Muriel's love life should shift the limelight, don't you think?" She pulled the covers back and draped her leg over Katlin as soon as she lay down.

"I'm still trying to wrap my head around that one. My Uncle Dalton is probably spinning in his grave at what she's doing."

Merrick ran her hand down Katlin's abdomen and sighed. "We can't always pick who we fall for."

"But sometimes we can make sacrifices for the sake of what we believe in, if the person we choose doesn't respect it." She slapped Merrick softly on the ass and pulled her closer. "That's for Muriel to decide, though, and right now I'm not worried about her and her problems."

"How long will you be gone this time?"

"Just a few days while we close the Capri deal. You'll barely notice I'm gone."

Merrick laughed at the gentle teasing and decided to do some of her own by squeezing Katlin's upper thigh between her legs.

"Need help with anything?" Katlin asked.

"You're still here? I didn't notice," Merrick said, letting out a shriek when Katlin slapped her ass again, making it sting this time. The night would have to last them until Katlin got back.

CHAPTER TEN

"Tell me, Simon, why are women so complicated? You'd think I'd know since I'm a woman, but I've never been able to find an answer."

"That question has no right answer, since all women are different. The best solution I've found, instead of wasting my time trying, has been to give diamonds for every occasion and in any circumstance."

"I'll keep that in mind," Remi said as she walked through the Quarter to the address her assistant Juno had given her that morning.

Juno had worked for her mother in Cuba and defected with the Jatibon family. Marianna had accepted the young girl's relationship with the quiet Simon, who at the time was Ramon's bodyguard, for what she saw it, love. As Remi grew and her father gave her more responsibility, he also gave her Simon. The strong woman would kill someone, if necessary, to protect one of Ramon's beloved children. Juno came along as part of the package, and together they kept Remi's life centered and on schedule.

"Just remember we have to be at the airport at ten," Simon said as they stopped in front of a plain building on Bourbon Street.

"The cup of coffee I'm planning on should take ten minutes." Remi glanced back when Simon cleared her throat. "What? You think she won't like coffee?"

"I'm sure she loves coffee, but telling her you're taking ten minutes out of your busy schedule isn't going to win you any favors."

"You should write a self-help book." Remi smirked as she pushed the buzzer.

"Can I help you?"

Remi recognized Dallas's voice and was surprised she'd answered the buzzer. "Good morning, Dallas, it's Remi."

"I'm sorry, who?"

She took her finger off the intercom and looked at Simon. "Hell, ten minutes might have been an overestimation."

"In these situations groveling and heartfelt apologies work just as well as precious stones."

"Remi Jatibon," Remi said, returning to the paces Dallas was putting her through.

"Sounds familiar…hmm…have we met?"

"I have some aliases you might recognize." Remi shook her head and took her finger off the button, then pointed it at Simon to make her stop laughing. "There's 'dyke,' 'shit for brains,' and 'moron.' Did I leave any out?"

"You left out 'pervert,' I believe," Dallas said, then laughed. "You have to realize Bob suffers from a chronic case of foot in the mouth."

"Let's not waste our time talking about Dickey. Can I come in?"

A buzzer sounded, unlocking the door, and the plain exterior gave way to a beautiful courtyard and garden sprinkled with pieces of outdoor art and wrought-iron furniture. The place felt more like home than a temporary location rental. One of the chairs under the largest shade tree had a book on it, and Remi figured that must be Dallas's reading nook.

She stepped onto the patch of grass, curious as to what Dallas was reading, and smiled when she saw *Turn Back Time*, by Radclyffe, with a bookmark close to the end. "Now I'm more curious than ever," she whispered.

Footsteps on the slate floor made her look up to find Dallas wearing worn jeans and a loose white shirt, with her hair pulled into a ponytail.

"Good morning," Remi said.

"Yes, it is." Dallas stopped when she reached the edge of the grass. "You're here, we both know who we are, and no one's wearing a tux."

"Not much on studio parties, are we?"

"I'm more of a barefoot and jeans girl, actually."

Remi glanced down at the sandals. "You put on shoes for me? That's flattering."

"I figure if you're here to fire me, it would be more professional if I was dressed somewhat like an adult."

The reasoning made no sense to Remi, and she glanced back at Simon. "Your ideas on women are sounding better all the time," she said, then laughed and shook her head. "I'm not here to fire you, since at the moment you don't actually work for me, but I am here to ask you for a favor over coffee."

"Have a seat and I'll go make some."

"We can go somewhere for coffee. I didn't mean to put you out." She nevertheless picked up the book and sat down.

"I promise not to poison you. Drip or espresso?"

"Espresso, with lots of sugar, thank you."

Dallas walked away but left her sandals behind. It amazed Remi that for all the foot traffic outside, Dallas's little patch of garden was as quiet as a church. She enjoyed the stillness with her eyes closed. "Makes me want to sell the penthouse," she told Simon.

"Maybe you won't have to," Simon said. She sat close by with her head back.

"Do you read tea leaves down in Jackson Square in your spare time?"

"That's fun to do every so often," Dallas answered, making Remi's head jerk up. She put down the tray she was holding and handed Simon a cup first. "What can I do for you, Ms. Jatibon?"

"It's Remi, and I wanted to ask you out to dinner."

"That's the favor?"

"If you say yes, I could apologize for not coming clean about who I was when we met, and we can talk about your upcoming project."

"That's a new way of going about things."

"I thought it would be more relaxing and we could maybe get to know each other better," Remi said, catching a hint that the ice under her boots was cracking.

"And if I say no to the offer, which I'm sure comes complete with a casting couch?" The question was venomous, but Remi detected a history behind it.

"Then you and Bob can handle it with legal." Remi stood and put her untouched coffee back on the tray. "Thanks for the coffee. I'm sorry we disturbed you and that I've somehow given you the impression that your future with the studio lies solely on your back."

They were halfway to the door when Dallas spoke up. "And if I said yes, what did you have in mind?"

"Italian chicken at Irene's. You'll stay fully dressed, including your shoes, then I'll drop you off here and you can finish your book."

Dallas pointed at the tray. "Why not forget I'm an idiot, then, and finish your coffee?"

"I have an appointment I unfortunately can't reschedule, so I have to get going."

"Does that mean Susan Wilkins brews a better pot than I do?"

Remi was surprised when the usually quiet Simon started laughing. "I wouldn't know, and I don't see any future opportunities to try anything she's brewing," she said, finding Dallas attractive but irritating. But she was beginning to realize all kinds of things about herself, namely that no other woman in her life had challenged her like this, much less that she'd enjoy it. With Dallas if she wanted more she'd have to work for it.

Dallas glanced down at her feet, and when she made eye contact again, Remi read her facial expression as contrite. "Sorry, that was out of line."

"Don't apologize for being straightforward. It's refreshing," Remi said, meaning every word, but she glanced at her watch and saw her fun was over. She took a card out of her pocket and handed it to Dallas. "Thanks for seeing me but I really have to get going."

Dallas closed her fingers around it and watched Remi leave, her boots echoing along the slate. Her shoulders slumped as soon as the lock clicked closed. This had been her chance with Remi, and she'd blown it in spectacular form. Before she could get too depressed, she studied the heavy linen paper with raised ink. It showed only Remi's name and a phone number, no company and no position. She wasn't sure why Remi had given it to her until she flipped it over.

If you ever feel the urge to call me, I say go with it. Just promise me you won't put Dickey on the line once you've dialed.

"How about tonight?" Dallas asked, when Remi answered after she dialed the listed number.

"If I'm back in time I'd love to, but I really don't know when I'll be through."

"It doesn't matter, give me a call. If it's late I'll fix something here to make up for acting like I have no control of my mouth."

"That sounds like something to look forward to. I'll see you tonight."

❖

```
========================================
         KLEIN STATION APC 3
           7717 LOUETTA RD
        SPRING, TX 77379-9998

06/10/2010                  03:01:57 PM
========================================


              Sales Receipt
Product          Sale    Unit      Final
Description       Qty   Price      Price
_____

SARATOGA, CA  95070                $10.70
Zone-7 Priority Mail® Medium
FR Box
                            ========
Issue Postage:                     $10.70

Total:                      =========
                                   $10.70

Paid by:
DebitCard                          $10.70
  Account #:      XXXXXXXXXXXXX7692
  Approval #:     195758
  Transaction #:  976
  23-902140565-99
  Receipt #:      033043

APC Transaction #:          45
USPS® #                     488566-9553

              Thanks.
      It's a pleasure to serve you.

ALL SALES FINAL ON STAMPS AND POSTAGE.
REFUNDS FOR GUARANTEED SERVICES ONLY.
```

```
=======================================
        KLEIN STATION APC 3
          7717 LOUETTA RD
        SPRING, TX 77379-9998

/10/2010                    02:59:56 PM
=======================================


               Sales Receipt
  Product          Sale    Unit      Final
  Description      Qty     Price     Price
  _____


  SARATOGA, CA  95070                 $10.70
  Zone-7 Priority Mail® Medium
  FR Box
                                   ========
  Issue Postage:                      $10.70

  Total:                           ==========
                                      $10.70

  Paid by:
  DebitCard                           $10.70
    Account #:     XXXXXXXXXXXX7692
    Approval #:    195593
    Transaction #: 975
    23-902140565-99
    Receipt #:     033042

  APC Transaction #:          44
  USPS® #                     488566-9553

              Thanks.
      It's a pleasure to serve you.

  ALL SALES FINAL ON STAMPS AND POSTAGE.
  REFUNDS FOR GUARANTEED SERVICES ONLY.
```

"Ready to buy a casino?" Remi asked Cain as they boarded the plane.

"Can't wait." Cain paused at the door to wait for Muriel, watching her stare at the surveillance team boarding a nearby plane so they could tag along. "Want to talk about it?"

"Nothing to talk about," Muriel said as she quickly climbed the steps. "More like loose ends that need to be tended to."

"Rash decisions aren't your style."

Muriel clicked her seatbelt on and put her hand on Cain's forearm. "I'm not making any quick decisions, just trying to make the right ones. You'll have to trust me."

"You have my trust, but don't forget you have the right to ask me for help if you need it."

"I know that, but I'd rather take care of this myself."

For the rest of the trip the group discussed the pending deal. That morning they were sitting down with Richard Bowen to finalize the deal, but they weren't stupid. The Jatibons and Cain knew Richard no more owned the Capri than Dwayne, Steve, and Ross would after the sale. He was Nunzio Luca's front man in the casino and on paper.

"The fact that Nunzio Luca's willing to sell at all still surprises me," Ramon said.

"True, since from what I'm hearing he's partnering with Rodolfo Luis," Cain said. "After Stephano's retirement, and considering Nunzio's expansion plans, I would've thought he'd have kept the first stop in the supply chain."

"Maybe he's made other arrangements," Steve said.

"Not likely, and that's the only part of this situation I can't work out," Cain said, and Remi nodded.

"What's your best guess?" Dwayne asked.

"Nunzio's been lured by the quick buck. To rise to where he wants in the drug-lord food chain, he needs cash to build up his network."

"Have you met this guy?" Ramon asked. "I know Rodolfo, but haven't had the pleasure of meeting Nunzio."

"You're not missing much. I met him one night at my old club Emerald's. He reminded me a lot of Giovanni in that he thinks killing enough people will solve any problem."

Remi crossed her legs and looked from Ramon to Cain. "I've dealt with him on a few occasions, so I have to agree with your assessment. You really think we're financing his expansion?"

"Like I said, I haven't figured it all out, but we need to be vigilant. If that *is* Nunzio's plan, then he'll rely on intimidation to make us back down if we try to take his people out of the Capri. He strikes me as the have-my-cake-and-eat-it-too kind. We give him the money he needs and then bend on letting him continue business as usual."

"We don't intimidate easily," Remi said.

"Wait until you have a four-year-old," Cain said, laughing.

❖

As Remi got into the waiting black limousine, followed by Cain, Muriel, and Juno, she said, "I hate these things. They always remind me of either a funeral or a wedding, which is kinda the same thing when you think about it."

"I don't know. According to Simon, we may have you fitted for a tux before too long," Juno said.

"I just want to have dinner with her to discuss her upcoming project without that asshole around."

"You're not talking about the girl who made her completely forget her date last night, are you?" Cain asked Juno.

"If it is, I can't blame you for wanting to spend time alone with her, Remi, but I'm partial to blondes myself."

"Who in their right mind isn't, but this is just business," Remi said. "Speaking of, did you set up extra security for today, Cain?"

"Katlin left earlier this morning with Mano and a group from both families. With the guys we have with us now, we should have it covered."

"Nunzio would have to be stupid to try anything now," Remi said.

"True, but sometimes stupid is a way of life for these guys," Cain said. The van that pulled up alongside them on the main drag in Biloxi made her sigh. Shelby and her friends had made the trip just fine.

"Once this is done I want to move some of our security to the casino. I want the grounds cleared of any evidence of the Bracatos and the Lucas as soon as possible. Guido's moving on after today, but there's something about him I don't trust," Remi told Cain.

"Please don't call him Guido. His name is Richard, and he's an American," Juno said.

"I was just kidding. But this guy looks like he's seen one gangster movie too many. He should know we have a much better sense of style," Remi told her, making Cain and Muriel laugh. "It's the bad-girl image that drives the women wild."

The car pulled to the front of the Capri Casino, and Mano opened the car door. Remi pulled his goatee as a greeting and waited for everyone to get out.

"Did everyone make it?" he asked Remi.

"At least from our end. Is Richard up there?"

"Yes, and already in a pissy mood." He pointed to the trucks in the far section of the front parking lot, ready to start taking the Capri signs down.

"I could give a rat's ass about what kind of mood Richard's in," Cain said. "I'm sure he'll cheer up as soon as he gets the check."

"I left some of Muriel's staff with him in case he had any questions," Mano told them as he pressed the up button on the bank of elevators. "Think of how surprised Guido will be when we shut the place down for a couple of weeks once the sale goes through. There's no way I'm putting any of our people in there until we inspect the facility and check personnel backgrounds."

"Good, since Richard was running more smack here than dice," Cain said. "We don't need that kind of heat. The less often we have to go before the gaming commission, or give the feds any more ammunition to make our lives miserable, the better."

Their group moved toward a private elevator that went to the third floor where the management offices were located. Once they boarded, three of Cain's men stayed by the doors to deter anyone else from going up.

CHAPTER ELEVEN

C ain." Richard Bowen stood and extended his hand when she entered the conference room first. "And Remi, you look good enough to eat."

Ramon puffed his chest out, ready to call the man down for his obvious sexual comment when Remi beat him to it.

"Hello, Richard, you're looking good yourself. Love the suit. It's so shiny. You rented *Good Fellas* again last night, didn't you?" She slid into the chair to the right of the head of the table, which she waved Cain into.

"I'm sure we all have better things to do than discuss how great everyone looks," Cain said and smiled broadly. "How about you sign the papers so we can give you the check?"

"I find the changes to this contract totally unacceptable. My firm was supposed to provide security for the hotel and casino for five years, with an option to renew," Richard said, slamming the papers down on his end of the polished table. "Muriel and Mano agreed when we did the initial sit-down."

"The hell we did," Mano said.

"That's not going to happen, and I'd appreciate it if you kept your delusions to a minimum," Muriel said. "You and everyone down to the guy who cleans the ashtrays are out as soon as we hand over the check."

"I repeat, that's unacceptable. I have friends in this town who you don't want to piss off. It could be bad for business."

"Is that a threat?" Remi countered. "Because if it is, Slick, you've just rolled snake eyes coming out of the box."

"No threat, and you don't have the balls to keep that promise. You and Cain don't want to take me on, so tell your peons to put that into the agreement," Richard told her as he slid the contract back to them.

"This is a waste of time," Cain said as she stood up, followed by everyone at the table but Richard. "Our offer's off the table."

With that Remi picked up both copies of the contract and tore them in half, letting them fall to the floor.

"Sit the fuck back down," Richard said, pointing at Cain.

"And I suggest you lower your voice and your finger before I have Simon snap it off for you," Remi said. "We want what we want, and you do as well." She kicked the torn papers in his direction. "This proves there's no middle ground."

"There's nothing else for sale around here," Richard said in a softer tone.

Everyone on the other side of the table laughed. "Everything's for sale, Richard," Cain said. "If you think otherwise, then Muriel's right—you *are* delusional."

"Walk out and you'll regret it," Richard screamed.

"You need better lines than that if you want me to take you seriously, Richard, because you sound more pathetic than threatening," Cain said.

"I mean it." Richard put his hands on the table and leaned forward in what Cain took as a more menacing stance.

"You had an offer and now you don't," Remi said, mirroring him. "Make sure you get that part of the story right when you report in. We weren't the ones who backed away from the table first."

"Sounds like you might be the one who lives to regret something today," Cain said seriously, before she walked out. "Or if I know your boss, you might not live long enough to regret anything."

"That went well, don't you think?" Ramon asked, making everyone laugh as they got in the elevator. "Mano, call our friend with the DEA. It's time to play our part as good citizens and give our government friends some hints as to what's going on at the Capri."

"Anonymous calls are one of my specialties."

Ramon put his hands on Remi and Cain's shoulders. "We haven't heard the last of this."

"You're a gambling man, Ramon," Cain said. "I say we're back here in a couple of days and someone else is sitting next to Richard's chair with a gun pointed at his balls. Remi was right to call him on it. There's no way Nunzio gave him the okay to walk away from this deal."

"If that's the case, then the guy's got *cojones*," Mano said. "The Luca family isn't known for their forgiving nature."

"It's the only thing we all have in common," Ramon said, the three of them smiling at the truth of his observation. "But only when it's truly deserved. None of us would've let someone else talk for us today, no matter whose name's on the deed."

"Like I said, stupid is a way of life for some people," Cain reasserted. "Our problem is that Nunzio's not only stupid, he's also cruel. We just have to wait to see how he entices us back to the table and what the fallout is if we don't agree."

❖

"Our guys on the street say the storekeeps in the ninth ward want to know when we'll be back online," Muriel said. They'd arrived back in town early enough to go to Cain's office. "They're having to deal with one of the local suppliers and they're getting squeezed."

"Sure, *now* they see the benefits of working with me."

"You know all those guys love you, so cut the shit."

Cain put her feet up on her desk and folded her hands over her stomach. "They're going to have to hang on. We'll get back to business as soon as I shake your girlfriend off my ass, and since she's keeping us both in the dark as to when that might be, I have no choice but to lay low for now."

The sound of Muriel's pen on the page stopped and she looked up. "Not funny."

"You're not kidding." Cain threw a paperclip at her and laughed to bleed all the sarcasm from her statement. "But we both know it's true. Unless I want to do some jail time, and I don't, there isn't a whole lot I can do about it right now."

The fact that Shelby and her partners were listening to "Can't Get No Satisfaction" over and over again made Cain smile.

"I know how you feel about this, and I'm going to take care of it."

Cain dropped her feet and moved around her desk to sit next to Muriel. "Let's forget for a minute how I feel about the situation and tell me how you see it."

"Shelby's someone I enjoy spending time with, but I'm not stupid enough to forget the fact that it's like a guilty pleasure. Sort of like too much whiskey—tastes good, but overdoing it isn't a great idea."

"Don't think I'm not taking all that into account. I happen to like Shelby." The cotton of Muriel's shirt felt stiff under her fingers when she placed her hand on her forearm. "She's a good match for you."

"Is that an endorsement, because my father hasn't been so kind. If I get the Casey Clan rah-rah speech one more time about how I'm betraying my bloodline, I'm going to strangle him."

She squeezed Muriel's arm before leaning back in her chair. "If this is the life you really want, then I'll talk Uncle Jarvis off the ledge. But if you choose this, you know I'll have to change your role in the family business, and it'll have nothing to do with trust. You're my family and I love you, and I want you to be happy."

Muriel nodded. "I know that, but I also know that family or not, you can't take the chance, and I can't blame you. Shelby's a beautiful woman, but she's as driven as we are. She's not going to give up her job for me."

"Does she expect you to?" Cain was incredulous, thinking maybe Shelby had changed from the eager but earnest agent she'd met.

"No, and it's not something I'm going to do either, so don't go looking for my replacement yet. Like I said, I'll take care of it."

"Are you sure about that?"

"Positive." Muriel tapped her finger on her notebook. "Back to our problem."

"It's time to break out your Robin Hood tights, cousin."

"I look horrible in green."

"Then take the drab blue pants you've got on and tell the guys to make the rounds. Give our regulars something to help out with the added expense and tell them to be patient. It might take me awhile, but I'll think of something to get us back to a more normal schedule.

"I'll send a couple of the guys to pay a discreet visit to the suppliers our shopkeeps are being forced to use. I don't mind a little friendly competition, but I'm not going to tolerate anyone trying to squeeze blood from these folks just because they choose to do business with me. The guys can pick one supplier and make enough of an impression that the rest of them should back down."

"I'll take care of it." Muriel finished taking notes. "This did bring more heat than I thought."

"I expected it, but Annabel has to either produce something or ease off eventually. We're going to win when it comes to this waiting game. All that matters is that our debts are paid," Cain said, meaning the Bracatos.

Muriel nodded. "Uncle Dalton would be proud."

"Hopefully, but I still have some atoning to do." Cain stood and escorted Muriel to the door. "Remember to do what's best for you, and I'll accept your decision. If it's Shelby, I love you enough to dance at your wedding."

❖

Merrick was waiting outside the door. She had been guarding Emma, whose day usually wasn't as exciting as Cain's and didn't require much "muscle." However, Cain knew Merrick hadn't forgotten her dark side, and Cain planned to indulge it soon.

"Give me some good news, Merrick," she said, dropping back into her chair.

"Your pal Barney Kyle's attorney managed to schedule a court date to get most of the charges against him dropped. But his row got harder to hoe after a recent FBI investigation. They discovered evidence of his fat bank accounts and haven't allowed him bail."

"Is he going to attend this procedure in person?"

Merrick took the seat Muriel had vacated and crossed her legs. "The federal prosecutor's office wants to use a video link, but Barney wants to go. That's the story they're putting out."

Cain cocked her head back and laughed. "When you say it like that I have to guess there's an unofficial story."

"You remember Shakes Curole?"

"Don't you mean bad-luck Curole? He's the only guy I know who has worse luck at the track and the tables than our old friend Blue. What about him?"

"His son works at the Federal Building in the jail ward as a guard. Since they don't hold a lot of people down there, the kid's got plenty of time to keep an eye on Kyle." Merrick took a roll of mints out of her pocket, peeled the foil off the end, and laughed when Cain knocked on the desk to get her talking again. "More importantly, he's been able to keep an eye on Kyle's visitors."

"Who are?" Cain asked, trying to get Merrick to step up the pace.

"Agents who have offices in the Hoover Building, along with the federal prosecuting team assigned to the case."

Cain slammed her hand down and everything sitting on the desk rattled. "The guys trying to put him away are on his visitors' log? The bastards are going to cut a deal with this scumbag?"

"Shakes's kid said, from the size of Kyle's smile these days, they're willing to not just cut a deal. They're going to cut him loose."

"How reliable is this guy?"

Merrick shrugged. "Hard to say, but he *is* Shakes's kid, and he didn't cough all this up for free."

"What'd he want?"

The deep breath Merrick had to take made Cain figure she wasn't going to like the answer. "Shakes is into Ramon for ten grand."

"Tell me you didn't give that idiot ten large of my money?" Cain pinched the bridge of her nose. "Well?" she asked when Merrick didn't answer quick enough again.

"I paid the debt," she said succinctly, then stopped. When Cain only stared at her, she finished. "He came to me and volunteered it in exchange for Shakes's debt. I believed him because I figure he knows not only Kyle's upcoming schedule, but what'll happen to him if he lied."

"Anything else?"

"Kyle might not have a court date with the feds, but there's still the matter of the state charges against him. He'll have to keep that court date until the feds talk the DA's office into playing along."

"When is this happening?"

"Tomorrow morning at nine."

Cain locked eyes with her and it had nothing to do with a power play. "Then I expect you there before nine. Is that good for you?"

The question made Merrick exhale as if she was exasperated. "You asked me that why?"

"Because I just finished talking about how my business is shit, and because you're getting used to making big decisions without me. This has to get done, but it has to be done without a glitch."

"It *will* be, no matter what time it is, and I'm up for it. You might want Katlin for this, but I'm just as good."

Cain walked around the desk, stood behind Merrick, and rested her hands on her shoulders. "Actually, I want you for this. It's the reason I sent Katlin to Biloxi. I love Katlin, but between us, she isn't at your level yet. I might not have explained this to you before, but that's why you're with Emma."

"Nothing's going to go wrong, but I want you to reconsider visiting Barney later today." Merrick put both feet on the ground and turned around. "Why turn up the heat if you don't have to?"

"My father always said that sometimes the safest place is in the middle of the fire. It burns off all the shit that would otherwise drown you." Cain returned to her office chair and laughed. "And I'm going to visit Barney today so I can start the flames that will change the landscape the FBI has drawn up for us. It's time to give the bloodhounds a new scent."

"I don't doubt you, but considering how relentless they've been lately, I don't know how you can pull that off."

"Merrick," Cain came forward and rested her elbows on her desk, "I didn't need somebody's kid to tell me that the FBI would be willing to cut Kyle loose. Barney wasn't going away, because he did something very few of them have been able to achieve."

"Infiltrate?"

"Giovanni gave Kyle a free pass because he knew Kyle didn't represent his badge when he showed up. Kyle wanted to bring me down, and he wanted more than a ribbon and a gold watch as pay. Now the feds are going to give him a free pass if he teaches them how to do it."

"If you know all that, then why risk going to see him?"

"To make sure. I'm not questioning myself, at least I try not to very often, but I'm willing to be proven wrong when it comes to something like this. I realize my actions may cause some fallout, but I can't take a chance on being wrong one way or the other."

"I'll get back to work, then, and leave you and Lou to it."

Once Cain was alone, she fit her steepled fingers under her chin. The planning that it took to make her life work was tiring at times, but it was as necessary as what had happened to Giovanni. She took a deep breath and felt like life always put her in situations where she had to climb out of ruts that others dug.

"Da, I hope Emma's right and you're looking out for us. Every so often it's hard to gauge how the bear will react when you shove the stick up its ass."

CHAPTER TWELVE

N unzio." Rodolfo purposely made the simple name sound more exotic. "I hope you're doing well." He glanced out the window to the pool. Juan was once again indulging in his sun worshipping.

"Rodolfo, I'm glad you called. I assume you've heard about our plans for the casino."

"My man gave me the news." That Nunzio was so matter-of-fact about it made Rodolfo hit his thigh with his fist. "Because of our alliance, I would've expected to hear it from you."

"My father and I decided that to turn the kind of profit we'd like to see from our product, we'd need the capital from this sale. Nothing we worked out between us has changed, so don't worry."

Rodolfo fanned his fingers out and took a deep breath with the receiver away from his mouth. He needed to relax so his voice wouldn't reveal his aggravation. "Are you planning to bring in our product some other way?"

"I don't see any changes, no matter whose name is on the deed, Rodolfo. We have enough muscle between the two of us to ensure that. Like I said, I'm handling things."

"Who's taking over?"

"We aren't partners in everything. Who we're doing business with has nothing to do with our arrangement with you. Just know that we picked someone we can easily control and had the ready cash. I'll be in touch once everything's been finalized."

When Rodolfo heard the dial tone he felt free to curse. Perhaps for once he should listen to Juan's ranting and investigate what was going on. He wasn't about to hand over most of his inventory to a man who couldn't be up-front with him. And now he knew that Nunzio didn't even have the capital for the deal he'd made. If Nunzio had withheld that piece of information, Rodolfo wouldn't be able to trust him and his father about anything.

❖

Nunzio muttered a few expletives as he gently put the phone down. The call from Rodolfo had interrupted Richard Bowen's explanation of why he wasn't handing over a check. "So you just walked out?" Nunzio asked, making Richard fidget more. "Are you a fucking moron?"

"Remi and Cain ran the meeting and they wouldn't sign the contract that let us provide security so I pushed, thinking they'd cave." Richard pulled at his collar as if he were having trouble breathing. "I thought you'd appreciate me taking the chance, since I thought it would go our way. I was just looking out for you."

"I don't pay you to fucking think. I pay you to go over there and *pick up a fucking check*. How difficult is that?" Nunzio had stood up, but he was using his lower, more menacing voice.

"Cain and Remi were running the meeting and you expected them to cave? My dog could've told you that wasn't going to happen. All you had to do was kiss their ass for five minutes and we'd have worked around it. I don't need those bitches' permission to do business." He looked at his nails while he delivered the threat.

Nunzio glanced back up and laughed at the total fear on Richard's face. "Now the only question is what happens to you, since you haven't exactly proven your value to this organization."

"If you give me another chance, I'll get them back to the table."

"One more chance means one more. I don't have to explain the price of failure, do I?" Richard nodded quickly at Nunzio's question. "Make it your priority to get them to close this deal, and, Richard, start praying they do. We might have to shave off a couple mil, that's not important, but we do need the bulk. Do we understand each other?"

"Yes, sir, we do."

"Good, get on it." He walked out of the room and headed to the office he kept in the house.

Nunzio Luca III, like Cain and Remi, had gone into the family business and had recently taken over most of the operations that his grandfather had started. The old man, Nunzio Sr., was now living in a gated community in southern Florida and leaving the business to his son in New York and his grandson in Biloxi. He had put in his time after a life of work that began after entering the United States as an immigrant from Naples.

Junior, Nunzio's father, had moved him to Biloxi to establish the family in that market. He had set his son up by buying property in other people's names so there wouldn't be a problem with the Biloxi Gaming Commission, which cringed at the mention of organized crime. That's why Richard was the "owner" of the Capri Casino.

The Luca family wasn't interested in gaming, though. It fronted the cocaine, heroin, and crack they sold across the country. The casino had been a good way to launder money without tipping off the authorities to the real source of the cash. With Nunzio's work in Biloxi, the family had enough police and politicians on their payroll that the family no longer needed the casino. Now they planned to use the capital from its sale to expand the drug pipeline they'd established from Florida to California.

But Cain and Remi had walked away, taking all their money with them. They weren't his favorite people, but cutting a deal with them was his best option since they had the money up front, and it would have been the quickest sale, considering Ramon's connections with the commission.

Richard's stupidity had set things back, but Nunzio figured he could fix the situation once he made his buyers see reason. If not, he would eliminate the weakest link in the chain and deal with what was left.

Putting away his opinions he picked up the phone and called his father. "Pop, how are you?"

"Tell me how heavy that check feels in your hand, son. Now that you have it, don't make any plans for next week. We're taking a trip south of the border. I set up a meet with some of Rodolfo's competitors. They want to break the stronghold he has, and that's good for us. Any war between the big suppliers will make the price drop there, but go up on the street here."

"I'm not holding a check, but let me explain before you get all crazy. Richard pushed them on the security issue, and Cain and Remi pulled the plug."

"If I didn't feel like looking for a new front man to hold the paper on that place, I swear I'd cut that idiot into little pieces myself. And as for that fucking Cain and Remi, they're just like Dalton and Ramon, which means nothing but headaches for us."

"I was thinking what our next move should be, but I wanted to run it by you first." Nunzio laid out his plan, his father grunting his approval every so often.

"That sounds good, but remember that we need this," Junior said.

"Don't worry. I'll take care of everything."

"Why doesn't that make me feel better?"

❖

"Is this part of the Caseys' legitimate business too?" Agent Joe Simmons asked Shelby. The team, now led jointly by Shelby and Joe, sat in a room they'd managed to lease in the building across the street from Cain's offices.

"Even though Anthony's on leave, I could close my eyes and imagine him asking me the same thing." After watching Remi and Mano disappear into the warehouse, she let her binoculars down. "If you have a problem with my personal life, then be up-front about it. The snide remarks are getting old."

"First off, don't compare me to that asshole, and assume from now on that if I ask you a question, that's all it is. I don't expect your answer comes from some inside track because of who you have dinner with every so often." Joe bumped shoulders with her and smiled. "If anyone gives you shit about anything, let me know."

"Thanks. After this morning I wasn't in the mood for any more ragging."

"Then let's take a walk and set some stuff straight."

There were only a few people walking along the sidewalk in front of Cain's place, but Joe noticed the guards posted on the roof stop pacing and follow Shelby and his movements as they headed for the café Cain frequented on occasion.

"To answer your question, we'll probably be seeing more of the Jatibons, which means we should have a meeting with the agents assigned to them."

Joe held up two fingers when the waitress picked up the coffee pot. "Cain's going into business with Ramon?"

"I think so," she told him about the party the night before, "but I've tried to stop speculating when it comes to Cain. It can give you whiplash when she takes a turn you're not expecting."

"There *is* one thing I'm expecting, but I'm not sure how she's going to pull it off."

"You're talking about Kyle?" Shelby poured some sugar into her cup and stirred it in slowly. "I don't think so."

"Why?"

"In this case we're working to put away a guy who shot her. I'd think she'd get some satisfaction knowing he's serving time and we're the ones who'll be taking him down."

Joe nodded, then just as quickly shook his head. "You have to consider that Barney talked Emma onto that plane to the frozen North while she was pregnant with that cutie we've been seeing. If he'd done that to me I'd be tempted to put a bullet between his eyes, and I have more self-control than Cain seems to." He put his hand over Shelby's on the table and whispered, "If she does try, that might be the way we finally pin something on her."

Both their phones rang simultaneously, so Joe threw a five on the table and followed Shelby outside when he got the message Cain was on the move. "Speak of the devil. Let the fun begin," he said to Shelby as they climbed into the back of the surveillance van. He had barely closed the door when the driver floored it to catch up to Cain's vehicle.

"Looks like a trip downtown," Lionel Jones said. He was fooling with a piece of equipment with one hand and holding a headset to his ear with the other. "If she doesn't turn that damn song off I'm going to put in for a transfer."

"I'm working on it," Claire Lansing said.

They all had to hang on as they came to an abrupt stop in front of the Federal Building.

"Get the feeling we won't have any trouble hearing her next conversation?" Shelby asked as Cain, flanked by three guards, made her way up the stairs. "Claire, you might want to call the boss and give her a heads-up."

"You got it. The guys inside said she just requested a visit with Kyle."

"Good," Joe said. "Maybe he'll talk to her since he hasn't done much of that since we locked him up."

As their driver pulled into the parking lot so they could get inside and in front of a monitor, Shelby asked, "What were you saying about fun?"

CHAPTER THIRTEEN

Remi dismissed the car and took the same walk through the French Quarter but couldn't get rid of Simon, who strode silently beside her. She rang the bell and waited while she looked at the throngs of tourists making their way down Bourbon Street and taking pictures every other foot of the decadence that made New Orleans such a fascinating city.

The gate opened and Dallas stood there, still in her casual outfit from the morning, though she'd let her shoulder-length hair down. "What, you couldn't stay away?" Dallas asked.

"Just wanted to come by and see if you'd changed your mind, and since I'm back early we can go out. It'll save you the time in the kitchen."

"And they say chivalry is dead." Dallas leaned on the open door and smiled up at her. "Would you like to come in and have a drink?"

"You're drinking already? Bad day?" She followed Dallas back to the courtyard.

"I was having hot chocolate, but if you'd like something stronger I'll go see what I have."

"Hot chocolate?" Remi asked, making it sound like something she'd never heard of. "Sounds great."

"What can I get for you?" Dallas held her hand out to Simon.

Simon shook it briefly and bowed her head slightly. "Simon Jimenez, ma'am, and don't bother with anything for me."

"I'll be right back then."

"We'll wait over there." Remi pointed to the chairs under the trees. She sat and leaned her head and tried to make out the noise from the street, but had a hard time.

"I've been thinking about you since you left this morning," Dallas said when she returned with two more mugs, clearly ignoring Simon's wishes. "Not the least bit curious?" she asked when Remi didn't say anything.

"Infinitely so, but there are two possibilities."

"Which are?"

Remi took a sip, then leaned forward, holding the mug between her knees. "It's either a good thing or a bad thing."

"I see." Dallas folded her legs under her and sat back on the double seat she'd picked next to Remi's. "Which are you leaning toward?"

"From the welcome I got, I'd go with a good thing, with a little bad mixed in."

"Is that a description of the situation or of you, Ms. Jatibon?"

"Maybe some of both."

Dallas nodded and ran her finger along the seam of her jeans. "I *am* curious about one thing."

"Ask away."

"Why is it I've never seen you, and just recently heard of you and your family, but you own the studio?"

Simon cleared her throat as Remi put her mug down. The leather of her alligator cowboy boots made a stretching noise as she crossed her legs so she could put her hand on the familiar leather bumps. "My family isn't the kind that craves attention."

"You're in the movie business and you don't crave attention." Dallas's laughter made Remi think she wasn't being taken seriously. "That's rare, because usually everyone in this business craves attention."

"Even you?" Remi said with a hint of humor.

"Once I get to know you better I'll tell you why I'm in the business, but for now, I'm perfectly content to sit here in my little secret garden and read books that let me escape for a while." Dallas pointed to the basket filled with books next to Remi's chair.

"So you only don the dress clothes and fake smile when the occasion calls for it, huh?"

"The dress was a last-minute decision and the smile was real, thank you very much. I see my new boss isn't easily impressed."

"After you sign the new contract I'll be happy to tell you what impresses your new boss, but for now you'll have to figure out any new information about her over dinner."

The gate opened again, making Remi stop talking and Simon stand, as was her training, in case the unexpected entry was cause for alarm. "I see more than one person shares the secret garden."

"Excuse me for a minute, would you? And no, I live alone."

Bob stopped at the edge of the flagstone and stared at Remi. The hatred she'd seen in his face before appeared only briefly, then was replaced by a smile so wide it made him appear freakish. If he intended to join them or to spend time with Dallas, the heated but short conversation Remi witnessed put those ideas to rest. That is, until they reached the gate again and Bob held the door shut with his palm.

"No fucking way, Dallas," Remi heard him say as she walked up.

"Dallas, you were getting your shoes," Remi said, never taking her eyes off Bob. "Are you about ready to go?" She stepped closer. "Unless you wanted something, Dickey?"

He opened his mouth wide enough for Remi to see the fillings in his top molars, but just as quickly closed it and took a deep breath. "Just a few minutes of your time to discuss Dallas's contract."

"I'm sure Dallas isn't going to have a problem getting a fair deal for the sequel, but I'm not in a position to discuss that right now." She lowered her eyes to where his hand was wrapped around Dallas's bicep. "Anything else I can do for you?"

"Since you're new to this business, let me give you a word of advice." He yanked Dallas closer to him. "It's considered taboo to speak to someone without their representative present. Keep that up and no talent will want to work with you."

"I appreciate your concern when it comes to my family's business, but since you're not familiar with the way we operate, let me give *you* a little advice." Remi held her hand out to Dallas, which she quickly accepted, making Simon step forward. The actions made Bob let go.

"We don't respond well to threats. If you don't like the way we conduct ourselves, then I suggest you suck it up and do the best by your client, and leave your personal feelings outside the negotiations. If you can't, then I'll give Dallas some free advice—to find new representation."

"Dallas doesn't go anywhere or do anything without me," he said, pointing at Remi. "She knows how long her leash is and isn't likely to do anything stupid."

Remi squeezed Dallas's fingers when she began to say something and cocked her head in the direction of the house. Dallas took the message and started for the door, but stopped to look back every so often. "Something tells me you have a story to tell, Dickey. Do you plan to tell it willingly, or is it going to take a little persuasion on my part?"

"I did a little digging on you, and you and your family don't scare me. You should be afraid of what I can do to you."

His jabbing finger came within an inch of Remi's chest, and she shook her head in Simon's direction to keep her from doing anything. "Like I said, I don't respond well to threats. That's why I rarely issue any, but in your case I'll make an exception." She lowered her voice to a whisper. "I don't know Dallas very well…yet. But if I find out you're hurting her in any way, you're going to remember today. You're going to remember it because it's the day you had the chance to walk away and didn't. You'll be thinking of that opportunity as your scariest nightmare unfolds, and it's worse than anything you could dream up."

"Big talk, Ms. Jatibon, but where I come from we don't take people like you seriously. We take you for a walk in the woods and get rid of the problem ourselves. I don't need any backup." He pointed to Simon.

When Remi started laughing, Bob's face got red. She heard the screen door open behind her, but Dallas didn't move from the doorway unless she was still barefoot. "I'll keep that in mind, and I look forward to talking to you again soon. Now I believe you were leaving."

As Remi finally turned around to see where Dallas was, the gate closed behind Bob. The last thing she needed was someone with baggage, and she had a feeling Dallas came with a cartload. Her mother came to mind, though, and she headed toward the girl with her hand out. Ramon had taught her to be strong, but her mother had tempered that quality by preaching justice and charity.

Dallas Montgomery was beautiful, but she was clearly a woman in need of both.

CHAPTER FOURTEEN

"Come to gloat?" Barney Kyle walked into his side of the drab room and sat in the only chair facing the glass that separated him from the free world.

Cain spread her hands out and shrugged. "God knows what you would've dished out if I was on your side of the glass."

"What in the hell do you want?"

She laughed at his impatience. "What's the rush? It's not like you don't have tons of time on your hands, and only that little cell to run back to."

"Actually, I'm glad you're here." He leaned forward, almost pressing his nose to the glass. "If only to tell you how much I enjoyed that night I pulled the trigger. Seeing you down and bloodied was the highlight of my career." His smile widened when she lifted her fingers to her chest where the scar from his bullet was. "No matter how hard you try to forget me, that hole will make it impossible."

"When you're sitting on your cot, do you ever think of what a waste your life has been? That you worked so hard for something but you're a complete, miserable failure?"

"Ha." He slapped the thick glass but it didn't move. "You think this is over?"

"In more ways than one, actually," Cain said with a smile, enjoying the exchange. This was the first time she'd actually talked to Kyle face to face.

"Tomorrow I'm going to court, and when I'm done the federal prosecutor's not going to have any choice but to let me go. I'm too valuable to lock up, and if that argument doesn't work, then I'm still in a good position. I know too much for them to take the chance of pissing me off." He sat back, looking to Cain like a man who was about to begin to enjoy all the rewards of his wrongdoings. "Annabel doesn't have the balls to take me on."

"Spoken like a man who's spent his life observing it from under a rock."

"What the hell is that supposed to mean?"

She sighed and reached in her coat pocket for something to hand to the guard on her side. "It means that you've spent your life in shadows watching other people live theirs, only you did it for your own gain and not for the reasons you took an oath. You made a pact with a demon to bring me down, but if I had to guess, Giovanni has done his best to disavow you. Your patron, if he shows his true colors, has turned his back on you and will do everything he can to destroy you before you get the chance to do the same." She stopped so the guard could hand Kyle the gift she'd brought him. "You're all alone, Barney, and that's not a good position to be in when you're in jail."

"What the fuck is this?" He held up the gold-embossed prayer card Bishop Andrew had gotten for her after she'd asked for it. On one side was a novena written in scrolling letters and on the other was St. Michael in the pose most people were familiar with—his foot on Satan's head and his sword raised in his right hand ready to strike.

"Just a reminder."

Kyle held the card to the glass as if she'd forgotten what it was. "Of what? A reminder to pray for good things to happen to me?"

"I'm not that presumptuous, and I could give a fuck about your soul, so no." She tapped her finger to the picture he still had pressed to the glass. "This is to remind you that before you go hunting the devil, you should know your own demons."

"Getting religious on me, Casey? If you think that'll get these assholes off your ass, you're crazy."

"I don't waste my time on wishful thinking, and I've finished what I came for today."

"So you're not here to gloat and only come bearing gifts?" He put the St. Michael card in the pocket of his gray jumpsuit. "This doesn't make us even, and it sure as hell doesn't make us friends."

"For once, Barney, you're right on both counts. After meeting you, I can honestly say I'm rooting for the feds this one time. You don't deserve anything more than a small cell and time for everything you've done." She stood and buttoned her jacket. "Take care, and perhaps with everything you're facing, prayer wouldn't be such a bad thing. My priest tells me confession is good for the soul, and if you're contrite enough, the folks who control your future might just show compassion."

"After tomorrow you should just worry about yourself and that pretty bitch who shares your bed. As a matter of fact, Emma might be one of the first people I visit when I get out of here. I gave her a way out and away from you, and she spit in my face."

"Best of luck to you then. I'll have a whiskey waiting." Cain chuckled at his baffled expression, but she didn't add anymore. She'd gotten what she came for, which was to meet the man who'd brought her such misery in both his time with the FBI and in Giovanni's employ. She knew her demons, so now she could bring her sword down on this snake with no remorse.

With one last wave she stepped out and headed toward the waning sunlight. She gazed back at the building, wondering if, when your time came to an end, it would be better to know or more peaceful to never see the bullet coming? Whatever the answer, she would ask Kyle when she eventually met him in hell.

❖

"Can I call you back?" Shelby asked as soon as she answered her cell phone, not bothering to see who it was. Her eyes were glued to Cain's retreating back as she quickly navigated the steps of the Federal Building on the way to her car.

Muriel answered her. "I'll be in the office until seven, then I have an engagement tonight for work. Try me before then or wait until tomorrow."

"Wait," she said, but was too late. The call had dropped from Muriel's end. "Shit."

"If you have to get going, I'll brief the next shift," Joe said, waving her toward the door. Since they were essentially back at the office, their cars were only a few blocks away and Shelby could get to Muriel's quickly.

"I'll take the morning briefing then." As she drove to Muriel's office, she tried to phone three more times, but the assistant said she was on a conference call. She stepped out of the elevator on the second floor over Emma's, Cain's newest nightclub, and was escorted into Muriel's office right away. She was still talking and pointed Shelby into one of the chairs facing her desk.

"A few more days is what I'm guessing, so sit tight and keep your eyes open. Call me if you get anything new and I'll let Cain know what you said," Muriel finished and hung up. "Don't," she said when Shelby stood and started toward her.

"So much changed since last night that I can't touch you?"

"Things haven't changed, Shelby, but they're clearer than they were last night. I pride myself on not going out of my way to make mistakes, but I didn't do that well this time," Muriel kept eye contact with her. "I made a mistake and it's time to rectify it, because no matter what promises we make, our lives aren't going to change, and our priorities sure as hell aren't. It's time to end this before we get any more involved."

"You think it's that easy to walk away?"

Muriel took a deep breath and shook her head. "It's far from easy, but neither of us has much choice. It was my mistake to think we could make this work, but our worlds are too far apart, and there's a fence dividing them that neither of us is willing to cross. To do that, we have to betray something that means more to us than what we have now."

"You're making a mistake, Muriel," Shelby said, her fingers wrapped so tight around the arms of her chair her chest was aching. "No one expects you to sacrifice so much for family honor. This isn't the Stone Age, for God's sake."

"I'm saving us both from facing now what's going to be inevitable eventually."

"What the hell are you talking about?" Shelby asked, her swelling anger making her want to hit something.

"Tell me that Annabel or someone else in the Bureau hasn't made an issue out of who you're seeing, and I'll back down."

"No one of import—"

Muriel slammed her hand down on her desk. "You lie to me now and you can get out, we're done."

"It doesn't matter to me who said what about you, baby. I don't owe my life to the Bureau, just like Cain doesn't own you. Don't throw this away for things that won't matter to us in the long run."

Muriel's phone rang four times before she reached over and picked it up. All Shelby did was watch as she held it to her ear and said nothing. Muriel wouldn't utter a word as long as Shelby was sitting in the room, so she put aside any notions of begging. It would do no good unless she was willing to toss aside everything she'd believed in up to then. Clearly Muriel wouldn't, no matter how much she cared for her. The realization hit her like a hurricane in August and she walked out.

"Muriel, did you hear what I said?"

"Sorry." She pressed her fingers to her forehead as if the pressure would erase the image of Shelby leaving. "Start from the beginning, T-Boy."

"This is a safe line, right?"

T-Boy was a gambling addict who knew more about the city than the people who supposedly ran it, but he was smart enough to know when to stay quiet. His call meant either he was broke and looking for some fast cash or he was banking for the future with something Muriel and Cain would find valuable.

"Safe is always relative, isn't it?"

"Just heard from my buddy that works at the airport."

Muriel picked up her pen, ready to start writing. "New tourists in town?"

"Your uncle and his boy are back from south of the border. Got in about an hour ago and got detained in customs, but from what I hear, it was so they could get fitted for a new suit. Custom job like from where your family shops."

Muriel wrote down that Rodolfo and Juan Luis were back and already under the watchful eye of the FBI and DEA. "We'll have to get together soon. Thanks for letting us know."

"One more thing."

"Yeah?"

"There's a new player in town looking for work, and considering his resume there's been plenty of interest."

Under the Luis names she put a question mark. "Can you come by in the morning? I'll stop and pick up my father's favorite."

"I'll be there."

"Shit," Muriel said as she fell back in her chair. Their future was a little more complicated. She wanted to wait to tell Cain, but thought better of it considering how Cain felt about Juan.

She called the house and found out where Cain and Emma had gone out for the evening, then drove to the Quarter to Galatoire's, one of the oldest restaurants in the city. Outside was a no-parking zone that the police patrolled regularly, so the paneled van that had been trailing

Cain was parked down the block. Muriel was sure the group on duty was crammed inside because you couldn't get a table here without a subpoena, and even with one you'd have a hard time.

They were sitting in the corner of the back of the place, with Lou and a couple of guys at the next table enjoying iced tea. "You look like you could use a drink," Cain said when Muriel sat down. "Rough day?"

"Tied up loose ends and some more unraveled—typical." Muriel quickly drained the glass Cain pushed toward her. "Expecting someone else?" She pointed to the other empty chair.

"Remi called and invited us, and I thought it was a good night to go out. To be seen, as it were." Cain signaled the waiter for another round and another place setting and glanced at her watch; it was a minute to eight.

They continued to chitchat until Remi arrived with her date. The room quieted for a moment as Dallas followed Remi to their table, but just as quickly the other diners went back to their own conversations.

"It's great to meet you, Dallas," Emma said.

"I figured she'd like having dinner with all of you since she thinks I'm only interested in sleeping with her," Remi said, clearly teasing.

"Then come to the restroom with me and I'll give you some pointers," Emma said to Dallas, making the others laugh.

"I'd find a hobby," Cain told Remi once the two left. "If Emma's persuasive, and she is, then sex is a long way off, if that *is* what you had in mind."

"And I thought this was a good idea," Remi said.

Cain looked at her watch and the second hand was sweeping past the two, on its way to mark nine o'clock. In her mind's eye she could see the armored van leaving the underground parking facility. The drive wouldn't take very long, and that's why it was being done at night. Less traffic meant fewer hassles from point *a* to point *b*.

She looked up as Emma and Dallas headed back, walking closely together and already appearing to be best friends. Cain loved seeing Emma like this, alive and happy, and she was willing to do anything to keep her that way. Even if it meant crossing a line considered taboo for so very long, no matter what city you did business in.

CHAPTER FIFTEEN

"Comfortable back there?" Agent Martin Chesterfield asked through the open porthole between the front seat and the back section.

"Just drive, asshole. And shut the fuck up." Barney Kyle stretched his hands upward but found that the shackles would stretch only an inch past his knees.

"I can see you're going to charm everyone in court tomorrow, but don't get too comfortable with the accommodations. Once you plead to the state charges against you, we'll pick you up for your next court appearance. It's a good thing you look so good in that federal gray, since you'll be wearing it for years to come." Martin laughed as they drove under the interstate. "Just ten more blocks now. How's it feel to be so popular?"

"Fuck off."

"Be nice or I'll tell our brethren over at central lockup to put you in with the general population. You know how those local guys feel about us. Then I'll ask them to pin a note to your back so everyone knows what you used to do for a living. I bet those guys won't care that you don't work for us anymore."

The driver pulled up to the gate on Broad Street and handed over the necessary papers. After a glance the guard pressed the button and the gate rolled slowly back, powered by a motor that sounded like it was on its last breath.

"Wait here, I'll be right back," Martin told the driver, getting out and walking to the back with the key. "Come on, Mr. Kyle." He unlocked the chain looped through his cuffs and put his hand under his arm to help Kyle down. "We'll be back for you tomorrow around ten." Martin let him go as the sheriff's officers responsible for the jail population walked toward them.

Merrick waited until Kyle was standing between the two groups before she set up her shot. The night-vision scope on the rifle she was using clearly outlined his head in the crosshairs. She took a breath and had started to put pressure on the trigger when he looked up at her as if he knew she was there. The last thing she saw as she squeezed all the way was his brows going up in what appeared to be confusion.

"Cover," more than one of the police around Kyle screamed as the back of his head sprayed into the rear of the van he'd been transported in.

Merrick took advantage of the chaos to remove the scope and lean the rifle on the half wall surrounding the old Jax Beer brewery. The rear fire escape looked rickety, but she took the steps at an alarming rate, not wanting to get caught anywhere in the vicinity when the cavalry started streaming out of the jail yard. Only Cain knew where she was and why she was there, and she had every intention of keeping it that way.

Once she was on the ground, she headed toward the downtown area at a normal pace, until she got to the convenience store where she'd parked the car she'd picked up for the job. As she drove toward Jarvis's, she kept under the speed limit, not that the police cars with their lights and sirens blaring would have noticed her.

"Now it's a matter of waiting," she said as she turned into the used-car lot. She slid the keys under the front seat and took her scope before walking to her own car parked behind the office. "Because it's only a matter of time before the feebies come a-knocking."

❖

"So you live in the city?" Emma asked Dallas as the entrées were brought out. "I'm shocked we haven't run into you, since Cain has a business down there."

"We've probably crossed paths, but I'm not famous enough for you to recognize me." Dallas nodded her thanks to the waiter and took a sip of wine.

"Hopefully this next film will take care of that," Remi said. "Then you can tell us if being noticed is more a curse than a blessing." She picked up her fork and used it to point at Cain. "What's your opinion?"

"It's a curse, but I think Dallas will handle the fame a little easier than we do. We're more apt to end up on the cover of some rag, but the public won't see it unless they mail lots of packages at the post office. After tonight I'm sure Emma agrees with me that we made a wise investment choice."

"I'm not sure what you mean by your fame, and the investment choice isn't registering either," Dallas said.

Remi smiled at her. "You'll understand the first part soon enough if we have more than a couple of minutes together, and the second one's easy. Meet the forty-nine percent owner of the studio."

"You all are a well-kept secret then, because I haven't heard of you either," Dallas told Cain. She was about to say something else but stopped when the smile fell away from Cain's face as she stared at the front of the restaurant. "Friend of yours?"

Emma reached for Cain's hand. "She's more like a termite. Hidden away most of the time and swarms only every so often, but just as destructive."

"Finish dinner and I'll be right back." Cain rubbed Emma's hand between hers, then stood. She waved off Lou and Muriel as she strode toward an agitated-appearing woman, who stood at the door. "Are you here for the crab cakes?"

"Cut the shit, Cain. You know exactly why I'm here," Shelby said in a harsh whisper. "I want you to come in for questioning."

"If it's about the crab cakes I'll be happy to, but I'd rather finish dinner first." People were seated near the door waiting for tables so their chatter was loud enough to cover Cain's conversation. "But if it's about something else, then you're going to have to fill me in since I'm sure you think I did it, and I'm sure I know nothing about it."

"Cain, your food's getting cold," Muriel said as she walked up. "And, Agent Philips, unless you have a warrant handy, then I suggest you scuttle back to your little cocoon outside."

"So your client knows nothing about…never mind." She pulled her hair back in apparent frustration. "I'm going to central lockup on Tulane Avenue, and if I find one thing tying you to tonight, pack your toothbrush in the morning, because I'm taking you in, Cain. As for you, this is what you really want?" She looked at Muriel. "If it is, then I don't know what to think of you anymore. And I'm not sure I'll spend any time worrying about it. Cain, expect me in the morning."

"I'll have coffee and biscuits ready," she responded, laughing when Shelby came close to saying something else but instead chose to storm out.

"Stop antagonizing the help," Muriel said.

"I'm just trying to figure out if she's more pissed at me or at you."

"Are you going to tell me what she's so upset about or do I have to guess?"

Cain put her arm around Muriel's shoulders and started back to the table. "What am I always telling you about time and place, cousin? The time right now is for crab cakes. When we get home I'll tell you a bedtime story."

"Everything all right?" Remi asked.

"What were we saying about fame? Or should I say notoriety?" Cain cocked her head in the direction of the door. "Something obviously happened tonight, and for some reason I'm the first person they blame."

"A Girl Scout like you? Hard to believe," Remi said as they all laughed.

Cain picked up her fork and took a bite of her crab cakes. She hoped whatever they'd served Kyle that night before shipping him off to hell was something he halfway enjoyed. Because if Father Andrew was right, he'd be up to his neck in pig shit for the whole of eternity, a fantasy that would let her sleep better at night.

❖

"You have nothing?" Shelby asked Martin after leaving the French Quarter and arriving at the jail.

"If you want to call the remodel job on the transport van and Kyle's new hairdo nothing, then I'm sure I can't talk you out of it. But if you're talking having someone in custody, then you're on the money. We have nothing."

A member of the FBI's forensic team walked up with a rifle in his hand. "We found this across the street on the roof, ma'am. We started there since it was the only logical spot after we figured the trajectory of the shot."

"Take it in and find out what tree the stock came from by morning," Annabel said. She'd left her house in jeans and a sweatshirt after Shelby's call. "Shit," she said, after taking a look under the sheet covering Kyle. "I didn't agree with what he did, but he deserved better than this."

"I hate to say this," Shelby said, squatting down next to Annabel, "but for once I have to agree with Anthony. This has Cain written all over it, and we need to find the connection that leads back to her. No one but a handful of people knew we were transporting tonight, and one of them had to have talked. Find that link and we finally find our way to a warrant with the name Casey on it."

"Make your list then, and keep me in the loop. If Casey is involved she went too far this time. Kyle wasn't on the right side of the law, but he was our responsibility until the process had run its course. I don't like being made a fool of."

"If it's there, we'll find it."

CHAPTER SIXTEEN

If you check around, Mr. Luis, you won't find anyone who can help you deal with problems better than me." Anthony Curtis had forgone the dark suit for a pair of khakis and a black leather jacket. He'd made it into the Luis suite at the Piquant, but Rodolfo still appeared wary.

"Tell me how a member of the FBI can help me except maybe try and bring me down." Rodolfo flicked his cigar in the direction of the ashtray but missed. The fat ash that landed on the light-colored carpet didn't seem to concern him, though, like a man used to others cleaning up after him. "And please don't try to deny who your employer is. One of my associates in the city pointed you out."

"I'm not going to deny that the FBI *was* my employer, but not anymore. I was dismissed recently, so I'm looking for something new to keep my interest. You and your nephew came to mind when I figured we have a common problem."

"Sounds interesting. Let's hear it."

Rodolfo crossed his legs and started puffing on his cigar again, so Anthony felt comfortable enough to sit down. Behind Rodolfo's head was a perfect view of the city's night skyline. "Derby Cain Casey."

"That's it?" Rodolfo laughed. "I met Ms. Casey on my last trip. She's rather abrupt in her conversation, but I doubt she's a problem to me."

"Really?" He mirrored Rodolfo's relaxed pose by crossing his legs. "Your business hasn't suffered any setbacks recently?" Rodolfo flinched and tried to hide his reaction, but Anthony saw it. His fish had taken the bait, so he stood up and shrugged. "Sorry I bothered you. I must have you confused with someone else."

Rodolfo shrugged as well. "You have to see it from where I'm sitting, Mr. Curtis. If I admit to having a business problem, as it were, then if you're just on *temporary* leave I might have a problem when you decide to return to work. A man like me stays in business by making sure of his moves before he makes them."

"I agree you have no reason to trust me, but you also would be a fool to turn me down. I'm no longer with the Bureau because of that bitch, so if the only way to bring her down is by working on the other side of the law, I'm willing to take my chances."

"Let me think about it and I'll get back to you." As soon as Rodolfo finished speaking, one of his men stepped up and stood behind Anthony, ready to escort him out of the room. "If I do agree to your offer, there's one thing you should keep in mind."

"What's that?" Anthony could see himself starting to reel in slowly because he knew the hook was now in place.

"If I'm disappointed in your job performance, I'll handle things differently than your previous employers. I'm not a man who tolerates disappointment well."

"Understood." Standing in the hall, Anthony felt his confidence crack a little, but he knew he could work around it. He was doing this to prove a point, and because he wasn't about to spend his leave in his apartment sulking until Annabel felt he was ready to come back. When Cain was out of the picture and Rodolfo was sharing her fate, he'd give Annabel her wish and transfer somewhere else, but so would she when he proved just how incompetent she was.

"We're going to use him, right?" Juan asked, coming into the room when he heard the front door close.

"What we're going to do, or at least what you're going to do, is everything I tell you to. I haven't been thrilled with your behavior lately, so unless you're ready to let me know what's on your mind that's made you lose your control, consider yourself on a short leash." Juan was dressed as if he was going out for the evening. "If you choose to disobey me, then take what I told Curtis to heart. I won't allow you to bring this family down for whatever it'll take to satisfy you."

"Papa, I may be many things, but I'll never turn against you or disappoint you. You have my word on that."

"If you're so loyal, tell me what's bothering you."

Juan stared at him for awhile without saying anything, just rocking in place. He reminded Rodolfo of when he was a little boy thinking of the best way to put something so Rodolfo wouldn't get angry.

"The last time we were here…" Juan said, sitting next to Rodolfo on the sofa so he could keep his eyes on his shoes. He told Rodolfo of his attempts to talk to Emma and how she'd laughed and humiliated him. The more he spoke the more venomous his tone became, and Rodolfo could easily read between the lines.

Juan had found something he wanted, and for once in the privileged life Rodolfo had given him, he couldn't have it. The realization was making Juan crazy, and crazy men were dangerous, in Rodolfo's opinion.

"You're my son, no matter who fathered you," he said, putting his hand behind Juan's neck, "and I love you. But get that woman out of your head. Cain Casey may be a woman, but she's a viper I'd rather leave alone. If you do anything to Emma, Cain won't stop coming until she's destroyed all of us. You bring that down on us, and you won't have to worry about her. I'll take care of you myself, no matter how much I love you."

"You'd take her side over mine?" Juan tried pulling away from Rodolfo but couldn't break his grasp.

"If you see it that way, we're going to have a problem. If you respect nothing, then you'll live your life without honor. In this case you have to respect Emma Casey's wishes and her commitments to someone else. So promise me you'll do that." Juan tried to pull away from him again. "I said promise me."

"I promise, Papa."

Rodolfo let him go and did nothing as Juan bolted from the room, followed by the men assigned to him. When they came back, he'd have to talk with the men guarding his nephew. He hoped he wasn't too late, because when a man made a promise he looked you in the eye. Juan had said the words, but they had no truth in them.

"No matter how hard I tried, I guess I couldn't knock your father's influence out of you. He was the same type of man when it came to women, and look what happened to him." Rodolfo spoke aloud as he gazed out at the city. "Even from the grave he has more of a hold over you than I do."

The glow of his cigar reflected in the glass, and he considered his next move since he hadn't been able to contact anyone in the Bracato organization. His business was important, but the smartest first move he could make was to contact Cain. They would never be friends, but he could prevent her from becoming an enemy.

❖

"What are you still doing up, sweet pea?" Cain asked Hannah when they got home and she found Carmen holding her in the den.

"I miss you and Mama," Hannah said as she did her best to wriggle away from Carmen.

"We missed you too, but it's way past your bedtime," Emma said, not sounding amused as she scooped Hannah up before she got to Cain. "Time for bed, and you," she pointed at Cain, "don't start without me."

"What would be the fun in that?" Cain kissed Hannah's forehead and headed to Jarvis's study. To give everyone more privacy and room, Jarvis had given Cain the use of the whole house while he took an extended vacation in Florida. Carmen followed Muriel into the study and poured them a drink without being asked. "Carmen, is Merrick in?"

"She's waiting in the pool house for you, but I called for her when I heard the car pull up," Carmen said, pouring the last glass and putting it next to the empty seat in front of the desk. "Will you need anything else?"

"No, thank you, Carmen, and good night."

"Want to fill me in on what's going on?" Muriel asked. "If Shelby's coming back in the morning, I'd like to be prepared."

"And I want you to be, but let's wait for Merrick."

A moment later Merrick asked, "Did you enjoy your evening?"

"Had dinner, enjoyed the company, and got shaken down by the feds...you know, a typical night in the life of Cain Casey," she said, laughing. "If I had to put on my guessing cap, I'd say Shelby's visit tonight means you were successful."

"You can be sure the past has been put to rest." Merrick lifted her glass in a toast. "Here's to the future."

"Don't knock the past, my friend, and don't give the future so much credit." Cain lifted her glass and drank anyway. "The past is known, but the future can sometimes be troublesome."

"I'm tired of troublesome myself," Emma said from the door. "I'm in the mood for slow and easy." She sat on Cain's lap and kissed the side of her head. "Merrick, you didn't tell me you were taking the night off."

"Merrick wasn't slacking, lass. She was paying our friend a visit."

"I swept the room before you got here so you can tell her if you want to," Merrick said.

"Friend?" Muriel asked.

"A bit of unfinished federal business," Cain said. "Merrick took care of it, and I feel better that it's a subject we'll never have to discuss again."

"You can't be serious?" Muriel said. "If that's true, the surveillance we've seen up to now will seem minor. They'll be relentless, Cain."

"What did you want me to do, ignore it?"

"You could've waited until it was done. Something arranged from the inside would've have been easier to cover. We have enough to worry about, and after a call I got today you can add some more."

"I talked to the bastard today, and he gloated about being cut loose. It was only a matter of time before he worked the system and they let him go. His first planned visit was with Emma to pay her back for what he viewed as her betrayal. And when it comes to Emma and assholes with a grudge, I'm not willing to gamble at all." The statement earned her a kiss from her partner. "The feds might have been that generous but I'm not."

"You're crazy, but a genius," Muriel said.

"No one is dumb enough to visit a condemned man, right?" Cain laughed. "The thing about playing within the parameters others put up for you is they aren't as challenging as the feds think they are. They think I'm stupid, and I'm okay with that."

"Sure you are, because you have the freedom to be your smart, cute self," Emma said. "What call, Muriel?"

"T-Boy called and the Luis family is back in town. I would imagine that the recent blows to their business here, and the wrench you threw into their operations to the east, needed a hands-on approach."

"Merrick, don't lose sight of Emma, and pass the word to Mook that I need more guys on the kids."

"You got it, boss." Merrick stood and nodded. "See you in the morning."

Muriel said good night as well and headed up to her suite.

"I want you to swear you'll tell me if that asshole comes within twenty feet of you," Cain said once they were alone.

"I think he got the message I wasn't interested, honey."

Cain shook her head. "Guys like Juan never get that message until two seconds before death takes them from the severe beating that kills them. If he comes near you, I want you to call me no matter what. I'm serious. I'm not taking any chances with you."

"I'll tell you, but I think Merrick's going to beat me to it. If Lou's with me, I'll call you from the bank while I'm drawing out his bail for shooting the little bastard."

"Just remember that Juan isn't someone I want to second-guess."

"I was being serious too. You've built a fortress around us, so I'm sure we'll be fine."

"I'll make that true no matter what."

CHAPTER SEVENTEEN

The car stopped in front of Galatoire's, but Remi studied the street in both directions before she opened the back door for Dallas. A few tourists were still walking around and the ever-present van was parked a block away, but otherwise, it was quiet.

"Ready?" Dallas asked from behind her.

"Sorry, old habit." Remi took her hand to help her in. On the seat lay a bouquet of Chinese orchids.

Dallas picked up the flowers and closed her eyes as she smelled them appreciatively. "How did you know these are my favorite?"

"I cruised the Internet this afternoon and found your official Web site. All it took was a call to the president of your fan club. She told me your favorite color, food, and sexual position, as well as your favorite flowers. I'm not going to press you as to how she came by her information." Remi smiled.

"If I have an official Web site, it's news to me, and if I did, I sure as hell wouldn't share that much."

"The woman did sound like someone with way too much time on her hands. To reward her, I did tell her that since I'm a fan too I'd do some research and get back to her if anything was off base."

"I hope you're not the kind to kiss and tell." Dallas laid the orchids across her lap and smiled. "Thank you for these. It's been awhile since anyone's given me flowers."

"Is it all right that I did?"

"Why wouldn't it be?"

"If you were with me, I'd mind if someone else went to the trouble. I don't want to do that to someone else. Despite my reputation, that isn't my style." Remi thought of Bob and what part he played in Dallas's life.

"There's no one," Dallas answered, taking Remi's hand. They rode the rest of the way to Dallas's home in silence. When they had to stop a block from her door because of the nightly barricades the police put up so Bourbon Street could become a pedestrian street, Simon got out and walked ahead of them.

"Does Simon always go everywhere with you?"

"Because of our business it's necessary, I'm afraid." Remi had about a hundred feet to come up with an explanation that wouldn't send Dallas screaming away from her. Dallas had to realize the risks involved with entering a relationship with her, if they decided that's what they both wanted.

Simon interrupted her thoughts. "I'll wait at the car. Call when you're ready."

Dallas unlocked the door and led Remi into the house. "Would you like anything?" She opened one of the kitchen cabinets and took out a vase. "If you don't want to tell me anything, it's okay. Just forget I asked."

"If you want to know something, I want you to ask. I'm having a hard time because I've never bothered to explain my situation to anyone." She watched Dallas's hands as she trimmed the tips off the stems and placed the flowers in the vase.

When she finished, Remi accepted the hand Dallas held up and followed her into her living room. The house contained a mixture of antique and comfortable pieces with tasteful artwork, but very few pictures. The style fit the little bit of Dallas she'd come to know.

"Are you sure you don't want anything?" Dallas asked as Remi took a seat next to her on the sofa.

"Just a few minutes to talk would be good." Remi studied their hands pressed together. Compared to hers, Dallas's hands were small and delicate, but her grip was strong. "I like spending time with you, but you need to know what you're getting into. Once I'm finished, if you feel like you can't or don't want to continue, you'll still have a future with the studio. You have my word. The woman who disrupted dinner tonight is with the FBI."

Remi gave her a tame but clear explanation as to why she and her business associates would bear federal scrutiny, or at least why the federal authorities thought they did. Dallas could have gathered these facts from reading the newspaper stories about them. Fair warning was one thing, but blatantly confessing to someone she didn't know much about was pure insanity.

In the middle of her account, Dallas turned away, then reclined against her and pulled Remi's arm around her. Remi was surprised but kept talking until Dallas had a clearer picture why she'd never heard of her and Cain, and why they fought so hard to keep it that way.

When she finally stopped, Dallas asked, "Are you done?"

"That's enough for one night."

"I have a question." She moved so they could face each other. "Did you tell me all that because you don't want to be here anymore?"

"I told you because I wanted to give you an out, if you want one."

"Truthfully, I'm looking for an in." Dallas had started to return to the spot at Remi's side when she sat back up. "You haven't been accused of selling drugs, have you? You didn't mention that."

"No, we've never been under scrutiny for that. If you work for my father, it's actually the quickest way to get fired. That's also true for the people we deal with, like Cain."

"I only have one more question," Dallas said, turning within the circle of Remi's arms to get comfortable again. "Am I just another notch on the famous bedpost of Remi Jatibon? I might not have known you, but I've heard a little gossip in the last few months."

"No, you aren't, unless you want to be. I won't deny my reputation. I do have one that I truly deserve."

Dallas faced her again and ran her hands up Remi's arms. Reaching her collar she slipped the fingers of one hand into the curls at the base of Remi's neck and pulled her down, stopping before their lips met. She ran her index finger lightly over Remi's bottom lip, waiting to see if she would object. When she didn't, Dallas let herself do what she'd wanted to since they met. She kissed Remi and slid her fingers through Remi's hair.

The kiss lasted until Remi's hands landed on her back. Then she pulled back and wiped her lipstick off Remi's lips. "Don't get mad, but I want to take this slow. I think it'd be prudent since we just met, and I don't want you to get the wrong impression."

"I gave you flowers, doesn't that count?"

"That was sweet, but it doesn't mean I'm going to sleep with you." Dallas moved to the buttons on Remi's shirt, plucking at them nervously.

"We could just have sex. No sleeping has to be involved," Remi whispered in her ear.

Dallas tapped the end of Remi's nose with her finger and laughed. "We could, but we're not."

"That restroom break must have been very informative," Remi teased. "But we'll go as slow as you want. Kiss me good night then."

"It's still early." Dallas kissed her chin. "And I have a few more questions."

"I'm sure you do, but I'm trying to impress you with how good I am. How about we get together tomorrow?" Remi stood up, taking Dallas with her. Without her heels their height difference was more noticeable.

Before leaving, Remi pulled Dallas close enough that almost the full lengths of their bodies were touching and she kissed her. "Good night."

"Sure you won't stay a little longer?" When Remi shook her head, Dallas sighed and kissed her one more time before letting go. "Good night."

"I'll see you in the morning," Remi said as she opened the door.

Dallas locked it behind her, confident Remi could make her way out, and got ready for bed. She thought about Bob, knowing he wouldn't be thrilled with this development, and realized he was the reason Remi had asked earlier about cutting in on anyone.

It shocked her that Remi hadn't asked outright about him, but it was just a matter of time. Lying in bed she tried to relax enough to get to sleep, figuring it would be a waste of time to start worrying now. She didn't want to piss Bob off, but she didn't want to miss out on getting to know Remi.

At 4:01 her eyes were still open. "I'm going to look like hell in the morning." The ringing phone on the nightstand scared her out of her musings. Dallas picked it up, thinking it was a wrong number, and tentatively said "Hello."

"Hey," Remi's voice rumbled from the other end. "I didn't wake you, did I?"

"It's four in the morning," she said, dragging out the word morning.

"I couldn't sleep and figured you might be in the same boat."

"Actually I was lying here watching the time tick away."

"How about that drink you offered me?"

Dallas sat up and laughed. "You want a drink right now?"

"You did offer, but if you're tired, I'll understand."

She put her robe on. In the kitchen she began to brew some espresso. "Where exactly are you?"

"Across the street. The idea of picking your lock crossed my mind, but I didn't want to freak you out."

She laughed, then realized Remi probably could do it. "If you want coffee, I suggest you get to it." As she poured, she heard the lock on the back door give way to whatever Remi had done, and she smiled as she put Remi's cup down. "You could come in handy if I ever lock myself out."

"You're an interesting woman," Remi said as she picked up her cup.

"I'm actually a woman who gets a little upset if I make coffee and don't get a kiss in return." She took her cup and headed for the sofa.

They sat together on Dallas's sofa until the sun came up, finally finding sleep. Right before Dallas gave way to her dreams, she thought of what Emma had told her earlier. *Give in right away and you'll be what she knows. If you want a future, then set yourself apart by respecting yourself and demanding the same of her.* After she had discovered how wonderful it felt to be in Remi's arms, she wanted a future with her.

She'd worry later about everything that could spoil things for them. And at the top of that list was something that could break her quicker than Bob could.

Would Remi accept her once she knew the whole truth?

CHAPTER EIGHTEEN

Richard drove from Biloxi to Cain's offices on the riverfront, drumming his fingers on his steering wheel and trying to center himself and rev up his bravado. Nunzio had impressed on him what he needed to do, and his palms were sweating as he thought about what he'd pay if this meeting didn't go well.

"Hello, sweets, you want to tell your boss I'm here," he told the receptionist. "The name's Richard."

The attractive brunette rolled her eyes, looked down to see where Richard's eyes were glued, then rolled them again at the frank way he was staring at her cleavage. When she got instructions from someone, she merely pointed. "Bitch," Richard thought, and strolled down the mahogany-paneled walls into the office, located almost in the center of the building for Cain's protection.

"What can we do for you, Richard?" Cain asked, not rising from her seat, and neither did Remi, Mano, Ramon, or Muriel.

"Thanks for agreeing to see me," Richard said softly.

"After thirty phone calls, we thought we'd agree just to get some quiet around here," Cain said, sounding like she wasn't kidding. "What's on your mind?"

"Wanted to chat and maybe do a little business. About our last meeting—I may've been a little adamant in my views. You all were right on the personnel issue. Once I sell, the place is yours to do whatever you want, so I'll go along with the contract as is." Richard folded his hands over the girth of his stomach. "If you have the papers ready, I'll sign. I could provide the best security for you, but if you want to do your own, then have at it."

"If that's why you wanted to meet, you should've mentioned that in all your messages and saved yourself a trip," Cain said. "We're looking into another property with a less colorful past, one that wouldn't require the kind of pest control your place needs."

"Don't be too quick. I'm sure we can work something out." Richard sat up, thinking his life wasn't worth much without a deal.

"It's too late to work something out. Besides, the location we're looking at is newer and connected to other sites we could get an option on after we're up and running. You did us a favor turning us down. In the long run this location makes more sense for us," Remi said, and everyone nodded.

"You all were hot for this a couple of days ago, so cut the shit." Richard was on the edge of his seat, wiping his brow with his handkerchief. "I know the business, and nothing but my place is for sale. I don't know what kind of scam you're trying to pull, but it won't work."

Ramon laughed as he twirled his lighter between his fingers. "Your sales pitch needs work. You of all people should realize everything's for sale if the price is right."

"If I walk out now, the deal's off. I don't care what you offer me after that, I'll sell to someone else," Richard said, trying to control the slight waver in his voice. "I'm not kidding."

"Then unless my partners disagree with me," Cain said, the springs in her chair creaking a little as she slowly rocked, "we're out." When Richard sprang out of his chair she put her hand over her letter opener.

"You'll be sorry, Cain. I can promise you that."

"I'm already sorry I've wasted this kind of time on you." Cain stood up and leaned on the handle of the letter opener. "If there's nothing else, get out of here, Richard, and take your empty threats with you."

When he turned to leave, Cain noticed the sweat marks under the arms of his suit. Considering the weather was still coolish, the reaction had to come from nerves.

"I figure Guido's about to piss his pants," Remi said, laughing. "If he's smart he'll point his car any direction but east and find a nice dark hole to slither into."

"If he's smart he'll give Nunzio a heads-up as soon as he hits the door. Once that happens and Nunzio knows we're not willing to deal on his terms, he'll contact us." Cain was still holding the letter opener that was sharp enough to cut through leather. "He needs us more than we need him, so he's not in a good position."

"That's the position of a desperate man, and we both know how smart that makes some people," Ramon said.

"You think he's there now?" Mano asked. "Desperate, I mean."

"That depends on who's supplying him," Cain said. "Your father and I both believe that the Luca family plans to move a lot of product soon. All that white powder makes money, but you have to pay up front," Cain said. "If Junior somehow talked his way around that, he might be in a crack now."

Muriel snapped her fingers. "Remi, Cain, that reminds me. Vinny asked for a sit-down with the two of you whenever it was convenient. After our recent reshuffle he's in position to start, but there's no way Vinny has the capital to compete with Luca."

"I'll be there whenever you can make it, Remi," Cain said. "Also, Muriel found out that Rodolfo and Juan are back in town, so let me know if he contacts you, Ramon. I want to keep an eye on the pissant, and that means every move he makes. I don't need to remind you what kind of problems he gave Emma the last time he was in town."

"We saw the headlines this morning," Mano said to Cain. "Someone took out Barney Kyle last night, and Remi tells us Agent Philips visited you right after it went down. Are you at the top of her list for a reason?"

"Whoever did this thing," Ramon said, holding his hand up to Mano, "they did us all a great service. You work for trash and sometimes bad things…they happen to you."

"I saw the paper too," Cain stabbed the morning addition of the *Times Picayune* and slid it forward, "and yes, Shelby Philips asked me some questions last night. She'll ask quite a few more before all this plays out, but I have a hunch the investigation will head in a direction she isn't planning. Kyle worked for Big Gino, and he has the most to gain from taking him out, not me."

"With what he did to your family, the feds will think otherwise," Mano said.

"If you have a problem with continuing our business together, now would be the time to tell me," Cain said. "You either trust me or you don't. I don't plan to consult you when I need to do something for the sake of my business or family, just like I don't expect you to consult me. I didn't think that needed to be said."

"I don't have a problem with you, and neither does my brother," Remi said as she cut her eyes to Mano. "I mean it."

"No hard feelings then." Cain stood and pointed them toward the conference room where she'd had breakfast delivered.

❖

Emma put her hand on Cain's pillow and sighed at how cold it was. Lately Cain had been forced to get up early too often. Emma was worried, since it really hadn't been that long since Kyle had tried to kill her. The wound had healed, but the memory of Cain's possible death remained vivid. She tried not to think about it, but the scar on Cain's chest represented all that she could lose.

"Don't dwell, Emma," she told herself, forcing herself out of bed and into the shower. "Time to move on."

The early spring weather was still cool enough for the sweater and skirt she'd picked up on her last shopping spree. Merrick was waiting downstairs, drinking a cup of coffee. The front page of the paper featured a large shot of the outside of the jail and more than one vehicle with the letters FBI stenciled on the side. At the bottom of the page was Kyle's picture from his days with the Bureau.

"Are they reporting on the hero killed last night?" Emma asked, tapping her finger on the photo.

Merrick folded the paper. "The op-ed piece was more like a laundry list of Barney's sins. For once the media got it right, so with a bit more digging our Dudley Do-Rights will surely pick up the correct scent and leave Cain alone." Emma sat down across from Merrick as she drained her cup. "What's on our agenda today?"

"We need to stop by the house first." She picked up a piece of toast and was about to butter it when she decided plain would be more palatable. "Then I need to make a few stops for Hayden's birthday party."

"Let's get to it then," Merrick said after Emma took one bite of the bread and threw it down with disgust. Per Cain's instructions, the car was waiting for them out back.

A few minutes later they reached the house and drove through the new security gate Cain had installed, along with a new brick fence that now completely surrounded the grounds instead of three-fourths of it as before. Inside, all the rooms had been painted, and the back of the house appeared as if nothing had happened. Cain's study had been restored to as close as Emma could get it to the original; even most of the leather from Dalton's office chair had been retained. The bulletproof glass was the one major change she'd made, so she could sleep better. Its cost had made even Cain's eyebrows rise, but she didn't care about anything but keeping Cain whole.

Jimmy Pitre the contractor said, "Just a few more touch-ups and you're ready to roll, Mrs. Casey. They're so minor, though, if you want to move in, go ahead, and we'll work around you."

Emma stood at the large window in Cain's office. The backyard hadn't changed much except for some playground equipment Cain had ordered installed for Hannah, but Emma could see those killers breaching the walls, intent on destroying her family. She shivered at the macabre memory and dwelt on the major difference between Giovanni and their other enemies.

Giovanni was a sadist with a penchant for ambush, but at least when he did come after you he approached in the open and you knew how to respond. Their home was repaired and safer, but now they needed to contend with the enemy who hid in dark places trying to catch snatches of their secrets. As Cain had said from the beginning— the feds operated without honor.

"Just one more thing, Mr. Pitre." Emma turned and faced him.

He glanced at Merrick before answering. "More changes?" He kept his smile, but Emma could tell he was close to cringing.

"Not on my part, no." A wave of dizziness made her sit at Cain's desk.

"I don't follow." He moved aside when Merrick bumped into him on her way to Emma's side.

"Are you okay?" Merrick asked.

"Just missing my morning coffee, I guess…I'm fine." She smiled up at Merrick, wrapping her fingers briefly around her wrist to keep her from moving away. "What I mean is," she said to Jimmy, trying to get back on track, "when you took this job we made a deal about who you'd allow to work here. You agreed you'd only use guys you could vouch for."

"I did."

"I'm not saying you didn't, but I'm having the house swept today. If I find the kind of devices that require the walls to be ripped up, I'm going to deduct five thousand for every one I find."

He took a step forward but stopped when Merrick put her hand in her jacket. "You can't do that," Jimmy said in transparent panic.

"I'm not," Emma said calmly, almost laughing at how he puffed out his chest, thinking she'd backed down. "I'll let my partner Cain collect however she sees fit. I love my privacy, but Cain is rather fanatical about hers. Once I'm done with the sweep I'll have Cain call you so we can settle our bill." She stared at him until he broke first and lowered his head. "Any problems with that?" Jimmy shook his head. "Anything you'd like to tell me?" He hesitated but shook his head again, only not as enthusiastically. "Thanks for stopping by, then. If there's a problem, like the fact you might owe us some money, I suggest you secure a line of credit before you meet with Cain. She's not only a stickler for her privacy, but she won't tolerate you owing us money."

As soon as Jimmy was out of earshot, Merrick started laughing. "It's going to take a week for his balls to fall back into place. Whatever happened to that farm girl I met not that long ago?"

"She found out the world is full of wolves, and they all wear gray suits. Thanks for putting that picture in my head."

Merrick sat across from her and leaned closer. "Are you sure you're okay?"

"I'm fine. Could you call in the guys and let's see what we're up against?" She whispered, figuring from Jimmy's subdued demeanor the bugs were not only there, but were operational.

"How'd you guess Jimmy would've taken the chance?"

Emma let out a short, sarcastic laugh. "He was in here working one day when I came by with the decorator. It was the Confederate-flag tattoo with the words 'live free or we'll take you out' that made me think he'd fall for the hype the feebies are always selling."

"He didn't look all that brave when he left," Merrick said.

"I grew up with guys like that and they never are, unless they're dealing with women or someone weaker. Confront them and they crumble like stale cookies, but for the most part they like to beat their chests and show the world how macho they are. Lucky for me I married the cure for jerks like that."

The guy standing at the door waited until she finished before interrupting. "You have a visitor, ma'am." He stepped aside so Dallas was visible.

"You said I could stop by if I wanted," Dallas said.

"I'm glad you did." Emma stood and smoothed her skirt.

Dallas appeared almost shy and unsure of herself, and she reminded Emma of the girl she was when she'd first arrived from Wisconsin.

Back then she'd never had Dallas's sense of style or level of success, but looking at Dallas, Emma could tell she had started something that excited and terrorized her.

Remi, like Cain, could devastate anyone with her looks and win anyone over with her charm, but she still had that dark side that couldn't be ignored. That side of both Remi and Cain could stop you cold if you thought too long about what they were capable of, but loving them meant accepting all of who they were. For her it was easy. Cain was ferociously protective, but she'd never felt that Cain committed the atrocities, as the government tried to define what she'd done, for pleasure.

Now, with Dallas, she had the chance to give someone the insight she'd had to gain for herself, after getting over her own mistakes. It would be nice to have a friend on a journey similar to hers.

"How about an early lunch?" Emma asked.

"That sounds great because I wanted to take you up on your offer to talk."

"Then how about an early lunch at our current address? If we're going to talk, I'd rather it stay between friends."

CHAPTER NINETEEN

M y uncle's stuck in the past," Juan said to Anthony Curtis. "He doesn't understand that the world has changed even though he refuses to." He shoved a forkful of eggs into his mouth, some of it falling and staining the napkin he had tucked into his shirt collar. "He said no, didn't he?"

Anthony crossed his legs and ran his finger along the top of his coffee cup. He couldn't appear too eager, because after reading the morning's paper he wanted in more than ever. If he played this idiot just right, he could use him to find his way in and eventually to Cain.

"Mr. Luis is entitled to his opinion and to whom he has working for him." He took a sip of coffee and shrugged. "His opinion of me isn't good, and yes, he turned me down. That's okay, though. I'm looking into other options."

"Why not work for me?" Juan dropped his silverware so quickly his plate almost shattered. "I'll take over for my uncle soon, and I could use you."

"I don't want to come between you and Mr. Luis."

Another mouthful of eggs wrapped in bread disappeared but were still visible when Juan laughed. "I'm sure that's your main concern, but don't worry about it."

"Then I'll be happy to help you out." Anthony nodded to the waitress when she removed his plate.

"Just one thing, Mr. FBI," Juan said, the others with him laughing as he carefully enunciated the three letters. "You in the big leagues now. If you're thinking of fucking me over, I'll feed your nuts to my dog with a bowl of salsa."

"I'll keep that in mind," Anthony said, pushing away from the table. When he stepped out of the restaurant, he took a page out of Cain's playbook and smiled wide enough to show teeth for the cameras as he put his sunglasses on. For once he felt in control instead of trapped being a watcher. "Twenty bucks dear Annabel calls before the day's out."

❖

"He's with who?" Annabel screamed into the phone as Shelby placed the ballistics report on the rifle they'd found at Kyle's crime scene on her desk. "Just stick with your assignment and I'll take care of it from my end."

"Problems?" Shelby asked.

"Not for long, but this couldn't have come at a worst time. We're stretched thin now, and I don't need another rogue agent on my hands."

"What?" Shelby sat down.

"We're splitting the investigation into the Luis family business with the DEA, and Mark Pearlman, the agent heading up their part, just called and said Anthony had breakfast with Juan Luis this morning and met with Rodolfo Luis last night."

Shelby fell back against the wood of the chair, feeling as if someone had hit her. "What's he up to?"

Annabel laughed as if Shelby had made a joke. "What's he up to? He's asking Rodolfo Luis for a job, of course, and since the old man was smart enough not to hire him, he accepted Juan's offer."

"What's he trying to prove?"

"I don't give a crap what he's trying to prove. He's about to compromise an ongoing investigation." Annabel picked up her phone, dialed her assistant, and demanded he find Anthony and bring him in. "What's the word on our gun?"

"The bullet we dug out of the back of the van was mutilated, but it does match the caliber of the rifle we found, so in all probability we have the murder weapon. The rifle itself had the serial number filed down, but the field agent shipped it to the lab at Quantico and they're working on it. Since this morning they've raised the first three numbers," Shelby said, reading from her notes.

"And?" Annabel glanced up at her from the top of her glasses.

"I ran that little information and got a list of possibles about a mile long. I took into consideration who the players were and narrowed the scope to one person."

Annabel put the folder down and smiled. "If you tell me you can trace it to Casey I'll nominate you for agent of the year."

"It's never that easy, ma'am. Giovanni Bracato, Sr. has a rifle of that caliber registered to him. He also has a license to hunt deer, which is what the rifle is most commonly used for. I won't know for sure it's his until they give me the entire serial number."

She thought of Cain's face as she confronted her the night before. No matter what, she was always relaxed, but never really smug like a person who always knew all the answers before the questions were really asked. "Not what we were expecting, but nothing ever is for me."

"Then keep at it. All we need is one lucky break."

Shelby pointed to the file on the rifle's owner. "Some would call that one."

"No, this is a dead end. Cain's been lucky up to now, but that can't last forever."

Shelby laughed as she stood up ready to head out again. "I wouldn't go that far. When it comes to the Casey family and luck, they have a lifetime supply. What you should maybe wish is for a little luck of the Irish to come our way."

❖

"Where'd you hear that?" Muriel asked. She was sitting at a table in Le Madeline Café across from St. Louis Cathedral. She wore a pair of dark sunglasses that gave her the freedom to study her surroundings.

After putting the last bite of croissant in his mouth, T-Boy brushed the crumbs from his fingers and pants. "My buddy told me he heard it from the man himself. Said the bitch running the show cut his balls off, and he wanted to work for someone who'd appreciate his talents."

Muriel had forgone the French roasted coffee and ordered a carton of chocolate milk. It reminded her of a simpler time in her life when all she had to worry about was appeasing the nuns who taught in the school Jarvis and Dalton had picked for her and Cain to attend. "Anthony Curtis is out for hire?"

"To the highest bidder, and from what I hear, that Mexican dude wants to get his hands on him first. I thought Cain would want to know right away."

She reached into the pocket of her leather coat and pulled out a roll of bills. "Thanks for the heads-up. Call me if you hear anything else."

He wrapped his fingers around the money and nodded.

After he walked away, Muriel called Cain and told her what was going on. "Want me to dig some more?"

"You might have broken up with a certain agent too soon. Annabel probably figured you were her inside track to me, but sometimes information flows both ways."

"That spigot's been shut off permanently, so we'll have to figure out something else." Muriel started walking to her office, glad to see she wasn't being followed.

"I'm not worried about Anthony yet."

"That guy's got it in for us, so you should worry." As she reached Canal Street, a car pulled up and stopped, blocking her path. When she leaned down to see who it was, she figured her opportunity to find out what was going on had come.

"You know me, there's more than one way to face a problem," Cain said.

Muriel looked at Shelby and smiled. "For once I believe you."

CHAPTER TWENTY

I haven't been here in a few years," Remi said, gazing out the window as Cain's driver took them farther into the ninth ward. Outside, the houses were getting smaller and thinner, perfect examples of shotgun homes—if you shot a gun through the front door, the bullet would pass through every room before it went out the back. "What do you have in mind?"

"We're here to introduce Vinny to our mutual friend."

"So there's soul food in my future?" Remi stretched her legs out as she laughed.

They turned right and four large African-American men stood in front of some street barricades. When the oldest-looking one tapped on the back-window glass, Cain lowered the window and stuck her hand out.

"How are the kids?"

"Costing me a fortune keeping them in shoes." He shook her hand, then waved to Remi. "Good to have you two back in the neighborhood."

"Does Maude have some chicken stew on?" Cain asked.

"She even changed into her best apron when she heard you were coming." He looked behind them. "Go on in and we'll keep the rats out."

Cain peeled four hundred dollars from her wallet. "Thanks, and here's something for your boys and your Nike fund."

The barricades were moved aside just enough to let the car through, then quickly put back into place, stopping the van as it pulled up. The agents were about to learn a lesson about private property and how close you needed to be to a location to make the trip down here worth your while. The street and every house on it belonged to Jasper Luke, and the people who worked for him knew better than to let you in if you weren't invited. The agents and their surveillance equipment were out of commission.

Maude's Kitchen stood at the end of the drive. Jasper's aunt was the chef and served from a large pot of whatever she felt like cooking. The front was jammed with cars, and Remi and Cain shook hands with the guys hanging out near the door.

As soon as they stepped inside, Maude said, "I been waitin' on you all morning." Cain had been enjoying Maude's cooking since she was a teenager and tagged along with Dalton when he came down to talk business with Jasper.

"Sorry to keep you waiting, sugar." Cain kissed both her cheeks and laughed at the strength of Maude's embrace. "Miss me?"

"I'm waitin' for you to leave that skinny blonde and take me out of that hot kitchen."

Cain hugged her again and kissed her forehead. "We're trying for number three, so she won't be skinny for long."

"Just don't forget me if you're looking for a change. Now get your butt to that table and let me feed y'all."

Remi reached the table first and accepted Jasper's hug. Neither she nor Cain could be considered small, but standing next to Jasper, Cain felt like a child. He was tall and built like a solid wall of muscle, topped with a completely shaven head so shiny it looked polished.

"Tell your dad I'm pissed I haven't seen him in awhile," Jasper said to Remi.

"You know how he is when he's got something going on. He did say there's a pair of dice waiting for you at the club."

As Jasper gave Cain a similar hug, Vinny Carlotti stepped out of the restroom. The four sat down and smiled at Maude when she carried out four bowls of chicken stew, ruffling Cain's hair when she got to her.

"What's on your mind, Cain?" Jasper asked. He emptied half a bottle of hot sauce into his portion.

"We've got a problem, but this time around it's not just our problem."

"Something I can help you with?" Jasper asked.

After a few bites of the spicy stew, Cain sipped her beer. "I'm sure Vinny's already clued you in on some of the stuff he's got in the works.

He's going into business on his own, with backing from Remi and me. That'll help some, but he needs a network to deal with the competition. That's not something Vincent, Remi, or I am equipped to provide."

"Stephano's let his business go to crap, and his father's never took off," Jasper said. "Some say they're coming back and others say they're not. But some young punks looking to make a name are stepping in." He dipped a piece of French bread into the bowl and put it in his mouth. "Makes no difference to me. Been a lot of killing down here, though, because they're not taking care of things."

"It's time to rein it in, Jasper, if you're interested," Remi said. "We all agree nobody can fully control this business, but it'll destroy us all if we don't try."

"You want my boys working with you?" Jasper asked Vinny.

"It's the only way to make sure you're not answering to Rodolfo Luis in a few years."

"What's yours and Remi's cut?" Jasper asked Cain.

Cain lifted her spoon and finished her meal. "I'm just here making introductions, my man. What you and Vinny work out is up to you two. Remi and my interest lie elsewhere. We did agree on a price for our unique form of protection, but that's coming out of Vinny's part."

"You're not interested in Juan Luis then?" Jasper laughed when Cain bent her spoon using just her thumb. "Thought so. Little shit was here earlier asking to make the same deal."

Remi pushed her plate away and put her hand on Vinny's forearm when he pulled his chair out. "Are we wasting our time?" she asked Jasper.

"I let him down the street because I was more interested in the company he's keeping. First time that white boy been in this neighborhood, if I had to guess. Five-O was quiet, but he's a guppy swimming by hisself in a pool of angry alligators." Jasper stood and led them to his office upstairs.

"You let Curtis in here?" Cain asked.

"He was too busy making sure nobody got behind him to get a good look. Butt head who brought him had to figure I wasn't doing business with someone who's setting a trap for me."

Cain almost cracked up at the thought of Anthony trying desperately to fit in. "What'd you tell Juan?"

"Told him to fuck off and the donkey he rode in on. We'll work the particulars out, Vinny, so stick around. And, Cain, keep an eye on Emma. Our boy's got a crush and he's looking to prove his manhood. He mentioned your lady more than once."

"Thanks, and remember I owe you one. Call if you need anything."

Remi and Cain left after a stop in the kitchen. When they got to the car they had a message that Nunzio Luca wanted a sit-down.

"How long do you want to keep him waiting?" Remi asked.

"Couple of days should leave him in a mood to talk business. Right now I've got snakes to flush out of their holes."

"Need help?"

"Are you sure? Mano sounded gun-shy this morning."

"My brother is the cautious one, but he'll learn you can't always be too careful. Do that and it makes you seem weak. None of us can afford that."

"What are your plans for tonight?"

When the car stopped in front of Remi's building she put her hand on the door handle. It was the only complex in the downtown area built on the river. "I don't have any yet," she said, chuckling. "Will I need a date?"

"Have anyone in mind?"

"I'll think about it. Where'd you want to go?"

Cain pointed at the van behind them. "Someplace fun where I can forget I'm an exotic pet worthy of observation."

"Emma does tell tales of some impressive feather rustling when you do your mating dance."

"Get out," she said, teasing, "and we'll meet you at eight. Feel like steak?"

"Eight at the Steak Knife. Better make sure you bring cash for some fun later. If you want to attract attention I have a good way to go about it that involves a set of dice."

Cain nodded and waved as Remi got out and shut the door. As they started moving again Cain let out the air in her lungs, tired from the large lunch they'd had. "Lou, if anyone calls at the office asking about what we're up to, give them what they want."

"Are you sure?"

"I'm not losing my mind." Cain let her head fall back and closed her eyes. "I'm just helping Juan make his first move. If he's going to make one, I want to see him coming."

❖

"Need a ride?" Shelby asked through the open window of her car.

"My office isn't that far. I'll walk since I wouldn't want you to go out of your way."

"How about a ten-minute truce?" She rested her head on the seat back and closed her eyes briefly. "Try to conjure up how you felt about me the last time you were in my house."

Muriel opened the door and got in. Shelby turned in the opposite direction of her office. They headed back into the French Quarter and pulled over behind the French Market.

"What's on your mind? Or did you have a sudden craving for Loretta's Pralines?" Muriel asked. She turned in her seat and pressed her back into the door.

"I want to know what happened." Shelby took Muriel's hand. "I can't stop thinking about you, and I can't concentrate on anything."

"You know what happened. Last night when you stepped into that restaurant should've been explanation enough, if I didn't do a thorough job. Something happened, and with no proof that my family was involved, we were your first stop anyway." She put her other hand over Shelby's, squeezed, then pulled away. "Your world doesn't fit into mine, and no matter how much we want to pretend, it never will."

"You want to just give up?"

When Shelby's lip trembled slightly Muriel couldn't resist holding her. "I care too much about you to lie to you. Do you really want to share your life with someone you'd have to censor yourself around? All that's left is the physical aspect, and you aren't that kind of girl."

"How do you know?" She moved closer into Muriel's embrace. "If it's all I can have, I wouldn't mind."

"But I would." Muriel moved back so she could see Shelby's face and put her palm against her cheek. "You deserve better than that, and so do I."

"Wait a minute." Shelby took a deep breath. "Stop trying to think for me, and don't decide things that will change my life. That's definitely something I'm not looking for in a partner."

"I'm not doing that. I'm only trying to be honest and tell you what I want. This isn't easy, Shelby, but it'll be ten times harder if we put it off." She kissed Shelby in the most chaste way she could manage.

"Things are moving too fast, and I'm having a hard time keeping up with it all."

The strange non sequitor made the skin on the back of Muriel's neck prickle. "Give it a couple of weeks and I'm sure you'll be fine. It's not as if we won't be seeing each other, considering our jobs," Muriel said as a joke to loosen Shelby up.

"Do you ever feel everything is being turned upside down and nothing makes sense?"

"Like I said, give it time and you'll see I'm right," Muriel tried again.

"Give it time is your best advice?" Shelby reached for her hand again and smiled when Muriel didn't rebuff her. "I've lost you, and work is crazy with Anthony going to work for the Luis family."

Muriel wanted to call Cain immediately and tell her she was right, but she wasn't ready to face that humiliation. She wasn't used to being stupid, but that's exactly what her attraction to this woman had reduced her to. "I'm sure that isn't a cause for concern," she said, trying to keep from screaming. "Your organization puts people undercover all the time. Some go about it more enthusiastically than others."

"What's that supposed to mean?"

"That Anthony will probably enjoy this assignment." It took all her willpower not to add "as much as you enjoyed yours in my bed."

"It isn't an assignment, Muriel. He was suspended and he's retaliating against Agent Hicks." She paused and sighed for what Muriel took to be effect. "Have you heard anything about him?"

"I need to retire," Muriel said, laughing. "Because I've gotten so dumb I actually fell for this crap." She opened the door and narrowed her eyes when Shelby tried to touch her.

"You think I only wanted to see you to get information out of you? Do you really think that little of me?"

"Save the indignation, sweetheart." Muriel stepped out, then leaned her upper body back into the car. "And you're right to say my advice is crap. I'll get over this in a flash. Thanks for going out of your way to make it easy for me." She slammed the door so hard she expected the window to shatter.

"Fuck," she said as she started walking in the direction she'd started. Her job had always kept her on the periphery of the family business and she'd accepted her position. That was about to change, though, because now she was willing to do anything to bring these people down. Shelby's ulterior motives had seen to that.

CHAPTER TWENTY-ONE

I want you back at the casino. Sit in your office and don't talk to anyone no matter what." Nunzio Luca paced in the sunroom in the back of his house. "Don't try anything to get your ass out of the crack it's in—understand?"

"Just one more chance, Nunzio. That's all I'm asking."

"Richard, your part in this is over. Consider yourself lucky you'll live to think about your brush with being a wise guy." Nunzio noticed Kim Stegal, the head of his security, at the back of the room when he turned around. "Try to remember that one simple thing, and stop trying these cute stunts. Your stupidity has cost us plenty already." He cocked his head toward the door, dismissing him.

"Do you need anything new on that front?" Kim asked, referring to Richard.

"Soon." Nunzio glanced back at her as she headed to his office. "He's a dumb ass, but until I get his name on the dotted line for the sale of the Capri, he's a valuable dumb ass. Have somebody good keep an eye on him, though. Richard has a talent for getting himself deeper into shit."

Kim pulled her blond hair out of the band that kept it tied back and reordered it. At five-eight she was an inch taller than Nunzio and had gotten her job by proving how persuasive she could be collecting from bad gamblers.

"I'll take care of it today." Kim stopped to pop one of the mints Nunzio kept on his desk into her mouth. "I did hear from Muriel while you were dealing with Richard."

"And?" He stopped flipping through the mail and looked up. Kim was good, but she had an annoying habit of making him beg for information.

"Neither Cain nor Remi are available right now." She brought her hand up when he took a breath and opened his mouth. "She didn't give me any idea when Cain would be. I didn't bother with Remi since I figure the Jatibons aren't available either."

"What's the fucking problem?" Nunzio punched the top of his desk, then had to shake his hand out. "They were willing to cut this deal a few days ago."

Kim nodded. "Cain's going to wait now. You haven't dealt with her as much as you have with Remi, but they have a lot in common. A few days ago you had something they wanted. Granted, they negotiated a good deal, but you had the edge. Richard handed it back to them on a silver platter." Kim delivered the explanation with little emotion, a technique she had perfected so he wouldn't have to bear the blame for anything. "You have to realize you don't have to sell to them, and they don't need the deal."

"This isn't like selling my car. If I have to start over with new buyers, my father isn't going to blame Richard."

"Then you wait until Cain and Remi think you've stewed long enough."

"That isn't the option I pay you to give me." He hit the top of his desk again, this time with an open palm. "Convince them it's not in their interest to wait. I don't care how you do it—just get it done."

"I have your permission to be creative?"

"As much as you like, but maybe start with Remi. The Jatibons are successful, but they aren't as organized as Casey. Stephano gave me the lowdown on Cain, and I don't need any more problems." He told her what he'd discussed with his father and she nodded again.

"I'll see what I can do," Kim said with a laugh, waving her fingers over her shoulder as she walked out.

He usually found it comforting when Kim was in such a good mood, but he had too much riding on the outcome to start laughing yet.

❖

"I had a wonderful day with Dallas Montgomery," Emma said. She hadn't gotten a lot done all day, but she thought she'd gained a new friend. "She seems nice and really interested in Remi."

"Well, Remi goes on about her a lot." Cain unbuttoned her shirt and threw it in the hamper. "Dallas might just be the woman who tames the wanderer in her."

"I gave Dallas a few pointers on that score today." Cain's naked back was too tempting, so Emma gave in and ran the tips of her fingers from her shoulders to the small of her back where Cain's pants didn't let her go any farther. "It's weird, though."

"What?" Cain stepped out of the pants next.

"For someone as accomplished as Dallas, she acts like she's running from something. She's kind of skittish." Before she could return to her exploration, Cain put on a pair of khaki pants and a sweater. "You're no fun."

"I promised Hannah and Hayden chocolate milk and beignets. You don't want me to break a date, do you?" Cain turned around and lightly pinched Emma's nipple. When Emma hissed she immediately let go. "Sorry, lass."

"It's not you, just a little sensitive today." She pressed Cain's hand flat on her chest and laughed at her hopeful look. "Way too early to tell that, love, and no, I don't want you to stand the kids up. Mind if I tag along?"

"That's like asking if I mind breathing."

"You're so sappy, aren't you?"

They loaded into two cars so Lou, Merrick, Mook, and a few others could come. Emma still wasn't comfortable with that level of protection, but she rarely said anything, knowing she'd never get Cain to bend on the subject. And rightfully so, she'd come to realize.

Since their return to New Orleans, Cain took this outing with them at least once a week. Emma would laugh the entire time, as Hannah always managed to cover her ever-patient partner in powdered sugar before they were done.

"Navy sweater, mobster." Emma plucked at Cain's top and shook her head. "Not a smart choice."

"Those little handprints are going to look good on you too." Cain patted her backside, referring to her black skirt.

Hannah led them to a table close to the entrance, wanting to listen to the older gentleman playing a saxophone right outside on the sidewalk. Emma was sure their little girl loved these outings with Cain and Hayden because New Orleans was so different from what she'd known, and Cain indulged her need to explore. Hannah was finally having the childhood she deserved, which hadn't been possible living with her grandmother.

"Chocolate milk and donuts, Mom," Hannah said, her hands on the metal railing and a smile on her face as the street musician played something with more pep.

Cain ordered for all of them and ran her hand along Hannah's back, clearly enjoying her enthusiasm. Then the relaxed set to Cain's mouth evaporated so quickly that Emma followed her line of sight and saw Juan Luis standing there staring at them. From the way his lip was twisted into a snarl, she could tell he was disgusted by what he saw.

"Cain." She took hold of Cain's hand as she stood up. "Leave it alone. Let Lou handle it."

"I just want to talk to him, lass," Cain said, the proof of T-Boy's information eyeing her from behind Juan. Anthony Curtis was smiling so widely he looked almost idiotic. "Just a talk, I promise."

She waved Lou off and stepped out, stopping five feet from Juan and his new employee. "Slumming?" she asked Anthony. "If you're this hard up for work, I have openings at Emma's for dishwashers."

"Still trying to pretend you have a pair, Casey?" Juan said, finally locking eyes with her. Through the entire exchange up to now Anthony had been staring at Emma. "After seeing your little bastards, though, I'm almost convinced you might not be pretending. Or is it that the slut you—"

Cain grabbed Juan, spun him around, and slammed his head so forcefully into one of the café's pillars, it split his lip. He pushed back in what she assumed was an attempt to get away and retaliate, but she easily held him in place.

"Listen up, because I'm only going to say it once," she whispered in his ear, driving his head into the pillar again to make him stop squirming. "You do whatever you need done and get out of New Orleans. Come near my family while you're here and I *will* kill you."

"What was that, Casey?" Anthony asked, finally coming to Juan's defense. "Assault in public isn't usually your style. Want me to call the cops, Mr. Luis?"

Juan straightened his clothes and pressed the handkerchief Anthony offered him to his lip when Cain let him go. "Fuck off, Curtis. You," he pointed at Cain, "got lucky today."

She grabbed his finger and twisted up so much he screamed and dropped to his knees. When it was clear he wouldn't resist anymore, she bent over and put her lips close to his ear again. "I don't have to pretend to be a man as much as you do, *hijo de puta*." She laughed and twisted his finger toward his wrist even harder, bringing tears to his eyes. "That's the correct term, isn't it? Your father wanted a quick fuck and your mother was quick to spread them, you son of a bitch." The rage in his eyes bloomed stronger than the pain and she laughed harder. She let him go and stepped back to anticipate his next move. "Oh, yes, you're not the only one who did a little digging into family trees."

"I'm going to kill you for that," Juan screamed as he lunged at her.

This time she opened a cut over his left eye when she slammed him into the pillar again. "Today is me being merciful, so remember what I said," Cain told him. Behind her, two cars screeched to a stop, followed by slamming doors.

"Anthony, I'm going to have to ask you to come with the agents behind me," Shelby said, pointing to the second car being driven by Joe Simmons.

"Cain Casey," Shelby said next, sounding official, "I'm going to have to ask you to come with us."

"Why? Am I under arrest for something?"

"Just a few questions, but with the assault on this gentleman we just taped I've got enough to cuff you. Don't make me do that in front of your kids."

"Emma, head home and call Muriel," Cain said calmly. Juan had given Shelby and her ilk the opening they'd been wanting. Letting her temper loose was satisfying, but the consequences had just arrived and were the reason she told Hayden over and over why such behavior was never wise, no matter how good it felt. "Don't worry. I'll be back home soon."

"Mom," Hayden said, moving close to her.

"Take care of your mother and your sister. That's your job until I get back," Cain said, putting her hand on his shoulder. "I'll be home soon."

"How can you be so sure?" Shelby asked as she held open the back door of the black sedan she'd arrived in.

"Because Mr. Luis won't press charges, and you're just fishing."

"Wow." Shelby slammed the door and got in the front. "Did you consult one of the fortune-tellers before I got here?"

"No, you're as easy to read as a Dick and Jane primer."

Shelby turned around, not appearing pleased. "Go ahead and enlighten us."

"Juan is the nephew of one of the largest drug runners in Mexico, but has the mentality of a gang banger. It'll be a long time before he achieves the polish Rodolfo has, if ever. He's not pressing charges for tripping in the street and accepting my assistance because that would make him lose face more than he has already," Cain said with a shrug, as if it should've been obvious. "Hispanic men don't take kindly to having a woman beat the shit out of them."

"And us just fishing?" Claire Lansing asked.

"That's the easiest one of all, Agent Lansing." Cain chuckled like she always did at their shocked expressions when she knew them by name. "If something goes wrong in the city, you guys throw your nets in my direction. You're just fishing because that's all you ever do. Call it the law of average behavior."

"Don't you mean the law of averages?" Shelby asked.

"Unlike you, I always say what I mean. There's nothing new in your pattern, so your behavior is average, predictable, non-imaginative, and whatever other word you care to apply."

"It must be a burden to always be right," Claire said.

"The bigger burden would be to always be wrong." Cain sat back and laughed. "But that's only a guess. After all the training and money the government's invested in people like you, I'm sure you know what you're doing."

"It might be wise for you to listen to the part that says you have the right to remain silent," Shelby said.

"You haven't read me my rights, but you're correct. Who am I to tell you how to do your job?"

CHAPTER TWENTY-TWO

Comfortable?" Shelby asked Cain when she finally picked a seat that gave the folks behind the mirror a good view of her face.

Cain just stared, wondering what was bothering Shelby so much that she sounded pissed. "What are you hoping for here, Agent Daniels?" She drummed her fingers in an uneven beat that made Shelby glare at her hand.

"It's Agent Philips, Ms. Casey. I know how much you pride yourself on getting our names right," Shelby said, her voice lower than before and her face paler.

Cain whispered right into her ear, after jumping up quickly and grabbing her head, "Tell them to turn off the built-in sound system until my attorney arrives or, trust me, it's going to be entertaining for me and interesting for them." Joe Simmons magically appeared at the door, gripping the frame.

"Shelby?" he asked when Shelby looked straight at him but didn't try to move away from Cain.

"It's okay. Tell them to turn off the equipment until Ms. Casey's attorney gets here." She pointed at him and in a serious voice repeated, "I mean it, Joe, turn it off."

Cain straightened up and laughed. She knew better than to believe Simmons would stop the tape. "Are we alone now, Agent?" Shelby stared at her but stayed quiet. "Is it safe for us to share all our dirty little secrets?"

Shelby barely shook her head. She saw it, but doubted anyone else looking in would. Of course it wasn't safe. And one word from Cain about the night she'd first met Shelby and convinced Vincent to spare her life, and Shelby could lose all she'd worked for. Her fear was written all over her face. Shelby Daniels was the name she had given Cain on that flight when she agreed to lie in exchange for her life.

"It doesn't matter, though, does it, that I have nothing to say. That I've done nothing to warrant you dragging me away in front of my partner and my children like a common thug simply because you can."

Cain moved closer again and lowered her voice. "Power is intoxicating, Agent, but like anything else, too much of a good thing isn't healthy. You wield it indiscriminately, and I'll show you how it's done. I'd love nothing better than to teach you all how to take away little by little everything that's important to the lot of you. I'll talk, and you know the Irish, we can weave a tale, we can. Do we understand each other, Agent Daniels?" Cain's lips were so close to Shelby's ear she could smell her perfume.

"Perfectly."

"Good. Then to answer your question, I'm comfortable." It was the last thing she said until Joe walked in with Muriel.

"Why is my client here?" Muriel said. She sat next to Cain and crossed her legs. When Shelby and Joe stayed quiet she snapped her fingers. "Now would be a great time to answer."

"Your client assaulted a gentleman on the street. We brought her in for questioning in that matter and about a few other topics."

Cain smiled and shrugged when Muriel glanced at her. "Let them tell us what I've done now, Muriel. It'll probably save time."

"Let's start with your altercation with Mr. Luis this afternoon," Joe said.

Cain leaned back in her chair. "Did he press charges or define it like that?"

"He didn't have much to say on the subject, but after more conversations he may change his mind," Joe said, his hand resting on another file. "There *is* another matter." He patted the file.

"Would it create more tension if you played dramatic music?" Cain asked, making Muriel snort.

Shelby bristled. "This isn't funny, Ms. Casey."

"You're right, this is serious business. Go on, Agent Simmons, let's hear it."

"Agent Barney Kyle was murdered last night."

"I'm aware of that," Cain said, never losing eye contact. She laughed when he leaned forward. "Don't look so eager. I do know how to read. That was the headline story in this morning's paper."

"You visited Agent Kyle yesterday in jail," Shelby said.

"You would know. You did, after all, follow me there from my office and had someone analyze every word we exchanged. Not to mention study every blink I made, and every facial expression. I visited Barney, but I don't believe that's a crime."

Shelby nodded. "Considering your past relationship with Agent Kyle, why bother seeing him?"

"Just a couple of things before we go on," Muriel interrupted. "Cain's 'past relationship' consisted of Kyle shooting her with the intent to kill. And why do you insist on calling him Agent Kyle? The guy was in jail facing some serious charges."

Shelby and Joe dropped their eyes to the table and didn't dispute her right away. The door opened again and Annabel took a deep breath before pointing to Shelby. Without hesitation Shelby gave up her seat and left the room.

"We meet again, Agent Hicks." Cain offered Annabel her hand.

"Thank you for agreeing to come in," Annabel said, accepting the handshake.

"You're welcome, even though it wasn't exactly voluntary."

"Before I arrived, Ms. Casey asked a question about Agent Kyle, and I'm here to answer it," she said, ignoring what Cain had stated.

"We're all ears," Muriel said.

"Agent Kyle was in the sheriff's custody when this happened, but in light of the report released today, I seriously doubt the District Attorney's office would've filed charges."

"Why is that?" Muriel asked.

"The FBI concluded that the incident with your client was an accident." Cain put her hand on Muriel's leg to keep her quiet until Annabel finished. "Furthermore, there was no evidence that Agent Kyle was working for, or affiliated with, the Bracato family. As far as the federal government was concerned, he was free to go as soon as he finished with local law enforcement. I understood Agent Kyle planned to retire after this to pursue other interests."

"He almost kills my cousin, and you're telling me it was an accident? Did your investigators bother to interview everyone in that warehouse that night?"

"Trust me, the investigation was thorough." She opened the file Joe had brought in. "We have the murder weapon used last night."

"Let me save you some more time in this little charade," Cain said. "Is it a Remington shotgun, silver barrel engraved with Irish roses, circa 1942?"

"No, it isn't," Joe said.

"Then it isn't mine. That's the only firearm I own. If you don't believe me, check."

"The gun used belonged to Giovanni Bracato," Annabel said.

"Then I suggest you find him and ask him why he decided to use Agent Kyle for target practice." She said Kyle's name with as much sarcasm as possible. "Wait, I forgot. There's no link between Kyle and Big Gino. At least not anymore. It sounds like Bracato made sure of that."

"I'm trying to locate Mr. Bracato and his sons, but haven't had much luck," Annabel said.

"And what? You want me to help you?" Cain stood and laughed. "Call the investigators you put on Barney's case, Agent. After what you told me today, they should be more than capable of finding things that are lost, because so far they've done a beautiful job of finding things that weren't there at all." She tapped Muriel's shoulder and started for the door.

"We're not done, Ms. Casey."

"Sure we are, Agent Hicks. You don't need help with anything. If it doesn't exist or doesn't fit in the hole you created, you make it up as you go along. So much for honor and duty, huh? You and your minions are nothing but a pack of lying dirt bags." She opened the door and faced them once more. "And you call me the criminal. If I was I could learn something from you, because compared to you, I'd be a rank amateur."

❖

Anthony waited in the next interview room, sitting down in the same position Cain had. He showed no emotion when Annabel walked in and sat down. "I never thought I'd be on this end of things," he said, trying to be flip.

"Shut up and listen. This isn't an interrogation and it isn't an interview," she said. "There are people who learn from their mistakes, Agent Curtis, and then there's you."

"What—" he jumped in his seat involuntarily when she slammed both her hands on the table between them and stood up, so he had to crane his neck back to see her.

"I said for you to be quiet. You're suspended, Mr. Curtis. If you're too stressed or feeble-minded to realize that means you're supposed to stay home and contemplate where you went wrong—consider this your warning." She leaned farther in, making him back up more in his seat. "Your new friend is under scrutiny from two agencies. If you do anything, and I mean anything, Mr. Curtis, to interfere in or screw up those ongoing operations, I *will* mount your head on my wall."

"It's my time to do with as I please," he said, louder than necessary, trying to intimidate her. "You said so yourself."

"You're not involved in this situation in any official capacity, and if something goes wrong I won't be able to protect you. Surely you know what that'll mean to your career? Why take the chance?"

"At the academy they kept saying if you don't take chances every so often, you'll never get anywhere. I'm tired of not getting anywhere." He slid his chair back, tired of the uncomfortable position. "Juan hates Cain and has some big hang-up about Emma Casey. Eventually one of them will reach the boiling point, and I plan to be there when that happens."

Annabel sat down and stared at her hands like she'd written her next words on her fingers. "You aren't taking a chance for the good of the team. You're set on revenge. I studied your file more closely and it led me to your father."

"Leave him out of this," Anthony said with menace. "They never proved he did anything wrong."

"You know how the Bureau works sometimes. They never publicized his case, but that doesn't mean nothing was there." She sighed like she knew she was wasting her time. "Something like that could cast a long shadow if you let it."

"My father wasn't on Bracato's payroll," he screamed.

"You're right, he wasn't on Bracato's payroll. He was on Vincent Carlotti's. A lot of evidence proves that. You can live in denial, but it won't do you any good to fall into the same situation, even if you have good intentions."

"Why are you doing this to me? This is my father you're talking about like a common criminal."

Annabel rested her crossed arms on the table and lowered her voice. "I'm not trying to humiliate you, but I'm still your boss and it's still my job to protect you."

His anger ratcheted and he jumped up and towered over her, but Annabel didn't flinch. "You're protecting me by tearing down my father? How convenient that he's dead and can't defend himself."

"I'm protecting you by telling you not to accept a salary from Juan Luis, though I doubt he'd take you seriously if you offered to work for free. But if you go that route, you'll be vulnerable because you're dealing with a monster and you have no backup." She stood and shook her head. "If we find stashes of cash in your accounts or in your possession when we're done, don't be surprised if we conclude it's another case of 'like father like son.' Once that happens you'll never throw off the suspicion."

He took a step toward the door, knowing he could leave whenever he wanted, but he wasn't ready. "And if people suspect you of something, it's got to be true, right?"

"That's Cain Casey's argument, Anthony. You're better than that."

"Maybe she's not completely full of shit. I consider myself warned, but you don't own me or my time. If you think I'm doing something wrong, arrest me. If not, I'm leaving." He stormed out without exchanging a word with anyone.

"It doesn't look like that went well," Shelby said when she joined Annabel.

"Something in him has changed, and I can't reach him," Annabel said. "I'd like to, though. We don't need another person to watch, but that's what we're faced with." She closed the door and made sure the monitors were off. "Meet with Mark Pearlman at DEA quietly and give him a rundown. That's all we can do for now."

"Something's got to be driving him."

"Until he decides to share that with me, my hands are tied." Annabel stared at the closed door Anthony had walked through and sighed. Some days she wished she cut grass for a living. They were supposed to be the good guys, but after talking to Anthony and reading the report on Kyle, she knew those strict lines of right and wrong weren't always so clear.

"On another subject," Shelby said, sounding hesitant, "how did the investigation into Kyle's murder ignore the mountain of evidence we had?"

"They only shared their findings with me, not their rationale. Kyle probably offered them more as a free man than a convict. Sometimes the higher-ups think it's a good idea to bargain someone's freedom for information."

"That's not fair. We put some work into that case."

"No, it isn't fair, but there's nothing I can do about it."

Shelby nodded. "What does it matter now? Kyle traded whatever he had, but last night wasn't the outcome he expected."

"Some would call it justice, though."

"When they're standing trial, I doubt they'll feel so sanctimonious."

Shelby said it, but Annabel could tell she wasn't confident that would happen. If Cain had something to do with Kyle, one more secret would eventually be buried with her, because Casey gave new meaning to the strong, silent type.

CHAPTER TWENTY-THREE

Y ou need to breathe or you're going to pass out," Cain told Muriel. They were headed home since Cain knew Emma would be a wreck until she arrived.

"Hicks was serious, wasn't she?" Muriel's voice was low and tight, both signs that she was angry. "They were going to let that asshole go."

"From what I understand, yes. Kyle was Giovanni's flunky but he was smart enough to figure out his operation. He definitely had a unique insight into Giovanni's dealings, since he was carrying out some of them himself. If Kyle ever got caught, he'd turn on him." Unlike her cousin, Cain felt as relaxed as if they were talking about the weather.

"You knew, didn't you? That's why you went to visit him. You knew."

"You're upset right now, Muriel, and because you are I'll try to explain something so we never need to have this conversation again. Somewhere in the building we just left, I'm positive, is a thick file containing a psychological workup labeling me a psychopath. A textbook example of a murderer so thirsty for blood I'll prey on the innocent just to get my fix."

When Muriel shook her head as if to disagree, Cain put her hand behind Muriel's neck and squeezed. "Sometimes when I decide on a course of action, you don't agree with it, but you never say anything."

"That's not my job," Muriel said.

"I always make those questionable decisions alone, because if I don't, the results will harm my family. My decisions," she said, speaking in broad terms, "are necessary. I'm no butcher, but I *am* a realist. Our world is full of bad people, but as long as I'm here I'll make as many hard choices as necessary so that you, Emma, and the kids are safe." She pulled Muriel forward and kissed her forehead. "That answer your question?"

Muriel nodded, then described her earlier visit with Shelby and explained she didn't believe Shelby's story of Anthony not being undercover. "She thought I'd just start talking, I guess."

"I can't believe I'm going to say this," Cain said, exhaling loudly, "but you need to withhold judgment on Shelby. She's working against us, but she can listen to reason when necessary. Don't completely alienate her yet."

"I don't want a relationship with a liar, Cain."

"I don't want that for you either. Just be cordial. I think she's partly right. Anthony isn't working for Annabel. He's working to see all of us go down. If that's true, he's twice as dangerous."

"Then let me help you," Muriel said. She turned in her seat and stared at Cain so intently Cain could tell her emotions were still fueled by the day's events. "I'm tired of sitting on the sidelines while you take all the chances. This is my family too and I want in."

"We put you on the sidelines for a reason, Muriel, so I want you to really think about what you're asking."

"You're willing to start teaching Hayden to take chances and give Katlin a chance, but not me?"

"We're all born into our roles for a reason, but no one forces you to follow the path we think is right for you. You already take plenty of chances, so why the sudden change?" Cain put her hand on Muriel's knee and did nothing when she slapped it away.

"I'm not a child you have to protect."

"How about a deal?" The offer made Muriel's head come up again. "Take a few days off, I mean really take off somewhere, and forget about the office. Then if you still feel the same way, I'll consider broadening the scope of your job."

"No more arguments to get me to change my mind?"

"I'll not force your path, Muriel, but I do want you to consider it before we veer in that direction." Cain would honor Muriel's decision, but it was like a cold wind slicing through her soul. She couldn't restore Muriel's innocence once she lost it, no matter how much power she wielded.

❖

Emma didn't say anything when Cain walked through the door. She'd been standing in the foyer since Cain had called that she was on the way home, and she didn't smile until she actually saw her. "Welcome home, baby," she said when Cain put her arms around her and lifted her off the ground.

"You okay?"

"I'm fine, and I missed you, but you do have some damage control waiting for you upstairs."

"Hannah?" Cain put Emma down.

"Hannah's young so she was easy. No, it's Hayden. And it's not me he wants to talk to about what happened." She ran her thumb along the crease in Cain's forehead. "He wasn't rude, and it's not because he doesn't trust me with his feelings. He said it was man stuff between the two of you."

Cain laughed a little. "That might be problematic since we're a man short, but I'll go up and talk to him."

"He's serious," Emma said, but smiled anyway.

"I'm not laughing at him, lass, but after dealing with Muriel we might get a group rate on anger-management classes before this is over."

"Come on, then, let's go upstairs. I have a date to dress dolls with Hannah." Emma led her up the stairs and kissed her in front of Hayden's room.

"They just let you go?" Hayden asked before Cain could even offer a greeting. She sat next to him on the bed and waited to see if he had anything else to start off with.

"They couldn't prove I did anything so they had no choice." She sat with her hands on her knees. For once she felt as if she'd let Hayden down. Hannah, Emma was right, was too young to know what had happened, but not him. She never wanted him to see her being taken away by the police. "I'm sorry you had to experience that."

"That didn't matter to me. I'm just mad." He smashed his fist into the palm of his other hand.

Cain took his wrist before he could repeat the action. "I'm still sorry you had to see that, but it happened. And if you want to talk about it, I want you to."

"There's nothing to talk about," he said, but hadn't made eye contact with her yet.

"Are you sure about that?" She moved her hand to his knee and waited. "You don't sound like you're okay."

She could hear Hannah talking to Emma. Hayden stayed quiet, but he turned his head slightly and looked at her hand. "Why?" he finally said.

"Why what?"

"Why did you go if you didn't have to?" As he asked he brought his eyes up.

"My father once caught me fighting with this neighborhood kid. I was beating on him because he called my father a useless killer."

Hayden blinked a few times then shook his head. "Did he get mad at you? You had a good reason to whale on the kid."

"He didn't stop me, but he didn't talk to me about it until the next day. Before he left for work he asked me to think about why he was disappointed."

Hayden stared at her like he couldn't believe what she'd said. "You defended him and he was disappointed in you? Why?"

"When that kid said that, I got mad and reacted—that was my only defense to my father. Because I was mad, I didn't notice he was smaller than me and said it because his friends goaded him into it."

"Why tell me that?"

She smiled and moved her hand to his cheek. The older Hayden got the more he resembled her father. "I want to explain why I did what I did today. But before I do tell you, why do you think I gave in?"

"I thought—" he stopped and cut his eyes down again.

"Say it," she said. "When it's you and me by ourselves, don't be afraid to say what you're thinking."

"You gave right in. That didn't make you look very strong. It's almost like you were afraid of those guys, and you were innocent. You're supposed to stand up for yourself no matter what."

"Son, being strong is knowing when to give in. I didn't go because I was weak and scared." She ran her fingers through his hair and sighed. "I was trying to be strong and show no fear. I unclenched my fists and used my head, like I should've done with that kid a long time ago. It's like I always tell you."

"I know, don't let anger rule your brain."

"Maybe I should have you talk to Muriel," she said, laughing, and shook her head when he looked at her like he didn't understand. "And remember, it's all right to be afraid. Don't try to live thinking nothing will ever scare you, because that'll only make you more reckless than some hothead."

"I'll keep that in mind, thanks."

Cain stood up and hugged him, liking how solid he felt in her arms. "Thank you for taking care of your mother and Hannah until I got back."

"You said it was my job, but I like having them here to take care of."

She smiled and left him to his video games to join Emma and Hannah next door. Emma was sitting on the floor surrounded by the doll clothes Cain had bought for Hannah's new favorite companion. At the moment the doll Hannah had named Becky was naked and hanging upside down in Hannah's arms as the little stylist struggled to get her shoes off.

Cain stood right outside the door and watched Emma. Her blond hair was a little longer than usual, so as she studied the outfits she had to brush it back more often. During their talk Hayden hadn't asked what did scare her, but here in this house was her greatest fear—that someone or something would take away these moments by either locking her up or harming Emma and the kids.

That fear made her wish she'd had that talk with Dalton. How did he balance his business obligations with keeping his family whole?

"You okay?" Emma asked from right in front of her.

The question brought Cain back from where her mind had flown to. "I hate to break up this play date, but how'd you like to have dinner with me? It's a double date with Remi."

"What's the special occasion?"

"I was planning to bait Juan, but any more of that and I might land in central lockup."

"Forget about him." Emma lifted her hand and kissed her fingertips. "He's not important enough to worry over."

"Whatever you say, Mrs. Casey."

"Worry about finding something for Miss Becky to wear, or you might have to go shopping again." Cain laughed and followed Emma into the room.

Juan, no matter what Emma thought, did warrant worry, but that was Cain's job. The role she played and accepted with all her heart was to worry, fix, and eliminate concerns and threats so her family could have these carefree moments. Perhaps that's what Dalton's answer would've been.

CHAPTER TWENTY-FOUR

Remi's phone rang right after she pressed the buzzer to Dallas's front door. "Change your mind?" she asked about their double date with Cain and Emma for dinner, recognizing the number.

"Don't you wish," Dallas said. "Could you work your charm on the lock again? I'm almost ready but not quite."

Simon stood with her back to Remi as Remi quickly unlocked the gate, and as it closed behind them it seemed someone flipped a switch on the noise as well. The door to the house was open, and when they stepped in they found the drinks Dallas had poured.

"She's a great hostess," Simon said, taking a seat in one of the wingback chairs by the fireplace.

"True," Remi responded automatically. Since Dallas was still upstairs she walked slowly around the room.

The house, or what parts of it she'd seen, were comfortable and so tastefully put together they could be in a magazine layout. Beautiful artwork hung on the walls, and mementos of Dallas's work sat on the mantel and other pieces of furniture.

"You're snooping."

Remi put down the badge Dallas had been issued for *Lady-Killers* and sat across from Simon. "I finally figured out what's off about this place."

"Looks good to me."

"It's great, but you could move in here and not feel like you're invading anyone's space."

Simon lowered her drink and leaned forward so they could keep their voices down. "What are you talking about?"

"She has great art, but no photographs of any kind except a few recent ones. There's stuff that must've meant something to her from work, but nothing else. She could leave here tomorrow and pack it in a small bag, because the rest is replaceable."

"Is that what you're afraid of?"

On the coffee table was the one piece that didn't fit—a rock with no markings and no recognizable shape, lying next to a vase of roses. "I don't have any hold over Dallas—I'm just curious."

"You have to care about her, because otherwise you wouldn't give a damn one way or the other." She waved her hand at Remi. "Don't try and deny it. I've known you from the day you were born." Remi heard movement at the top of the stairs, and Simon stopped talking. The size of Simon's smile made Remi stand and turn around, because Simon rarely smiled like that except at Juno. She whispered to Remi, "Tell me again later how you don't care. I'll wait for you outside. Good evening, Miss Dallas," she added before leaving.

Dallas stopped on the last step, wearing a tea-length black dress with a slit up the side past her knee. If she expected any kind of reaction, Remi disappointed her by just standing there and staring. "Is this all right? If not, I can change."

"I'm sorry," Remi said, moving closer. "Please don't change a thing. You look beautiful." She put her hands on Dallas's hips and kissed her neck.

"People tell me that all the time, and I never put a lot of credence in it. But when you say it, you make me believe it."

"I wouldn't say it if I didn't mean it."

"I believe you because you have nothing to gain from the compliment, and because you've taken the time to want to know me."

"That process has just begun, take my word for it." Remi let her go and took a step back. "Shall we?"

"I'm looking forward to it."

The answer, Remi thought, applied to a lot more than a dinner invitation.

❖

"She doesn't exist, Papi, and I've looked. She pays no taxes, collects no checks, and owns nothing in her name. The information we have on file is bogus. The schools, the birthplace, nothing checks out. It's as if she appeared one day, then made up a life," Mano told his father as he held a folder in his hand full of the information he'd gathered on Dallas. "I'm sure no one's checked before because, once they break in, everyone in this business changes their name to something more marketable. It's strange, though, that none of the tabloids have picked up on this. They live for these types of stories."

"Dallas hasn't gone for roles that would catapult her into a career that would bring extra scrutiny. Those vultures spend their time on the truly famous, and she's hovering at the cusp of that category."

"I give her credit then."

"How does she get paid?" Ramon asked.

"The money goes to the manager, Bob, who, as far as I can tell, must dole out an allowance, since I can't even find a bank account in her name. If I hadn't seen her at the party, I'd say she didn't exist, because I haven't been able to prove it."

"If we can't find anything, we might have a problem. Remi won't admit it, but she cares for this girl. If she turns out to be something she's not, your sister could end up getting hurt." Ramon glanced over the papers Mano had handed him. "Concentrate on the casino deal and leave this to me. I'll check on a few other things and see what I can find. The last thing I need is to open up something that could put us in the spotlight."

"I'd like to look somewhere else before I quit." Mano handed Ramon another folder. "Instead of hunting for something we may never find, why not start with the person who made Remi want to know about Dallas in the first place?"

The folder had the name Bob Bennett on it. Mano had already started the search for answers about Dallas through the only link they had. "This one has a few more pages," Ramon said, quickly flipping through the whole thing.

"It's a lot more interesting reading too. Bob's tried to distance himself from his beginnings, but he didn't go about it as intelligently as Dallas did."

"To tell you the truth, I didn't think we'd find anything on either one. The fact that Dallas is such a mystery disturbs me since your sister is busy spinning theories of her own."

Mano stood up and clicked his briefcase closed. "Are you sure you don't want my help?"

"I trust you with my life, and if Remi was here, I'm sure she'd tell you the same thing," Ramon said. He put the files in his top desk drawer and locked it. "But maybe this is something you shouldn't know on the off chance Remi gets serious with this girl. You'd never betray her, but if you knew the whole truth it might embarrass both Remi and Dallas, and that might come back to haunt them."

"Let me know if you run into a dead end, or if you need my help."

Ramon walked with Mano to the side door of his office that led outside and kissed his forehead before he opened it. "You'll be my first call. Stay out of trouble."

"Are things still on track? I didn't mean to insult Cain at our last meeting."

"I'm sure your question didn't put Cain off, unlike some of the others we deal with. She likes everyone to be upfront, just like your sister. If she's got a problem she won't hesitate to bring it up."

"I'll keep in touch with Muriel then, as soon as we're ready for the next step."

Ramon nodded and watched Mano walk to his car. Of all the deals he'd made since arriving in the States, this one had the most twists and surprises. When Ramon added what they didn't know about the one girl Remi had ever shown an interest in for more than one date it only added to the unknowns he had to deal with as they tried to close the casino deal. He figured his retirement wouldn't be anytime soon.

CHAPTER TWENTY-FIVE

The Steak Knife was famous for all its infamous patrons. Those who didn't personally know the owner always had to wait six months for a reservation, but they waited because for one night it didn't matter if they were accountants or podiatrists—they could sit next to someone they read about all the time. These were the people who, no matter what, never followed the rules.

The owner stood by the host stand, a smile breaking across his face as Lou held the door open for Emma and Cain.

"You finally decided to grace me with the company of this beautiful woman," he said to Cain as he held both of Emma's hands and kissed her cheeks. "Welcome back, bella Emma."

"Thank you, I missed you," Emma returned his welcome. "And we brought friends." She stepped aside so he could see Dallas and Remi.

"One of these days you two are going to have to share your secret for finding beautiful women," he said, kissing Dallas hello. Four waiters stood behind him ready to escort them to their table and start bringing out drinks. "But let me feed you first."

"Do you all come here often?" Dallas asked. The whispers and the not-too-discreet finger-pointing had begun as they made their way to the table.

"Not enough to raise our cholesterol," Remi said as she pulled Dallas's chair. "This is one of those places that's like family. It doesn't matter how often you come, they're just glad you're here."

"Then for once the whispering might not be about me. How long did it take you to get used to this, Emma?" Dallas asked. "Going somewhere with Remi is like realizing I'm the only person in the city who didn't know her."

"Part of me will forever be a dairy farmer's daughter who won't get used to the attention, but for the most part I'm so in love it doesn't bother me. I just enjoy my life and the interesting people in it because of Cain." She ran her fingers through Cain's hair. "Given your career choice, being noticed must be commonplace."

"It's not something you really ever get used to," Dallas said, clicking her mouth shut so quickly Emma figured she had more to say on the subject.

She'd stopped when Lou rose from the next table and stood behind Cain so he could whisper in her ear. "Katlin called from outside. It's about to get crowded in here."

Cain didn't need to ask who, since she could see Nunzio Luca making small talk with the owner, and Rodolfo and Juan Luis hanging back and scanning the room. Juan's face held signs of his recent run-in with her, with a bruise around his mouth and one over his eye.

"This might answer how long Nunzio was willing to wait," Cain said, cocking her head in the direction of the door so Remi would turn around. "The mountain has come to us, Mohammad."

"Too bad he brought the trash with him," Remi said. "It looks like Juan either pissed somebody off or hit a brick wall with his face."

Emma put her ice water down and laughed. "Maybe a little of both, but you have to admit my brick wall is cute." She smiled at Cain.

"Cain—Remi." Nunzio stopped at their table. "I was hoping to run into you when I got to town. Lady Luck's on my side."

"Or maybe you called my office on the off chance someone would tell you where I was," Cain said. She wiggled her fingers in Juan's direction and smiled.

"You really should warn them about that," Nunzio said, stepping in front of Juan. "You never know who's calling."

"Your concern is touching, but I'm sure you'd rather enjoy the menu here than worry about my employee disclosures." Cain picked up her drink and took a sip.

"Before I head back, I'd like to meet with all the parties involved in our deal. It's time you spoke to me directly about this issue with employee problems before we have any more misunderstandings." Nunzio nodded, and Kim led Juan and Rodolfo away. "Is tomorrow good for the two of you?"

"I'll talk it over with my father," Remi said, "but I'm afraid we might search out new options. Of course, I'm only speaking for my family, though I'm confident Cain will join us on this venture."

"Remi, I've never known you to be hasty." Nunzio was leaning over trying to keep their talk private, but it was difficult in such close quarters. "Why not give me a chance to negotiate?"

"I know Ramon seldom does business on Sundays," Cain said, glancing at Remi, who nodded once in return. "So make it Tuesday at my office. We'll have one of our guys pick you up and drive you. No sense in giving the feds any more clues, right?"

"You want me to come alone?"

"I actually don't want you to come at all," Cain said, and Emma laughed. "You're the one who wants to meet."

"Until Tuesday, then." Nunzio's smile appeared forced. "Ladies, it was a pleasure," he said to Emma and Dallas.

As he walked away Dallas shivered so noticeably Cain couldn't help but ask, "Are you all right?"

"He reminds me of someone I used to know. The same dead eyes." Dallas shivered again and rubbed her arms as if she were really cold. "Sorry. Remi, I'm sure you and Cain have some stuff to talk over. Do you need us to head to the ladies' room?"

"Let's not give them a choice," Emma said. When she rose, Lou stood up with her. "Merrick?" She looked at her guard.

"We flipped a coin and Lou won," Merrick said. "He's the only person who hates Juan more than Cain does and would love to add matching bruises on the opposite side of Juan's face."

"Come on, Lou, you two spent so much time fighting over me, I really do have to go."

Cain laughed and watched them walk away. Since the owner had put Nunzio and the Luis family in the next room, she didn't have to look at them. "It's a good thing we're going to Pescador's after this."

"You want to talk to my father?"

"More like I want you to talk to him—I already know how I'm going to handle Nunzio." Cain stopped talking when the waiter arrived with a fresh round of drinks.

"You backing out on us?" Remi asked, but Cain could tell she wasn't angry.

"I gave you my word and I'd never back out, but I don't like this guy. Nunzio's going to tell us whatever we want to hear just to get his hands on the money. Once that happens, we'll have to deal with the consequences of the monster we'll have helped create."

Remi nodded. "I agree but don't see a lot of options here. If we want what he's selling, we can either talk him down or move on to something else. Mirage Properties will probably hold their noses and deal with him if they can add another property to their holdings."

"I'm sure we'll think of something," Cain said. She stood as Emma and Dallas made it back. "We have until Tuesday to come up with a better deal."

"Have you solved all the world's problems?" Emma asked. She kissed Cain's chin before sitting down.

"Everything okay?" Cain cocked her head in the direction of the restrooms.

"For once it was a bathroom trip without incident." Emma laughed at Dallas's look. "Long story that I'll tell you the next time we have lunch."

Their appetizers had arrived when Juan strode toward the front of the restaurant. He stared directly at Emma, puckered his lips, and blew her a kiss. He laughed when Emma put a restraining hand on Cain's shoulder, but stopped when Lou stood up as if waiting for him to pass. He stayed at his table for the remainder of the meal.

After dinner Remi led them to Ramon's club, where it was hard to miss Shelby and Claire having a club soda at the bar. But the agents were stuck there as Remi took her party up the stairs to the private section.

Dallas looped her arm through Remi's as they walked toward the cashier's cage. After Remi signed a voucher, the girl pushed a stack of chips toward her, repeating the process when Cain laid her money down.

"Craps?" Remi asked Cain.

They played, sharing their chips with Emma and Dallas, who, by the time Ramon arrived, were doing better than they were. Ramon gave them some hints on how to bet, obviously enjoying Dallas and Emma's enthusiasm.

"Nunzio Luca's in town and wants a meeting," Remi said as she and her father moved to the bar to get water for everyone.

"What answer did you and Cain give him?"

"Tuesday, if he comes alone. But Cain's not sounding too hyped about this deal anymore." Remi waved the bartender off, wanting a few more minutes with her father.

Ramon draped his arm around her shoulders and kissed Remi's cheek before letting her go. "I've taught you everything I can, and I know you weren't sure why I wanted to partner with Cain on this and the studio. Doing business with her will give you a new perspective. Cain surprises a lot of people all the time, but I'm seldom in that group because I seldom underestimate her."

"So you don't think she'll back out?" Remi asked.

"She gave us her word—to Cain that still means something. Before we're done, we'll own the Capri. It just might not come from the deal Nunzio Luca has in mind. If that's the case, we'll end up with a bargain we didn't expect."

When the waiter appeared again, Remi nodded. "How about the other thing I asked you to work on?"

Someone shouted from the craps table, and Ramon turned around as Dallas clapped and laughed. "I met with Mano about that this morning. We haven't found anything yet, but after I started reading what he has so far, I can see what made you curious."

"Nothing," Remi said, staring at the Evian bottles.

"Let me check one more thing before you jump to any conclusions. For the most part, she's who she says she is, and she's got the talent to back it up. That part is more than clear. But we don't know how she got there."

Remi cracked open one of the bottles and took a gulp, then wiped her mouth with the back of her hand. She joined her father in watching Dallas and her friends having a good time. "Sometimes it's easy to identify a woman with no past," she said, making Ramon step closer to her again.

"Give me a couple more days," he said in a gentle tone.

"If she's undercover, you're not going to find anything except what whoever she's working for wants you to find."

"I don't think that's it."

"Why not?" Remi waved back when Dallas made a motion for her to rejoin them. "She's got the perfect cover. Damsel in distress under the thumb of an overbearing manager. I was bound to notice her sooner or later. Our taking over Gemini has been in the works for a couple of years, so it hasn't been a secret. I'm not saying she's a cop, but if she is, you have to give them credit for the elaborate setup."

"If it's there, I'll find it. If there's anything to find."

"I trust you, Papi. Let me know, and follow the money trail. Her work experience isn't extensive, but this last film has been lucrative."

"Go on." Ramon handed the tray over and pushed her in her date's direction. "You've spent so much time with me you're being rude."

"And about Tuesday?"

"Tell Cain I'll be glad to follow her lead."

CHAPTER TWENTY-SIX

"Dallas, it was great seeing you again," Cain said as they came down the stairs of the club. Shelby was still sitting on her stool, but Claire was nowhere in sight. "Have a good night." She shook hands with Remi before accepting a friendly embrace.

"I'll call you tomorrow," Remi told her before she stepped back.

"Whenever you like, we'll be home."

Remi and Cain stood back as Emma and Dallas said their good-byes. They hadn't known each other long, but Remi could see they were becoming good friends. The conversation she'd had with her father returned to her, and suddenly the possibility of Dallas not being who she said she was hit her in the gut. If there was even a remote chance, Dallas would be betraying not only her family and her—she would also get to Cain via her partner.

Taking her aside, Cain asked, "You all right?"

"I need your help." Remi hoped her father was right about Cain's creativity. "My father and Mano are working on something, but they haven't had much luck."

"Remi," Cain said, winking at Emma when she took a step toward them, "we've known each other a long time. If you need anything, just ask. It's that simple."

"This has nothing to do with business." She glanced at Dallas before giving Cain her full attention. "But until we talk, please tell Emma to be careful on any future lunch dates."

"You know how I feel about Emma. Give me a hint so I can sleep tonight."

"Not here, not now, but I promise first thing in the morning." Remi pointed to Shelby, not caring if she could see her. "I have your word it'll stay between us if I'm wrong?"

"You've got no worries, no matter what it is. Go on and get Dallas home, and we'll talk tomorrow."

Emma kissed Remi's cheek before following Cain out to the car. "Anything wrong?" she asked when the door closed, leaving them alone in the back.

"If there is we'll have to wait until tomorrow to find out. You had lunch with Dallas, right?"

"I told you about it, remember?"

Lou headed out of the Quarter but wasn't driving them to Jarvis's. They were going to their house. "Did she ask any strange questions? Anything on the verge of snooping?" Cain asked, not questioning their direction.

"You mean more about business and less about girl talk?"

"I'm not asking to be insulting."

"I know. You're asking because of that serious and sudden talk you just had with Remi. What's the problem?"

"I don't know if there is one, but it sounds like Remi's trying to find out some information on Dallas, or she has Ramon working on it."

"How romantic," Emma said, clearly being sarcastic.

"Something must've prompted it, lass. Don't go crucifying her yet."

"Did you do that to me?"

"I didn't have to." Cain laughed at the menacing glare Emma had plastered on her face.

"Why's that?"

"After our first date, I knew all I had to about you, and I was right."

"So I didn't send off warning bells in your head?" Emma moved closer and lifted Cain's arm around her shoulder.

"In my head and in other parts of my anatomy," Cain teased. "I saw past the clumsy waitress and into my future and the mother of my children. I had no reason to question what was in my heart."

"You," Emma ran her hand up Cain's leg until she reached her crotch, "are a very romantic soul, but I think you took a little longer to see all that in me. The night we met was more of a question of whether to fire the hayseed or not."

"And give someone else a shot at you? Not on your life," Cain said, then tapped on the window. "Are we going to study more paint swatches?"

"We're going to study something, and eventually it'll require more painting, but it's more to rev you up for a threat I made today."

"Why do I get the feeling I'm not going to like this, Mrs. Casey?"

"Trust me, baby, you can't be any madder about the situation than I am. I wanted to show you something, then I want you to talk to our contractor in the morning. However you decide to handle the situation I'll gladly back you, but it needs your unique persuasive charms."

They drove through the new gate and Cain spotted the van across the street already in place. The guards waited in the car as Emma took Cain's hand and led her through the front door. From the time they made it inside until they stopped at the stairs, Cain counted over a hundred holes in their walls, most of them in her study.

"What about upstairs?" Cain asked Emma.

"The maid hasn't made it up there yet, since this part took so long after I left here this morning," Emma said. "I'm sure it's the same mess."

Cain smiled finally and kissed her. They stood outside the house now, but the bugs inside were undoubtedly operational. The agents in the van were probably testing them.

"Let's get going then. I wouldn't want you to come down with something," Cain said.

As soon as they were back in the car Emma said, "His name is Jimmy Pitre, if you remember, and I told him you'd call when I had the sweep done. This is going to set us back some."

"I'll take care of it, lass, even if I have to make a trip to Home Depot and fix it myself. What kind of deal did you offer this guy?"

Emma told her about the five-thousand-dollar penalty for every device they found.

"You should've set an extra charge for every one you found after a hundred," Cain said.

❖

"Thanks for inviting me tonight." Dallas held Remi's hand as they walked down Bourbon Street toward her house. "I really like Emma and Cain."

"They're a great couple who've already had their share of heartache. It's good to see them together again."

"Together again? Were they separated?" Dallas took her key out of her small evening bag and handed it to Remi.

"It's a long story." She unlocked the outer door and held it open for Dallas. "Maybe next time I'll get into it more. I don't like to talk about my friends out of turn."

They stopped at the door to the house, and Dallas placed her hands on Remi's shoulders. "It's still early. You have time now if you want to come in."

"I have some meetings in the morning so I have to get going." She unlocked the next door. "I'll call once I'm done."

Dallas moved her hands up until they were behind Remi's neck. "Why does that sound like a brush-off? Did I do or say something to upset you?"

"I have a lot on my mind, and I'm not brushing you off. As soon as I'm done I'll give you a call." Remi kissed her, then waited for her to slide the deadbolt on the door into place. When Dallas's expression had turned to one of sadness, she'd almost given in. *That's something I can't allow myself to do until I know all your secrets, Dallas Montgomery.*

❖

"Where in the hell have you been?" Bob said menacingly as he dug his fingers into Dallas's arm when Remi's footsteps faded away.

He'd been waiting for her inside the door in the shadows, she was sure, so he could keep out of sight if Remi had accepted her invitation to come in. She didn't answer and tried to pull away, not in the mood for Bob's games. "Answer me, or do I need to remind you who owns you, sweetheart?" he asked, tightening his hold. "I'll put the bruises where no camera will ever find them."

"You remind me so much every day, I'd think you'd be tired of it by now." Dallas winced as the pain got worse right before he let go. Taking no chances that he'd touch her again, she moved around him and put as much distance between them as possible. "I had dinner with Remi Jatibon. It was a spur-of-the-moment invitation, so I didn't have time to call you. Since you told me to be nice, I thought you wouldn't mind."

"You're finally using your head and appealing to her more basic needs. I'm glad to see you're not playing hard to get. We both know better. But make sure you check with me before you go making any stupid moves."

"I leave all the move-making up to you," she said, suddenly feeling tired. Now that Remi was gone, she just wanted to be alone.

"Think you can smart off now? What, you get one dinner invitation and you believe you've found a guard dog to protect you from me? Do I need to remind you she didn't even make it through the door?"

"Not everyone is out to get something. This was dinner, and unlike most people I have to deal with, Remi wasn't expecting me to pay for it on my back." She glanced at the rock on her coffee table and took a deep breath. "Those days are over, if I can help it."

"I'm out to get all I can, and we're taking another step next week. The studio called, and we have an appointment. Let's hope your little girlfriend hasn't moved on to a newer flavor by then, and you end up with a more lucrative contract than before." He crossed the room and stopped in front of her, then ran his finger down her cheek to her neck. "Whatever happens, don't start thinking this perverted bitch can help you get rid of me, because that'll never happen. We're partners for life, baby. I've seen to that."

When Bob left, the air in the room seemed to return. Dallas slumped against the chair she'd been standing by and gave in to the tears she seldom shed in front of anyone, not anymore. Bob was an ass, but he wasn't wrong about a whole list of things. She belonged to him; he wasn't going away voluntarily, and Remi had already moved on.

Something had happened while they were in Pescador's that had changed Remi's demeanor toward her. If she'd ever had a chance with Remi, something had snatched it away before anything came of it. Too tired to climb the stairs to her room, she stretched out on the sofa and cried.

Dallas had learned early that life wasn't fair. Fate showed her glimpses of what was possible, then just as quickly took them away. She would've done better never to know any kind of happiness was possible, because then she'd have nothing to compare the misery to. She wouldn't have any memories of her mother singing her to sleep, picking wildflowers in the meadow near their house, or how good it felt when Remi held her on this same couch.

That's all they were, memories so fleeting she could almost convince herself they were simply strings of fantasy.

CHAPTER TWENTY-SEVEN

The mansion off the road in Long Island had been in the same family for three generations. Guards carrying machine guns and large dogs roaming the grounds dissuaded unwelcome guests from impromptu visits. The beautiful gardens and buildings were purchased with blood, drugs, and no conscience.

Junior Luca sat on a bench that overlooked the water, the one place on the property where he felt comfortable to talk freely because of his staff's constant sweeps for listening devices. "Nunzio, you in New Orleans yet?"

"I just got back from dinner with Rodolfo and Juan. I thought I'd call before I take a shower. After spending the night listening to that idiot Juan, I can use one."

"Yeah, well, while Rodolfo's making nice with you, he's breathing down my neck about money. We're tapped out, and I can't bleed any more cash out of the East Coast operations. What kind of timetable are you looking at down there?"

"I ran into Remi and Cain at dinner tonight, and they said they'd sit down with me Tuesday. They acted pretty chummy, and they're both holding the line that they're negotiating some other deal." He stood at the window peering out at the night sky. "I talked it over with Kim, and she's ready to go when it comes to what we talked about before."

"Boy, the last fucking thing we need is to get into a pissing contest with Cain Casey. Tell Kim to rework her plan and get back to me, but I can tell you right now, Tuesday's too late."

"I think you're wrong there, Papa. Tuesday will give me all the time I need to put things into motion not only for this deal, but for our future dealings in the South." The glass felt cold against his hand, but he'd flipped the air conditioner on. He couldn't sleep unless it was cold.

"What's on your mind? Or should I say who?" Junior Luca asked.

"If I move, it'll be with the help of the Colombians."

"I don't want to owe anyone any favors after this plays out."

"Look at it this way, if they help us they're going to be doing us a favor. But if I let them take care of business when they're here, then what they'll owe us in return is going to be so much more. We have a lot of enemies in common, and letting them get involved on our terms will drive our price down in the end."

"Don't forget to keep me in the loop, and if not Cain, then who?"

"Remi. That'll make Cain and Ramon see it's in their best interest to talk to me," Nunzio said.

"We'll see."

Nunzio threw his phone on the bed and took one last look at the view before he closed the curtains. The phone landed near Kim, and she placed it on the nightstand as she turned up the volume on the television. "He doesn't agree with you," she said.

"He doesn't trust me. That's different than disagreeing with me." He sat down so hard the mattress bounced.

"Give him a few days to fully appreciate how this plays out. When Junior gets everything he wants and is making more money than he ever dreamed, he won't take you for granted again."

Nunzio laughed and scrubbed his face with his hands. "This is Junior Luca we're talking about, right? He's not about to give in that easily, no matter how successful I am."

Kim pointed the remote at the TV and turned it off. "Then how about if I take your mind off it some other way?" She rolled toward him, put her hand on his crotch, and squeezed.

The blatant come-on made him forget his father, Remi, Cain, and, most importantly, his wife.

❖

"Am I too early?" Remi asked when she was led back to the dining room to find Emma and the children having breakfast. "Or is Cain just sleeping in?"

"Cain's meeting with our contractor this morning, but she said she wouldn't be long, so please join us." Emma was cutting up a waffle for Hannah, who was doing a good job of shoving bacon in her mouth. "Hannah, slow down before you choke and Remi thinks we're not teaching you any table manners."

"Cain tells me you've got a birthday coming up, Hayden," Remi said. "What's on your wish list?"

"A Corvette, but Mama says I have to wait a few years," he joked. "Think Emil would consider helping me out with some boots?"

Remi crossed her feet at the ankles and gave him a good view of her black alligator boots, polished to perfection. They'd been a gift from her father's personal guard Emil, who knew as much about trapping gators as he did about keeping Ramon safe. "I'm sure if we ask him real nice, he'll put you in some new footwear." Remi opened her arms when he came around the table and hugged her.

"Thanks, Remi, and if you're not busy, come to the barbeque Mama's putting together. You can meet my Grandpa Ross. He's making the trip down from Wisconsin."

"I wouldn't miss it."

Hayden kissed Emma next and waved to Hannah before he walked out.

"He's getting tall." Remi smiled at Hannah, who'd moved on to filling her cheeks with waffle. "And this one just gets cuter. I can see why Cain talks about them all the time."

"They're beautiful, but they're a handful since they don't just *look* like Cain. She keeps telling me it's the strands of bad Casey grass running through them."

When Hannah lost interest in her plate, Emma wiped her mouth and put her on the floor. Hannah stopped and gave Remi a hug as well before she followed Carmen out.

"If you're good enough for Hayden," Emma explained. "That's her litmus test." She stood and poured them a cup of coffee. "It gets a little more complicated once we get older, doesn't it?"

"That's because the older we get, the better we get at hiding who we are."

"Can I be honest with you?" Emma sat down across from her and added cream to her coffee. "This is decaffeinated," she said when Remi nodded. "I hope you've had a real cup already." Her attempt at humor worked and Remi laughed. "I had lunch with Dallas, and I noticed something about her."

Emma sounded so serious Remi hesitated before answering. "If she made you feel uncomfortable—"

"Remi, she didn't make me feel uncomfortable. I felt sorry for her.

Dallas is running from something, and the last thing she needs is for you to disappear."

"What makes you think I'll do that?" Her coffee sat forgotten, but Remi did run her finger along the cup handle to have something to do while she lay under Emma's microscope.

"How do I know? Are you kidding?" She laughed, and some of the hair in her ponytail pulled loose. "I might have graduated from Tulane with a degree in English, but I have a doctorate in life when it comes to understanding Derby Cain Casey. You two are at different points in your lives, but in here," Emma stood up and placed her hand over Remi's heart, "you're the same. It's this," she tapped the side of her head, "that gets in the way when it comes to situations like this."

"You sound like you *do* know about it." Remi stood and followed Emma to the sunroom. Outside Hannah was running around chasing the last of the falling leaves.

"If you just change where we're from, Dallas and I aren't that different either. In the end we're all running from something. If you care even a little about her, you need to find out what it is and make her want to run toward something."

Remi smiled as she gave Emma a quick hug. From the time Cain had introduced them, Remi had liked the little firecracker. Suddenly she saw the allure of having only one woman in her life. "My mother could take lessons from you."

The teasing comment made Emma chuckle. "How do you know I haven't taken some from her? I'm just practicing. With a true-bred Casey upstairs and another one coming up right behind him," she pointed to Hannah, "I can use all the experience I can get. Once all those hormones kick in, our house is going to be a zoo."

"I'm sure you'll do fine." Remi opened the door to the yard and waved her through. "How about if I get some practice with a four-year-old until Cain gets back?"

"If everything works out you could use that."

Emma was kidding, but is that what she wanted? She had a home, but she had never considered filling it with a wife and children, like Cain had. And if she did consider it, was Dallas the one who, like Emma, could make the perfect partner?"

The answers were like a fortune cookie, wrapped in secrecy. She just had to crack through what Dallas was hiding.

CHAPTER TWENTY-EIGHT

Jimmy Pitre stood in Cain's office breathing like he'd sprinted a mile. His eyes darted from Cain's face to the multitude of holes in the walls. This room had been gutted first during the renovations because of all the bullet holes, and Cain was sure the FBI had taken full advantage of the missing drywall to wire the room in which she most likely did business.

"Beautiful day, don't you think?" Cain asked him after fifteen minutes of silence. She gave him credit for keeping his mouth shut since he'd arrived. Usually the sobbing started five minutes in.

"I guess," Jimmy said, his voice wavering.

"When you were dealing with my wife, she said you were always certain," Cain said, staring at him until he dropped his eyes to the floor. "You remember my wife, don't you? The cute blonde who gave you some pretty straight-forward directions."

"I did my job, Ms. Casey. The house is almost finished. I fulfilled Emma's wishes, and I didn't leave any room looking like that." He pointed to the holes.

"I see." Her leather chair creaked when she sat back. In the quiet house it sounded even louder than usual, but still she could hear Jimmy's breathing. "Do I look stupid, Jimmy? May I call you Jimmy?"

He whipped his head up and nodded vigorously. "No, ma'am, you don't look stupid."

"Then maybe when Emma hired you she misunderstood exactly what kind of work you do, or maybe you forgot to tell her about all those little things that set you apart from the other guys she could've gone with. Which do you suppose it was?"

He spread his hands out in front of him and smiled. "I do go that extra mile to make sure you're satisfied. But don't worry—there's no charge for that."

"I see," she repeated and pulled away the kitchen towel she'd grabbed before he'd arrived, then rested her hands on the edge of the desk. "I imagine, then, that the main control for these is somewhere in the house. When you submitted your final bill, I didn't notice any mention of them, so now that you're here, explain them to me."

"Those aren't mine, and I don't know anything about them," he said, his voice going up an octave.

"We'll get to who they belong to and how they got here in a minute, but first let's talk about your last chat with Emma. Do you remember the fine she mentioned?"

"She said five thousand per infraction."

"Right here then we have five hundred and eighty thousand dollars worth of infractions." She had laid every bug Katlin had found in neat rows on her desk. "And we're talking the first floor only." She stopped and picked up two that lay to the side of the others. "Do you know where we found these?" She held them up and Jimmy shook his head. "On the new playground equipment I put up for my daughter. I realize some people consider me a monster, but do you really think if I were, I'd show that side of myself in front of my four-year-old?" She slammed the devices back down on the desk.

"I don't know who did that." His lip trembled as he spoke.

"We have a problem, Jimmy. My math tells me that you owe me over a hundred grand at the moment." She went on talking over him. "Did you bring your checkbook?"

"No." His eyes were glassy now, but the tears were holding steady.

"That's okay, because I'm not finished tabulating." Cain saw Lou's chest shake in quiet laughter when Jimmy appeared so relieved he took a small step forward. "Like I said, these were downstairs, and once I start on the second floor, the fine will be the same unless I find any in the master bedroom."

"What happens then?" He sounded as if he had to choose between being disemboweled or burned alive.

"Are you married, Jimmy?"

"Five years."

She nodded. "Any kids?"

"A three-year-old boy."

"Uh-huh." She picked up another bug and studied it. "How would you feel making love to your wife and sharing lovers' conversations, only to have a bunch of people you don't know listen in?"

"I wouldn't like it."

"Good for you, that was the right answer. Your wife would be proud." She glanced up at him again and stood. From the way his eyes widened, she was sure he was surprised that she was taller by a few inches. "Back to our talk about the master bedroom. For every one of these I find up there," she picked up another one at random, "it's going to cost you a little bit more."

"How much?" His tears had started and ran down his face almost as if he didn't notice they were falling.

"Lou, you know Emma," Cain said, addressing him for the first time and making him step closer to Jimmy. "How much do you think her dignity is worth?"

"A lot more than five grand, boss."

"You're right, but let's give our boy here a chance to redeem himself. How about it?" she asked Jimmy. "One simple question and, if you tell me the truth, we call it even."

"I've been telling the truth." If Jimmy intended to protest anymore, he clicked his mouth shut when he felt Lou's hand on his shoulder. "What do you want to know?"

"How many of these are in our bedroom? Tell me the truth and I'll wipe your slate clear of debt for the second floor. Lie and it'll cost you fifty for every one I find."

"I don't know anything about this, and I don't have that kind of money." Jimmy's tears fell faster when she put her hands on her desk, she leaned over, and took a deep breath.

"Does that answer fit the question I asked? Do I need to explain how much I dislike repeating myself? And asking you if I look stupid is repeating myself." Cain finally let go of some of her control and started screaming. "So answer my damn question."

"None," he blurted. "There's none up there."

Cain pointed at Katlin and the room fell silent again as she went to test his answer. For ten minutes Cain drummed her fingers in her usual uneven beat on her desk, and Jimmy continued to wipe his nose on his sleeve. A moment later they heard a loud noise, followed quickly by another—the sound of a hammer going through a wall. Katlin finally made it down and added another six to Cain's collection.

"You're not a very honest man, Jimmy," Cain said. She scraped her nail along what she assumed was the speaker, hoping the idiots listening in had the volume turned up. "You owe me another three hundred thousand."

"Are those on?" Jimmy asked, suddenly sounding like the panic was really setting in and he'd had a brilliant idea. "Is anyone listening to this?"

"If you want to yell for help, go ahead," she said, handing him one of the bugs. "I ripped them out, but I didn't destroy them. I'm guessing, but I think destruction of government property is a crime, and that's not what we're about. And if you want to know if anyone's listening, the van you passed on the way in here is probably full of your new friends witnessing the crack your ass is in right now. Only if they come barging in here like the calvary, they also have to admit these belong to them."

She leaned over and spoke directly into the new ones Katlin had brought down. "They're not going to do that for you, Jimmy, because they're after the big fish." She pointed her thumb toward her chest. "And they don't care how many little guppies go down in their pursuit. You know what they're hoping for out there while they're crammed in the back of that van like cockroaches?"

"What?"

"That I, in a fit of anger, blow your brains out all over the new rug Emma picked out for me. Then, believe me, they'll come running, but only if that happens."

"Can I go home?"

"Just one more thing." Cain walked around her desk and grabbed him by the collar.

"Please don't hurt me."

"I'm not going to hurt you. Like I said, I'm not a monster, Jimmy. Today was just about talking to you and getting our finances straight. See, you shouldn't have believed what other people said about me instead of asking me directly." She smiled at him and tightened her hold on his collar. "I want you to divide the pile in two." She dragged him forward and pointed to her desk.

"What for?"

"You're going to swallow anything on the right, so keep that in mind when you divide it."

His hands shook as he stretched it toward the pile. "Are you sure they're working?"

Cain crooked her finger at Katlin so she'd run the locator over her desk. When she did, the needle on the meter jumped completely to the right. "They're all working, and the calvary isn't coming. Think about that when you pay your federal taxes."

Jimmy peered at her with bloodshot eyes and mucus draining out of his nose. "But why?"

"In situations like this, you're either a pawn or a prized target. You're under a lot of stress and obviously not paying very close attention, so I'll repeat myself so it'll sink in. They're waiting for the target to kill the pawn. Then they'll rush in here. Now I do believe we've established that's *not* going to happen. You can cry and beg all you want, but they'll just sit and wait for the gunshot."

"Only the ones on the right?" he asked. He made his cut as if ready to get it over with.

"About twenty-five," Cain said when he was done. "Not enough to get sick on but enough to show me you're trying. One more thing—strip."

"What?" he gazed up at her again. "Why?"

"Because I asked you to. Don't make me ask again." He took his shirt off first, displaying the tattoo Emma had described, then removed his pants and underwear. "Bon appetit."

Jimmy started with the small ones first and gagged on the larger ones. He coughed and held his stomach on the last one but managed to get it down without throwing up on Cain's desk. "Finished," he said.

"Not quite."

For the next part Shelby and the other agents on duty listened as Jimmy grunted and cried, but they couldn't hear any other voices or noise. Cain must have written her directions.

"Shelby," Claire said when the front door opened and a naked Jimmy stood there.

He ran across the street and tapped on their back window. When no one inside answered, he banged on the glass again until the van started swaying.

"Open up, you sons of bitches, or I swear I'll break it," he screamed.

Lionel was closest to the door and gave in before the neighbors called the police. "You're okay now," he told Jimmy, who was holding his hands in front of his genitals as if trying to preserve some of his dignity.

"Shut the fuck up and give me a map of where you put all your shit."

Shelby tried to calm him down. "We can't do that, Mr. Pitre. We went over this, remember?"

"I owe that crazy bitch a bunch of money unless you give me a map. If you don't, who's going to pay?"

"We'll figure something out, but first we need to know what happened," Shelby said.

"You know what you need to figure out? The quickest route to my house because I forgot my pants in there and I'm not going back. And once you drop me off, stay the hell away from me." He got in and grabbed his stomach as soon as he was past Lionel. The momentum landed him in the middle of them. "Oh God," he said in obvious pain.

After that, everyone but Jimmy dashed for the back and piled out into the street. Cain's car stopped as it came through the gate and she rolled the window down.

"Problem?" Cain asked, smiling.

"You know damn well what our problem is," Shelby said.

Cain craned her head to see in the van. "I really don't know, but that," she pointed to the van and the stains on their pants, "is the true meaning of listening to shit."

CHAPTER TWENTY-NINE

A few cars were parked in front of Jarvis's house when Cain got back, but she assumed Remi and her family were there. Emma was waiting at the front door and took her hand and led her into the kitchen.

"Giving cooking lessons?" Cain said as a joke as she kissed the side of Emma's neck. "Not that I don't want to be alone with you, lass, but don't we have company?"

"If you weren't so big I'd spank you. We have company, but not all of it is who you were expecting. Nunzio Luca's here and Remi's keeping him company."

"Did she ask you to call Ramon and Mano?"

"Not yet, and she didn't ask me to leave, so I've been making small talk to help her out. Honey," she held both of Cain's hands, "this guy's a creep. I didn't think anyone could be a bigger ass than Juan, but after spending an hour with Nunzio, I have to admit I was wrong."

"He's not only a creep, he doesn't know how to take directions. Today isn't Tuesday." She kissed Emma and turned to join Remi.

"Hey," Emma said, stopping her. "You were gone longer than I thought. How'd it go with Jimmy?"

"He owes us some money, and after our talk," Cain couldn't help but laugh, "I'm sure he had an ass full of me and all those bugs we found."

"You didn't."

"You're right, I didn't, but Jimmy sure did. After he was done I suggested he return them to their rightful owners. I'm sure they can be used again, but I hope they disinfect them first."

Emma was laughing so hard she was hanging on the counter. "Thanks for putting that image in my head, and thanks for taking care of it. I feel like an idiot that I didn't post someone over there."

"When we finish the sweep, go ahead and call Jimmy back. He can work off his debt while Lou or one of the guys follows him around."

"Are you sure?"

"Positive." Emma moved closer and Cain met her halfway. "After today's meeting, I'm sure he doesn't want to go through another negotiation session with me. Let me go see what Nunzio wants, then let's take the kids out for something fun."

Nunzio stood and extended his hand when Cain joined them in the sunroom. He and Remi were sitting across from each other so Cain took the sofa between them. Remi looked like her anger was simmering just below the surface.

"I didn't expect to see you for a couple more days, Nunzio. Did something change that I don't know about?"

"Remi and I started without you, and I was explaining that I'm willing to shave three percent from the final price, but I need your answer by today. I've got some business out of town, and today is as long as I can stretch it."

"I see." Cain crossed her legs and glanced at Remi. "Talk about anything else?"

"I was just telling Remi what a lucky bitch she is to be seeing Dallas Montgomery. I'm a fan and sure as hell wouldn't mind tapping into that."

"Remi?" Cain said her name, but kept her eyes on Nunzio. "Since you all started without me, what's our answer?"

"No deal even if he cuts the price in half."

"That's why I waited for you, Cain. I thought you might be the levelheaded one here." Nunzio clapped his hands and laughed. "If I insulted you by mentioning your new playmate, I'm sorry, Remi. This is business, though, tell her, Cain."

"I believe you've got our answer. Is there anything else?"

"You and I both know you need this." Nunzio's face twisted into a snarl and he pointed at Cain.

"Why would you think that?" Cain asked.

"Because the Bracatos were a pack of idiots, but you're playing in a whole different ballgame now. The enemies you're making are smarter, stronger, and more widespread than Big Gino. With the casino, you and the Jatibons have a fighting chance to keep what you've got now." He stood up but didn't take a step toward them when Simon stood as well. "In the coming weeks, if you were hoping for backup from Vinny, I wouldn't count on that. He doesn't have his father's savvy, and the competition will eat him alive."

"Simon, would you be so kind," Cain said. Simon bowed her head slightly and walked Nunzio out.

When they were alone Remi's head fell back and her hands clenched into fists. "I'm sorry if you wanted this, but I'm not having anything to do with that guy."

"We'll deal with this soon enough. Let's talk about the favor you wanted to ask me."

"Are you sure? We put a lot of time and effort into this."

Cain took a deep breath and released it slowly. "We did, but there'll be others. We need time to think over our next step, but that's for later—tell me what's on your mind."

"It's Dallas." Remi lifted her head and leaned forward. "I asked my father to investigate her past to see where her life intersected with her manager Bob's. This guy's a total dick, and there's some reason she hasn't dumped him."

"What did Ramon find?" Cain accepted the cigar Remi offered her and led her outside.

"Nothing yet. The trail stops at the beginning of her career. That's when Dallas Montgomery was born, and she effectively buried whoever she really is."

Cain accepted Remi's clippers and lighter to prepare her cigar. After she blew out her first stream of smoke, she sat in one of the chairs around the pool. It would be awhile before anyone used it, but Jarvis's people kept it pristine. "Until you find out, what are you concerned about?"

"Think about what you were doing this morning." Remi lit her own cigar. "Since I doubt you've taken a sudden interest in decorating, you met with your contractor for some other reason. You and I both know there's more than one way for these bastards to get in."

"And because you're guessing she's some sort of cop, you're going to just let her go?"

"Please tell me this isn't one of those keep-your-enemies-closer lectures?" Remi joked. "Isn't that what you'd do?"

"Barney Kyle turned, even if it was temporarily, the one person in my life who should've been rock solid. Because he was successful I missed my wife, the birth of my daughter, and a very long time period that I'll never get back." Cain remembered vividly how she felt then. "I could've been sure that she wouldn't betray me again by not letting her back into my life, but I would've missed out on what I need to make all this worthwhile."

"This is different. Dallas isn't Emma."

"I'll work on this personally, and if I find something, I won't tell anybody but you. Until then if you don't give a shit about her, don't let this eat away at you, but if you do, then don't be afraid to move forward."

"And if she turns out to be a cop?"

Hannah came running across the yard, and Cain stood and grabbed her before she got within twenty feet of the pool. "I'll give you the same advice I gave Muriel." She tossed Hannah into the air, loving the squeal it always produced. "Don't talk in your sleep."

❖

Muriel sat in the famous piano bar in Pat O'Brien's on Bourbon Street, having a scotch and listening to the woman performing. It was a tourist destination, proved by the number of folks with a multitude of different accents sitting nearby, but the place filled up every night because the musicians were so good. Cain had told her to get away from everything, and this was as much of an escape as she was willing to agree to.

As she brought her glass up, one of Vincent Carlotti's men joined her and put his beer down. Almost everyone in the room was singing the refrain from "American Pie" when he asked her to go outside to the patio.

"The boss is keeping an eye on Vinny and his business," the guy said as a start.

"So are Cain and Remi. Does he have a problem with something?" Muriel leaned against the brick wall at the back of the open space.

"More like he wanted to give you guys a heads-up. Vincent's been talking to Hector Delarosa."

"The Columbian Hector Delarosa?" Muriel asked.

"That's the one. He called tonight so Mr. Carlotti would be watching for a particular plane soon."

Muriel put her hand up to keep the waitress away. "Before you go on, tell me why you're not talking to Cain."

"I did. Cain told me where I could probably find you. You can call her if you want, but she said for you to take care of it."

She closed her eyes and shook her head. The guy standing before her represented Cain's way of giving her what she'd asked for. If she said no, that would've been acceptable too. Her role had been defined for so long, not only with her family but with the others as well, that no one would've thought less of her for keeping to her place.

"That's okay. Just tell me," Muriel said.

"When people like Hector need something taken care of, especially in the States, they use one guy. Hector said his name is Jorge Cristo, and according to Hector, he's a killing machine."

"When's he get here?" Muriel asked. The couple sitting closest to them left and Muriel sat down.

"That's the easy part—this Friday, AeroMexico's last flight is coming in from Mexico City." He cocked his bottle back and drained the last of his drink. "What we need to figure out before then is who his target is and who hired him."

"That we do, since it sounds like he sure as hell isn't coming for the seafood. Tell Vincent thanks for the information." The guy stood up and shook hands with her. "Did Delarosa describe him?"

"Mr. Cristo likes to fly AeroMexico out of Mexico City because usually only about ten Americans are on the flight."

Muriel put her hands up and shrugged. "And?"

"The rest of the deplaning passengers are Mexican and other South Americans. It's a good way to blend in."

"I take it Hector didn't give him up completely."

"Hector sees potential in dealing with Vinny because of his father and his friends, but no, he didn't give us what you're asking. Down the line he might have a problem or two he needs solved. He burns Jorge, and who's he going to call to fix it?"

"Nothing's ever easy, is it?"

CHAPTER THIRTY

The sun was creeping along the floor, slowly making its way toward the sofa where Dallas had been lying since the night before. She didn't feel like this very often any more, because she refused to let things she couldn't change drag her down, but on mornings like this she didn't have the strength to try.

Her tears started again, but she was so exhausted she didn't move to wipe them away. When the phone rang she ignored that as well until the machine picked up in the kitchen. She'd never recorded her own message so a robotic-sounding voice asked the caller to leave their name and number.

The sound of Kristen's voice got her on her feet and to the phone before her little sister hung up. "Hey, just wait for the stupid thing to click off," she said.

"Out late? You usually pick up by the second ring."

Kristen always sounded light, as if her essence was sunlight. They'd started in a horrible place, but Dallas had taken the weight of that darkness so Kristen's memories would be easier to bear. She was the one person who knew all of Dallas's secrets and still loved her without reservations.

"I was sleeping in." Dallas headed for the kitchen and the coffee pot. "We went out last night, but my date was a perfect gentlewoman and deposited me on my doorstep at a decent hour."

"She didn't stay for coffee?"

Dallas heard people shouting and having a good time in the background, so she figured Kristen was sitting outside somewhere on campus. "She had a busy morning, she said."

"What's wrong?"

"Nothing's wrong," Dallas said quietly. She pinched the bridge of her nose and placed the coffee pot under the faucet to fill it. "Nothing's wrong," she repeated when Kristen stayed quiet.

"Are you finished hiding your feelings? I recognize that tone. Something's wrong, and it'll be easier in the long run if you go ahead and tell me what it is."

"I'm disappointed Remi didn't stay."

"And?" Kristen prompted.

"Bob was here last night—waiting for me." She opened the canister of coffee and inhaled the aroma before scooping out a couple of spoonfuls. She'd started the ritual the first time she could afford to buy good beans. "He was in one of his moods, but he said the studio called, and I've got an appointment this week."

"Remi saw that asshole there and left anyway?"

"She never saw him. She's not like that."

"It doesn't matter what's she's like. You need to be more careful. One of these days Bob's going to really hurt you trying to prove how far he can push you, and then he'll just move on to the next person he can exploit."

"We don't have a choice, Kristen. If Bob makes good on his promises, what happens to you?" She poured a cup of coffee and sat on a stool at the counter.

"I don't care about me. I want you to walk away. We have enough to live normal lives and don't need something glamorous. That's not who we are."

"Honey, it's not that simple. I've done a lot I'm not proud of, but humiliation never killed anyone. If I'm serving twenty to life and have to leave you all alone, that would kill me, but the jail time wouldn't bother me. I've hidden you as much as I can, but I can't guarantee that someone like Bob won't find you." The buzzer for the gate cut her off and she came close to ignoring it. "Hold on, somebody's here."

"If it's Bob, tell him to go to hell."

Dallas laughed as she reached the intercom by the back door. "Can I help you?" she asked.

"I wanted to see if you were free for breakfast," Remi said as a greeting.

She'd been depressed because Remi had left, but now a sense of panic seized her. Last night's wrinkled outfit and running makeup spelled a troubled woman, and Remi wouldn't be attracted to that kind of person.

"Dallas?" Remi's voice came through again.

"Go open the door and say yes," Kristen said.

"I'm not looking too good," Dallas said, feeling disgusted with herself.

Kristen said jokingly, "Even if you slept in pig slop, you're beautiful. It's your curse, so learn to deal with it. I'm hanging up so let her in, make her wait while you shower, and go out for pancakes. And call me when you get back."

"I love you." Dallas gripped the phone, wanting to hang on as long as she could.

"I love you too, and it's time you took a chance on being happy. Whether it's Remi or not, you need to open your heart to someone other than me."

"Thanks, and I'll call you later." She took another sip of coffee, more as a delay tactic than needing the caffeine, before she walked outside to the gate. "Good morning," she said, opening the gate a little.

"Good—" was the only word Remi got out before she stepped forward and put her arms around Dallas.

"I wasn't expecting you," Dallas said. She kept her arms tense, like she didn't want to get too comfortable against Remi's chest.

"My meeting wasn't as long as I thought." Remi held her a little apart from her so she could see Dallas's face. Most of her makeup had been wiped away during what looked like a bout of crying. The blue eyes were rimmed in red and Dallas appeared tired. "Is everything okay?" She ran her thumbs along Dallas's cheeks and stopped breathing for a moment when Dallas started crying. "Hey, it's going to be all right."

Remi held her, hoping Dallas would calm down, but when she only cried harder Remi picked her up and carried her to the chair Dallas used to sit in and read. With Dallas sitting on her lap, Remi held her until the outburst burned itself out.

"You must think I'm a nutcase," Dallas said, her voice raw.

"I deal with nutcases all the time, and you're not even close." Remi leaned back when Dallas snuggled closer. "Want to tell me what's wrong?" She wiped away the wetness on Dallas's face.

"Just fighting old demons," Dallas said, then shook her head as if anything else she was thinking of saying died in her throat.

"It's okay. You don't have to tell me if you don't want to, but I've probably faced worse nightmares than whatever haunts you. We haven't known each other long, but if you need me, I'll be happy to help you carry that heavy load."

"I know you would." Dallas put her hand behind Remi's neck and kissed her cheek. "But this is something I...I have to deal with myself."

"Like I said, no pressure, but let me at least try to take your mind off it by treating you to breakfast."

"Just the two of us?"

"I gave Simon the rest of the day off, so it's just you and me." Dallas finally smiled at her fully and started to move off her. When Dallas stood in front of her with the sun shining above her, Remi noticed her arm—a complete set of fingers outlined in a vivid bruise on Dallas's right bicep. "Who did that?" Remi asked, consumed with tempered rage.

"I had a little disagreement, but it's nothing," Dallas said, her words rapid and nervous sounding.

"Anything that leave that kind of marks isn't nothing, Dallas." Remi stood and held one of Dallas's hands. "Who did that to you?"

"It was Bob, but really, it's okay."

"Did he hurt you in any other way?"

"Please, Remi, forget it. You may not understand certain things, but I can't afford to change them right now."

"You're going to have to learn to trust me a little." Remi held her other hand as well. "I'm not asking to use your answers against you."

"I know that, but I'm under contract with him, and I just want to go back to work. When I'm filming, Bob usually entertains himself doing something else."

She sounded like a battered wife who was used to making excuses for her deadbeat husband. Remi didn't understand why Bob would still be in Dallas's life, since no contract was that ironclad anymore if someone in Dallas's position wanted to break it. The information her father had given her the night before at first made her think this was a setup, but now, looking at Dallas in the morning light, Remi thought Bob seemed more like a pimp than a law-enforcement partner. "If you want, I can arrange for Bob to entertain himself permanently away from you."

Dallas shook her head and grabbed the front of Remi's shirt until she was wrinkling the material. "What do you mean?"

"I'm more of a manager than an attorney these days, but I'm sure if I asked Dwayne and Steve, they can make any deal Bob struck with you go away. Loyalty to someone who helped you get started doesn't mean they have the right to do this to you, Dallas." Remi skimmed the tips of her fingers over the bruise. "No one has the right to do this to you, for any reason."

"You may not think I'm all right, but I am. If you want to help me, forget about this and leave Bob out of it."

Remi didn't move back, and even though Dallas was pressed up against her, she was out of reach. It would take more than one talk to get her to see reason, if she ever would. Bob had been there from the beginning of Dallas's career, and God only knew how long before that. It'd take drastic measures to flush him out.

"Do you want me to go?" Remi asked. She was willing to wait until Dallas was ready.

"I wouldn't blame you," Dallas said in a whisper. "This whole thing is my problem, and you don't need to get involved."

"That's not what I asked." Remi combed away some of the hair that had fallen into Dallas's face. "We'll take this slow, but it's important for you to tell me what you want, so…" She gently brought Dallas's head up by putting her fingers under her chin. "Do you want me to go?"

"I want you to stay."

"Good, now how about a shower, a comfortable pair of jeans, and a stack of pancakes from the Camellia Grill?"

"You like pancakes?"

"There's nothing in the world maple syrup can't cure." They held hands to the door, and once they were inside Remi noticed the discarded coffee cup. "Go on and I'll make you a fresh cup." As Dallas reached the stairs, Remi couldn't help but give in to her impulses. "While you're up there, why not pack a bag for a few days?"

"Where am I going?"

"Some place where I know you'll be safe."

Dallas closed her eyes and held her breath for a long while. "Are you playing savior today?"

She didn't ask the question in anger or disgust, and Remi didn't take it that way. "If I said yes, I'm guessing that'd be the wrong answer."

"Not if it's the truth. I'm just wondering what happens tomorrow when you put your cape away?" she asked like a woman used to disappointment. "Maybe you should take your own advice to go slow."

"How about we make a deal instead?" Remi walked across the kitchen and held her hand out. "I won't jump to any conclusions about you, if you give me the same consideration. If we try to do that, tomorrow won't be a problem."

"Deal." Dallas shook her hand.

Remi watched her climb the stairs and smiled at how relieved Dallas had appeared right before she left the room. She still had her doubts, which made what she had in mind totally ludicrous, but that wasn't important right now.

"I was raised by a gambler," she told the coffee pot, "and Ramon always says to be a good gambler, you have to take chances." Letting Dallas in this much would definitely qualify.

CHAPTER THIRTY-ONE

What time do you want me there in the morning?" Anthony asked Juan as they headed to the airport. Because of Rodolfo's displeasure that Juan had hired him and their dinner the night before with Nunzio Luca, Rodolfo was sending Juan home. In the short time Anthony had spent with Juan, though, he knew Juan would never go, and he was right.

"You weren't paying attention, Mr. FBI?" Juan asked, sounding pissed. Since they'd pulled away from the Piquant, Juan had stared out the window and slapped his hand against his leg. "I've told you a hundred times already, and if you didn't understand, maybe I fucked up by hiring you. Maybe Casey was right when she said you're all a bunch of dumb fucks."

"Cain Casey is about as smart as a bag of shit. She has more luck than brains, I assure you." Anthony tried not to let his bias show, but when Juan smiled at him for the first time that day, he knew he'd failed miserably. "Do you want me to do anything about her while you're gone?"

"Don't worry about Cain. I've got that covered."

"But if you're not here, don't you want to make sure it's done right?"

Juan quit staring out the window and faced him. "You just worry about what I asked you to do and forget the rest."

The Spanish accent made Juan's *y*'s sound like *j*'s, but he spoke so slowly Anthony couldn't mistake the words as well as the threat behind them. Perhaps he wasn't as much of an idiot as Anthony had believed; perhaps Juan really had learned something from Rodolfo.

"I just wanted to help since I thought that's why you wanted me around," Anthony said, trying to appease him. "Cain isn't someone to take on lightly."

"Didn't you say she's just lucky?"

"She is, but you have to give her some credit. If you go after her and fail, remember she's hot-headed. She'll come after you with all she's got, and if she's joined forces with Ramon and the evil twins, they could be dangerous."

Juan laughed and reclined farther into the seat. "Who said anything about going after that bitch?"

The question made Anthony pause. Juan obviously had a plan, and Anthony was running out of time to try to figure out what it was.

"Sounds interesting," Anthony said, fishing for more information.

"Tomorrow at nine," Juan said as the car stopped at the AeroMexico terminal. Rodolfo's man Carolos Santiago, carrying Juan's ticket and passport, emerged from the front seat and held the door for him. "Be here or don't fucking call me," Juan added before getting out.

"Your uncle expects you to stay home until he returns," Carlos said in Spanish. "He has your mother waiting at the house."

"For what? To babysit me?"

"As soon as he's done with his business here he wants to talk to both of you," Carlos said, obviously not caring to respond to Juan's sarcasm. "He wanted me to express how disappointed he'll be if you choose to ignore him again."

"He could've told me himself."

"You and I both know it'll be better for you if he cools off." Carlos handed him his papers as another man lifted his luggage out of the trunk. The other guard waited to walk Juan in. "Jesus will wait with you until your plane leaves."

"I can get on a plane by myself, Carlos," Juan said with aggravation.

"I used to think you could do all sorts of things to help out Mr. Rodolfo, but you proved me wrong so I'm not taking any chances."

"Remember that my uncle won't live forever, and one day you'll work for me. When that day comes, I won't forget this one." Juan shoved his ticket into his jacket pocket and stormed off, with Jesus trailing him.

In the car, Anthony stayed quiet, trying to decipher some of the conversation. It took him a second to realize that Carlos was still standing there holding the door open. He started to get out, since he figured these goons weren't about to give him a ride back to the city.

"Agent Curtis, you don't think we'd leave you stranded?" Carlos asked, almost as if he'd read his mind. He had his hand up, blocking Anthony. "Sit back and let us give you a ride."

"You don't have to bother, I can catch a cab." Anthony tried to get out again, but Carlos leaned farther in, his jacket flapping open to the gun he wore. Someone else opened the other passenger door, slid in, and pressed a pistol into Anthony's side before he could reach for his.

"Mr. Luis would like to talk to you, so I insist on giving you that ride," Carlos said before he slammed the door shut.

The guy sitting next to him had to have come from another car, since Anthony had never seen him, and he froze as the guy removed his gun and handed it to Carlos. After that his new friend patted him down and removed the other weapon from his ankle holster. He slipped that one into his jacket pocket. Then he ran his hand along Anthony's body for any surveillance equipment, going so slowly and doing such a thorough job that he felt violated enough to crave a shower.

"What does Rodolfo want with me?" Anthony slapped his hand to the side of his head as soon as he asked, trying to rub away the pain of the blow the guy had delivered with the butt of his gun. When he took his hand away his fingers were bloody. "What in the hell was that for?" he asked louder than he'd intended.

"I've worked for Mr. Luis half my life," Carlos said, never turning around, "and I'd never disrespect him by calling him by his first name. Pedro was just giving you a lesson in manners."

Unarmed and bleeding, Anthony sat quietly for the rest of the ride. He kept reminding himself that he was smarter than all these people combined, but he had to stay calm if he was going to get out of this alive. As they exited the interstate, a car accident had backed up traffic, a perfect chance to escape, but his watcher must have sensed the same thing and pushed the barrel of his gun so viciously into his side that Anthony winced.

As they finally approached the hotel, sweat accumulated under his arms and down his back. Would anyone even notice if these idiots killed him and took him out with the trash?

"If you cause a scene in the lobby, Agent Curtis, I swear on my mother's head you *will* live to regret it," Carlos said.

The threat made him behave until Carlos swiped his key card at Rodolfo's suite door. Rodolfo was sitting in the same spot he'd chosen the last time they met, only this time the drapes were closed. Anthony sat down.

"No one asked you to sit, Mr. Curtis," Rodolfo said, then crossed his legs. "You aren't a very mannered man, are you?"

"My manners are fine, I just have a headache," Anthony said as he pointed to his head where he'd been hit, but stood after Rodolfo's reprimand. "That would put anyone in a bad mood."

"You're just an innocent victim in all this, I'm sure." Rodolfo laughed. "You can tend to your head in a bit since I'm not planning to keep you long."

"If you want to offer me a job—my dance card's full." Carlos came closer and he almost expected to get hit again.

"My nephew's not very smart and seldom thinks, but don't put me in the same league. I don't want to offer you a job. I want to give you fair warning." Rodolfo got to his feet and stepped close enough that Anthony could smell his cologne. "Go home and tend to your head and be grateful that's all that happened."

"I don't work for you, Mr. Luis, so, with all due respect, I don't have to take orders from you." He heard the whoosh of air behind him just before the pain in his head drove him to his knees. When Anthony could open his eyes, Carlos stood over him, holding his own gun to his head.

"Supposedly you work for my nephew, but you and I both know who you really work for, so I want you gone. If you talk to Juan again… well, I'll leave that to your imagination." Rodolfo pressed his fingers to the oozing wound and looked at them before he painted Anthony's cheek with the blood that coated them. "Like you said, though, you don't work for me, but I want you to remember one thing."

"What?"

"The next time I call you in for a talk, don't beg for mercy or cry for salvation, because there won't be any."

Anthony was still on his knees, which made Rodolfo seem taller when he peered up at him. "If you believe I still work for the FBI, isn't treating me like this stupid?"

"Do you think anyone in this room but you is going to admit this meeting took place? Go home and back to your job, Mr. Curtis, and you won't have a thing to worry about. If you don't, you won't be of consequence to anyone for long."

Rodolfo left the room, and Carlos picked Anthony up and handed him to Pedro. "Now you can take that cab, Agent Curtis."

"What about my guns?"

"You know what I think?"

"What?"

"That this won't be the last time we talk." Carlos suddenly grabbed Anthony's crotch and squeezed so hard his eyes welled with tears. "When we have to talk again, I'm going to shoot this off first and send it to that pretty lady you work for." He squeezed harder. "Then I'm going to put a bullet between your eyes with your FBI gun that I'm keeping to show my friends." Carlos laughed before throwing him out.

Out in the hall Anthony leaned against the wall well away from the suite, trying to get his heart rate down. He needed to concoct a new plan before Juan returned the next night. No matter what it was, Carlos, Rodolfo, and Pedro were going down.

"And when that happens, you son of a bitch, don't beg *me* for mercy," he said, referring to Rodolfo. "Because I'm going to pull the fucking trigger three times, and it's going to feel sweet."

CHAPTER THIRTY-TWO

Y ou ready to go, lass?" Cain yelled up the stairs while Hannah climbed to the fourth step and jumped into her arms. It was the third time she'd gone through the process of climbing and jumping, adding a step every time.

"If she tries that with me when you're not home, I'm going to be pissed when I call you from the emergency room," Emma said from the landing. She'd changed into a simple-cut dress and low heels.

"Hannah's smart enough not to try that with you, Mama," Hayden said as he passed her on the way down.

"Why do you think that?"

"Because when I was four I was smart enough to know we'd both be in trouble if I tried it. You're our mom, but you're kinda shrimpy," he joked.

"Good to know, son." She started down, keeping her eyes off Hannah, who was leaping from the sixth step now.

This time Cain caught Hannah and kept her in her arms. "Let's go pick up Grandpa," she said, having to use both hands to keep Hannah still. "Wait until you see what he got you for your birthday," she told Hayden.

"He let you know what it was?"

"He called for hints, and I told him you missed your milking duties so much he smuggled a cow on board."

"You're so funny. You're just jealous I know how and you don't."

"Your mom promised to take me in the barn for a private lesson when we go up for a visit—" Emma put her hand over Cain's mouth and pointed to the door.

Cain drove them to the airport, with Lou, Merrick, and Mook following. Ross had planned the trip to sign a contract for Cain, and for Hayden's birthday. The airport was busy as the influx of Sunday afternoon flights arrived, so it took Cain a while to find two parking spots close to each other.

They waited at the Delta section, and Hannah ran around them. Cain split her time watching her and Emma, who had her eyes plastered to the long concourse but had been constantly smoothing down her dress in a nervous-tic way.

"Are you okay?" she asked Emma.

"It's weird, but I'm not. I've felt like such a disappointment to him for so long that sometimes I don't know how to act around him."

Cain put her arm around Emma's waist and kissed her temple. "I've talked to your father quite often since we got back, and he certainly isn't disappointed in you. Ross is proud of the life and family you've built, lass. With his separation from your mother, he feels freer to express himself, and he's looking forward to spending more time with us. It's time for him to get to know his grandchildren and his little girl. You two need to move past the shadow of what happened with your mother and stop wasting time dwelling on what could've been."

"He did mention that Maddie and Jerry agreed to take over the farm," Emma said. "With the help from their new silent partner, Jerry's planning to put together a bigger herd for the coming season." A crowd was making its way up the main corridor, meaning a flight had just deplaned. "With any luck we can talk him into staying with us during the winter months. What do you think?"

"That we need to get the house finished so he'll know we have a place for him." Cain jutted her chin in the direction of the security stand and the first guy through it. "Go tell him hello."

Ross stopped halfway to them and put his bag down so he could pick up Hannah, who was running toward him at her usual rapid pace. It was the reception he'd been hoping for, and only got better when Hayden was right behind her.

"You both have gotten so big," he told them after giving both a kiss.

"I missed you, Grandpa," Hannah said as she wrapped her arms around his neck and squeezed.

"Hello, Daddy," Emma told him. Cain was next to her and took Hannah from him.

With his hands free, Ross didn't hesitate to put his arms around

Emma and hang on until a lump formed in his throat. "You have a beautiful family, sweetheart," he managed to say, and Emma simply nodded against his shoulder.

"Let's get out of here and go catch up," Cain said as she patted Ross on the back. "If you're not too tired, the kids want to treat you to dinner at their favorite place."

It didn't take long to get to Jacquimo's on Oak Street. The restaurant started by a merchant-marine cook was in an old shotgun house, and the kids loved it because they got to walk through the kitchen to get to the dining area out back. None of the plates or utensils matched, the drinks were served in Mason jars, and the wait staff looked rather Bohemian, but they made the best fried chicken in the city.

Ross barely had to speak as Hannah and Hayden filled in what they'd been doing since he'd seen them last. By the time they reached coffee and dessert, Hannah was asleep on Cain's lap.

When they got home, Ross watched Emma and Cain work together to put Hannah to bed and smiled as he remembered how Barney Kyle had described Cain. This gentle soul didn't resemble the rabid beast in Kyle's stories at all.

"Looks like Hannah's forgotten your mom," Ross told Emma.

"Thank God for that. You want to call it a night or join Cain downstairs?" Emma pointed in the direction Cain had headed. "I put a pair of Cain's sweats and some T-shirts on your bed to sleep in. Hopefully they'll find your bags by tomorrow."

"What, she doesn't own pajamas?" he asked, then laughed.

Emma blushed but laughed along with him. "There's a spare toothbrush in there too."

"Sorry, I couldn't resist, and I can go to bed if you want. You look tired." He combed Emma's hair back, an old habit he'd developed from the time she was a baby.

"Cain's just finishing up some stuff, and I'm going to bed, don't worry." Emma kissed him on the cheek. "I know you like talking to her, and when the kids are wound up like that it's hard to cut in. I'm happy you're here, Daddy."

"You might get sick of having me around now that I'm retired."

"We'll see about that." Emma kissed him again and headed for their bedroom.

Ross found his way to the study and stood outside until Cain finished her phone call. "Staying up past nine might take some getting used to."

"We'll citify you in no time," she said, then laughed. "And I hope you do come to like it here. Emma's been redecorating our place and your rooms are ready."

"I told you I'd sign for you on that casino thing, no need to butter me up. The last thing you need is some old codger hanging around."

"I'll have plenty of time to convince you otherwise, but for tonight how about a drink and a comfortable bed?"

They talked close to an hour over a couple of glasses of aged whiskey before Cain walked him to his room. "Give a yell if you need anything."

Cain stopped at the children's rooms to check on them before joining Emma. When she opened their door, a candle burning on the nightstand gave off just enough light for Cain to tell Emma was naked. With a flick of her fingers she locked the door and started stripping off pieces of clothing, leaving a trail to the bed.

"We'll talk about my father later, okay?"

"Want to talk about something else?"

"Actually I don't want to talk at all," Emma said, as she encouraged Cain to cover her with her body. "Just touch me."

Later she'd have to ask Emma what she'd been thinking about while she'd been downstairs with Ross, because when she put her fingers on Emma she was wet. From that first touch Emma spread her legs wider and lifted her hips to meet her touch.

"Go inside, baby, please," Emma whispered in her ear.

As Cain slowly gave Emma what she wanted, she dragged her nails from the small of her back upward. As quick as a summer rainstorm, Cain was soaked. She tried to go slower, but Emma wasn't having any of it. Emma set the pace with her hips, and Cain merely smiled and complied. Emma's orgasm didn't stop her, and she pressed Cain closer. That near, Cain could hear her breathing deepen and quicken.

"You ambushed me," Cain said when Emma was done.

"Not yet, but that was in my plan."

Cain laughed but soon moaned as Emma left her arms and disappeared under the covers.

When Emma wrapped her lips around her clitoris and sucked hard, she grabbed a handful of the sheets. At this rate she wasn't going to last long, but she felt so good she did nothing to slow Emma down. Emma brought her to the brink then stopped, making Cain's eyes fly open.

"What's wrong?" she asked, out of breath.

"Nothing." Emma put two fingers in, then pulled out slowly.

"Not a good time to be stopping, lass."

Emma didn't respond but lowered her head again, this time using only the tip of her tongue. Soon Cain was at the same level of excitement, and her clit felt so hard when Emma stopped again she thought it would pop.

"Set on torturing me then?" she asked. "Did I do something wrong?"

"You should be asking yourself what you've done right." Emma ran her flat tongue upward this time. "And you should be asking yourself what's it going to take," she did it again, "to get what you want." The third swipe of her tongue made Cain lift her hips so far off the bed chasing Emma's mouth that she could feel her calf muscles tense. "What do you want, mobster?"

Cain lifted her upper body up and grabbed Emma, making her squeal. Carefully she turned her around so her mouth was just below Emma's opening. "What I want is to even the score." She lifted her head slightly and kissed the glistening lips. "Just remember one thing."

"What?" Emma asked, lowering her head and repeating Cain's actions.

"If you stop, so will I." If Emma thought to say anything or ask a question, Cain emptied her mind as she sucked her in. "Understand?" She repeated her actions and Emma pressed herself closer. "Do you understand?"

She came close to laughing when Emma still didn't answer, but that notion died abruptly when Emma put her mouth back on her. This time Cain could tell as the pressure built that Emma wasn't going to stop. She could sense how Emma felt about her in every touch, and Cain felt so good she had to force herself to concentrate on giving Emma pleasure. It didn't take long for her orgasm to wash over her, but she didn't stop touching Emma until she reached the same peak.

She helped Emma turn around and ran her fingers gently along her back, since Emma had collapsed on top of her. "Tell me what I did right so I can keep up the good work," Cain said softly. The mattress bounced slightly when Emma laughed. "Because I certainly do like your rewards."

"I wanted to thank you for making me so happy and," Emma lifted her head and bit down gently on Cain's chin, "because I didn't want you to think we were going to stop doing this just because my father's in the house. I thought I'd nip that in the bud before you got goofy on me."

"Considering we're going to try and convince him to retire to warmer climates, I'm not that crazy."

"Do you think he'll be happy here? He's used to running a farm and being active."

Cain stopped her hands and held Emma closer. "I'm sure we can keep him busy, and I have some ideas of how to keep him involved with the life he's used to."

"Don't worry is your answer, huh?"

"And get a good night's sleep." She kissed Emma and got her more comfortable by rolling over and sliding behind her. "I love you."

Emma lifted their joined hands and kissed Cain's knuckles before she moved Cain's hand between her breasts. Before Cain gave in to sleep, she hoped all their problems could be settled so easily. But she was serious about trying to keep Ross nearby, if only to have one more person willing to do anything to keep Emma and the kids safe. Cain would have a problem with Ross being there only if he invited his wife to join him.

CHAPTER THIRTY-THREE

"Cain, the airport called," Carmen said as she poured herself a cup of coffee in the kitchen. Cain was leaning against the counter downing a bottle of juice after her run. With Hayden in school she shared her runs with Merrick and Mook. "Mr. Ross's luggage finally made it, and they offered to deliver it, if you want."

"If we take them up on that, Ross will never see his underwear. Call and tell them I'm sending someone." Cain glanced out to the foyer and spotted one of the young guys Lou had assigned to the house and who had been out with them to various restaurants. The tall blond named Rick Greco was somehow related to Mook and had earned Lou's trust by never turning him down, no matter what Lou asked of him. Lou was thinking of putting Rick with Hannah when he had a little more experience.

"Rick," Cain called.

"Morning, boss."

"Do me a favor and take one of the cars and run out to the airport. Ross was missing a bag and it just made its way from Hawaii, probably."

"Sure, let Lou know where I am."

"Actually, I'll drive you," Lou said. "We ordered some new scanning equipment and it's at the FedEx office out there. I'll drop you off, pick the stuff up, and come back for you so you don't have to park. Come on, kid." Lou put his hand on the back of Rick's neck and guided him toward the door. Cain shook her head at their roughhousing. It was one of the ways Lou acted when he really liked someone.

"Is Emma up yet?" Cain asked Carmen.

"Not yet, but Hayden's almost ready to go."

Outside, Lou got behind the wheel of one of their SUVs and laughed as Rick told him about his last date, which had turned out disastrously. At the airport he dropped Rick at the baggage claim and waved to him as he drove toward the freight area.

Rick walked to the Delta office and rested his elbows on the counter since the place was empty. A pile of bags sat outside next to the carousel and in the office, so he was content to wait, not wanting to check every tag himself.

This section was the airport's newest addition, and from where he stood he could see the new customs office. A group of Hispanic men loitered outside the solid door, and the shortest one in the bunch piqued his interest. Rick thought he'd seen him before but couldn't place where or with whom. He moved closer to the glass wall for a better look at the guy with the ponytail. The men stood in a circle talking and laughing at something one of them had said, but none of them were facing out.

One other guy sat on the other side, and Rick could see his legs and his black dress shoes, but not his face. He moved closer to the door, trying to get a better angle to see the guy and hoping that whoever it was would trigger the memory of where he knew the long-haired man from.

When he moved to the open door, the short guy turned in Rick's direction and, from his facial expression, Rick guessed he'd recognized him right off. The guy said something, the others looked too, and then Rick could see the man seated. Anthony Curtis locked eyes with him, and Rick fumbled in his pocket for his cell phone. Lou's number rang twice before the men reached him, pulled his arm down, and pressed a gun into his back.

The action made Rick remember where he'd seen the little guy with the long thick hair. He was one of the men standing outside the Steak Knife the night Juan Luis went there with Nunzio Luca and his uncle.

"What you doing here, hotshot?" the men behind him asked him in a heavy accent. Rick took a slight step forward when the gun was jammed harder into his back. "I asked you a question."

The door behind them started to open, but before the airline employee made it in, the men hauled Rick toward the bathroom close to the escalators. Anthony watched the whole time but didn't move.

One of the four guys checked the stalls, while another one stood at the door to prevent anyone from coming in. The guy Rick had recognized was screwing a silencer to his gun and the sight of it drove his pulse up, but he showed no outward emotion. They were probably just going to scare him a little after luckily finding him alone.

"How you know we here, cowboy?" the little guy asked as he pressed his gun to Rick's forehead, having to hold it at an odd angle to reach.

"I'm picking up a bag, asshole, and I don't really give a shit why you're here."

The last guy kicked him behind the right knee, making him lose his balance and fall to his knees. "You don't got no backup, cowboy, so be good."

"You need plenty of backup, don't you, little shit?" The last word had barely left his mouth when his head exploded.

"What in the fuck was that, Jesus?" Oscar, who'd been standing behind Rick, jumped back and reverted to Spanish. The back of Rick's head sprayed him from head to waist, and he wiped his face and visibly shivered as his fingers found solid particles that couldn't be blood. "This is going to bring the kind of heat Juan is paying us to avoid."

"Shut up and let me think and keep everybody out." Jesus Vega took his gun apart and paced by Rick's body. He couldn't go back to Rodolfo after this, which made him feel sick to his stomach. "Merda," he said as he stared into Rick's open, dead eyes. Before Juan had been sent home, Jesus had reluctantly cut a deal with him as a way to assure his place in the future. Rodolfo was more level-headed, but he wasn't going to live forever.

"They're starting to let people out," the guy at the door said.

"What do we do, Jesus?" Oscar asked.

"Put him in the last stall," Jesus ordered in Spanish. "And change clothes with him. We'll get stopped for sure if you try to walk out like that." He pointed to Oscar's blood- and brain-splattered suit.

"Somebody's going to find him eventually, and when they trace it to us we're dead," Oscar said.

"None of you are going to tell Juan what happened, so it's not a problem. Get me?" Jesus glanced around the space, trying to remember if he'd touched anything. The others arranged Rick so he wouldn't fall forward.

"And get us all killed? Don't worry," Oscar said as he cinched Rick's belt as tight as it would go.

Anthony was gone when they walked out, but a crowd of people were waiting for their luggage after they'd cleared customs. The four turned toward the wall as Lou rode past them on the escalator. Jesus saw Lou glance back at them as if he'd noticed something. Lou had most probably come in because Rick wasn't answering his cell, which they'd heard ringing and dropped in the toilet they'd sat him on.

"Did someone claim Ross Verde's bag?" Lou asked. He snapped his phone shut in irritation when Rick's went to voice mail again.

"I've got it right here." The guy placed it on the counter.

"You didn't see a blond kid in here?" Lou punched the redial button only to get Rick's recorded message instantly, as if the phone was now turned off.

"Some people were leaving when I got back from my break. I called out but they went that way." He pointed toward the men's room.

"Fuck," Lou said, taking off at a run. The restroom was crowded with guys who'd gotten off the Mexico City flight. He bent down and looked under the stall doors, wanting to throw up when he saw the feet adorned only with a pair of socks. That's what was weird about the guys on the escalator. One of them had on a suit that was way too big. The guy had stripped Rick for some reason and worn his clothes.

Lou kicked the door of the stall in and yelled "No" so loud that most of the men headed for the exit. Rick was slumped on the seat, his eyes still open and a bullet hole in his forehead with a single line of blood coming from it.

"Get security," Lou screamed at the man standing next to him staring, "now." The command got the man moving, and Lou took advantage of being alone to make a phone call. "Cain," he said, hearing Emma and Hannah's voices in the background. "Rick's dead and I need you to stay put until I can figure out what's going on. With Katlin gone I don't need to worry about you too."

"How?" Cain asked.

"Somebody shot him and stripped him in the restroom. It might've been random, but I did see some guys who acted hinky on the way out." Four security guards ran in and Lou stepped away from the stall. "I'll call you later."

Lou closed the phone but made no move to put it back in the holder on his belt. "You need to call the police," he told the group as he held his hands slightly upward. He knew the pose would make his gun holster visible, but he thought it would be better to get the fact that he was armed out of the way. "It's my friend."

He made no attempt to fight when the guards came forward and pushed him to the floor face down. The force they used to pull his hands back into cuffs made Lou exhale, but he stayed quiet otherwise. At least one of his captors was calling the police, and Lou took one last look at Rick as he was escorted out. The security personnel had laid him in the spot where Rick had been killed, and Lou noticed some of his blood was smeared on the front of his shirt.

They had already compromised and contaminated the crime scene, and Lou thought he was losing valuable time dealing with such incompetence, but this wasn't the place to flex his muscle. He didn't want to spend any more time than necessary cuffed by the pretend-cops. He wanted to hunt down the idiots who'd done this.

As the police arrived, Lou was escorted to a windowless room close to the customs office. They sat him in a chair, leaving his cuffs on, and only one of the guards stayed with him; the others, he was sure, were going back to take another look at the men's room.

"Don't I get a phone call or something?" Lou asked.

"We're waiting for a unit to come pick you up, so shut up and get comfortable."

"I have a permit for the gun you took off me, and if you bothered to check, it hasn't been fired recently."

The guard closed his eyes and sat back in his chair, evidently sure Lou wasn't going anywhere. "You can save your innocent routine for the guys who'll arrest you. I'm not interested."

Lou didn't have a choice but to wait, so he closed his eyes as well and tried to remember anything about the guys he'd seen on the way in. He had a gut feeling they were responsible for what had happened to Rick, and he intended to find a way to ask the questions that would get Rick the payback he deserved.

CHAPTER THIRTY-FOUR

Since telling Dallas good night the previous evening, Remi hadn't thought about anything but her. At least she was still sleeping behind the closed door, or so Remi guessed, since she hadn't heard a sound from the room all morning. She reread the first line of the lead story in the morning's paper for the twentieth time and still didn't have an inkling of what it said.

She put the paper aside and decided to concentrate on the view instead. Maybe she could do that while trying to organize her jumbled brain. When the elevator doors opened, Remi was so startled she almost went for a kitchen knife. Simon and Juno lived a floor below her, and they were the only ones who occasionally popped in unexpectedly. But Dallas stood in the foyer wearing a T-shirt and a pair of sweat pants, and judging from the perspiration running down her face, she'd been out exercising.

"I thought you were asleep," Remi said as she tried not to put her hand to her chest and calm her heart to a steadier pace.

"Sorry, I checked with Simon and she let me down and came and got me so I could take my morning walk. I would've let you know but you were still in your room, and I didn't want to bother you."

"You shouldn't go out this early alone," Remi said, putting her finger up to keep Dallas from wandering off since the phone was ringing. She looked at Dallas after she picked up but didn't say anything once she pressed it to her ear.

When Dallas pointed in the direction of her room Remi shook her head, not wanting her to leave. "Do you have any idea who?" Remi finally said, then fell silent again and listened. "You need me to send someone out there? Call me if you change your mind."

"Something wrong?" Dallas asked when Remi hung up.

"Someone killed one of Cain's men this morning at the airport."

"God, that's tragic. What happened?"

"Whoever it was made it look like Rick got rolled and shot, but people usually don't get mugged in an airport."

Dallas kept her distance and wiped her hands on her pants like she needed to dry them. "Do you need to go see Cain? I could sit with Emma if you want me to come along."

"You might want to stay here," Remi said, then cleared her throat as Dallas neared.

"I'd like to help."

"I know," Remi said, and exhaled deeply, "but you might not want to get too involved in this."

"Why am I here, Remi? I mean really here?"

"We've been over this already. You staying home isn't a good idea right now, if Bob has some problem with you."

Dallas laid her hand flat on Remi's chest and looked into her eyes as if trying to find something in them. "That doesn't answer my question. If that's the only reason, there are plenty of hotel rooms in this city where it would've taken Bob a year to find me. Why am I here?"

"I'm not sure what answer you want, because that's the only one I've got," Remi said, dropping her gaze to Dallas's hand. It appeared delicate against the green, heavy silk of her robe.

"You have another one, but maybe you're not ready to share it with me." Dallas moved her hand up until she reached Remi's shoulder. "But that's okay." She stood on tiptoe. "I'm willing to wait you out until you're ready." She put her hand behind Remi's head, encouraging Remi to bend down so she could reach her lips.

They'd kissed before, but for Remi this one was like turning the page of a book and finding out something new about the character she thought she knew. Dallas might have been an enigma, but when Remi pressed her lips to hers, she got a dose of passion and compassion all in one act. For all her doubts, Remi relaxed somewhat, because in her experience, no one could fake something like this.

"You're here because you need someone to stand up for you, since you can't or won't for whatever reason," Remi said when they parted. Dallas opened her mouth in an almost perfect *o* and had taken the breath to push out whatever word she had in mind, but Remi kissed her again. "You're here because I want to be that someone. Not because I owe it to you, or because you asked me, but because I want to."

She pulled away and headed toward her bedroom to get dressed, but stopped as she reached the hall. When she turned around Dallas was standing there touching her lips and appearing dazed. "If you want to, I'm sure Emma would appreciate the company. If you want to stay, that's okay too. But promise you won't go out alone until I know what's going on."

❖

Muriel quickly made it from the parking garage to the airport with only one thing in mind. As much as what had happened to Rick upset her, she was concerned with the living, and she hadn't been able to reach Lou since he'd hung up with Cain. She'd spent the morning calling all of their police contacts and was still in the dark.

While she tried to find Lou, Cain had made a few calls of her own and had gotten their people back from Mississippi. Katlin was there in two hours and had volunteered to escort Muriel to the last place Lou had been, so Katlin, along with a few more men, walked with her, making almost a human cage of protection as they entered the chilly interior of the main corridor.

"Did he say where in the building he was?" Katlin asked.

"They were here to pick up a damn bag," Muriel said, disgusted. "Nothing worth getting killed over."

"Let's start there."

At the bank of escalators three police officers stood in front of a line of police crime-scene tape to keep anyone from going down. "Who's in charge?" Muriel asked the first one who looked her way.

"Captain Hallman, but he's too busy to come up right now."

"I don't want him to come up, I want to go down." Muriel pointed at the escalator that someone had turned off, the steps frozen in position.

"They're still working the scene, so that's not going to happen."

"Either you call him and get me cleared or I'll call his boss and get the same thing, your choice."

"Let her down," a man screamed from the floor beneath them. "Alone."

Muriel took the steps two at a time and stopped in front of Paul Hallman. He was two years from retirement, and to Muriel, he always appeared tired. "That your guy in there?" He jerked his thumb over his shoulder.

"Rick worked for my cousin, Cain Casey, and he was here picking up a bag for a family member. When you're finished with your investigation, call my office so we can arrange to pick him up and take him to the funeral home."

Hallman scratched his head, then tried to order his thinning hair with his fingers. "That's mighty agreeable of you, Muriel. All the years I've known you, I pegged you for someone whose nails we need to shove bamboo under while we drip water on your forehead to get you to admit to your name. I do believe that's the most I've ever heard you say at one time."

"I'm feeling generous, considering the situation, but that's not why I'm here. Our family will take care of Rick later. I'm here for Mr. Romano."

"Who?"

She laughed at the way he crinkled his brow. "Don't start playing dumb now, Paul. You're too old for that. Lou Romano is in your custody, if I had to guess. Unless you have reason to hold him, I want him released to me."

"Lou's last name is Romano?" Hallman laughed and led her to the security office. "I sure as hell didn't know that. Never heard him called anything but Lou."

"Why is he still here?"

"The guys told me he was the one who found your boy, and he volunteered to give a statement." Hallman opened the door, and the same security guard that had put Lou in the chair still sat across from him. Lou was still cuffed. "Why in the hell didn't you take those off, you idiot?" The guard came close to falling backward when Hallman screamed at him.

"You okay, Lou?" Muriel asked.

"Just great." Lou rubbed his wrists and stood up. "Am I free to go?"

"Did you give a statement?" Hallman asked.

"That's going to have to wait. I need to go to the hospital and have my hands checked out from being cuffed so tight for so long."

Paul nodded. "I'll cut you some slack, but I want you in my office no later than tomorrow."

"I'll have him there," Muriel said.

They had started to leave when Hallman's gruff voice stopped them. "You didn't see anything, did you, Lou?"

"Just my friend with a bullet hole in his forehead."

"Let's say I believe you for now," Hallman said slowly. "Don't go doing anything crazy, okay?"

"Crazy isn't our style," Muriel said as she wrapped her hand around Lou's bicep to keep him quiet.

"I'll see you around, then." Paul stuck his hand out and offered it to Muriel first, then Lou.

"Let me know if you find anything that points to who did this," Muriel said. "Cain's putting up a ten-thousand-dollar reward for information. That should help with the investigation."

"I'll pass that along, and you remember to do the same. If you find something, phone me."

Muriel just stared at him before smiling. "I'm sure you'll be my first call."

"You're full of shit, Muriel, but I like you anyway."

She bowed her head slightly and just as quickly quit smiling. The cops had their job to do, and they had theirs. Whoever had killed Rick would face endless court dates or only one quick date with death. It depended on who won the footrace—Hallman or them.

CHAPTER THIRTY-FIVE

"You know what this might mean, don't you?" Cain asked Remi. She was staring at the spot where Rick had been standing just that morning. After asking Merrick earlier she knew he was twenty-six years old. At that age she'd never thought about death much, until it became such a frequent visitor.

"The start of a war? If it is, it'd be nice to know who we're fighting."

"We're fighting the future, Remi, and for once I don't know if we can win this fight no matter how hard we go at it." Cain exhaled and shook her head to force herself to look away.

"You want to give up before we even start?"

"I'm tired, that's all. I've changed because I wanted peace. I wanted to enjoy my family and my wife without some asshole constantly taking shots at me."

Remi placed her mug in the sink and leaned against the counter. "I can't see you retired and knitting booties somewhere."

"But I can see her feeding cows somewhere for about a week," Ross said, interrupting them. "After that, all your energy would drive you mad."

"Are you wondering deep down if perhaps Carol was right? Your daughter could've picked safer," Cain said.

"My daughter picked with her heart. Your life isn't always perfect, but unlike what that guy Kyle told me, the fight seems to always come to you without you looking for it. This would be the time to get up, brush yourself off, and kick the shit out of someone."

"You know..." Cain did something she'd never done to Ross. She walked over and hugged him. "You asked me once if you were anything like my father." She'd never been this close to him, and while he wasn't a large man, he felt strong and solid. "If he'd been here, that's exactly what he would've said." The kitchen door opened and Lou walked in, his shirt still stained with Rick's blood. "You look like a man who could use a drink," she told him.

"Later on I'd love one, but right now I want to talk to you."

Lou followed her out to the yard and stood in the center, well away from the trees. "Any idea who did this?" she asked.

"I dropped him off and went to pick up our stuff." He coughed and had to stop, and Cain suspected it had nothing to do with the weather.

"We can do this later," Cain offered when he pressed the heels of his palms to his eyes.

"It was a fucking bag," he yelled. "We could've sent anyone in there…I could've gone."

"You know *what-ifs* don't accomplish anything. What we need now is to honor Rick's life by taking care of his family and finding the bastards who did this before the cops do."

"While I was sitting in that fucking room with my hands on my ass, I tried to remember anything that would get us closer to the shooter. I saw this group of guys leaving when I went in to check on Rick. I could swear one of them was wearing Rick's clothes, and when I found him he was in his underwear. His shoes and cell phone were shoved in the can."

"Did you get a look at their faces?"

"They were staring at those ads the airport puts up so I didn't think anything of it then, but later I thought that was weird."

"No faces, okay, anything else?"

"It was their hair that gives me an idea where we need to start looking."

Cain glanced at Lou's face and saw that his eyes had watered. "What about it?"

"Black, thick, slicked back, and one of them had a ponytail."

"Tall or short?" Cain asked the questions the police were probably trying to squeeze out of whoever was within a ninety-mile radius of the airport.

"Short sticks in my head. They remind me of those guys we saw always hanging close to Juan and his uncle."

"Rick was with us the night we went to the Steak Knife, wasn't he?" Cain felt like someone had given her a shot of adrenaline.

"I had him tag along so he'd get used to being around you guys. If we eventually put him with Hannah, I wanted him to get used to the family's routine."

"Good work, Lou. You're right. We know where to look first." She put her hand on his shoulder and squeezed briefly. "If I'm right, Rick was at the wrong place at the wrong time for all the right reasons. It sounds like these guys panicked, so I'm sure Rick never saw it coming when they got him in the bathroom."

"What about his family?"

"I'll take care of that myself. Rick was loyal and needs to be repaid, if not to him then to his mother."

"Take Mook with you," Lou said. "He's another good kid, and she's his great-aunt. I'm sure it'll make her feel better to have some family around."

Cain nodded and led him back inside. "Clean up and I'll call you if we're going out, but don't worry. That won't be for awhile yet."

"Don't start without me."

"More importantly, I don't plan to finish without you."

❖

From the sunroom, Emma watched Cain and Lou talk, and she could tell Lou's face was wet with tears. She was trying not to give in to her own grief again, since it wouldn't help Cain take care of things. When Cain had told her about Rick, she'd cried for the loss but had selfishly given thanks it hadn't been Cain or one of her children. If she burned in hell for that, then so be it.

"This doesn't happen often, does it?" Dallas asked her.

"Not really, but it doesn't make it any easier when it does. Could you excuse me for a minute?" She stood next to the window until Cain noticed her. She knew that once Cain started to strike back, they wouldn't have much time alone.

When Cain's eyes finally found her, she smiled and waved her out. As Emma hurried to where Cain was standing, she stopped and put her arms around Lou and kissed his forehead when he bent down to return the kindness. "I know you're not going to listen to me, but you need to lie down for a while. This wasn't your fault, Lou."

"It might take a bit for that to sink in, and I couldn't sleep now unless someone cold-cocked me."

"I'm in no position to tell you what to do, but can I ask you for a favor?" When he straightened up and she dropped her head back to still see his face, she had to shield her eyes from the brightness.

"You know you can."

"Lie down for at least an hour. When Cain decides to move, she'll want you with her, and I want you at your best. You won't be protecting only her, but my heart as well. That's a really corny thing to say, but it's true."

"You're a tough opponent, Emma." Lou hugged her again and headed to the pool house. After Katlin had moved out, the guys used it as a sort of bunkhouse when they kept long hours and needed to get some sleep.

"Undermining my authority, lass?" Cain asked, but from the relaxed set of her eyes Emma could tell she was kidding. "I'm glad he listens to one of us."

"I just told him the truth. He does go out everyday with my heart in his care." She leaned against Cain and put her arms around her hips. "One thing I've learned about you big ruthless types is that most of you are closet romantics who can't fight it no matter how hard you try." Cain laughed and scratched Emma's back. "Did Lou give you any clues?"

"I needed a point to start from, and I think he provided that. Sounds like three or four guys waiting for something else jumped Rick and killed him. From Lou's sketchy descriptions they sounded Hispanic."

"Rodolfo's guys?"

"I can't answer that right now, but give me some time and maybe I can narrow it down."

"Before I lose you to the people waiting inside, remember that I love you, and I'm here to take care of you."

"I love you too, and even though I'm working, I want to see you."

Emma pressed her cheek to Cain's chest and laughed. "See what I mean about you big ruthless types."

They walked back to the house hand-in-hand, and Emma saw Dallas standing at the French doors of the sunroom watching them. Aside from when they arrived, Emma hadn't seen Remi and Dallas together. She was looking forward to it, if only to see if there was anything worth celebrating.

"Ramon and Mano arrived while you were out there with Lou. I put them all in the kitchen since there aren't enough chairs in the study, but don't worry. I'll keep the kids out of the way."

"Thanks, lass." Cain kissed her and nodded to Dallas as they entered the house. "Why don't the two of you join the kids upstairs and watch some television?"

Emma rubbed the small of Cain's back to let her know she'd understood the request. No one minded Dallas being there, but she was still a wild card in Cain's opinion as well as Remi's. While they wouldn't send her home, Cain didn't want her too close to the upcoming meetings.

"Call up if you need anything."

Cain waited until she heard the door to the den upstairs open and close before she entered the kitchen. She spotted Muriel first and noticed the anger twisting her face. "I need you to contact T-Boy and get with him, Muriel. Tell him it's worth a lot to me to have today's list of all the passengers who flew in and had to go through Customs."

"There's something else you should know," Muriel said hesitantly.

"This isn't the time to withhold any information, no matter how trivial it is."

"One of Vincent's men came to see me last night after he talked to you. Somebody's bringing in a shooter, but we don't know the target."

"Or who hired this guy?" Remi asked.

"That's probably easier, since we can narrow it down to two people we're dealing with right now. It's the why that'll take more time," Cain said as she cracked open a soft drink from the refrigerator. "What do you think, Ramon?"

"I think like you that it's Nunzio Luca, but what does Rick have to do with that?"

"The shooter isn't due until Friday," Muriel said.

"That's why today didn't have anything to do with Luca," Cain said after she'd sat between Remi and Ramon.

"Then with whom?" Mano asked. "If we're going to be targets I'd like to have some idea why before one of us gets killed."

"We have to work together to answer that question, before anyone else gets hurt. I'm guessing, so you can't take what I say for fact."

Remi nodded and butted shoulders with Cain. "When you guess, you're usually in the ballpark, so let's hear it."

"Today was like I just told Lou. Our guy Rick was in the wrong place and someone recognized him. To hide the fact that Rick knew who they were, they killed him." Cain stopped and glanced at Muriel. She didn't appear as upset now, but no way could Cain let her leave now if she was so angry she couldn't think straight. "I'm not discounting the shooter and whatever reason someone has for bringing him here, but it had nothing to do with today."

"I think we can all agree that today, while tragic, is over. Our new problem is Friday and why this guy's coming," Mano said.

"Today isn't over. No one walks up and kills one of my people for no reason, and he'll pay. Friday has to do with Nunzio Luca and how he plans to break us."

"What if you're wrong?" Mano persisted.

"Then we sit and wait to find out which one of us Nunzio's planning to knock off and afterward come up with a plan. I don't know about you, but that's not one choice I'm going with."

"Cain," Ramon said with his hands spread out on the table in front of him.

Cain raised her finger for Ramon's patience and studied Mano and his posture. "I want to hear what you have in mind. I've been doing all the talking, and I haven't given you a chance."

Mano glanced up and Remi nodded her head, brought her hand up, and curled her fingers over so he'd start talking. "If this is Nunzio Luca, he's going after the weakest link as a scare tactic to get us to deal. He's tried being nice, so now he's going to try the other plan available to him."

"You should speak up more often, Mano. I agree," Cain said, lifting her can in his direction.

"So you think I should just sit around and wait for someone to put a bullet in my head?" Mano asked.

Muriel covered his hand with hers and patted it before sitting back. "It'll be a shot through the heart. That's Jorge's signature. He likes the chest shot so whoever's lucky enough to have him as an assassin can have an open casket. That way your family can look at you before you're buried and realize it's their fault they put you in the ground."

"Is that supposed to make me feel better?" Mano asked, laughing finally.

"I don't think Nunzio hired this guy to kill you, so you should feel better," Cain said.

"Forgive me if I'm still a little on edge," Mano said.

"You're assuming you're the weakest link in the chain, and in this case you're not." Cain peered first at Ramon then at Remi.

Mano didn't take his eyes off Cain. "What are you talking about?"

"Mano, you're Remi's right hand, or you will be eventually, but unless she gives over the reins, you won't be the head of your family." She spoke softly and with as much compassion as she could muster, not wanting to hurt his feelings. "I'm not telling you this to hurt you, and it shouldn't be a surprise to you."

"You're right, but that's not something I'm worried about. Remi will take over for my father one day, and I'm fine with that."

"Then you have to consider that this chain has three links." She put her right hand on the table and slid it in front of Remi. "There's Remi," she put her left hand toward Ramon and repeated the motion, "there's your father, and there's me. Out of those three, if you were some clueless idiot who let somebody they've never met before take care of their business, who would you hit?"

"Remi?"

"Remi," Cain confirmed. "I don't agree with the assessment, but Nunzio's thinking like a man chasing something he had, and because he again let that idiot Richard handle his business he lost it, and now he's desperate. If he takes Remi out, he sends the message that none of us are untouchable if he wants to strike."

"Then why not you or my father?"

"I told you before, I'm only guessing. I'd kill me, followed by your father, then Remi. You and Emma would be left, and the grief would make you easier to control."

Mano leaned forward and rested his chin on his hands. "I can see why my father thinks you're fascinating. You have an interesting way of thinking."

"Your father's a smart man, but so was mine. Dalton never thought of anything as having only two sides, but layers. If Nunzio tries to hit me or Ramon and misses, let's just say he's an idiot, but he's not totally stupid. If he misses the two people who are the most insulated, then the fallout would be a tad more stepped up, and he knows that."

"I still don't understand why he wouldn't think that anyway?" Mano said.

"Because your sister's death would send a message to me more than to Cain," Ramon said. "If he goes after Cain, she's in a more powerful position to strike back. We're partners, though, not family. If he hits Remi, then it could break us, since he considers us the weaker opponent."

"You'd stand by and allow that to happen?" Mano said, sounding as if he were loath to ask the question.

"You aren't my family, Mano," Cain said, and saw his head lower. "Not by blood, but remember this. What we agreed to isn't just for today. Our deal is for the future of both our families. Because of that, you'll one day sit at a table where my son is sitting with me. I would never put Hayden in a situation that would leave him vulnerable in any way." She waited until he looked her in the eye again. "That means you're not my blood but I welcome you into my family, and I'll watch over you like you were my own."

"We have a couple of days then. What do we do?" Mano asked.

The sun was starting to set and Cain stood up from the table and threw her can away. "I have to deal with Rick and his family, Muriel has some information to gather, and it's getting late. How about if we call it a night and meet again tomorrow afternoon?"

"There's nothing you want us to do?" Remi asked.

"I need you to do a couple of things in case I'm way off on this." Cain came up behind Mano and spoke in a low voice, making him nod a lot as she went down the list. "Before you go, Remi, I need to tell you something as well." She led Remi to the study.

"Are you going to share what you told Mano?"

"Your brother's got that under control, and I'm sure by morning he'll be at your place with my shopping list of stuff, but this has to do with Dallas."

"You can't have found something already." Remi sat in the chair across from the desk, and Cain sat beside her.

"Mano and your father followed the money. Not a bad plan but it would eventually lead back to Bob, thus a dead end."

"And you? What trail did you follow?"

"I'm a criminal, my friend. Not a common criminal, mind you, but still a criminal, so I decided to think like the dark side does."

Remi laughed as she twirled her cigar lighter between her fingers. "What in the hell is that supposed to mean?"

"Running isn't in my nature and it isn't in yours, but Emma said something interesting when it came to your girlfriend. She keeps feeling that Dallas is running from something or someone." She took a slip of paper out of her shirt pocket and read the name she'd written down. "The thing about running is you have to start somewhere, and it's a little easier to do when you find someone to help you create a new identity that lets you hide in plain sight."

"You found her already?"

"More like I found her possible track coach." She handed over the paper, then took it back and put it in her pocket again. "If I'm right, he gave her all the necessary paperwork to create Dallas Montgomery and the life that went along with her."

"How long before you know?"

"I invited him to New Orleans for a couple of days. Like I told you, I'll take care of it, and in a few days I might have the answers you're looking for. If it helps any, I exhausted my leads into the cop angle. I wouldn't swear on my mum's grave yet, but I don't believe she's undercover in an official way. It's more a survival kind of way."

It was suddenly noisy on the other side of the door, meaning that Emma, Dallas, and the kids had come down, probably searching for food. "And Bob? Did you find anything on him?"

"I think Bob's an opportunist who found her secret and used it to his advantage." Cain reached out when Remi started to stand up. "We'll deal with him soon enough, but Bob has a lot in common with Nunzio Luca. I want nothing more than to take care of Nunzio, but first we have to strip away his own secrets so that when he's dead—he's dead. Once he is, we don't have to worry about anything coming back from the grave to haunt us."

"Bob's not that smart."

"Does Dallas buck him in any way?" Remi shook her head. "Does she act like a woman who thinks her troubles are over now that you're in her life?" Remi shook her head again. "Then stop and think about what he has over her that's kept her as compliant as a puppy for years. When someone like Bob sinks his claws into someone, it takes a special meeting to dig them out. Be patient, and once we have most of the answers, we'll deal with him."

"And that's everything?"

Cain hesitated, then nodded. "Everything I know so far."

"You gave me your word."

"I've told you everything I'm sure about. I won't put rumors in your head to drive you insane."

"I want to know." She put her hand on Cain's shoulder to keep her in her seat. "I'm not asking because I want to replace Bob in her life."

"I'd never think that of you, but why torture yourself if you don't have to?"

"How can I help her if I don't know the truth?"

Cain stood up, making Remi break her hold. "I promise. Then if you want, I'll tell you everything I find out."

With a stiff nod Remi thanked her and left the room. Cain followed her out to the den and saw Emma and Dallas talking and sharing a laugh. She had every faith in Remi, but she prayed she could look past Dallas's actions enough that they wouldn't interfere with whatever relationship they established. Sometimes knowing something only allowed doubt to make Swiss cheese out of your brain, and Dallas deserved better than that.

CHAPTER THIRTY-SIX

S imon opened the back door for Dallas and Remi, and they rode to the condo in silence. Remi stared out the window, but she didn't seem to see the houses they passed.

"Are you okay?" Dallas asked. She took a chance and held Remi's hand. "Emma told me about Rick and how young he was. It's horrible that someone did that to him."

"Our world is sometimes a horrible place," Remi said without taking her eye off the window.

"Do you want me to go home? You have a lot going on, and you don't need to worry about having me around."

"You aren't in the way, and I don't want you out alone."

"I appreciate that you care, Remi, but I've been on my own for a long time."

"That doesn't mean you have to spend the rest of your life that way." Remi intertwined their fingers and faced Dallas. "If you don't let me in just a little, I can't help you."

Dallas couldn't maintain eye contact with her and dropped her head to stare at their joined hands. "It's not that I won't let you in. It's just hard. I've survived this long because I don't let myself get hurt."

"I'm not asking because I want to hurt you." Remi put her fingers under her chin and lifted her head.

"I wouldn't blame you for losing patience with me, but I can't express in words exactly how hard this is." She put her hand on Remi's cheek, then outlined the dark brows with her fingertips. "I've truly never taken this kind of chance."

"I want you to stay even longer than you might've planned for. I'm not comfortable letting you go home, and with our time together, maybe you'll start believing I'm the best problem solver you'll ever meet."

"I already know that."

Remi smiled and leaned closer and kissed her.

"Why do you want me to stay longer? Not that I mind spending time with you."

"Cain and I have a theory as to what's going to happen next, and the guy who'll be responsible for any more bloodshed saw us together. If he thinks we're a couple, he won't hesitate to hurt you to get to me."

When Remi lifted her arm, Dallas took the invitation and moved closer. "It's that guy that stopped at our table, isn't it? The one with the dead eyes?"

"Nunzio's more known for his dead heart, but yes, that's the guy." Dallas smiled when Remi kissed the top of her head, because she felt that Remi had done it unconsciously. "Until I know you'll be safe on your own, I want you to stay with me."

"Do you think it'll take long?" Dallas rested her head on the front of Remi's shoulder and put her hand on her abdomen.

"Could take years." Remi laughed.

"I don't know, having you as my jailer might be like winning the lottery."

"Don't worry. I won't keep you captive in your room, but I do have something in mind, and I want you to think about it before you say no."

"I'll go along with whatever you think."

"I might get used to such cooperation."

Dallas laughed also and ran her fingers down Remi's leg. "I wouldn't do that, if I were you. After all, Emma keeps preaching to me that making you work for it makes it that much more rewarding."

"I'm more than capable of doing heavy lifting when it's required, ma'am," Remi said as she picked Dallas off the seat and sat her on her lap. "I need you to be okay so I can prove myself as a worthy companion."

"If you offer references to that fact, you could end up with a few bruises." Dallas held up her thumb and index finger in a pinching position.

"All my references would be glad to tell you how much fun I am for about two dates, then how hard it is to get in touch with me, so I'll pass."

"You're hoping for more than two dates here?" Dallas dropped her hand to Remi's neck and came close to holding her breath, waiting for an answer.

"You know where I live. That makes it harder to avoid you, but that's the last thing I want to do. I want to take my time and get to know you. Hopefully, once that's accomplished, you'll have learned something about me as well and won't be running for the hills." Remi smiled at her before she lowered her head and kissed her.

"Hopefully you'll feel the same way about me," Dallas said as soon as their lips parted. "I don't want to disappoint you."

"The only way that'll happen is if you don't give this a chance." Remi kissed her again, only this time it was longer and laced with more passion.

"And you don't mind going slow," Dallas said, her voice dropping lower and her breath speeding up.

Remi combed Dallas's hair back and placed her finger over her pulse on her neck. "I'm looking forward to the long scenic route, Ms. Montgomery," she said, then replaced her fingers on Dallas's neck with her lips. "I'm sure it'll make arrival much more enjoyable."

"Uh-huh." Dallas tilted her head back as encouragement for Remi not to stop. "You aren't going to make this easy, are you?"

"I wouldn't want you to lose interest along the way."

For the first time Dallas felt like she was glimpsing what it would've been like to grow up in a world where people dated and fell in love. She was no innocent by any means, but spending time like this with Remi was showing her what being respected and courted was all about. If anything could help heal her soul, she was certain Remi would go out of her way to give it to her.

"I don't think there's any chance of that," Dallas said to Remi. They spent the rest of the trip in each other's arms.

❖

"If you were hoping for the easy answer and an even easier target, you're out of luck," Muriel said as she dropped the list of passengers that had arrived the day before. "Juan isn't on the list. Well, the name Juan is on the list, but only because it's as popular as John is in the States."

"Then your Jorge arrived early and his welcoming committee put a bullet in Rick's head," Cain said in return. She flipped through the pages and dropped them on her desk in disgust. "It's either that, or new players have joined the game and no one gave us a heads-up about it."

"I talked to Katlin and she's trying to find out. If there's something to know, somebody on the street will tell us eventually."

"Eventually might be too late." Cain stretched before standing up and waved Muriel into her chair. "Make some more calls and see if we can't speed up the process before we end up planning someone else's funeral."

"Where are you headed?"

"To visit Rick's mother and to see a man about a fake ID," Cain said, waving as she left.

The first visit was short, but Cain sat with the grieving mother as long as the woman could keep her emotions in check and went willingly into Cain's arms when she could no longer keep her tears at bay. She'd lost her son, but Cain promised that her daughter could stay in college, and they wouldn't lose their home now that Rick was no longer the main breadwinner. Lou had only been able to shake her hand and step back to the doorway, unable to say anything. It wasn't that he didn't want to pay his respects, but Cain knew Rick's loss had made Lou feel guilty.

As Cain started to leave, a young woman in her early twenties stopped her at the door and asked to speak to her. "You're Cain Casey, aren't you?"

"Yes, I am, and you must be Sabana. I didn't know your brother long, but he did a good job of describing you." Cain held out her hand but, from the angry set to the redhead's mouth, didn't expect her to take it. "I'm sorry for your loss."

"My father worked for yours when he was alive."

"I remember him." Cain brought her fingers together and dropped her hand when Sabana ignored it. "He died too young as well."

"After my dad died, getting cancer was Rick's biggest fear, since everyone always said how much alike they were. I guess he should've worried about getting killed doing something he really liked." As Sabana spoke, she sounded as if her throat was closing with emotion. "Can you promise me something before you go?"

"I'll try my best." Cain accepted the hand that Sabana now held out.

"I know you talked to my mom and you're not going to forget about us. But you don't have to feel like you're responsible for this, because you're not." She held Cain's hand in both of hers. "I know you can make this right. I want you to get justice for Rick."

"Help your mother through this and call me if you need anything. Leave the rest to me."

She pulled slightly on Cain's hand as if she were desperate for her to listen to what she was saying. "I know you think I'm too young or too naïve to know why this happened, and the FBI has already sent a couple of guys over here to see if me or Mom would roll on you, but I'm not and we didn't."

"Your mother didn't mention that," Cain said, trying not to sound surprised.

"I stopped them before they got to the door. Rick always told me they'd be the first ones over here if something happened to him, since those maggots are always looking for a way in, no matter what's going on."

"If they bother you again, will you call me?"

"I'll call if you consider something else."

Cain had to smile at this girl's grit. "What's on your mind?"

"I promised Rick I'd finish school, but when I'm done I want to work for you. I'd have asked sooner, but I gave him my word I'd graduate first." Sabana let go of Cain and stood up straight. "Before you give me your list of reasons why I can't, remember this has nothing to do with what happened to my brother. If I'm with you, though, I can help you catch whoever did this."

"I'm not turning you down, but I expect you to honor your commitment. When you're done, call me and we'll see what we can work out."

"This isn't a brush-off, is it?"

From the inside pocket of her jacket Cain took out a card. "A brush-off consists of me saying something close to what you want, then going on my way. I want you to finish like Rick wanted, because by then you might've changed your mind. But if you don't, I'll see where you fit in with us."

"Thanks, Ms. Casey, you won't be sorry."

"I'm sure I won't, but remember to call sooner if your new friends come back."

"They didn't stay long, so I'm sure they won't be back."

Cain nodded and was about to leave when it struck her that Rick hadn't worked for her long enough for the feds to have picked up his scent.

"Just one more thing, Sabana. Who did the feds send to talk to you?"

Cain waited while Sabana went into the other room and a minute later came out holding up a card. "Only one of them did the talking. The other guy stood there and scanned the yard because I wouldn't let them in the house."

The name on the card was Shelby's, so it wouldn't be hard to narrow down who she'd brought with her. "What did she ask you? Try to remember the exact words."

"She told me what had happened to Rick and asked if I knew he worked for you. No matter what she said I stood there and stared at her and never opened my mouth, unless it was to tell her that she couldn't come in and talk to Mom."

"Nothing else?"

Sabana closed her eyes as if that would make her recollect better. "She did ask me something weird, or at least I thought it was. She asked if Rick had ever mentioned a guy named Anthony something."

As soon as Cain heard the name, she shot Lou a glance to keep him quiet. "Was it Anthony Curtis?"

"Yeah, that was the name. Was he the one who shot Rick?"

"I don't think so, but I want you to do me a favor. The funeral's tomorrow, and after that I want you and your mom to get away for a while. Do you have family anywhere you'd like to see?"

"We'll be fine here."

"Sabana, if you want to work for me, remember that when I make a friendly request, most of the time it's for your own good. I don't want whoever killed Rick to connect the dots back to you and your mother, if they think Rick might have talked about him." As she spoke, Cain took out her cell and called Muriel to send over a couple of guys to sit on the house. "Is that all Agent Philips asked you?"

"I cut her off after that question, and I promise your name didn't come up again after she asked if I knew Rick worked for you."

"I believe you and I'll see you tomorrow. Have your mom ready to go after the funeral, and I'll get you both home as soon as possible."

"What's on *your* mind, boss?" Lou asked when they were in the car headed back to the city.

"After our next appointment we're going hunting, Lou, and I'm not going to stop until I get my fill of trophies." Cain glanced down at Shelby's card, sure that Sabana hadn't noticed that she'd taken it. The fact that Shelby had gone to Rick's family right after his death and the question she'd asked made Cain more sure than ever that Rick's death had been an unfortunate incident, and one that had been totally preventable.

"Some I'm going to hang on my wall, and the rest I'm going to lock in little cages for the rest of their miserable lives," Cain said. She tore the card in two, crumpled the pieces together, and threw them on the floor of the car.

❖

"Think the kid will tell her we were there?" Joe asked Shelby as they watched Cain disappear into the house.

"I'm sure she'll be more talkative since Cain just offered to keep them on the payroll in exchange for Rick's life. She'd have to kill a litter of kittens on live television for these people to see her for what she is," Shelby said as she worked on her daily surveillance report.

"Even if she did that, she'd have a good reason that'd still make her out the hero." Through his headphones Joe could hear Rick's mom crying, and nothing else. "Do you think she knows what went down?"

"We can't piece together what happened for sure. What makes you think she can?"

Cain's voice came through again and it startled Joe. As much time as they spent watching and listening in on Cain, it still surprised him when they actually heard her voice. It was like sighting the Loch Ness monster.

"I think she's motivated," Joe said when Cain stopped speaking.

Shelby finally slammed her pen down and broke the silence. "And you think we're not?"

"We are, but you know how it is when one of your own gets killed. If Cain's not careful, though, this could turn into an epidemic. We're motivated but she's driven."

Their subjects were quiet again, and Shelby scanned the outside of the house. Then Joe noticed her stop her sweep.

"Why aren't you inside?" Shelby asked, almost to herself.

"What?"

"Second oak outside. She acts like she's looking right at us, like she knows we're here."

Joe glanced from Sabana, who was leaning against the tree, to the front door, where a few of Cain's men were standing, staring at their van as well. "If she's waiting to talk to Cain, all she can say is that you came by and tried to ask some questions. It's not like you broke the kid."

Sabana straightened out and took a step in their direction before turning and heading into the house. From inside they could hear Cain telling the mother good-bye and not to worry about anything, followed by Cain's talk with Sabana. Everyone in the van was quiet as they eavesdropped on the hushed conversation, and then came Cain's question of "nothing else?" As Sabana started to answer, Cain cut them off so quickly they didn't even catch the first word.

Joe saw Shelby press her fingers to her forehead as if trying to remember what she and Joe had said after that. The door opened and the group, followed by Lou, stepped out. They could see Cain's lips moving, and she appeared as tight as a bow.

"I asked her if she knew or heard the name Anthony next, didn't I?" Shelby asked him. "My notes are back at the office."

"It was, but there's no way in hell Cain puts him at something like this. Anthony's not that stupid."

"Willing to bet your badge on that?"

"Not quite yet, when it comes to Anthony." Joe's cell phone vibrated on his hip and he answered it. "Call in our backup unit to stay with Cain. Agent Hicks arranged a meet with the other teams we'll be running into as we work our case. Mark Pearlman from DEA and the crew investigating the Jatibons are due in the office in thirty minutes. It's time to start sharing information."

"Tell them not to lose Cain," Shelby said. "Whatever that kid told her sparked something, and we *do not* want to miss the fireworks once they start."

CHAPTER THIRTY-SEVEN

Cain had her driver stop in front of the Piquant, and she and Lou walked quickly through the boutique section to the elevators. From the lobby on the third floor, they crossed to the bank of elevators and punched the eighteenth floor. When the doors opened they headed for the stairs at the end of the hall and jogged down a couple of flights in case their tagalongs made it in on time to see what floor they'd gone up to. By the time they ran background checks on the guests on eighteen, Cain planned to be home.

She could hear the television when she opened the door of the room farthest away from the elevator, but closest to the stairs. Katlin was sitting with Nathan Mosley, who was in town at Cain's request, and when they were done he'd be on the next flight to Los Angeles. She wanted him gone as quietly as he'd come.

"Mr. Mosley." Cain walked in and offered him her hand. "Cain Casey, and I want to thank you for agreeing to meet me."

Nathan was an even five foot, slender man with the reddest hair Cain had ever seen on an individual, and judging from his age someone had concocted the color for him in a bottle. He was stylishly dressed, wore a pair of wingtips whose heels were higher than normal, and glasses that overall made you want to peg him as an eccentric accountant.

"Your bonus made it hard to refuse." After turning the television off, he sat back down and Cain took Katlin's seat. "And don't worry. If anyone looks, the room was occupied by Edward Miller. Just another tourist from the Midwest and no one anyone will concern themselves with."

"I'm sure that as long as no one actually gets a look at you, you're right. Your work, after all, speaks for itself."

"I love a woman who knows how to flatter an old guy like me, but I doubt you went to all this trouble for that alone."

"That's not why you're here, Mr. Mosley, but before we start I do need to know if you're as discreet as you are talented."

Nathan picked up a gold-plated cigarette case and held it up before taking a stick out. When Cain nodded once, he lit his smoke with the matching lighter. "I've been doing this for close to forty years, and I haven't had a problem yet. The whole purpose of coming to me is that you want to start fresh. If I give you up the first time someone asks, what'd be the point?"

Cain smiled at him because he showed absolutely no fear, considering who he was sitting across from, and she wasn't alone. "Before we're done then, both of us are going to have to bend a little and trust a lot."

"Agreed, Ms. Casey. I can assure you that if anyone asks, we've never met. What can I do for you?"

"Dallas Montgomery."

He took some drags from his cigarette and stubbed it out in the crystal ashtray the hotel provided. "Actress, I believe, with relatively good success recently."

Cain's laugh was heartfelt. "You're discreet all right, or do you work for *Entertainment Tonight*? I know who she is. What I don't know is if she's a former client of yours."

"Tell me first why you need to know."

"Where she started from doesn't matter to me, but Dallas has recently come to mean something to a friend of mine. Like I found you because of what you do, I'd hope you know who I am before you accepted my invitation. If you do, then you realize in my world I can't afford to let someone with no past in without question. My friend is in the same position."

He lit another cigarette and seemed to be strategizing his next move. "Why are you here and not your friend?"

"She ran into your carefully constructed brick wall and asked for help. In my opinion, there are ways through it, no matter how well built or how high you made it."

"Are you a blaster, Ms. Casey?"

"If the situation calls for it, but not today. What I want today is the key to the gate, and I believe it's up here." She tapped the side of her head then pointed at him. "Is Dallas one of your creations?"

"I'm not saying I won't answer, but one more question before we move on. Is your friend good at keeping secrets? Dallas is a lovely girl I won't have hurt."

"Remi Jatibon is as honorable as they come, and you have my word Dallas won't suffer from this."

Nathan waved Cain closer and started to talk. In a low murmur he told Dallas's story, or as much of it as he knew. When he finished he fell back in his seat and spread his hands in front of him. "I've had all kinds come to me, and she was the first I almost did for free. It's good to know the papers I forged have worked up to now."

"I know how I broke through, but how did Bob Bennett?"

"Dallas never did give up all her secrets, but I think Bob was there before she came to me. He's got time and history on his side." He pulled a black book from his bag. "I'm not sure if he's aware I drew up more than one set of papers for her, but Remi needs to know if she wants to help her." His finger went down the page and stopped near the middle. "Dallas Montgomery wasn't the only one who I gave birth to that day. There was a Kristen Montgomery as well, but her I never met."

"On the documents you forged, what was their relationship?"

"Kristen is her younger sister, or at least that's what she was when I was done. She's a better-kept secret, though, than who Dallas really is."

"Thanks for your help, Mr. Mosley. One more thing," Cain said as Nathan repacked his stuff. "Because of who Dallas has become, you might get other requests similar to mine. Before you're tempted by the money, I want the chance to counteroffer."

"After today I plan to destroy any connection between us."

The decision made Cain raise her brows. "She must've really made an impression."

"She did, but that's not why. What Dallas paid me was a fraction of what you offered, and your money finished burying who Dallas was and whatever she did. If anyone finds out what I told you, it won't have come from me."

"Still," Cain said tapping her finger on the briefcase where he'd put his book of potential blackmail, "sometimes the money's hard to pass up."

"That's true, but let me play the devil's advocate." Nathan picked up his gold case and lighter and slipped them into his front pocket.

"What happens if I renege on our agreement? No amount of cash is worth gambling my life. Your friendship guarantees her past stays buried."

"It's been a pleasure," Cain said as she shook his hand. "If social security doesn't cut it for you, give me a call."

"I'll do that. If you've got the occasional job it might be good to stay in practice, in case I get bored out of my mind playing shuffleboard." Before Cain opened the door Nathan had one more thing to say. "If Dallas finds out I told you, could you apologize for me."

"Because of you I'm going to wield whatever power I have to wipe her slate clean. Instead of requesting an apology, she'll probably want to send you a thank-you card."

"You're an interesting woman, Ms. Casey."

"It's the romantic in me I didn't know existed until my wife came along," she said, making him chuckle before she disappeared behind the door.

CHAPTER THIRTY-EIGHT

The walls of the third-floor conference room in the Federal Building were plastered with crime-scene photos of the first-floor bathroom located in the airport. Rick resembled a large broken doll as he sat with his eyes and mouth open, his hands crumpled on his lap.

Annabel Hicks came in and sat at the head of the long table and waited for everyone to follow suit. "A few months ago we thought we had a war on our hands when the Bracato and Casey families squared off. What we ended up with was a stealth operation conducted by Cain Casey, resulting in the disappearance of Bracato and his four sons. A lot has changed in a few months, but what we avoided then I'm afraid will soon be a reality, considering how many players we've added to the game."

Shelby used a laser pointer and aimed it at the picture of the stall. "The death of Rick Greco yesterday might be the fuse that starts it." She then gave a brief history of Rick's work record. "Because of where in the airport this happened and how exposed it was, none of us had someone inside. The closest team was Mark Pearlman's from DEA. Mark." Shelby turned it over to him.

"We're mostly assigned to major players in the city but are reassigned whenever Rodolfo Luis is in town. The street vendors are one thing, but Luis is one of the big heads of the snake. Cut him off from moving his crap in and we put a serious hurt on supply." He turned on the projector connected to his laptop, and one of his guys dimmed the lights. "Yesterday we followed four of Rodolfo's men to the airport. When security sounded the alarm, we started to move a group in to pick these guys up on their way out, since video from their exit shows one of them in different clothes that are too big for him and a bundle under his arm.

"But that's not the only thing we captured on surveillance after the pandemonium that this caused." Mark advanced to the next picture. As soon as it came on the screen, Annabel and the rest of her agents leaned forward. Anthony Curtis and Juan Luis were getting into a car on the lower level of the airport.

"Anthony was in there when this happened?" Shelby asked.

"If he was, we didn't pick him up with the other four, but we weren't really looking for him," Mark said. "We spotted Anthony and Juan seconds before security called for help. Having Juan come back so soon leaves us with more questions than we have answers."

"Like what?" Joe asked.

"The name Juan Luis appears nowhere on the manifest from the flight he took, he hasn't gone anywhere near his uncle since he came back, and neither have the four idiots who probably did this. I don't think Rodolfo knows his nephew is back. I just don't know why, so we let everyone go and stepped up the surveillance on them."

"He's splintered off from Rodolfo, that's why," Shelby said.

"There's no way that's true," Mark said. "Rodolfo runs that family with no tolerance for dissension in the ranks, and Juan will be lucky to keep control once the old man goes down."

"But Rodolfo sent him home why?" Shelby asked.

"From what we could gather," Mark said, "because your guy's gotten in the way."

"Rodolfo, probably for the first time, hasn't given in to Juan's whims, and because of Anthony he feels emboldened to defy his uncle," Shelby said. "You're right. Rodolfo doesn't know he's back, but it's only a matter of time before Juan does something to announce his arrival. When that happens, Juan and everyone who helped him will get off easy if all that happens to them is a bullet in the head."

Mark turned off the projector and the lights came back up. "You're doing a lot of guessing, and we can't afford to be wrong. You may know your subjects but we know the Luis family. After watching this guy, we're positive Rodolfo won't put up with anything from anyone, especially his nephew."

"Juan may love and respect his uncle," Joe said, "but something stronger is pulling at him now."

"Since you two have all the answers, how about you share with the rest of us," Mark said.

"His hatred of Cain Casey, that's why he's back, and in Anthony he's found the perfect ally."

"Find Anthony and bring him in. If he was there yesterday and stood by while this went down, that's his ass," Annabel said. "And Shelby," she added as the meeting started to break up, "make sure your team reads him his rights as soon as you find him."

"Yes, ma'am."

"At this point it might be better to leave him on the street with the rest of them," Mark said. "If your guy's been able to get close to Juan, he's going to be easier to squeeze when the time comes. Pick him up now and we blow the opportunity."

"I want regular reports, if that's the case," Annabel told Mark.

"You got it, since we're putting a team on Juan."

Joe placed his hand on Shelby's arm and led her to an interview room while Annabel finished up with the other agency. "If Sabana Greco told Cain that you asked about Anthony, we better find him first."

"There's no way Cain goes after an agent."

"Shelby, are you crazy? Anthony was standing next to Juan when he confronted Cain. In her mind that changed the rules of the game."

"That goddamn moron," Shelby said, letting her anger out. "If something does happen to him, it's his own fault."

"At this point I'm not sure who he has to be more afraid of," Joe said as he scratched the top of his head, "Cain or Hicks."

"You know the answer to that one, Joe." Shelby stared at the chair Cain had occupied recently when they'd brought her in. "Hicks might reprimand or maybe fire him, but Cain…that's a different punishment, isn't it? If Cain puts him there, Anthony's going to be joining Giovanni and his sons, wherever that may be. We'd have better luck finding Jimmy Hoffa or having tea with space aliens."

❖

"You're looking smug today, mobster," Emma said as they descended the stairs together the next morning. "Not that you shouldn't, considering what you're able to do to me most nights," Emma teased until she saw her father waiting for them on the first floor.

"Have I ever mentioned how beautiful you are when you blush?"

"Don't you bruise easily?" Emma shot back, smiling the entire time. "Morning, Daddy."

"Morning." Ross opened his arms to Emma and kissed her cheek. "You look beautiful this morning."

"It's always a good day when everyone's this nice to you," Emma said, feeling happy. "Do you want to do some sightseeing today, Daddy?"

"I'd rather go start on some of the house repairs Cain told me about." He nodded when one of the women who worked for Jarvis held up a carafe of coffee.

"We didn't invite you for that," Emma said. "Tell him, honey."

"Ross, you aren't here to repair our house," Cain said dutifully.

"I know this place is huge, but tell me you both aren't ready to get home. And you know I built the majority of the house you grew up in," he told Emma. "Besides, Hayden's birthday's in a couple of days. He's going to feel more comfortable having his friends over if he's home."

"If you promise not to work yourself into the ground and take some help with you," Emma said, "then knock yourself out." She put her hands on her hips and tapped her foot on the floor when she heard Cain laugh. "What's funny?"

"It's good to see where that well-developed stubborn streak of yours comes from."

"Ha." Emma picked Hannah up when she ran to her. "I'm mildly persistent compared to you."

"Compared to Mom you're not what?" Hayden asked. He was dressed for school and Mook was right behind him, carrying his book bag.

"I'm not stubborn," Emma said.

"Uh-huh." Hayden dragged out the phrase. "She's got a good sense of humor, huh, Granddad?"

"Good imagination too."

"What happened to the highly complimentary group from earlier?" Emma said.

"You're stubborn, lass, but incredibly beautiful." Cain kissed the side of her neck. "I've got to head to the office, but I'll call later to see if Ross needs any help."

"Are you putting on a tool belt?"

Cain didn't answer but did gently swat her on the butt. "I'm heading over to Rick's funeral as well."

"Are you sure you don't want me to go with you?"

"I'd feel better if you kept low for a few days." Cain kissed her again and headed out.

On the way to the riverfront warehouse Cain took out the list of passengers from the day Rick was killed. She would find the answer to what had happened in one of the names, she was sure of it. Lots of *Juan*s, Muriel had been right about that, but not one *Jorge*. She had no idea about this situation yet, but at least Dallas Montgomery wasn't such a mystery anymore.

Instead of having the driver go into the building as he usually did, Cain had him stop in front. "Cain, this isn't a good time to break with routine," Lou said. It was the first time he'd spoken all morning.

"I want to grab a cup of coffee, not dare someone to take a shot at us."

"There's coffee inside," he pointed out. "All Rick was doing was picking up a bag and look at what happened."

"I'm working on that because I don't want it to go unanswered, and not because of the insult to me. Rick was a good kid and deserves to be avenged."

"Still, there's coffee inside."

"But our friendly federal agents aren't likely to wander into our kitchen, are they?" Before Lou could wave out some backup, Cain put her hand on his shoulder. "Just you and me, Lou. We don't want to scare the timid things away."

The café across the street was crowded with guys who worked at the various docks close by, but the waitress wiped off a table in the back corner and smiled at Cain as they took a seat. She ordered a sweet roll to go with the coffee and acknowledged every greeting the other patrons offered.

"What'd you get Hayden for his birthday?" Lou asked. After Cain cut her sweet roll and offered some to him, he picked up half of it.

"A hunting trip he asked about a couple of months ago. I told him how much my brother Billy liked the sport, and he wants to try it out."

"You're going hunting? When was the last time you did that?"

"I've only been once, so it's been awhile. Hayden seemed excited, and I didn't have the heart to let him down."

"He's excited about spending time with you, Boss." Lou accepted a refill and another roll.

"I spend time with him," Cain said as she brought her brows together, not understanding what he meant.

"I know you do, but he's got to share you now. When Emma and Hannah moved in, he didn't have you twenty-four-seven like he did before." He brushed his hands off and finished his coffee. "Not that he'd change things, but I think he still misses it a bit."

"Thanks for telling me, and I'm glad we're going away for a few days. The trip's not until the fall, but maybe we can squeeze some fishing in when it gets warmer."

Lou's face became devoid of emotion as he nodded. "You're about to get a bite now."

"I sure made that intro easy for you," Cain said with a short laugh. Throughout their talk she'd kept her eyes on Shelby and Lionel, who were seated at the counter returning the favor.

"What do you think it'd take for these guys to stop watching?"

"That's an easy one too, Lou. They'll stop when I give them what they want, but that won't be today."

"Cain, could we join you for a minute?" Shelby asked. The two empty chairs at their table had their backs to the door and were in the way of the wait-staff traffic to and from the kitchen. They were the worse seats in the place, making Cain smirk when she pushed Shelby's chair out with her foot.

"Are you here for the sweet rolls?" Cain asked, and Lou smiled slightly.

"Good place to get coffee." Shelby sat down and laid her hands on the table.

"Just happen to be in the neighborhood, or are you planning to join the longshoreman's union?"

"Could we call a truce until we finish our coffee?" Shelby asked. "You know why I'm here."

"Sure, what can I do for you?"

"We wanted to talk. I don't know if you've met—"

"Special Agent Lionel Jones, computer guru and boy genius? No, we haven't met, but I've heard so much about him."

"How did you..." Lionel acted like he didn't know how to finish the question.

"I've always believed if I have to show you mine, you have to give some up as well." Cain shrugged, then folded her arms in front of her chest and sat up straighter. "Maybe once Shelby starts on her second career as a longshoreman I'll do something new as well. I might try my hand at writing. Think anyone would be interested in a book about what FBI agents do on their days off? What cute little sites on the Internet their boy geniuses visit when no one's looking?"

Cain had to laugh when Lionel blushed visibly, despite his deep olive complexion. Sometimes she really enjoyed these guessing games that took only a little information and a lot of imagination.

"Stop picking on Lionel," Shelby said as she looked from Cain to her coworker.

"If I do, will you return the favor?" Cain said, her smile not diminishing. "And to save time, don't bother to tell me you can't. We both know it's your life's work to follow me around skulking in shitty little vans and dark rooms. What's brought you out of your cocoon next door?"

"We wanted to give you our condolences for what happened to Rick Greco. I realize you had nothing to do with it, but you did visit his family yesterday."

What Shelby had said made no sense to her, and because it didn't, Cain stayed quiet as she sorted the puzzle pieces in her head. No matter their past dealings, Shelby didn't often crawl out of her hole to interact with her, so something had spooked her. Cain might've crossed the street to fish, but so had Shelby.

"Do you mean if Lionel here meets some tragic end, you wouldn't bother to visit his family to offer your respects? Tsk," Cain shook her head slowly, "I thought you were raised better than that, Agent Philips."

"I didn't say it was wrong." Shelby seemed hesitant.

"You must've found something objectionable about it, considering you were most probably listening in, which reminds me." Cain turned her attention to Lionel. "What's your favorite song, Lionel? You don't mind me calling you Lionel, do you?"

"No, I don't mind," Lionel stopped to clear his throat, "and the theme from *Bonanza* is my favorite song."

"How manly of you, but back to Shelby's problem."

"I don't have a problem, Cain," she said, sounding as if she was losing patience.

"I went to the Grecos' to reassure them they won't be thrown out on the street after what happened to Rick. After his father died he was supporting his mother and sister, and I'm sure that was worrying Mrs. Greco. You beat me over there, but Sabana didn't get the impression you came to hand off a list of government agencies ready to help them pay the mortgage."

"Rick worked for you," Shelby said.

"As do a lot of people. Lou here works for me," Cain said, tired of their cautious verbal dance. "What does that have to do with me wanting to help out? That's supposed to be part of your life's work, to protect and defend, or whatever your slogan is, but you didn't do such a bang-up job when it came to Rick, did you?" Then it hit her why Shelby was here with the most unintimidating member of her team, and the shock stopped her cold.

Shelby wanted the answers to the questions she'd asked Sabana, and bringing Lionel was supposed to make Cain relax enough to give them to her. Cain couldn't believe she was right this time, but there was only one way to find out.

"We weren't watching Rick," Shelby said.

"You and your friends weren't watching him, but somebody was, weren't they? Do you allow an agent to sit by and let someone get killed? Or was he there to participate?"

The café was noisier now, but from the way Shelby blanched Cain knew she'd heard the question. That's not what surprised her, though. She was shocked that Anthony Curtis had been at the airport and that's why Shelby had asked Sabana about him. Cain didn't know what he was doing there or if he actually had anything to do with Rick's murder, but obviously neither did Shelby.

"What are you talking about?" Shelby finally asked.

"Curtis was there, and since we all know how he regards me, I'm sure he felt justified in taking out someone tied to me." Cain stood up. "Don't bother denying it."

"Cain, wait, this isn't a game. You have to tell me how you know that."

After she handed their waitress a twenty, Cain turned around, and Shelby and Lionel were both standing. "If we're playing a game, the rules have changed, don't you think?"

"No one's going to give you the benefit of the doubt for going after an agent, no matter how justified you think you are," Shelby said.

"Not like they would you for going after me and mine? Don't worry, Agent Philips. I'm not known for stupid flights of fancy." Before Cain walked out she saw Shelby's lips move, and even though she couldn't hear her, the word "fuck" was easy enough to make out.

"See, Lou, now we know who we're fishing for," Cain said to him softly as they walked toward the office. "Get with Katlin and find him."

"Will do, boss. You want us to bring him in for a chat?"

"You heard Shelby. No one's going to forgive us for taking care of this problem. I've got other plans for him."

"Anything else?"

Cain stopped at the door of the warehouse and glanced at the window across the street where the feds were lurking. "You heard the man, cue up *Bonanza* for him."

CHAPTER THIRTY-NINE

"Thanks to the smart guys you've got working for you, we're all in deep shit," Anthony said to Juan. After Juan's arrival they'd moved to a hotel in the French Quarter and hadn't left the room.

"Don't you mean *you're* in deep shit?" Juan took another bite from the shrimp cocktail he'd ordered from room service. "Nobody knows I'm here. You, though, were right in the middle of the action, but that's what you kept saying you wanted. Ain't no going back to that gray suit, Mr. FBI."

"This isn't some joke. Your guys killed a man for no reason."

Juan pointed at him with a jumbo shrimp and laughed. "Jesus said Cain had sent him to spy on us. In my book that means Jesus did the right thing. What I want to know is how did you let Cain know I was back? You're the supposed expert on laying low."

"I didn't," Anthony said through clenched teeth. He got up and stared out the window again. At check-in he'd insisted on a room with a view of the street. If any of his co-workers were out there, he hadn't spotted them yet. "Did you ever consider that Jesus isn't being completely straight with you?"

"You want out, then get the fuck out," Juan screamed, and pushed away from his plate.

"I'm trying to keep us all out of jail."

"Forget about that shit. I got something for you to do."

The tone of Juan's voice made Anthony think his gamble was finally paying off. "What do you want?"

"Emma Casey," Juan said when Anthony sat down across from him. "I want to know everything about her, but most importantly I want to know her schedule."

"Why?"

"Who paid you to think? I want to know, and I need to know if you can do it."

"That should be easy," Anthony said slowly, as if talking to a mentally challenged person, because that's what he figured Juan was. If he didn't want what happened at the airport to end his career, he had to stick with Juan, though. He needed him to knock down the rest of the dominos.

"I don't know. Cain's better at picking up a tail than you ever imagined. Just a warning before you start. If Cain finds you sniffing after her whore, she can have you to do whatever she likes." Juan laughed as he picked his teeth with the nail of his pinky. "I've found nothing motivates Cain more than when any man keeps his eyes on that piece of ass too long."

"Don't worry about it. I'll start this morning, since they'll be easy to pick up at the funeral. While I'm doing that, why not have a talk with Jesus and see if he tells you what really happened at the airport." Anthony tried to relax and sound as if the outcome of this meeting wasn't particularly important to him. "And you have to trust me."

"You don't think I trust you?"

"You order me around but you don't tell me what for. That means you don't trust me." Anthony put both of his feet on the ground and pushed out of his chair. "If you don't trust me, then what the hell am I doing here? Like you said, if you want me out, then tell me to get out."

"What do you want to know?" Juan asked as soon as Anthony had made it halfway to the door.

"What's so important about Emma Casey?"

"My uncle always preached to me that everyone has a weakness—the one thing you can use against them to make them fall to their knees. For Cain it's Emma and those bastards they have together, but in this case I can't blame her for letting this woman make her weak."

One of the brass bands that played for tourists in the Quarter went under the window, and Anthony wished he was one of those people milling around down on Bourbon Street with nothing to worry about except where to eat that night. "What are you talking about?"

"I want to kill Cain, but I want to keep Emma for myself. What happens to the kids isn't my problem, but I want her alive and whole."

The way Juan went down his to-do list as if he were planning a trip to the grocery almost made Anthony's hands shake. "She'll never do that."

"Who, Emma? You may have played nice all this time because it's what you do, but there's more than one way to break a woman. When I'm done she'll beg to stay with me." Juan turned so Anthony could see his face. "And every time she does get that pleasure, it'll only remind her how much time she wasted with that bitch."

"How's your uncle going to feel about your plan?" Anthony tried to talk him back from the brink with the one thing Juan still feared. "It'll take more than killing Cain to convince her friends and those loyal to her not to come after you."

"My uncle should've listened to his own advice. He's trying to be something he's not, and the more he tries, the weaker and more pathetic he becomes."

"What do you mean?"

"Rodolfo thinks he's a civilized man, but he's not. He's just an old man chasing some sort of respectability that no amount of money can buy."

Anthony had to laugh because, for once, Juan's reasoning was right on the mark. "And you don't care about being civilized?"

"All I care about is winning and control. If that's not what you want, run back to your job or to my uncle. Whoever you pick won't give you the respect and the freedom to do what you need to when it comes to beating Cain." Juan stood and put his hands in his pockets. "We have a deal?"

"That we do, Juan."

❖

"Are you sure?" Remi asked. They were on the way back to her condo after a walk through the Quarter. Dallas had knocked on her bedroom door that morning, and instead of their usual forty-five-minute jog, Remi and Simon had gone for a brisk walk. "You could come in to work with me."

"I checked my phone this morning, and so far I've gotten about sixty messages from Bob. To keep the peace I thought I'd have him meet me at my place, and we'll go to the studio from there." She wrapped her hand around Remi's bicep and squeezed. "Please don't be mad. I'll call if I need to change my plan."

"If that's what you want to do, I'm fine with it, but don't you think it's strange for someone to call you sixty times a day?"

The breeze was picking up along the river, and Dallas moved one hand down and took Remi's, then pulled her hair away from her face with the other. As they approached a bench, she pointed to it and Remi nodded. "I know you don't understand why I don't tell him to get lost. I would if I could."

"Why can't you tell me?" Remi lifted their hands and kissed the back of Dallas's. "No matter what it is, I'll still want to be with you."

"Let's get through this meeting today, and tonight we'll talk." When Remi moved closer and kissed her, Dallas went willingly. "You make me feel so much."

"You can trust me, Dallas. Even if you decide this isn't for you, I can help you get to a better place in your life, no strings attached."

"I'm not sure how I lucked out by having you be so kind, but I'm grateful. I'll tell you as much as I can and after that, the same applies to you. You can walk away—no hard feelings."

Remi kissed her again before she stood up and helped Dallas to her feet. "Let's get ready so you can get home to meet Bob."

"Considering how you feel about him, you're being good about this."

"I trust you to handle Bob, after all you've been doing it for a long time." She had to laugh when Dallas peered up at her like she didn't totally believe her. "I'm sending some added insurance, and before you turn me down, remember you said you'd go along with anything I wanted."

"You're saying I might regret that promise, aren't you?"

"I'm sure you'll be fine." They crossed the intersection between the aquarium and the Riverwalk Mall, and Remi spotted Emil sitting on the rim of the fountain in the middle of the courtyard that led to her building. When Emil stood up and started toward them, Dallas moved closer to Remi. "See, I told you. You'll be fine because that's the reaction this big guy always gets." Remi smiled.

"You know him?" Dallas asked, still glued to Remi's side.

"Dallas, let me introduce you to Emil, who works for my father. Actually he's his Simon," she pointed back at her own guard, "and until things calm down, he's going to work for you."

"I appreciate your thinking about me, but there's no way I can accept."

"This doesn't have to do with Bob, but with what happened to Rick and what it means to me and our business. Things happen that I can't control, and if something happened to you, I wouldn't be able to accept the fact that I could've prevented it."

Emil stood with his hands behind his back until Remi finished. "Ms. Montgomery, you're not even going to notice I'm around." Remi had to cover her mouth with her free hand when he said that.

"Do you really think someone's going to come after me?" Dallas asked.

"You met Nunzio Luca. Do you think he'd be the type to do that?" Instead of having this talk outside, Remi walked them toward the elevator. "Once this is over we'll go back to normal, if that's what you want, but please consider my proposition."

"Does he have to start today?"

Dallas glanced back at Emil, and Remi could tell she wasn't thinking of her well-being, but of Bob's reaction. "If you have to, blame it on me and the studio. Tell him it's a new section of your contract."

"As long as you think he won't have to stay with me forever." Dallas looked back again and smiled at Emil. "Not that I have anything against him, but this is a bit out of my norm."

Dallas kissed Remi good-bye, still feeling uncertain as Emil followed her out. When she met Bob, she asked Emil to wait outside for a minute while she explained his presence. Emil agreed to stand outside the door but not to a closed door.

He explained, "Not that I don't trust you, Ms. Montgomery, but I can't do my job if we have too many barriers between us."

"Everyone at the studio is getting their own security?" Bob asked in a low voice.

"That's what they told me when they sent Emil over here."

Bob got close enough to put his lips to her ear. "Before the day's out, find a way to ditch this guy so you can tell me where you've been. You know how much I don't like it when you disappear and don't return any of my calls."

"Ms. Montgomery, are you all right?" Emil asked, poking his head in the door.

"Fine, thank you." Dallas pushed away from Bob.

"This isn't going to work for me," Bob said.

Dallas held her hand up toward Emil. "Just a few more minutes and we'll be ready to go." She took a deep breath before facing Bob again. "My next job is the sequel, and if I want to do that, I don't have much choice. Do you have a better idea?"

"Let me do all the talking at the meeting, and I'll take care of this."

The studio offices had been set up one block into the French Quarter in a building that had started as a coffee-roasting plant. Like Remi's condo, it had a good view of the river, and the top floor, where the management team was housed, was opulently decorated. After walking around the waiting area to admire the collection of movie posters, Dallas stopped at the large window at one end of the room and tried to forget the two men watching her intently for two different reasons.

They had driven over with Emil and hadn't spoken a word, and Bob acted more uncomfortable than when he went off about something. She pressed her fingers to the glass and thought about her relationship with him and how it would affect her relationship with Remi.

"Hello, Dallas," Steve said, then turned his attention across the room. "Dick, I hope you haven't been waiting long."

"We just arrived, thanks," Dallas said, returning Dwayne's wave.

"Can we get you anything?"

"No, thanks. How about you, Bob?" she added, to be nice and avoid an argument on the way home.

"Actually we need to borrow Dickey for some preliminary stuff that we don't need to bore you with," Steve said.

"Then I shouldn't keep you. Should I wait here?" she asked, earning a glare from Bob when she didn't correct his name.

"Enjoy the view. Let's go, Dickey, we're set up in the conference room," Steve said, and slapped him on the back so hard the much-shorter Bob stumbled.

"If you need anything, Dallas, just ask," Dwayne said, and winked on his way out.

Dallas walked to the windows overlooking the river and watched the steamboat make its way downstream. After a few months off she was anxious to return to work. Getting swept up in a new project would help clear her mind of everything wrong with her life, like it always did. She was a good actress because she could pretend to be something she wasn't. Before she got too lost in thought, she felt the heat of a taller body behind her and knew instantly who it was.

"Do you have an appointment to see someone?"

"I'm here to see the boss, as a matter of fact." She placed her hands over the ones that had pulled her into a hug from behind.

"Are you okay?"

"Are you asking if Bob hates that you've hired Emil to keep an eye on me? I'm okay with it and he's not, but we'll all have to deal with it, won't we?"

"Would it make you feel better if most of the time I'll be the one keeping an eye on you? Unless you go home because you're sick of my company. Now that Emil's with you, you can do that if you want." Remi turned her around, not letting go of her hand, and walked Dallas to her office. Once the door closed, she pressed Dallas to her and kissed her.

Dallas could immediately tell Remi had let go of whatever was holding her back and kissed her like she wanted her in her life. "You're safe for now, since I'm not quite ready to go home. Not that I'm afraid of anything, but I don't want to give up the time with you. The one thing we have to talk about, though, is this cigar-smoking thing," she said, looking at the smoldering cigar in an ashtray on Remi's desk.

"I'll try to keep that in mind, but bad habits are the worst to break." Remi led her to the sofa in the office and offered her a seat while she put the cigar out. "The fact you're here is a good sign you'll renew your contract."

"You had doubts about that?"

"After dealing with people in this business, I'm learning anything's possible."

"I want this part, so no worries from this talent. Bob might not be so easy on you, but I'm going to enjoy having you as one of my bosses."

"It's good to know someone likes me. I've made more enemies in the last week than I have since I started working for my father, and that's going some. Let me walk you to the conference room and get you squared away on the paperwork, and we can take off early." Remi kissed her forehead, then ran her thumb over Dallas's lips. "Can I interest you in a quiet evening at home with me?"

"Best offer I've had all day."

When Remi led Dallas into the conference room, all the occupants looked up. Dallas had never known Bob to appear so full of hatred, but it oozed off him as he watched Remi pull out a chair for her.

"Since you're talking about her, I thought I'd let her come listen in."

Bob forced a smile and held his hand out. "Hi, Remi, nice to see you again. I'm looking forward to working with you on the upcoming project."

"We're looking forward to having Dallas on this project," Remi said.

He let his hand fall since Remi never accepted it. "I also wanted to apologize for any misunderstandings between us. This is a generous offer you've proposed for Dallas, and I don't want any of my attempts at humor to stand in our way."

"If you've been trying to be funny, your act needs work. Guys, take care of the paperwork and call me if you need anything. Once you've gone through all the fine points, we'll arrange to have the contract delivered to Dallas for her signature, but unless you need us we're taking the rest of the day off." Remi held her hand out for Dallas, who readily accepted it.

"Self-righteous bitch," Bob hissed under his breath, though loud enough for Dwayne and Steve to hear him.

"If you'd like any contract signed with this studio in the near future, you'll keep your opinions to yourself. Do I make myself clear, Mr. Bennett?" Steve asked from his side of the table.

"Crystal." Bob enunciated the word clearly, making it obvious how he felt about Remi. "As long as Remi understands that anything to do with Dallas comes through me."

"I'm sure she has Dallas's best interests at heart," Steve said. "Maybe that's something you can learn from her."

"Is advice part of the contract?"

Steve shook his head and twirled his pen through his fingers.

"Then drop it. It's not like you and your boss are lily white."

"That might be true, but we're worlds apart from you, Dickey." Dwayne pushed the contract back in front of Bob and pointed to where they'd left off. "Do you have any questions so far?"

"How do we lose the big ape following Dallas around? She said she doesn't like it, and I don't think it's necessary."

"The studio hired him and he's a reality, so learn to live with it," Dwayne said. "Think of it this way. Dallas will have to get rid of you before she gets rid of Emil."

"I'm not going anywhere."

"There's your answer then," Steve said. "Everyone's staying put for now."

CHAPTER FORTY

Muriel had been watching the monitors they had trained on the building where the feds were housed. She wasn't surprised that Shelby came out right after Cain, but she was surprised that she still missed Shelby. "Learn anything at the café?"

"So much I could take the rest of the day off and still feel like I accomplished something," Cain said in a joking tone. "But right now we need to get to the bat cave and go over a few things."

"What, no hints?"

"Better yet, I'll give you the whole story, but first, Lou." She glanced back at him.

"Name it, boss."

"I need Katlin in here." They stepped into Cain's office and she pointed Muriel into a chair. "Before she gets here, are you sure you want to be included? I won't stop you from doing something you need to, but once you cross the line you can't turn back."

"I want to help, and I know what that means."

"When we're done, we can go back to the way things were, but in here," she tapped over her heart, "and up here," she tapped the side of her head, "you won't be able to undo it."

"I can handle it."

"I've got to worry—you're my family."

"Boss," Katlin said from the door.

"We're done, come in," Muriel said.

Cain nodded and told them what she'd just learned from Shelby. "I need a few things from you all. Katlin, I want one of Rodolfo's guys that was outside the day we went to the Steak Knife, the one with a ponytail."

"You want to talk to this clown?"

"I'm interested in a long, private conversation."

"We'll go tonight and take a look. If you're in for the night, I'll take Lou with me and maybe he'll recognize him." Katlin leaned her hip against the side of Cain's desk, and Muriel saw how she didn't hesitate to follow Cain's orders.

"Muriel," Cain said next. "I'm going to have some of the guys work with you."

"I can handle it myself."

"In law school did they teach you how to break into someone's house and not have them notice you've been there?"

"Breaking and entering? Since when are we involved in petty crime?"

"Think of it this way," Cain said, not sounding upset with Muriel's question. "If we get caught, it'll be much easier to defend me against that than tax evasion and bootlegging."

"Who are we robbing and how do I fit in?"

"Anthony Curtis—"

"Agent Anthony Curtis." Muriel was shocked that Cain would even consider such a move.

"Is it time for you to go up to your office?" Cain asked, not quite slamming her hand down, but getting Muriel's attention.

"I'm not trying to piss you off, just keep you out of trouble. Don't you think they're waiting for you to go after Curtis?"

"I'm always thinking, and if something goes wrong, don't worry. It'll be my ass in the vise, not yours."

The set of Cain's mouth was proof that Muriel had pushed too far and shouldn't have initiated this conversation with Katlin and Lou in the room, but she didn't let up. "Don't you think I know that? That night in the warehouse you were supposed to be the only one in the line of fire—Emma was a surprise. And look at what that almost cost us. If you want this family to survive intact, get used to the idea of me taking care of you."

"I appreciate that, but if you want to get involved in all the business, remember there's only one person in charge. And you have to trust I know what I'm doing." Cain glanced up at Katlin. "Since what I'm asking is new to you, I'll put Katlin with you. I want someone in Curtis's house, but don't go near him. I need information, not the satisfaction of driving his nose into his brain."

Muriel locked eyes with Cain but realized she couldn't win. "What do you need?" she asked as her way of conceding.

After Cain started her list, Muriel realized she would have to go because it was the only way she could be sure they'd get what Cain needed. She knew without any explanation why Cain was asking and what she planned to do with the information.

"Cain." Cain's assistant came over the intercom. "I hate to bother you, but Remi Jatibon's on the phone."

"Any questions?" Cain asked the group in her office. She didn't pick up until she was alone. "Remi, where are you?"

"I'm helping Dallas gather a few things from her place. She's staying with me for several days since she's got a lot going on, including starting her contract negotiations today. It reminded me why I asked you for help with Bob."

Cain laughed at the frustration in Remi's voice. "I think it reminded you that you want Dallas all to yourself. I've been there, my friend, and it can make you crazy."

"I'm beginning to realize that."

"Can you talk? I've got something that might help you," Cain said as she opened the file she'd made on Dallas.

"Not right now, but I can swing by later."

"Come for dinner tonight and bring Dallas. We can talk about your problem and recap everything else we're facing."

Remi laughed. "What, you're not going to give me a hint? Did you find anything?"

"I had an idea and it panned out. Stop worrying. You'll have to learn to live with some things and forget others, but you can have faith in what she feels for you."

"Thanks, Cain. If you've got most of what I was looking for, I can call off my father."

Cain hung up and closed her eyes, trying to order her thoughts. The casino deal, Juan Luis, Anthony Curtis, and Dallas Montgomery were all on her mind, and with enough time she would have some solutions. She already had an idea about Dallas and Anthony, which would only take some finishing inquiries. Nunzio Luca deserved her attention more than all the rest, and she wrote his name at the top of a fresh sheet on the pad on her desk.

To most, Rick was a small cog, and she was almost certain what had happened to him at the airport hadn't been directed at her. That left two possible motives. Someone had managed to catch him unawares and mug him, or someone wanted him not to report something he'd seen. She circled "something he'd seen," then picked up the passenger manifest.

She grabbed the phone again. "Are you still in the building?"

"I'm in the parking lot."

"I need one more thing before you go." Cain sat and waited for Muriel to come back in. "Hector Delarosa gave us the assassin, Jorge, didn't he?"

"He went through Vincent, but yeah."

"Call Vincent and find out how I can talk to this Delarosa guy. It has to be a clean line, since we know DEA isn't limited to this country. If he's big in Columbia, he's being watched."

Muriel rested her briefcase on the visitor chair. "What do I tell Vincent if he asks?"

"Vincent isn't going to ask. He's either going to set it up or not."

"To satisfy my own curiosity, why do you want to talk to him?"

Cain wrote something down on the sheet and circled that as well. "A strange little man named Nathan gave me an idea. Now I need to talk to someone who can identify the shit that falls out of the Luis family tree when I shake it."

Muriel stared at her like she was waiting for her to say something else. "Is that supposed to make sense?"

"Hiding in plain sight—that's what I should've thought about when you handed me this, but what happened to Rick threw me off." Cain stood up and waved her away. "Don't worry about it yet. Scroll through that Blackberry of yours and see if you know anyone in Tennessee."

"Because…"

"I promise I'll be more informative after I talk to Remi about the Tennessee part. After that's done I'll have one less thing to worry about and we can concentrate on getting rid of the people out to harm us."

"I'll check and see if any of my classmates ended up in the Smokey Mountain State. See you at home later."

Before Muriel could move, Cain joined her on the other side of the desk and hugged her. "I might bark a lot but you're doing a good job. Remember to keep your head down and take time to think about what you want in the long run. Letting Shelby go sounds easy enough, but sometimes the hole it leaves is hard to deal with."

"Are you buying a couch for in here?" Muriel asked in jest.

"If I do, you're the last person I'd want on it." Cain laughed as she put on her jacket. It felt good to laugh before she headed to St. Patrick's Church to pay Rick her respects.

CHAPTER FORTY-ONE

S he didn't fire you?" Dallas asked, wiping the sides of her eyes after laughing so hard she'd teared up.

"Are you kidding? If I'd known how well spilling beer on her would turn out for me, I'd have dumped a pitcher on her head the minute she walked through the door," Emma said, kissing the pout off Cain's mouth. Remi took out the leather carrier she kept her cigars in and offered one to Cain. "If you must, then head outside, you two." Emma pointed to the back door.

They had finished dinner over an hour ago, but Cain hadn't had the heart to break up Emma's plans for after-dinner drinks in an effort to get to know both Remi and Dallas better. Emma had made acquaintances in New Orleans, but they weren't trusted friends. Aside from Cain, Emma didn't confide in anyone but Mattie, but she was in Wisconsin.

Cain thought that's why she was trying so hard to bring Dallas and Remi together. Though Mattie was Emma's best friend, she would never know what it was like to be married to someone like Cain. Their world was totally foreign to the wife of a dairy farmer, but Dallas, if it worked out, would be a true confidante.

"Before you tell me what, tell me how," Remi said. They stopped at the pool, but Cain took her into the empty pool house. "It can't be that bad, can it?"

Cain glanced around the place her inner circle of guards had made their own. "I want to make sure if you react to what I'm going to tell you, you don't embarrass Dallas. If you do, that'll stay between me and you."

"How do you know what you found out is right?"

Cain put her hand on Remi's shoulders. "Listen to me. Ramon followed the money, but that's not what drives this girl. We needed the key to unlock her past, and I found it."

The cigar in Remi's hand hung loosely in her fingers as she fell into a chair. "What was it?"

"Her name," Cain said. She pulled another seat closer and patted Remi's knee. "Katie Moores of Sparta, Tennessee, and she hasn't had an easy life."

"Katie?"

"I don't have the why yet, but Katie ran away with her little sister, Sue Lee, and ended up in Los Angeles. After she got there, she was too young and didn't have any experience to make a living that would support two people."

"She has a sister?"

"Kristen Montgomery, who's a college student up North. Dallas has done a good job of keeping her away from her job and out of the limelight."

"How did you find all this?"

Cain told her about Nathan and how he'd helped Dallas with the identity she'd used to build her new life. "If you couldn't find her, then I figured there were only a few ways she could've managed an identity that's stood up this long. I started with the best and lucked out."

"How'd she afford that?" Remi asked, sounding as if the answer was something she needed to hear but dreaded at the same time. "Something like that isn't cheap."

"You have to meet Nathan Mosley. He made a deal with her, and she kept her end of the bargain. Otherwise he would have sold her out. The new identity holds up only if Nathan keeps a client's secret."

"What's going to stop him now?"

Cain laughed as she headed to the bar. "My reputation is good for something, and Nathan seems to genuinely like her."

"After you get to know Dallas you'll understand why," Remi said. She accepted the glass Cain handed her. "And I imagine what you've told me so far is just the fluff of this story."

"You should've asked yourself how a girl you can't find ended up on the screen. Where'd she get her start?" Cain raised her glass and encouraged Remi to take a drink. "Nathan didn't know the whole story, but he knew enough to give me a place to start. Sweet China was the name she used in a short stint in the porn industry."

"What?" Remi screamed.

"Think about the position she was in, and imagine what drove her to have to do that. She took what she learned in that life and created one she could live out with a lot more dignity. What's wrong with that?"

"I'm not knocking her, but why in the hell did she think she needed to hide that? These days, she probably could've gotten bigger roles if people *had* known that's where she started."

Remi's rage was hard to miss, and Cain gave her a few minutes to calm down. "While I can see where she wouldn't be proud of that period of her life, I think she needed Nathan for another reason. To find that answer we need to go back a little further. This had to have begun in Sparta."

"Where in the hell does Bob fit into all of this?"

"From what Nathan told me, he was there from the beginning, but only Dallas can tell us what that beginning was. I assume Bob knows every secret she wanted to bury. But I don't think he knows about Dallas's sister." The cigar Remi had been holding was now in two pieces on the floor. "And we're going to work together to make sure it stays that way."

"How do we discover the rest?" Remi asked, pressing her fingers to the sides of her head.

"I'm going to have Muriel locate someone I can talk to."

"If you do, this will be in the tabloids by tomorrow afternoon."

Cain shook her head, pulled out a twenty, and handed it to Remi. "There's more than one way to keep someone quiet." She held up the bill.

"You can offer money to anyone, but if the story's good enough, someone's offer will be that much better."

"Remi, if I give you this bill and tell you something, you probably wouldn't tell anyone if I ask you not to, right?"

"You know it."

"But how could I guarantee that you wouldn't, legally, that is?"

"If I'm your attorney you could give me the money as a retainer," Remi said, shaking her head and laughing.

"Don't worry. I hit you with a lot tonight, and eventually you'd have figured that one out on your own. I'm going to hire a local attorney to do the digging for me. If the attorney-client privilege doesn't convince him to keep quiet, my threat to rip out his tongue with a fingernail clipper might do the trick."

Remi stood up and held out her hand. "Thanks, I owe you."

"You owe me nothing." Cain shook her hand and started for the door. "Does this change how you feel about her?"

"Not in the way you think. I've held back because I was wary of her, but now she's exactly what I hoped she'd be. If I'm lucky she needs me in her life just a little."

"I saw how she kept her eyes on you all through dinner. You don't have a thing to worry about."

CHAPTER FORTY-TWO

Remi passed the door of Dallas's room and paused before continuing to her favorite spot in the penthouse. With the lights off inside, the traffic on the river was easy to see, as was the skyline of the downtown area and the aquarium. Here, twenty floors up, she couldn't hear any noise from the Natchez Steamboat's organ or from the tourists milling around having a good time. The quiet in the midst of all the commotion let her think.

Since they'd gotten back from Cain and Emma's, Dallas had said little as she walked around and peered at the view. She seemed tired and withdrawn and hadn't wanted to talk after the conversation they'd had when they got home, so Remi had walked her to her room and told her good night. The one thing Dallas had accepted before Remi closed the door was a kiss and a long hug.

To get Dallas to trust her, Remi had done something highly unusual for her. She'd given Dallas a clear picture of who she was, and hadn't hidden behind innuendo or conjecture. If Dallas chose she could use the truth Remi had revealed to seriously damage her, but she couldn't expect Dallas to open up to her if she wasn't willing to do the same. She hadn't expected Dallas to answer her phone and clam up immediately afterward, though. She'd tried asking if she could help, but after their kiss Dallas had simply lowered her head and closed the door.

"Patience," Remi said softly to her reflection on the glass, "that's what Emma keeps preaching." From the pocket of her robe she retrieved her cigar clipper, opened the humidor sitting on the nearby table, and pulled out one of her favorite brands, ritualistically getting it ready to smoke.

For an instant, the darkness was broken by the powerful cigar lighter her father had given her, then blue smoke outlined in moonlight billowed over her head. She watched it rise and thought about Dallas and everything Cain had told her. Could she live with the truth of Dallas's choices? But who the hell was she to even consider judging her? Remi knew all about making difficult choices for the sake of taking care of her family.

The door of the guest bedroom opened quietly, and Dallas stepped out in bare feet, stopping at the end of the hallway, content to watch Remi smoke. She'd fallen asleep almost instantly when she lay down, wanting to escape the fear that had blossomed after she hung up with Kristen, but when her eyes opened again, something had energized her. The way Remi had so methodically laid out the truth meant they'd crossed some barrier Remi had mentally erected to keep her from getting too close. Dallas could imagine how her silence and sudden withdrawal had affected Remi. Most people interpreted silence as rejection, which was the last thing Dallas wanted.

As the smoke rings drifted slowly toward the ceiling she caught the slightest hint of the cigar, and while she'd never really cared for smoking, the aroma from the brand Remi was partial to wasn't unpleasant. The humidor's nearness to Remi told Dallas she sat here and smoked frequently. Taking a deep breath to settle her nerves, she walked until she stood in front of Remi, blocking her view. Remi's eyes roved slowly up and down, making Dallas feel like she'd been caressed.

That was exactly what Remi wanted to do—touch Dallas until she'd memorized every curve and inch of skin. Instead, she curled the fingers of her free hand until they pressed against her palm.

Dallas stepped closer, making Remi concentrate on the sway of her hips and how mesmerizing the movement was because of the long white silk nightgown.

"I thought I told you my feelings about smoking inside?" Dallas asked, placing her hands on the arms of Remi's chair. When she leaned forward in challenge, Remi had a delightful view down the low scoop neck.

Smiling up at Dallas she said, "I thought you meant inside your house."

As Remi began to take another drag, Emma plucked the cigar from Remi's fingers and ground it out in the ashtray next to the chair. "Inside means inside anywhere."

Dallas leaned in the final inches and kissed her until Remi was aware only of Dallas's lips against hers and her tongue pushing insistently against her own. The kiss ended when Dallas stood, and Remi froze as

Dallas lifted the soft silk enough so she could straddle her lap. When she got comfortable Dallas placed her palms under Remi's soft T-shirt and touched as much skin as she could reach, making Remi surmise she was trying to prove to herself this was real.

"I don't want you to give up something you love, but I want to take care of you, keep you healthy and happy so you'll be around for years to come. That's really important to me," Dallas said as Remi's hands slid up and under the pooled gown.

"What else do you want, besides limited smoking?" Remi asked.

"I want you." Dallas placed her hands on Remi's shoulders just under the neck of her T-shirt. "I'm sorry about how I handled tonight, but it had nothing to do with what you told me. What you said doesn't change how much I want to be with you. The truth of who you are is safe with me."

"I know that," Remi said, continuing upward under the silk gown, exposing more and more skin. She kept her eyes on Dallas's face until she raised the sleepwear over her head and dropped it to the floor. When Dallas was naked she gazed at her. She lifted her hand again to touch her, but stopped before she made contact. "You're so beautiful. Is it okay to touch you?" she asked out of respect for Dallas and their agreement to go slow.

"Please," Dallas said, and took a short breath when Remi circled her breasts, then drew an invisible line down her middle.

"Let's go somewhere more comfortable," Remi said as she helped Dallas to her feet.

Remi bent to get Dallas's nightgown and threw it over her shoulder. As she straightened, her robe opened further and Dallas tugged it off, dropping it and the nightgown.

"Leave it," she said.

The command made Remi forget about picking anything up except Dallas. They didn't exchange a word as she carried Dallas into the master suite and set her gently on her feet. Despite the room's fabulous view of the river and west bank because of the two walls of glass, Dallas's eyes never wavered from hers.

When Remi began to take off her T-shirt, she noticed Dallas finally glance around. She considered the room utilitarian, but she'd wanted to keep it simple, thinking the view was enough. When the shirt cleared her head, she saw Dallas looking at one of the two pieces of furniture.

The antique four-poster bed faced the windows and was a place she'd never shared with anyone until now.

"This room is a good reflection of you," Dallas said, and stepped right in front of her. "It's open," she whispered and stretched to reach Remi's neck with her lips while her hands stopped at the elastic of her boxers. With a good tug they fell to her ankles.

"You're incredible," Dallas said as she stood and stared.

Remi took advantage of Dallas's unfocused state to pick her up again and lay her on the bed. She lay next to her and wanted more than anything to touch Dallas but wanted to go slow, not because of their agreement, but because she wanted to savor their first time together.

Like a blind woman learning braille, Remi started at the crown of Dallas's head and moved her hand across her forehead to her cheek. Dallas closed her eyes when she reached her neck and pulled on the back of Remi's hair as she circled but didn't touch her nipples. When she continued southward, Remi flattened her hand on her stomach, inching down her legs until she reached the knee closest to her. That she lifted until Dallas draped her leg over her body, leaving her open to her touch.

She dipped her fingers past the hair that was more red than blond and found the evidence of Dallas's desire for her. "You are so wet," she said, making Dallas nod slowly as if she'd lost the ability to speak. "I'm glad we waited, but imagining you like this has made all that time difficult," Remi said as her middle and index finger caressed from Dallas's opening to just under her clitoris. There she opened them so they rested at the sides of the hard point and squeezed. Dallas lifted her hips and gasped in obvious pleasure.

Before Dallas could rock her hips, Remi again returned to her opening, wanting to keep her fingers wet. The more she touched Dallas, the more she chased Remi's fingers in whatever direction they headed, but then Remi stopped and coaxed Dallas on top of her and into a sitting position.

"You're stopping now?" Dallas asked, sounding breathless.

"I wouldn't define it as stopping," Remi said, falling back into the thick pillows to admire Dallas's flushed body. She ran her hands up the bare legs and reached Dallas's hips, then pulled her closer, encouraging Dallas to press her center to her middle. When she did, Remi pinched her nipples until Dallas moaned and pressed harder into her.

"If you want me, I'm yours," Dallas said as she leaned in and pressed their bodies together.

"You're mine now, and no one else will ever touch you like this, if I can help it."

The declaration seemed to double Dallas's wetness, and Remi gently rolled her to her back so she could cover as much of her as possible. She urged Dallas to spread her legs so she could fit her hand between them, but it wasn't enough.

Remi moved until her legs were hanging off the end of the bed, then ducked her head and ran her tongue from the wet opening to Dallas's clitoris. She smiled as Dallas's hips shot off the bed.

"Don't stop...don't stop," Dallas said as she ground herself into Remi's face. Then Remi inserted her fingers and curled them upward until she felt Dallas wrap intimately around them, almost willing Remi to be still for a moment as she reached the peak of her orgasm. Screaming Remi's name, Dallas fell back to the bed and tears rolled down her face, quickly turning into choking sobs.

Remi whipped her head up in confusion at the conclusion of what she thought Dallas wanted. She gently gathered Dallas into her arms. "I'm sorry. I didn't mean to hurt you." Remi kissed the top of her head and continued to whisper her apologies until finally Dallas's crying slowed a little.

With a rough voice, Dallas spoke but never lifted her head from Remi's chest. "You didn't hurt me, and I'm not sure you'll understand this, but this is the first time I've ever wanted someone to touch me."

Remi thought she was going to say more but Dallas stayed quiet. "Thank you for gifting me with that, and I'll do my best to deserve it."

"You probably deserve better, but thank you for not thinking I'm completely insane." Dallas wiped her face with the corner of the sheet Remi was offering her and laughed. "Not exactly living up to my image as someone who wants to do another action picture, am I? Becoming hysterical after something so wonderful isn't exactly sexy."

"You don't hear me complaining, do you?" Remi asked, as she playfully squeezed one side of her butt.

Dallas brought her hand between Remi's legs and smiled. "I don't see why you're not. You have every right to, judging from this."

"That you thought it was wonderful was all I need to know." Remi wiped away the last of her tears and kissed her. When Dallas pushed her into the pillows to return the affection, her knee pressed against Remi hard enough to make her moan.

"Something I can do for you?" Dallas asked, pressing into her again.

"If you want we can—" Remi couldn't finish when Dallas covered her mouth with her free hand.

"Let me show you how much I want to touch you in return," she told Remi before she kissed her one last time before heading to where Remi most needed her.

Remi instinctively grabbed a fist full of hair to keep Dallas from moving away when she put her mouth on her. "Right there, that feels so good," Remi said softly as Dallas quickened her pace, bringing Remi's orgasm on so fast she almost cried out in frustration as well as pleasure. Giving Dallas the same pleasure had left her more than primed.

When Remi was done, Dallas lifted her head and inched up until she had pressed her sex to Remi's hip.

"You feel okay?" Remi asked. She rolled Dallas onto her back again.

"I will if I get more of you."

Remi positioned herself so they were mound to mound and started to pump her hips into Dallas. "Do you want me to stop?" She held herself still until she saw Dallas shake her head. If that wasn't enough, Dallas spread her legs open as far as she could and pressed her heels into the small of her back.

The harder she pumped, the harder Dallas dug her nails into her back, until Remi felt the pressure building, begging for release.

"Yes, like that," Dallas said, her voice wavering because of the motion. As Remi sped her hips she felt Dallas press her heels down harder. "Oh God...I'm coming...coming again." Remi hung on until she felt Dallas tense and moan, her actions matching her words. Another climax so close to the first one left Remi drained, but she stayed put until Dallas opened her eyes and dropped her feet to the mattress.

When she did, Dallas's eyes and her hand rested at the top of Remi's right arm where it started to curve into her shoulder. Remi lay next to her as Dallas traced the outline of the tattoo she'd found.

"You're just full of surprises, aren't you?" Dallas asked as her finger continued to roam over the area. "What is it?"

"It's half of a snake head."

"Why just half?"

"Mano has the other half. Our nickname on the street is Snake Eyes, so we got inked as a joke, which my mother didn't exactly find amusing. When we're out doing a little gentle persuasion we wear sleeveless shirts to show our tattoos off. We try to stand shoulder to shoulder so the image that's our company logo is easier to see. Only on these, the pupils are dice in the *one* position as our tribute to our father's favorite game."

Remi kissed the tip of the finger Dallas had used before rolling off the bed to retrieve the blankets they had knocked to the floor.

"Would you be more comfortable if I went back to the guestroom?" Dallas asked.

"That isn't a serious question, is it?" Remi smoothed the covers over Dallas before taking her in her arms again. "I want you here. I want you to get a good night's sleep, and then I want to talk to you about where we go from here."

Dallas snuggled closer. "I feel almost selfish being this happy, because I realize I'm only going to complicate your life with all the crap I have in mine."

"We're going to work together to make your life as simple as possible, and we'll start in the morning. But you have to let me in and trust me. I'll wait until you're ready, if it's tomorrow or a year from now. Just promise me you won't disappear because you think you're doing me a favor."

"I'll be here until you tell me to go."

Remi tried to make her kiss show Dallas how much she cared. "Then it'll be forever before you go anywhere without me."

CHAPTER FORTY-THREE

Emma stood back as Cain finished reading Hannah a story. It was an hour past her regular bedtime, but Hannah had stubbornly kept her eyes open until Cain came upstairs. They made it through three-fourths of the book before Hannah was out for the night. The way Cain tucked the covers around Hannah and kissed her forehead made Emma sigh. Hannah was losing the haunted expression she often wore up North because she was afraid of doing something to make her grandmother unhappy.

"I love you," Emma said when Cain was close enough for her to put her arms around her waist.

"And I love you, lass." Cain placed her palms against her cheeks and kissed her. "Think we'll have another baby like that?"

"I'll tell you in a week or so." Cain closed the door and they strolled down the hall to their room. "Daddy started fixing the holes in our walls today."

"Did the guys finish sweeping?"

"We're bug-free at the moment, and they're going through again tomorrow with the new equipment Lou ordered." She turned around so Cain could unzip her dress. "On another subject, Remi looked pale when they left. What did you two talk about?"

"Dallas," Cain said, pulling the covers back since they were both naked. "I found what Remi asked me about."

"Which was?"

"Are you sure you want to know? I promised I wouldn't even tell her father."

When Cain clicked off the lamp the room went dark, the only light coming from under the bathroom door. "Is it something Remi can live with?"

"She'll have to." Cain pressed up against Emma's back. "She might not realize it, but she's in love with her."

Emma let the subject drop, knowing how Cain felt about breaking her word. She relaxed, listening to Cain breathing and the house settling, and hadn't realized she'd fallen asleep until the phone rang two hours later.

The receiver dropped from Cain's hand as she groped for it, and she cursed softly as she had to sit up to find it. She finally pressed it to her ear and said nothing as whoever was on the other line said something brief.

"Sorry for waking you, lass." Cain stood and went to into the bathroom.

"Who was that?" Emma rolled over with her eyes shut to keep from squinting.

"Katlin." Cain walked out still naked and headed for the closet. "I've got to go meet her, but I shouldn't be long."

"Just be careful, okay."

"You got it." Cain kissed her and pulled the blankets back up. "Go back to sleep."

The damp chill in the air made Cain glad she'd put on a sweater. Lou was already waiting for her outside the pool house. "Nice night for a chat, don't you think, Lou?"

"I was coming up to get you."

"Katlin called and woke me. What's going on outside?"

"The guys at the gate said the night crew's on. They changed when Remi pulled out."

They left a trail in the wet grass as they headed to the back of the yard. Jarvis had dug an exit, but with the light surveillance they didn't need to use it.

They scaled the wall and dropped to the neighbor's yard, virtually invisible in their dark clothing. Once they made it though the front gate, they walked two blocks to the car Lou kept parked on the street. He paid his nephew to move it a couple of times a week so no one would notice it.

"Where's Katlin?" Cain asked as she got into the passenger side.

"She didn't want to travel too much, so she's waiting for us at the Esplanade warehouse."

They drove aimlessly through the downtown area for twenty minutes before heading through the Quarter and into the Faubourg

Marigny neighborhood. With no tail, Lou made no more detours on the way to the storage warehouse Cain had owned for years. Only the deed was in Orlindo Adam's name. Considering he'd been dead since the 1980's, Cain figured he wouldn't mind as long as she paid his taxes on the property.

"It would be so much more convenient if we had these meetings in my office at home," Cain said as Lou drove to the back of the property and parked in the one covered spot. "Then I could throw on a robe and skip these late-night forays."

"Emma spent a month looking for the rug in there. She'd probably kneecap you if you messed it up," Lou said.

When Cain was upright she laughed and stretched, trying to wipe away the last of her grogginess. "Let's get going. I promised I wouldn't be long."

Katlin was sitting on the desk in the back office that at one time was probably the receiving manager's spot. The furniture had been left like it was, since Cain only wanted the place to store cases of wine. As shitty as the place appeared from the outside, including weeds growing in the cracks in the asphalt, the main space was totally climate-controlled.

The invoice Cain picked up read Brown's Dairy at the top, but the rest was too faded to read. "Where'd you find him?" she asked about the guy sitting in the chair staring down the barrel of Katlin's gun.

"Just have to know who to ask if you want to find somebody." When Lou stood behind the guy, Katlin put her gun away. "I asked the bellman at the Piquant."

"They gave him up? I thought they prided themselves on guests' privacy."

"I didn't ask about this clown. I asked where I could get the most authentic enchilada in town. Seems Pepe here likes the Taqueria Grill too."

"My name no is Pepe, bitch," Jesus said, then spit close to Katlin's shoe.

"What was he carrying?" Cain asked, ignoring Jesus for now and flipping through the wallet on the desk.

"Big man like Pepe needs a big gun." She pulled a forty-caliber pistol from her waistband.

"I say my name no is Pepe."

"What about it, Lou?" Cain asked. Jesus's ponytail swung back and forth as he swiveled his head, like he was trying to keep them all in sight. "Is it him?"

"Same hair, small build, same suit—I'm positive it's this guy."

Katlin handed Jesus's gun to Cain and stood next to Lou. "If he had friends with him when you saw him, Lou, they ditched him tonight. Pepe was enjoying his enchilada all alone."

"Bitch, you deaf or something? My name no is—" Jesus screamed so loud the veins at the side of his neck bulged. When Cain shot him he squirmed like a trout on a line.

"What's your name?"

"Pepe." He rocked in his seat but didn't lift his bleeding foot. "You call me Pepe if you want."

"I'm not interested in calling you anything, but I do want to know why you killed my man in the airport."

Jesus continued to rock and had started to sweat and pull at his hair, messing up his neat ponytail. "I know nothing what you talking about. Por favor, you believe me, I no there."

"Okay, calm down, I believe you. I'm sure Lou—" As Cain spoke, Lou stepped forward where Jesus could see him. "I'm sure Lou was wrong when he told me you were there, so let's try something else. Let's say you were there but you didn't have anything to do with what happened. You understand?" Cain asked, and Jesus nodded so fast he resembled one of those fake dogs with the bobbing head that people put in their cars. "Just tell me who did."

"I no there," he screamed, sounding beyond frustrated. When Cain pulled the trigger again, the gun sounded like a cannon, but Jesus's screams drowned out the echo. He wriggled in his chair like someone had hooked him to an electric current.

"Is your memory getting any better?" Cain asked him, raising her voice to be heard over his crying. "If it isn't, then maybe one here," she put the gun to his shin, "will improve it."

"It no was me, I swear…it…it was Oscar…Oscar Cardone. He kill that guy."

"See, you need the right persuasion," Cain told Lou. "I just have a few more questions so try and focus. What were you doing at the airport?"

"Senor Rodolfo, he send us, but Oscar go crazy and we have to go." Jesus's speech was becoming more rapid and he had to stop to throw up. "It hurt so bad."

"One more thing. Was Anthony Curtis there?"

"Who?" Jesus's eyes widened then shut as if he realized his mistake. When he opened his eyes again Cain's finger was moving back to press the trigger. "*Esperate.*"

The word "wait" was one of the few Cain recognized and she let the gun fall to her side. "It's late, Mr. Vega, and I'm tired. Not a good combination for you, so cut the crap."

"You know me?"

"Your mother might have named you Jesus," she did her best to pronounce it correctly, beginning the name with an *h*, "but she wasted it on you." She waved the wallet Katlin had taken from him in his face.

"Anthony, he was there."

"Were you all waiting for Juan Luis?" The gun was starting to feel heavy in Cain's hand as she bounced it against her thigh.

"Senor Rodolfo, he send us. I go where the patron say, and then Señor Anthony say kill that man, he see me."

The explanation was rough but understandable enough to Cain. She kept her eyes on Jesus as she handed Lou the gun. "You need me to stay?"

"I won't be long, but I want to finish and clean up. It's the least I owe Rick."

Cain picked up Jesus's wallet before leaving with Katlin. To get back to the house quicker, Katlin took the interstate, keeping two miles under the limit. The windows on the Tahoe SUV she'd taken out were tinted dark enough in the back that Cain made no attempt to get down as they drove past the van parked across the street from the gate. In the garage Cain waved to Katlin as she headed to the pool house for the rest of the night.

"Give Merrick my apologies for keeping you out so late."

"Sure thing," Katlin said, her voice sounding muffled as she walked away.

"Were you right or wrong?" Emma asked a short time later when Cain got back in bed.

"A little of both, I guess."

"Then more right than wrong, I hope."

Emma felt like warm silk against her skin. "Do you know why Napoleon lost his last war?"

"Honey, it's past three," Emma said with a trace of a whine.

"Supply chain. He stretched his troops too far for his supplies to reach the advanced divisions. No matter what the other theories are about the subject, that's my opinion."

"That's nice, and that has to do with tonight because?"

"I need to start figuring some of this out, or we're going to stretch ourselves too thin. There's no way to keep the feds on the other side of that fence and take down Nunzio Luca and the Luis family all at the same time, without falling short in one or more areas." Cain rolled onto her back and Emma went with her, covering half of Cain's body with hers.

"There's a way. You just haven't thought of it yet."

"Thanks, lass. It's nice to have someone who believes I know what I'm doing."

The room was still dark, but Emma obviously didn't have trouble finding Cain's lips. "I happen to think you're brilliant, but if you don't know what you're doing," she teased, "then leave me in the dark."

"That's a deal," Cain said, and laughed. Despite the hour she wasn't tired.

"Since we're both up, how about we have coffee and talk?"

"How'd you know I wasn't sleepy?"

Emma rubbed her stomach before she sat up. "I'm your wife, so I can tell the difference between alert and sleepy. Besides, if we get up now we can fit in a nap later today."

After Emma turned the coffee pot on, they sat together in the kitchen. Their hands were joined as they sat at the small table set in the bay window overlooking the gardens out back, and every so often they'd see one of the guards patrolling, leading a large German shepherd.

"Tell me what you know, mobster," Emma said.

"Which part?"

"Whichever part you think has the potential to do the most harm."

The coffee pot sputtered, signaling it was done, and Cain got up to fill the two cups Emma had set out with the added ingredients they liked. She picked them up and cocked her head in the direction of the sunroom. It was still three hours till sunrise, but they'd be more comfortable on the sofa.

"I had a talk with one of Rodolfo's men tonight, and he admitted to being at the airport with Anthony Curtis. According to him, Anthony ordered the group they were with to kill Rick because he'd seen them waiting for someone," Cain said. She was filling in the blanks for Emma, but by talking out loud she was seeing the information from a new viewpoint.

"Anthony ordered Rick killed?"

"If that was the case, my plan of action would be easy. No, Anthony's an ass but he's not dumb. He's playing some kind of twisted game of chicken, and at the airport the truck heading toward him creamed him." She put her cup down, then Emma's, so they could stretch out. "But Anthony's not out of this. He's hurt himself and is going to be more dangerous now."

Emma put her hand in Cain's robe and ran her fingers along her stomach again. "Why?"

"Because I don't believe he ordered anything, but he was there. He watched Rodolfo's dogs take Rick away and kill him. In Anthony's world that makes him culpable, and he knows that. But I don't think he's aware his employer knows he was there."

"That's the other thing I don't understand. Why was he there?"

"Jesus said Rodolfo sent them, but he didn't know for what."

Emma lifted her head and laughed. "Jesus told you? If you got to talk to him you should've asked better questions."

"Funny girl," Cain said, pinching one of her cheeks. "I don't buy that, but that's the story he stuck with no matter how many different ways I asked."

"How do you find out the truth? Ask the Virgin Mary?"

Cain had to laugh at that one. "You need more sleep if you're this punchy, but to answer your question, I see only one way. I'm going to ask Rodolfo as soon as I get a meeting with him."

"He'd just tell you?"

"Probably not, but I want to send him a message that he has a mutiny brewing in his house." Cain helped Emma up and put her arm around her shoulders.

"It's me, baby. Could you not be so cryptic?"

"The rabid dog he's been feeding and training all these years has finally decided to break his leash and bite his master. Anthony wasn't at the airport on Rodolfo's orders—he was there at Juan's. I think he's back and Anthony is with him." Cain smoothed the blankets over them and opened her arms to Emma once they were settled in the bed. "You wanted to know what could harm us the most. If I'm right, it'd be that."

"And if it really was Rodolfo?"

"If it was him I'm going to feed him that shit he sells until he chokes on it, then ship him back to Mexico in a crate of bananas to give his nephew a hint of what'll happen to him if he comes back here."

Emma rested her head in the bend of Cain's shoulder and kissed the side of her neck. "See, and you said you didn't have a plan."

CHAPTER FORTY-FOUR

"Where are you going?" Dallas asked from under the covers. She watched Remi walk out of the bathroom toward the bed, her hair wet from a shower. "After last night you're supposed to be in here with me."

"Can I tell you how good you look in sheets?" Remi joined her when Dallas held up the blanket.

"You smell nice." Dallas went willingly when Remi took her in her arms. "If you'd woken me up, I could've helped you get that way."

"What's wrong?" Remi combed Dallas's hair behind her ear and kissed her. "I'm sorry I got up without you."

"That usually means you didn't—"

Remi stopped her from saying anything else by kissing her again, only this time longer and more passionately. "I wake up early every day no matter what's going on, and since I'm a little ADD, I get restless. You looked so peaceful I didn't want to disturb you, but last night was wonderful."

"You're not sorry?"

"So sorry that I want us to repeat it tonight." Remi ran her thumb along Dallas's lips. "It doesn't have anything to do with sex, but everything with having you here with me."

"Can we have that talk today?" The night before, Dallas had lain in Remi's arms, and it had felt so good she came close to crying again. But like Remi said, it had nothing to do with sex. For once she felt safe enough to simply put her head down and rest. With Remi, the last thing she wanted to do was leave.

"Cain called and I've got to head out for a meeting, but I had Juno clear the rest of my day so we can talk." Remi ran her hands down Dallas's back to her butt, then lifted her closer. "While I'm gone I want you to do me a favor."

"What?" When Remi lay flat on her back Dallas was happy to spread her legs and straddle Remi's waist. The new position let her lick Remi's nipple, getting it wet. She blew on it and it puckered. "What can I do for you?" Her question had more to do with other kinds of favors, if Remi was interested.

"Make your Christmas list early." Remi's voice cracked on the last word as Dallas repeated her action on the other breast. "When I come back, I want you to tell me what you want changed in your life that would make you happy."

Dallas sat up and smiled. In the daylight she could see Remi's face and how much desire it held for her, but she saw more. Not only lust shone in the uniquely different colors of blue and green, that kind of caring was the biggest turn-on Dallas had experienced in her short life. And it evidently drove Remi's need to free her from whatever haunted her.

"When you come back?" Dallas asked as she rocked against Remi's lower abdomen, guaranteeing she'd need another shower. "I'll do whatever you like." She eased down and kneeled between Remi's legs. "But you need to come right now." She thought her play on words was lost as Remi moaned instead of laughed.

They touched, but their union was different in the light of day. It was still hungry, yet it felt like nothing Dallas had shared with anyone. For the first time she experienced what it was like for someone to make love to her. Remi touched her like someone who cared about her pleasure because she cared about her. Remi didn't want to possess her, but to express how much she wanted her in and out of bed.

As they stood in the shower together, Remi held her under the spray and kissed every part of her face with soft, gentle movements. "You know," she said when she kissed a spot over Dallas's left brow, "if you keep crying every time we do that," she moved to the right one, "I'm going to develop a complex."

"I wish I could explain it better, but I promise, you're not doing anything wrong. You're doing everything so right I'm having a hard time processing it." Dallas leaned back and ran her fingers along Remi's collarbone. "Does that make sense?"

"You make perfect sense."

They finished showering and Dallas borrowed Remi's robe to head into the kitchen. Surprisingly, the sight of Emil sitting at the counter having coffee and reading the paper didn't startle her as much as she would've thought. He was polite and pointed out where the mugs were so she could pour two cups of coffee. He stopped her as she started back.

"I almost forgot." He held up a small gift bag. "I don't know if Remi mentioned it, but I've got a hobby."

Dallas blinked a few times but stayed quiet as her brain flipped through the possibilities of what Emil would find fun, considering he looked like a brick wall. Granted, he appeared to have broken his nose a couple of times, and he had a small collection of scars on his face, one thick one that ran though his left brow, but it somehow made him seem more genuine.

"Is that for me?" Dallas asked.

"I thought you'd like it."

For such a big guy Emil had a soft voice. Dallas put the cups down and accepted the bag. Inside was a wide tan alligator belt with his name stamped in small letters on the inside next to the buckle.

"You made this?" she asked, getting a shy nod. "It's beautiful, thank you." Even though he was sitting she still had to tiptoe to kiss his cheek. "I love it." To her astonishment he nodded again and blushed.

"Morning, Emil," Remi said as she entered the kitchen. "That color looks nice on you." She pointed to his face.

"Leave him alone. You can't tease a man who comes bearing gifts."

"If you sweet-talk him while I'm gone, maybe he'll make you a matching pair of boots." Remi lifted her foot to show off her usual footwear. The black boots matched the pair Emil, Mano, and her father had. "You two relax and I'll be back in a couple of hours." Remi kissed Dallas at the door, then stopped a floor down to pick up Simon.

Cain had called that morning and wanted to review a few things she needed her and Mano to take over. She knew Mano had been working closely with Muriel to keep Richard in their sights until they closed the casino deal. Nunzio might have owned it, but it wasn't his signature they needed when it came time.

"We're not going to the house?" Remi asked when Simon turned right toward the Quarter.

"Cain's at the Pescador with your father. She said she had an outing last night and needs a meet with Rodolfo."

"She wants us there?"

"The last thing Cain Casey needs is a backup or someone to hold her hand. She wants your father to set it up since he knows Rodolfo better. If she has to talk to him, it's about Juan, and neither of them have anything to do with us."

Remi rested her hand on the top of her boot, since she'd pushed the front passenger seat all the way back so she could cross her legs. "I wouldn't mind going to do both, if she asked. I've enjoyed working with her. Cain's got a lot to teach."

At a light Simon glanced at her. "That's what you have Ramon for."

"True, and his advice is priceless."

The careful way she said that must have been why Simon laughed. "But? I have a feeling that's what you were going to say next."

"Papi has been a great teacher, but he teaches Mano and me to do things the way he would do them. He told me when he decided on these mergers with Cain that I should pay attention, and I have. Cain might've lost Dalton but she's sharp. She's had to learn the business on her own, using the foundation he gave her, but you can tell she's made it grow and get stronger."

"Uh-huh." Simon slowed as they turned on the block where Ramon's club was located. "When Dalton was killed, your father and Vincent both waited for her to fail or ask for help, which in their eyes would've been the same thing. Cain proved herself, though, by walking through fire to keep her organization together. I admired her for that, and I think Vincent did too. You know your father did, or he wouldn't be dealing with her at all."

"I think he knows something I figured out when I attended Dalton's funeral. No matter what happens in this city, Cain's too smart not to survive. If there's a war, the smartest play is to be on her side, no matter what the other guy offers you, because when the dust settles she'll give you just enough time to see death coming. It's that kind of thinking that Papi respects."

There was space reserved for them out front, and Katlin waved to them as Simon started to parallel park. Across the street a news crew was interviewing what Remi assumed were the new owners of the building being renovated on the corner. When the car stopped she took her sunglasses off and threw them on the dash, not wanting to have to carry them.

She opened her door as Simon opened the driver's side, and as soon as she stood up straight something flashed momentarily, making her glance up and to the right.

The single shot from the high-powered rifle was so deafening that everyone on the street stopped what they were doing. Simon heard Remi slam into the side of the car from the force of the impact. The scene seemed surreal to Simon as she watched Remi go down from a single shot that had hit her square in the chest. She ran without thinking to the other side of the car to see if she was alive, not caring that it put her in the line of fire. Katlin had drawn her gun and was scanning the area across from them, trying to spot the shooter.

"Oh my God," Simon heard the reporter across the street scream as the cameraman moved closer. "Who's that?"

"Katlin, help me," Simon ordered. Working together they picked Remi up and laid her across the back seat. "Tell Ramon," was all she could get out before she jumped behind the wheel and took off.

❖

The television on the security guard's desk was on as Emil and Dallas returned to Remi's building after a trip to the grocery store. When Dallas heard the woman say the name Remington Jatibon, she turned her head toward the TV. Next to her Emil stopped and looked too as the small screen cut to the front of the Pescador Club. The woman reporter was going on about the tragedy they'd caught on tape, and Dallas started to shake her head as a feeling of dread washed over her.

"Remington Jatibon, daughter of reputed mob boss Ramon Jatibon, was gunned down this morning as she stepped out of a car in front of the Pescador Club. Jatibon was taken down by a single gunshot. She never had a chance, as you can see from the footage." The picture changed to the one of Remi looking up, and then just as quickly she was on the ground. "With one single shot one of the more colorful lives in corporate America comes to an end. The family has offered no comment so far, but we will keep you informed." The talking head droned on while the shot played repeatedly.

"This can't be happening," Dallas said, having to hang on to Emil to keep herself on her feet.

"Come on, Dallas, we can't stay down here." Emil dropped the bags and practically dragged Dallas to the elevator.

"You want these sent up, Emil?" the security guy asked.

"Call for Juno and she'll take care of it." Once the doors closed, he put in the key for the penthouse floor, then held on to Dallas. She was glassy-eyed but seemed in shock rather than grieving. "Once we get upstairs I can make some calls and find out what's going on, but you have to hang in there. This isn't a good time to give up."

"She's not coming back," Dallas repeated, as if she were trying to convince herself it was true.

As they entered the penthouse, Dallas's cell phone rang and she answered it without checking to see who it was, thinking it could be news about Remi. "Hello."

"Have you been in front of a television today?" Bob asked. "If not, let me be the first to give you the good news. The dyke is dead and I want you back in the house by this afternoon, if you know what's good for you. I told you, sweetheart, we're partnered for life and no one can come between us."

Dallas dropped the phone and barely noticed as it broke in two when it hit the marble floor. She made it as far as the sofa before she collapsed and started crying.

Emil watched her and forgot about his calls, opting to sit with her and hold her. Since Dallas was pressed to his chest she never saw the tears that spilled down his face for the loss he was sure would destroy both Ramon and Marianna, but especially Ramon. His boss had been gifted with two wonderful children, but Remi held a special place in his heart.

Now that place was dark, and Emil was sure it would die away, taking Ramon with it.

❖

"Send the money. It's done right where you wanted it. Ramon should be able to give a proper farewell." Jorge Cristo spoke into the prepaid, untraceable cell phone. He was parked on Canal Street, studying the map from the car he'd rented in Houston. Knowing someone might be waiting on his arrival, he had landed in Texas a couple of days early and driven in.

"I'll wire it this morning, and since I'm getting to watch it on television, I might throw in a bonus." Nunzio watched the smug face on the screen contort with pain again. He had to remember to send the reporter some flowers for having the good fortune to be standing there when it all went down. If his father needed proof, he'd e-mail him the evidence. Watching Remi die on the news was as satisfying as good sex.

Getting a blow job while watching the bitch die again and again wasn't all that bad either. He put his hand on the back of Kim's head and pulled on her hair to get her to slow down. "Take it easy, babe, I want to enjoy this." He pressed the play button on the remote and watched Remi fly into the car in slow motion.

All he had to do was wait a few days for Ramon and Cain to get through the funeral, then make the deal. If Ramon refused, little sweet Mano would be next. He wondered how he could get that on tape as well, if it came down to having to call on Jorge for an encore.

"Oh yeah," he said as Kim sucked harder just as Remi's head turned upward in slow motion. "This is better than fucking to porn."

CHAPTER FORTY-FIVE

I want that hijo de puta's head on a pike," Ramon screamed as Katlin holstered her weapon.

"Ramon, you need to sit down," Cain said from behind the bar. As soon as Katlin had told them what had happened, Cain had watched the furor rise in Ramon, his face reddening and his chest heaving as if he couldn't get enough air in his lungs. "I'm sure she's fine. You need to stay calm when you call Marianna. Drink this, it'll help."

"She's fine?" The way he laughed, Cain was afraid he wanted to hit something, and she would have been as good as anything. "Didn't you hear what Katlin said? The bastard shot her in the middle of the chest. Since we know who pulled the trigger, it's almost certain it was through the heart."

"I considered that possibility and had Mano take care of something. You have to trust me." The phone rang, interrupting what Cain was saying, and since Ramon still appeared to be in no state to talk, she picked it up. "Marianna," she said, then took the receiver away from her ear. "What?" Cain searched behind the bar for the remote control. "Stop watching and call Mano to come sit with you. I'll have Ramon home soon."

She pointed the remote at the television Ramon kept on during sporting events for people who'd bet on the games. The station Marianna had told her about had returned to regular programming, and Cain was relieved Ramon would be spared for now. Later in the day it'd be the lead story, and he'd have to face the ugliness of what had happened.

As she went back to explain why she'd stopped to watch television, the phone rang again. Cain picked it up and listened to Ramon's employee from downstairs. "Stop them at the door and I'll be down in a minute. Whatever you do, don't let them anywhere near the stairs. Cops love situations like this to get into places they're not wanted."

"What now?" Ramon asked.

"Katlin, get down there and keep the cops company," Cain said first. "I'm sure the 911 system lit up like a Christmas tree after that cannon shot, and the city's finest is on the case. They're here and they want answers, since Simon hasn't shown up at any of the local hospitals."

"Why would she?" Ramon asked. He sounded like the rage had burned itself out and despair was starting to seep in.

"Ramon, go home and sit with your wife and leave this to me. I'll deal with the cops, but before you go, give me Simon's number." She dialed the number he gave her and it rang three times before Simon answered. "Tell me."

Ramon stood right in front of her and put his hand on the arm Cain was using to hold the receiver to her ear. "We're headed to the spot we talked about," Simon said.

"Talk to Ramon," Cain said, and handed him the phone.

Ramon listened to Simon and his legs buckled. The phone slipped from his hand and he fell against Cain, sobbing. "Call me when you get there," Cain told Simon before hanging up. To Ramon she said, "Get home and don't make Marianna wait for you any longer than necessary."

Cain took a deep breath and headed downstairs to give the cops as little information as possible. What had happened was over, and there was nothing for them to investigate. She'd take care of that. She walked down the stairs slowly to take in the bottom floor and see who'd drawn the short straw of getting the case assigned to them.

The group assembled around Katlin had their backs to her, making it hard to recognize the detectives. Since Katlin was her height, Cain was surprised to see the white-haired cop standing so close he could've head-butted Katlin. Obviously he liked to use his height to intimidate, a tactic lost on Katlin, who stood with her arms crossed and a smile on her face.

"If you have a problem with anything, take it up with my boss," Cain heard Katlin say when she was close enough.

"Then get their ass down here," the cop said. The voice stopped Cain on the last step since, while it was deep and rich, it was definitely not male.

"The ass is here, but you know me better than that, to have such a low opinion of me," Cain said.

Detective Sept Savoie turned around and put her hands on her hips. The straight cut of the light gray jacket did a good job of hiding anything that would give away her gender. Smart for her choice of career, thought Cain as she walked over to her.

"Cain, it's been awhile," Sept said, holding her hand out. "I'd love to catch up on old times, but I need to talk to someone in the Jatibon family." Sept spoke in a no-nonsense way.

"Sept, you were the same on the playground in kindergarten. You think if you bark loud enough someone will give you whatever you like, but that's not possible right now. You can talk to me or you can sit down here and wait until the family's available—your choice."

"Our friendship doesn't mean anything right now. This is official police business. Get Ramon down here or I'll have a team of cops here in less than ten minutes and take this place apart, including all those nice slot machines nobody wants to admit are up there."

"Ooh, forceful," Cain said as she pulled out her phone. "Muriel, yes, I'm already here. Be here in less than five minutes. Don't let me down. We're under the gun since they've sent in Wyatt Earp." The comment made Sept's almost black eyes narrow to slits.

"It's Detective Savoie, jackass," Sept said with a smile that made her appear sarcastic without trying. "And you haven't changed all that much from the playground either. You always thought if you make enough smart comments, you can get away with anything."

"Calm down, Sept. There's a huge line ahead of you trying to get me, and I'm sure you're as good as the feds."

"Do you have any idea where Remi Jatibon's body is?"

"No, I don't," Cain held up her fingers, "Scout's honor."

"You do realize she's been shot?" Sept said, stepping into Cain's comfort zone.

Cain had to cock her head back to make eye contact, but she smiled instead of showing any fear. To make Sept back down first, Cain moved forward in the little bit of room left until the tips of their shoes touched. "I've known since someone told me they watched it on television. What are you doing here instead of trying to find the asshole who actually shot her? Isn't that the way it usually works? Someone shoots someone else and the cops go after the one with the gun, not the one who took the bullet. Why are you wasting time trying to harass the Jatibons or slow dance with me instead of giving them justice?"

"I already know how to do my job, but thanks for the advice. Do you know how I can get in touch with Ramon Jatibon?"

"If you have a court order, it shouldn't be a problem to get him to come to the door. Since you won't get off your obsession to bother the Jatibons right now, you can wait outside," Cain said, and stopped smiling. "Good seeing you again, and tell your mother I said hello. At least she has a sense of humor, but I have a soft spot for people with absolutely none."

"My sense of humor's fine," they all turned around when Muriel came in, "when I find something funny," Sept said. "The day we finally put you away, I'll be giddy. I'll come over and play poker with you every so often, since I'll know where to find you." With a flick of her wrist she signaled for her partner to get going. "This isn't over."

"For once we agree on something."

Katlin waited until they left before looking at Cain. "Now what?"

"Now we light a candle and contact the spirit of Remi."

Katlin laughed. "You know Ramon looked mad enough to kill, so you might want to tone down the humor."

"You have to have a little faith, Cousin." Cain considered how to get out of there and lose the locals as well as the feds. "Let's take a walk."

"Not on your life," Lou said. "There's some nut out there with a scope."

"The nut finished what he came to do. The fact that he was early means I have to put my shit on hold and deal with this. We're walking, but not out that door," she said, meaning the front door. "I'm sure the feds have the back covered, but we're going out that way."

The back alley was deserted, but Cain could hear the sirens getting closer. She wasn't worried about the cops now, even if they did manage to push Muriel aside. It would take them a week to cut through the door Ramon had installed to protect the secrets of the second floor. His friends within the police department would come through way before then.

Cain had a lot to do but decided to start with the one person everyone else had forgotten about. Remi's relationship with Dallas was still in its infancy, but Dallas didn't deserve the pain she was in. She took her phone from the inside pocket of her jacket and dialed without looking at the pad. "Emma, meet me at Remi's as soon as you can manage it, but tell Merrick I want a wall around you from the minute you leave the house."

"You okay, honey?"

"I'm fine. Just thinking about my supply chain."

❖

It seemed like hours had passed since they heard the news, but Emil and Dallas were still sitting together on the sofa. Dallas felt drained, but she stood up and headed for the room Remi had put her in when she'd first come over. She looked from the hall to the front door and wondered how a day that had started so great had completely blown up in misery.

"Do you want me to get you something?" Emil asked.

"I need a ride home," Dallas said as she tried to think if she'd left anything in Remi's room.

"You need to hold up on that, but if you'd feel better going home I'm coming with you."

"Mr. Jatibon will surely want you back with him. Now that this has happened, there's no reason for you to stay." Her lip trembled as she tried to smile. His presence was comforting, but he also reminded her of Remi. Jealousy coursed through her when she thought of how much more time Emil had spent with Remi than she had.

"You only met Ramon once, but if you don't want me to get fired for leaving you alone, you'll accept that I'm staying with you. Remi's wishes are still in effect. You were special, and if something happens to you, that would—"

"What, kill her?" Dallas asked, but the words tasted like bile in her mouth. "That's already a reality, as much as I don't want it to be true."

"Come on." Emil put his arm around her and walked her to Remi's bedroom. "Try and get some sleep, and when you're up for it, we'll come up with a plan we'll both be happy with."

"I'm sorry for being so much trouble, but I don't think I can sleep." She got into bed anyway and Emil sat on the edge.

"Then close your eyes. I swear it'll make you feel better."

She grabbed his wrist as he started to leave. "How could this have happened?"

"That's what I don't understand. Remi knew what was coming, and even though it was early, she should've been more prepared. She's Ramon's child, and he knew she'd outshine him. Remi was smarter, savvier, and more vicious than Ramon, but she seldom showed that side. She understood the life's dangers, but whoever ended her life like this took the coward's way out."

"I wish I'd done a better job of telling her how I felt about her while she was here. I kept putting it off because I was afraid, and now it's too late."

Emil held her hand between his, and the differences in their sizes were so great, Dallas felt like an infant. "I think she knew. She told me to watch over you because you meant something to her. Do you know how incredible that is? Remi never let any woman get close. She loved very sparingly, but she didn't want you out of her sight for long. That had something to do with keeping you safe, but there was so much more."

"Thanks for saying that."

He stood up and nodded. "Get some rest, but call me if you need anything."

Emil left the door open so he could hear her if she did need him, but he kept going until he reached the sliding glass door out to the balcony. He wanted to call Ramon, but he didn't want Dallas to think he was anxious to leave. As he was about to dial, the elevator rang announcing a visitor. Cain and Emma walked in, followed by a distraught Juno.

"Lass, why don't you take Juno into the kitchen and make her some tea," Cain told Emma. When Emma looped her arm with Juno's, Cain put her arms around both of them. "Juno, I swear on my family that everything will be all right."

"It'll never be that way again. I've known Remi from the day she was born. She's like my own, and now this." She cried against Cain's chest, and Emma moved out of the way. "And I'm so worried about Simon. I haven't heard from her."

"Emil," Cain said, still holding Juno, "could you get Dallas in here. I've got news you all want to hear." Flanked by Emma and Juno, Cain led them to the kitchen where Juno told Emma where to find everything to make tea. Dallas fell immediately into Emma's arms, and Emma held her as she cried.

"Honey, you need to sit and listen to Cain or you'll make yourself sick," she told Dallas.

"I'm sorry you all had to watch that on television today," Cain said. "It was a fluke, but that can't be helped now."

"You said you had news," Emil said.

"Ramon and I talked to Simon earlier, and she's fine," Cain said for Juno's benefit. "She went to the one place I thought no one would think to look, and the one place you wouldn't appear out of place going to," she said to Dallas.

"Where is she?" Emil said, his face a clear picture of confusion.

"At Dallas's house in the French Quarter. Are you packed, Dallas?"

"I'm sure Remi would want her to stay here," Emil protested, and Juno nodded.

"What Remi's going to want when she wakes up is to see Dallas, Juno, and you. That way when you report back to Marianna that her baby's bruised but definitely breathing, she won't think you're insane."

"She's alive?" Dallas asked. She let go of Emma and grabbed Cain by her arms and shook her. "Is she?"

"We planned for the shooting, but not for the television coverage. She's alive, and I'm sorry you went through the pain of watching something that made you think otherwise. After seeing it I think it'll only help us, since it's so convincing."

"How do you figure?" Emil asked.

"Nunzio Luca hired someone to kill her, and according to the news he did that. If Remi's dead to the world, there's no reason for this guy to try again. Having Remi out of sight for a while will help us deal with Nunzio, and help find this Jorge Cristo who pulled the trigger. Nothing helps you relax like success."

"She's alive," Dallas repeated, but not as a question this time.

"She is, and in need of some TLC. Go pack, just to give the appearance of going home, in case someone's watching." Cain sent Dallas to the other side of the house with Emma.

"There's always someone watching, the bastards," Emil said.

"Simon's over there, but as soon as you get there she'll be leaving, since Ramon's going to need her help. You need to keep everyone out of there, Emil, including Dallas's manager Bob. Dallas and Remi haven't been seen together enough for you to worry about the cops, but if Bob finds out she's alive, the jig is up."

"I'll kill the slime myself before that happens."

"If you take that pleasure away from Remi, she'll never forgive you."

Dallas came back with her bag hanging from her shoulder, which Emil promptly took from her. "I'm ready, let's go."

"Emil, you heard the lady," Cain said. "Go on, and tell Remi she'd better keep out of sight until I call her. If she needs anything, we'll do it through Juno and Simon, but her ass doesn't move."

"Don't worry. If she won't listen to me, I'll find a way to smuggle Marianna in to deal with her," Emil said. "Having Dallas there is all the incentive she'll need to lay low."

"Dallas, again I'm sorry for putting you through this," Cain said.

Dallas kissed her cheek. "I have a chance to tell her how I feel, so you don't have anything to be sorry for."

Juno kissed her too before she followed Emil and Dallas out, leaving Cain alone with Emma. Katlin, Lou, Merrick, and the others were in the lobby.

"You know something, mobster?" Emma wiped Cain's cheek free of lipstick.

"What's that, my love?" Cain sat in one of the kitchen chairs and encouraged Emma to sit on her lap. After this she had to arrange a meeting with Rodolfo, and she wanted to enjoy the stillness of Remi's home with her wife before she bothered.

"Don't ever think of giving me a hard time about playing matchmaker again."

She laughed. "Why's that?"

"You fraud, you damn well know why. You've done everything you can to bring them together." Emma ran her fingers along her jawline before kissing her. "You're sweet."

"I've known Remi a long time, and after seeing them together, I was sure it was right. Up to now that's only happened to me once—when I saw the picture that guy took of us at Vincent's place. The way we were looking at each other made me realize that I had found my one and only love." They kissed again, then sat together until Cain's phone rang.

"I know you have to go, but remember one thing," Emma said, after Cain hung up with Katlin.

"Name it."

"I see or hear of you getting shot and there'll be hell to pay. Stay safe."

"Go home and I'll join you in a couple of hours."

CHAPTER FORTY-SIX

"Hola." Carlos Santiago answered the phone in Rodolfo's suite.

Rodolfo had been working the phones trying to find Nunzio or Junior Luca, but had come up empty. He was used to having people jump when he barked, so being ignored had left him in the mood to take it out on the people who still did listen to him, Carlos included.

"Who's calling?"

In the chair Rodolfo found most comfortable he gestured to Carlos to tell him who it was.

"A moment, Ms. Casey, and I'll see if he's available." Carlos put his hand over the mouthpiece and said, "It's Cain for you."

"Cain, what can I do for you?" he asked after ripping the phone away from Carlos.

"I need to arrange a meeting whenever you can spare the time. Tomorrow, if it's possible."

"How about here in the hotel?"

Cain laughed. "I'm already popular enough with the FBI. I don't need the DEA added to my alphabet soup. We can meet at my office if you want. I'll have someone pick you up."

"I'm an old man who's lived long enough to know not to go to dangerous places."

"We can make it someplace neutral if you like. I'd offer Ramon's place, but he's mourning the loss of his child. If you come to my office, we'll be able to talk freely, and I guarantee your safety."

"Send directions to my man Carlos and I'll be there," Rodolfo said as he stared at Carlos. "I have your word, and you have mine that I had nothing to do with what happened to Remi. If that's what you wish to discuss, I don't have any information."

"That's not why I need to talk to you. Until tomorrow," Cain said and hung up.

"Are you sure you want to do that?" Carlos asked as Rodolfo tapped the receiver against his chin.

"She gave her word on our safety, and to Cain that still means something. This isn't about threats or business, and I'm curious. The last person I expected to hear from today is Casey. She isn't the type to ask me for anything, so this has to do with either Juan or the Lucas." Rodolfo put the phone down and stripped off his jacket, since he wasn't planning to leave the suite until the morning. "Speaking of which, have you gotten Juan on the phone yet?"

"I tried the house again an hour ago and he's still not there. He's probably in the apartment downtown sulking for being sent home like a child."

The information only darkened Rodolfo's mood. "You sure this line is safe?"

"Nunzio's men checked it again today."

Rodolfo dialed the number to his house in Cozumel and asked the maid for his sister. "Gracelia, where's your son?"

"I don't get a hello?"

"You'll get thrown out of my house and off my bankroll if you don't answer my question. Where is he?"

"He said he needed some time alone. That's all he said when I saw him."

"You're sure you saw him and didn't just talk to him on the phone?" Rodolfo asked in a tone that dared her to lie.

"He's back, if that's what you're worried about. You should worry about how to get him to trust you again, after you humiliated him."

"Try your best to stay away from the coke and find him. You have two days."

"You can't blame me this time. He's gone because of you—you find him."

"I told Juan what it would take to stay in my good graces, and he pulls this. If you want me to find him I will," Rodolfo said, cracking his knuckles, "but if it comes to that, neither of you will like the outcome."

"You can't touch him and you know why."

"I've given him everything and he repays me with nothing but disrespect. Maybe it's time for both of you to learn how hard it is to make a living in this world." Gracelia was screaming something as he hung up.

"He's still not at the house?" Carlos asked.

"No, and my gut is telling me he's about to screw up this deal."

"If you give me permission to handle it, I'll send some guys to all the places he probably is. If they find him, I'll order them to escort him back."

"Do it. Find Juan before his stupidity destroys us."

❖

"Who?" Juan watched the afternoon news, the footage of Remi dominating the coverage.

Anthony sat, his eyes on the screen, so restless he felt like peeling off his skin. Instead of being in the middle of the investigation, he was stuck with Juan as the idiot made plans he wouldn't share. It had taken Anthony awhile, but he finally spotted the surveillance outside. The DEA carried out their operations differently, but they were still visible if you knew what to look for.

"I don't know. Considering it was Remi Jatibon, there's a long list of possibilities," he answered Juan. The loop they had the TV story on had gotten boring, so he stood up and cracked the curtain just a hair to scan the grounds in front of the hotel. The agent was sitting at the café on the corner pretending to read a book. Different guy, but he was still third in the lineup in the shifts. Unless you were trained to see patterns, you'd miss him.

"That's another bitch who should've learned to stay home and bake cookies."

"Things are going to get tight from a law-enforcement standpoint." Anthony came close to ripping the curtains off the hooks when he saw Joe walk up and join the DEA guy at the café. His being there had nothing to do with Juan and everything to do with him. "We have to get out of here."

"What are you talking about? You going crazy on me or something?"

"Look down there and tell me what you see."

"I don't see anything," Juan said, peering through the crack Anthony allowed him. "You break into my stash or what?"

Anthony let go of the drapes and put his hand on the box Juan was talking about. The teakwood had lotus flowers carved into it and resembled the jewelry box Anthony's grandmother had. But his grandmother kept the few pieces of jewelry she owned in hers, whereas Juan's was full of high-quality cocaine that he shared with his friends.

"The guy in the white T-shirt is DEA, and the other one's name is Joe Simmons. I used to work with him."

"How'd they know we're here?"

"Because you people travel in packs so it's not hard to track you. You couldn't trust me to pick you up, so the idiots you had meet me there ended up doing something to someone who works for Cain. That's not exactly the definition of laying low." He picked up his car keys, wanting to get away from Juan and think. The more time they spent together, the stupider he was becoming. "Did they fess up to what exactly they did?"

"We didn't hear about anything in the airport." Juan waved his finger between them. "You people can't help but splash your business in the news, and there was none from that day. Nothing happened."

"When it's blatant like today, that's true. But not when there are enough cops to contain it and it's to our advantage. But hey, what do I know?" Anthony hit his chest with his fists. "You're the guy with all the answers and I say, have at it." He opened the door to the room and the sound of the hammer on a gun cocking stopped him cold. With his hands up and out, Anthony turned around.

The desk drawer was open and Juan was aiming a 357 magnum at his chest. "You leave when I say you can fucking leave. You understand?"

"If you aim it you'd better be prepared to use it, and if you kill me—"

"What, I'm going to get in trouble for killing an FBI agent?" Juan closed his eyes momentarily when he laughed, but not long enough for Anthony to tackle him.

His question had him, though. He could stay and keep pretending, or he could admit why he was really here and get rewarded for his honesty with a bullet that could cut him in two. "I can't help you if you won't let me. If you don't want my help, then why the hell am I here?"

"Sit down," Juan said, "and close the door." The box's hinges made no noise when Juan opened it. He scooped a bit of the white powder onto the sight of his pistol and snorted it off before dipping his finger in and scrubbing it along his teeth. The drug, Anthony guessed, was what made him shake like a wet dog.

This behavior had surprised Anthony. He'd thought people like Juan sold this stuff but were smart enough not to partake. That was a myth. Juan and his men were all hooked, and the level of the box never went down.

"Do you need something?" Anthony closed the door and sat down as far to the left as he could to have a chance of reaching for his gun, if it came to that. "You haven't up to now. Between making jokes about me and whispering with your friends, you've got it all under control. There's no need for me to be here."

"You know why I haven't told you my plans?"

"Considering all I've given up to help you, I'd love to hear it." Anthony crossed his legs and clamped his mouth closed, trying to keep down the nausea as he watched Juan dip the tip of the gun into the cocaine again. He silently wished Juan just needed another hit.

"You with me, Mr. FBI, or you with G.I. Joe on the corner?" Juan neared and pointed the barrel under Anthony's nose. "You want me to let you really work for me?" He pressed the barrel to the skin of his upper lip. "Then show me you're with me."

Of all the things that could've popped into Anthony's head, his talk with Annabel Hicks came to the forefront of his mind. The Bureau always knew what you did wrong, no matter how much you tried to hide it, and they didn't care what your reasons were. This was his line in the sand. If he crossed it he could still go back, but the return would be tainted.

"My uncle's a fool, but he's right about you," Juan said.

The words weren't a commentary on the truth but, in Anthony's mind, a taunt. He looked directly at Juan and snorted the coke off the pistol, then repeated the action when Juan held it up on the opposite side.

Anthony felt like someone had pried shingles off his eyes and he was seeing the world in its true bright colors for the first time. The drug pulsed through his system and wrapped seductively around his brain, making him feel euphoric enough to question why he'd fought so hard to keep this away from whoever wanted to use it.

"Tell me," Anthony said. The barrel of Juan's gun was still pointed at his head, but he was flying too high to think about fear.

Juan put his gun down and his hand on Anthony's head. "Whatever you want to know."

Annabel and her warnings melted from his thoughts as he looked at Juan. He'd taken his chances and now was in the stronghold people like Shelby and Joe would never find. There was only one difference in his plans. He would take Cain and Juan out, but no matter how that went down, the teak box was his. No way was he giving up the chance to feel like this again.

CHAPTER FORTY-SEVEN

Hey, none of that." Remi tried to reach up to touch Dallas, but the movement made her grimace in apparent pain. "We knew this guy's signature, and Cain had Mano order the best body armor available for both of us. And the guys think I've been reading all those knight books for nothing."

"Why didn't you tell me?" Dallas tried to keep from crying, but having Remi on her back appearing so vulnerable made her realize that no matter how she felt about her, she could lose her. "When I saw that, I thought my heart would stop."

"I'm sorry. I never expected it. Once I was on the ground, Simon got me in the car and out of there." Remi held her hand and smiled. "We're really going to have to do something about that front lock of yours."

"I'm just glad you're all right. You're all right, aren't you?"

"I haven't been x-rayed yet, but our family doctor made a house call and said I probably have a couple of either bruised or cracked ribs. Don't worry. I'll be fine."

"Since I have you at my mercy, I want to have that talk with you before we take this any further. It's the only way I can make this fair to you. You need to know the real me before you commit to anything."

"Come closer," Remi said. Dallas lay down carefully and tried not to add to Remi's pain. "I want you to know how committed I am to you."

The phone next to the bed rang and Dallas picked it up, thinking it was Kristen. "Sorry," she said to Remi.

"I know you're home, so don't think about avoiding me. I'm just around the corner," Bob said, and disconnected.

"Who was it?" Remi asked.

"Bob, he wanted to see me, but it's—"

Remi moaned, and she obviously didn't do it out of pleasure, but she rolled over and kissed Dallas. "You don't want to—is that what you were going to say?"

"It's hard to explain, but I have to put up with him. You might think I'm insane for doing it, but like he keeps reminding me, he's not going away."

"I want you to let Emil deal with him. That way we can finally have that talk."

Dallas sat up and ran her fingers through her hair to try and order it. "Let me get rid of him and make him understand I need a few more days alone." She backed out of the room, but when Remi said nothing, she came close to getting back into the bed. "I'll be right back."

Halfway down the stairs, Dallas heard the buzzer to the gate and ran to press the button to release the lock. Even if she wanted Emil's help, she didn't notice him on her way out. Bob was already halfway through the courtyard and snarled when he saw her.

"You stupid bitch," he said, and grabbed her arm. "You honestly thought that dyke was going to ride in here and save you." He yanked her, making her lose her balance and stumble. "Know how I'm going to pay you back for going against me? We're going to call Johnny together and tell him where to find you so the sheriff can finally press charges for what you did. I can even give the sheriff the rock you used. What, you didn't think I noticed it sitting on your coffee table like some kind of trophy? Then you can tell dear old Dad where he can find your little sister."

"What are you talking about?" Dallas asked in a panic. Kristen was someone she'd been careful to hide.

"You're a riot." He laughed. "She was as easy to find as you were to figure out. From the beginning I made a point of getting to know the one person in this world who knows you, Katie Lynn. I called that sick fuck you call a father." He ran his finger down her cheek and across her lips. "You've made enough money for me, and it'll serve you right to start warming Johnny's bed at night again."

"Dallas, I'm sorry I took so long," Emil said. Bob didn't let go of Dallas. "Why don't you go inside and wait for me?"

"Dallas doesn't want you here. Tell him." Bob squeezed her arm harder and pressed up behind her. "Go back to wherever you came from."

"Dallas," Emil said gently as he wrapped his fingers around Bob's wrist. It didn't take much to break his hold, but when Dallas took a couple of steps back, Emil still didn't let go. "Go on inside," he repeated. "Bob and I need to have some time alone."

"Don't tell me you forgot what we were just talking about?" Bob said. His tight mouth showed Dallas he was trying to break Emil's hold. "There's only one way to keep me quiet, so think before you throw everything away. And that's what it'll be, Dallas, you throwing it away. When Johnny gets back what you stole from him, it'll be your fault, but I'm sure he'll take his time with Kristen."

Every word was like a nail pinning Dallas's feet to the ground. She couldn't move but she wasn't completely still. Bob's threats were making her shake like she did as a child and saw her father in the doorway of her room. Back then she didn't make a sound either, not wanting to wake Kristen in case her father turned his attention her way.

"It's going to be all right." Emil cocked his head toward the door.

Dallas took a deep breath and let her head fall back. Taking the step Emil was asking of her would free her of Bob, but he would savor taking her freedom away again.

"No, it's not going to be all right, and you know that," Bob said, his voice close to a hiss.

"Let me make it easy for both of you then," Emil said. He smashed his fist into the side of Bob's head. He fell like pins being hit by a bowling ball. "Sorry you had to see that."

"I would've been more sorry not to see it," Dallas said, her attention on the rise and fall of Bob's chest. He appeared to be in a deep, peaceful sleep.

Emil laughed at her observation. "Go ahead and join Remi, and I'll take care of this."

Upstairs, Remi pressed her hand to her chest and sat up, pausing when the pain made her light-headed. The phone Dallas had just used was next to the bed and she figured it wasn't tapped, but she'd keep the call brief on the off chance it was.

"I need something."

"Name it," Cain said.

"I've got a package I need delivered, and I've got a chance to go shopping."

"I'll send my best delivery guy. Wrap it up the best you can."

It took Cain an hour but she got Lou's nephew, Nick, to the alley behind Dallas's place. He sat for half an hour after that to make sure

Lou didn't spot anyone watching. Emil brought out the rug from the guest bedroom rolled up on his shoulder and dumped it in the back of the van. Nick then left to follow Emil's directions, confident that unless he was caught speeding no one would stop the produce van from one of the local markets.

The way Bob was taken out of her house didn't worry Dallas as much as watching Remi try to make it down the stairs. From the way she moved, Dallas could tell she was in pain, but what had happened had to be finished. She knew that without any explanation from Remi or Emil.

"Do you have to leave right now?" Dallas asked. She took a seat on the sofa, so Remi would have plenty of room if she needed to join her. "Before you go through all this trouble, I want to tell you a few things about myself."

"You don't have to."

"I want to be honest with you."

"Katie Lynn, we've all made mistakes. They're what make us smarter and stronger in the end. If you want my help, all you have to do is ask, but if you want me to condemn you, I can't."

"You know?" Dallas started crying again.

"Probably not everything."

"If you know, I'll understand why you can't stay. I'm so ashamed." Dallas couldn't help but let out all her insecurities.

"I'd be willing to bet your sins don't come close to mine. Your past is exactly that—your past. You had to invent Dallas Montgomery for a reason, and as soon as I get back we can start on that story."

"Why go through all this trouble for me?"

Remi couldn't lift her arms very high so she placed her hand on Dallas's knee. "If you don't know, then I want plenty of time to explain it to you. For now I'll give you the short version. I feel strongly about you. Last night wasn't about filling some base need, but more like filling one in my heart."

"Will you come back when you're done?"

"If it's okay with you, Emil and I will be your guests for a couple of days, or until Cain and my father find the guy who used me for target practice."

"That's good to hear." Dallas kissed her and helped her stand. By the time Remi and Emil walked out, Remi felt less stiff.

Emil opened the back door for Remi. As they left, Simon went in to stay with Dallas, but her eyes lingered on Remi like she was making sure she was okay. They drove out of the city, and Remi rested her head back and closed her eyes. She'd been to where they were going on a few occasions to help Emil during harvest. The location was remote, making any tail on them stick out like a naked whore at Sunday services.

The marina looked so dilapidated it appeared to be abandoned, but in the middle slip sat a new airboat with an alligator-skin driver's seat. Emil helped Remi board, and she nodded to Cain and Lou, who were already seated.

"Thank God we're doing this while it's still cool," Lou said.

"What's the matter? You don't like mosquitoes?" Emil asked. His laughter as well as that of the others was drowned out when he started the powerful engine.

The fan blade behind the cage at the back started spinning slowly as he backed out but cranked up when he closed his hand around the accelerator control. Two minutes into the trip they were in the blackness of the swamp, but Emil had made this trip thousands of times and swerved around the ancient cypress trees as if gifted with some sort of night vision.

Halfway there they started to see orange orbs glowing at the top of the water, quickly disappearing as the roar of the airboat neared. Remi had learned from Emil that the orange lights were the female gators floating at the top of the water waiting for a late-night meal. According to Cajun lore, only the female eyes glowed because they were the more cunning of the species, so God gave anyone who wanted to mess with them fair warning.

"Thanks for helping me out with this," Remi said as Emil brought them in slowly to the camp that appeared to be floating above the murky water. The small structure made of cypress wood from the trees surrounding it was built on stilts that raised it fifteen feet into the air.

Cain walked next to Remi as they ascended the ramp to the front porch. They were all dressed in black and blended in well with the worn wood. The two friends sat in rockers outside, and Cain dropped a bag between them.

"I know you don't especially like getting your hands dirty," Remi said.

"There's always an exception to every rule," Cain said, setting her rocker in motion. "I asked Muriel to put together the papers that would fix this. All we have to do is talk him into signing them. But talking to Bob is probably like that old expression about trying to teach a pig to sing. It's a waste of time all the way around."

"I want him out of her life."

"That's the wisest thing, but he still won't answer all your questions unless he's in a talkative mood. I think you and I should be the ones to get whatever we can out of Bob tonight. I know you trust Emil like I trust Lou, but this is the kind of guy who's going to talk just to watch you squirm. They won't forget what he might say, and you don't need to do that to Dallas," Cain said. She pointed to the bag. "What's in there goes with you after we're done, and to my grave with me."

"Then I owe you a debt."

"This is my wedding gift to you," Cain said with a smile. "At least that's what my wife tells me is going to happen with you two. The way you look at her predicts the future." She stood up and offered Remi her hand. "Let's get this over with."

Nick was sitting at the table with a gun in his waistband. Even if Bob had tried to run there was no way he'd ever find his way out, since he'd made the trip wrapped in a rug. Cain walked in and sat to his right.

"If you know what's good for you, tell this idiot to take me back," Bob said.

"What's good for me?" Cain tilted her head to the side, trying to decipher what exactly that meant. "I give up. What do you plan to do to me if I don't?"

"I'm not an idiot."

Cain knocked on the table with her knuckles and laughed. "That's negotiable." She waved Nick outside.

"I know who you are, and the minute I get back I'm sure the authorities would love to hear what you did to me."

"I'm here doing a favor for a friend, nothing more than that, but I thought we'd have a talk first."

"This is about Dallas and her trying to get rid of me. I own that bitch, and if you think this intimidation act is going to change my mind about that, it's not. Like I told that dyke that got herself killed, I've faced worse and lived to tell the tale."

"I'm no stranger to intimidation, Mr. Bennett, but that's not why you're here. Dallas happens to be a friend of mine, and you've taken some things that don't belong to you. I think it's only fair that you give them back. It's that simple."

"What things?"

"Just minor things like her house, her money, and some papers, and if you're cooperative I won't ask you how you got those away from her."

"Fuck off."

"I had my attorney draw up some papers that give Dallas legal right to the list I mentioned, and I'd like you to sign them."

"Are you deaf? I said to fuck off."

"Mr. Bennett, let me explain something to you in terms that even you can understand. You're going to sign. That point's non-negotiable. You can choose to do it now and save yourself a lot of pain, or you can play the macho role and hold out, which brings its own set of consequences. Those are the only two options. Now I'm going to ask you one more time, do you want to sign or do you choose to wait?"

"I want you to listen to me, fucker. I'm not going to sign those papers now, an hour from now, or a week from now. Dallas may have had some fantasy of your dead friend up on a big fucking white horse saving her from me, but that ain't going to happen now, is it? If you want an answer then here it is. Kiss my ass. What are you going to do now, beat me to death?" Bob asked, laughing.

"No, Dickey, she won't beat you, but I will." Remi's voice cut through the room, making Bob twist his head around.

"But you're dead. I saw it on television, you're dead." Bob paled considerably.

"You're not one of those people who believes everything you see on television, are you?" Remi sat across from him and took a cigar out of her shirt pocket. She sat that and her clippers on the table. "Do you smoke?" she asked Bob, who shook his head. "Too bad, there's nothing like a good cigar."

"Let me go and I'll check that out."

"You wanted to meet with me in the worst way to negotiate Dallas's new contract. Well, here I am, and there's no chance anyone's going to disturb us. Only anything having to do with Dallas's future is off the table. We're here for her past dealings."

"You don't scare me, so cut the theatrics."

Cain put her bag on the table. "Funny, she scares the shit out of me at times. You were right, he isn't very smart."

"More like an asshole who's made a living as a leech," Remi said to Cain, then turned to Bob. "Before we begin let me ask you something. Are you right- or left- handed?"

"What does that have to do with anything?" Bob was getting louder and his speech was getting faster.

"Because I can start with your dominant hand or not. The choice is yours."

"Right-handed."

"See, that wasn't too hard, was it? What we're going to play tonight is like a version of twenty questions my father taught me. It's a little messy but it gets results, and that's what we're here for. I'm going to ask you questions, and if you're lying or you get it wrong then," she paused and clipped off the tip of the cigar in her hand with the golden clippers for emphasis, "I'm going to start cutting your fingers off at each joint until you tell the truth or get it right. Any questions before we begin?"

"You're kidding me, right? I'm not falling for that bluff," Bob told her with a nervous laugh.

"Remi never bluffs," Cain said. "It's what makes her such a good gambler."

"Ready to play?" Remi asked without any humor. "Don't worry. I'm going to save your right hand for last so you can sign the papers Cain mentioned. Last chance, Bob. I'm not fucking around. We can skip all this if you sign."

"You don't listen very well, do you? This is what I'm going to do. As soon as I leave here, I'm going to drive to the closest rag and give them an exclusive on the past life of one Dallas Montgomery, aka Katie Moores. I'm sure her mug shot from when she got caught shoplifting will make a wonderful cover, and the skin flick she was in won't make *ET*, but the copies I own will be worth a fortune." Before he could continue, Cain placed the mug shot and a copy of the video on the table in front of Remi.

"Is this what you're talking about?"

"Those are mine. Give them back," he yelled, sounding like a small child whose favorite toy had been taken away. He moved to grab the stuff, but Cain was quicker. She stood and yanked him back by the hair, but it was the knife biting into his neck that stopped him cold. "If you try that again I'm going to gut you like a fish. Do you understand me?" Cain asked. He nodded his head, apparently too afraid to speak.

"Bob, I'm going to repay you every unkindness you ever heaped on Dallas, and so you know, I'm going to enjoy every moment of it. Are there any other documents I need to collect from you?" Remi asked.

"Yes, bitch, and I'm never going to tell you where they are." He watched her pick up the clippers and slip her fingers into the appropriate holes. "You don't have the guts to carry this out."

"What makes us better than the animals, Dickey?"

"Our ability to forgive and forget."

"Funny, who knew you had a sense of humor, but sadly that's a wrong answer. I did warn you what would happen if you answered untruthfully or wrong, didn't I? The right answer would be opposable thumbs, Dickey." With that said, she squeezed the blade shut. Just as quickly the agonizing scream that pierced the silence of the ancient swamp scared the sleeping white egrets off the branches overhead with loud squawks.

"Wait," Bob said, his voice raspy as Remi moved the clippers to his index finger. He seemed to be the only one horrified that his left thumb was sitting on the table. "Just wait."

"It's simple, like I said. Give me the information I want and this ends," Remi said, squeezing the clippers enough to touch the first segment of his finger.

"Why don't you leave me and Dallas alone? We were fine until you came along." He screamed just as loud when the tip of his finger landed on the table. "You won't get away with this."

Cain grabbed his hand as he tried to pull it back and slammed it back in front of Remi. "Do you think that's what Dallas would say if she were here?" Cain asked. "That she was fine working to hand over the lion's share to you? Because from what my people found in your house, that's exactly what's happened. She's worked her ass off and owns nothing in her name, but that can't be said of you, can it?"

"She wanted it that way. Dallas wanted me to look out for her and her money." The next segment of his finger came off as he finished, leaving only the nub up from the knuckle.

"That one might be a guess on my part, but I don't think you were telling the truth," Remi said as she moved the clippers up close to his palm. "Did you set up anything else for Dallas that I need to know about? Think long and hard, because you have only so many chances to get it right before we move on to the next body part that'll fit in this hole." She squeezed the clippers a bit to make him realize what she was talking about. "Like I said, we'll leave that right hand for last, but the rest is on the chopping block, as it were."

A few hours later the group took a much slower boat ride with a now-whimpering Bob in tow. Heading out into the blackness of the swamp and into the hunting grounds Emil used, Remi had him finally cut the engines. She slapped Bob on the face a couple of times to focus his attention and have her last conversation with him. "Wakey, wakey, Bob."

"What? Leave me alone. I told you everything you wanted to know, now leave me alone."

"One more question." He was already covered in sweat and started shaking at the question. "Can you swim?"

"Yes," he answered quickly, since stalling only caused instant pain even if the answer was correct.

"Good, since we had an agreement. I'm not going to kill you, but this is where we part ways. If you make it back to shore you're free to go, and I'll let you keep the money you have in the bank. But if you so much as look in Dallas's direction again I'll make you pray to die. Do we understand each other?"

"Yes, ma'am, we do."

"Good. Then strip down."

"You want me naked?"

"It'll help you stay afloat, trust me." Bob stood up, holding his hands to his chest, and jumped off the front of the boat.

Emil revved up the motor again but kept it slow enough that Nick could keep up in the mud boat he was steering. At Remi's feet was the bag with the remnants of a sad little girl born to a sadist. Katie Moores and her sister Sue Lee would finally disappear into the smoke of Dallas's fireplace as soon as she got back. Cain had put a copy of Dallas's first acting job on her back in the bag, but she had destroyed the other five hundred copies she found at Bob's place.

"Remind me never to piss you off," Cain said in a loud-enough voice to be heard over the engine.

"He got what he deserved."

"True. He'll be meeting some of Emil's future boot material before he has a chance to get his hair wet."

The marina came into view and Emil slowed down so he could back into his slip. Cain got out first and helped Remi onto the dock. "Give Dallas my best, and if there's anything else having to do with this business that'll bury it once and for all, make me your first call."

"You're a good friend," Remi said, putting her arms around Cain as best she could.

"One who cares about you, so keep your head down while your father and I finish our expedition. Jorge took Nunzio's money, so he'll keep coming until he finishes the job. Next time he'll probably vary from his usual shot and make it through the head. I don't want that on mine, so stay at Dallas's until we take care of that."

Remi followed her to the cars, the click of her and Emil's boots echoing. "Are you sure there's nothing I can do to help?"

"Stay inside and start on Marianna's grandchildren," Cain said with a smile. "That's it. If I see you out, I'll kick your ass myself."

"That sounds like a hardship, but okay. What are you going to be doing?"

Cain opened the passenger door of the truck Lou had driven down and leaned against it. "I have the edges of my puzzle put together. Now I have to fill in the middle."

"Sounds interesting."

"You can't see the whole picture until you fill in the middle. Once I do, it'll make tonight appear tame."

Remi shook hands with her and closed the door once Cain was seated. As Lou pulled away slowly, something her father had always told her about Cain came to mind. Cain's word was as good as a signed contract. That was why Ramon had done business with her. So Remi wondered what was in store for Juan Luis and Nunzio Luca.

"Whatever it is, I'm sure they'd pick hungry alligators over it."

CHAPTER FORTY-EIGHT

Are you sure he's not in there?" Muriel asked for the fifth time.

Katlin was working the lock, but stopped when Muriel asked again. "If you want, you can wait for me in the car. He's not here, and after driving around with you for the last three hours, I can tell you a certain cute FBI agent isn't waiting outside to cuff you and take you in."

"Is it a crime to want to be sure?"

The door opened and Katlin laughed softly. "No, but if you step through there it is. From crack lawyer to someone breaking and entering. My, how far you've come, Muriel."

The apartment was dark and smelled musty, as if Anthony Curtis hadn't been there in weeks. Though the place was small, Muriel could tell right off where he did like to spend time when he was home. A cleared space on the couch faced the television that was far too big for the space, and five beer bottles were lined up on the desk shoved into the corner.

"Okay, we're in. What are we looking for?" Katlin asked.

"I'll do the searching and you make sure no one's coming."

"Should I practice my birdcalls as a warning?"

Muriel closed the door and glared at Katlin. "That's not funny. Go through the bedroom and see if you can find anything having to do with Cain, the family, or Anthony's new friends, the Luis family."

"I'm sorry." Katlin squeezed her shoulder in comfort. "Just relax and we'll be out of here faster."

Muriel scanned the room to see if anything jumped out at her, but all she noticed was that Anthony was a slob, no matter how neat he appeared in public. The man in the pressed suits and shiny shoes didn't quite fit with the condition of this place. She sat at his desk and tried to go through the drawers without moving too much around, but they were so overfilled he'd probably never suspect anyone had been there.

It wasn't until she called Katlin to unlock the top right-hand drawer that Muriel found any order to the madness that was Anthony's life. There in neat files was what she was looking for. His bank records, retirement funds, and investments were in color-coded binders, and at the back were his social security number and birth certificate. For someone in law enforcement to have such sensitive information all in one place was crazy, but very considerate since that's what she was after.

Carefully holding a pen light in her mouth, she copied the numbers she needed in order, so she could put the pages back as she'd found them. When she got to the last folder, she fell back in the chair and was tempted to turn on the light to fully appreciate what she'd found. She rifled through pictures and meticulous notes of Cain and her schedule whenever he'd tailed her, all dated. The follow-up notes revealed different patterns he was working out regarding Cain. Most of them were from when Anthony was still with Shelby and her team, but the last ones had come after his supposed suspension.

"Find something?" Katlin asked.

Muriel held up the last picture in the file—of Cain the night she'd had dinner with Remi and Dallas at the Steak Knife. Cain was laughing at something Emma had probably told her, and Anthony had drawn a red circle with an x through her head.

"What do you think this means?" Muriel asked.

"Our boy's got a bigger crush than we thought. What other pictures did you find?"

Muriel took the file from the drawer and let Katlin flip through it. He must have collected most of the stuff when he was off duty, which could only mean that his hate ran deep. Katlin stopped when she got to a photo of Emma alone, or as alone as Emma ever was. She was standing outside Mr. B's restaurant in the French Quarter, and she and Merrick were waiting for the car to be brought out. Emma had just finished having lunch with Marianna Jatibon, since the two served on a committee to raise money for Children's Hospital.

"Cain, I understand, but why this one?" Katlin asked.

"The ones of Cain feed his appetite, but Emma has to do with his new boss. This one was recent, though, and Juan's supposedly gone."

A car door slammed outside, and Katlin quickly handed the file back to Muriel and stepped to the window. Anthony lived on the third floor of an old building uptown, which gave them the amount of time it would take him to climb the steps to get out, since he was heading in quickly.

"Put the file back exactly where you found it," Katlin ordered, then set out to lock the drawer. That one had been easy, but the ancient deadbolt on the door had been another matter. "Wait a floor up for me," she told Muriel, "and don't come down no matter what."

She had unscrewed the light on the second-floor landing and heard his footsteps slow down, but still the damn lock wouldn't turn. "Great, it's like some Hitchcock movie," she muttered to herself as she turned the picks trying to catch the locking device until finally feeling the satisfying click.

With her fingers to her lips, she stared at Muriel and stood just at the top of the steps leading to the fourth floor. If Anthony glanced up, he couldn't miss them.

She stood still as Anthony stopped but didn't hear the sound of the key going into his lock. His breathing, though, was hard to miss. He was puffing so hard he sounded like he had run a mile as fast as he could instead of having climbed several flights of stairs. Then he slammed his hand into the doorjamb and laughed.

Slowly, as if Anthony could hear the sound of fabric rubbing on fabric, Katlin raised her hand and stuck it in her jacket, resting it on the butt of her gun. The last thing she wanted was to shoot him, but she wanted to be prepared. When he finally unlocked the door and went inside, she brought it down just as slowly. It didn't take long for the muffled noise of the television to filter out to the hall.

Katlin turned to leave, but Muriel put her hand on her collar. "Wait."

"For what?" Katlin asked.

"If he finds anything out of place, he'll do it in the next five minutes."

After a while, Muriel pushed on Katlin a little, and they passed the doorway of Anthony's place just as quietly as they made it down the stairs. If he did notice anything, he was biding his time and not running out to see if the trespassers were still close.

"Are you going to the house, or home?" Muriel asked once they were on the street and walking toward their car parked three blocks away.

"I moved Merrick to your place until this is over, so we're going in the same direction, don't worry. I want to wait until tomorrow to tell Cain. It's late and I'm sure she's in for the night. This will hold until the morning."

"But not much longer than that."

❖

Cain entered the house and stood by the back door waiting for her eyes to adjust to the low lighting. She'd skipped dinner when Katlin had gotten back from Bob's place and showed her what she'd found after an extensive search that had included his attic. That's where she'd found the boxes of VHS tapes of Dallas's short stint in the skin-flick business. Sitting on top was the master tape Cain figured Bob had stolen to protect his interests. She'd given it all to Remi when she'd gone to meet her.

"His cash cow was too lucrative to throw to the wolves that prowl the entertainment business," she said softly as she opened the fridge. Bob and his dirty secrets were gone, making Cain wish she could solve all her problems so easily.

"I made you a sandwich," Emma said, turning on the light over the stove. "Have a seat and I'll get it for you."

"No hello kiss?"

She set the plate down with a glass of milk and pulled Cain's chair out for her. "I'd love to, but I just finished throwing up and don't want to gross you out."

"What's wrong?" Cain put her hand to her forehead instantly. "Do you need a doctor?"

"Hannah came home from preschool today feeling queasy, so I'm sure it's whatever bug she caught there." Emma kissed her chin and pointed to the chair. "Sit and eat."

"Are you sure you're all right?"

"I'm fine, but I feel horrible for Carmen. She made her mother's chicken recipe and thinks that's what did it."

They sat together and Emma watched her eat as they talked about their day. As they climbed to the second floor someone walked in and lingered in the foyer.

"Problem, Muriel?" Cain asked, her arm around Emma. She couldn't see who it was, but guessed it had to be Muriel.

"Just working late."

"I'm not buying that. Spill it and get up here where I can see you." Cain kissed Emma on the temple and patted her on the butt to get her moving toward the bedroom. "I'll be in as soon as I'm done."

Face to face it didn't take long for Muriel to tell her story. Cain was grateful she'd sent Emma to their room before Muriel told her about the pictures she'd found. "You didn't discover anything that'd lead us to Juan?"

"Not yet, but I got everything else you asked for, and someone to carry it out."

"Who?" Cain asked as she pulled her shirttail from her pants simply to have something to do with her hands.

"Nick. He's young enough and has the same physical characteristics. In an out-of-the-way location he'll pass, and he's not taking away anything. If he was, that might be more of a problem."

"Tell him to be ready tomorrow."

Muriel nodded. "He wants a more permanent job close to you."

"Nick's a good kid. I'll talk to him and have him work with Lou whenever possible, but he's not ready for a spot in our immediate crew yet."

"He's going to be disappointed."

"Disappointment comes when you don't have a chance," Cain said, echoing her father. "That's not what I'm saying. Once he's got more experience, he's got a shot."

"The only one that'll make happy is Lou's brother." Muriel walked with her down the hall. "He's a fireman with no interest in the life. Lou told me it's killing him that Nick chose to follow this path. He wanted better for his son."

"I can understand that. Every parent wants the best for their children, but he doesn't—"

Cain stopped talking and walking, and Muriel had to turn back. "Something wrong?"

Without saying anything else, Cain went back down and into the office. The list of passengers was in the top drawer. She'd been meaning to call Hector Delarosa in Columbia to pick his brain, but now she had only one question to ask him. After Muriel told her about Anthony's collection of pictures, she wasn't willing to wait for the answer.

With every counter-surveillance device turned on, Cain dialed the number. "Señor Delarosa, please." She paused as whoever answered said something. "It's Cain Casey from New Orleans."

She sat and indicated to Muriel to do the same. "Sometimes things are so easy it makes you miss them," she said as she waited.

"What's so easy?" Muriel asked.

Cain put her finger up as she heard a muted exchange on the other end. "Hello."

"Señor Delarosa, I'm sorry to call so late," Cain said with the sheet from the airline in her hand.

"Cain, please call me Hector," he said in refined English with a slight accent. "I've heard so much about you I feel as if we're old friends. What can I do to help you?"

"From my contacts here I understand you and Rodolfo Luis were business partners at one time." She picked up a pen and put a check mark next to every *Juan* on the page.

"Until Rodolfo became too important. Do you understand my meaning?"

"After meeting him a few times I understand perfectly."

"It's of no matter now. Rodolfo has chosen to do business with the Luca family, and we will deal with someone else. This person has a bigger network of friends, which means fewer enemies for me to deal with. In my business it's a better position to be in." Cain accepted the drink Muriel had poured her, as well as the fact that it was Remi and herself Hector was talking about, and rested her elbows on the edge of the desk. "But I'm sure you didn't call about my history. What else can I answer for you?"

Drugs weren't something Cain would ever involve herself in, but something about Hector made her like him. "My father always said that history was a good roadmap to the future."

"Then it is history we will talk about tonight."

"The story I'm interested in actually has to do more with Juan Luis than his uncle."

"Rodolfo will learn soon enough what a rabid dog he's raised, and unfortunately for him it will be a lesson he won't live to learn from. He punished his sister Gracelia for soiling his family name by taking Juan away from her to raise himself. That selfishness on his part has made both Juan and his mother unstable enough to turn on him."

That statement alone made Cain smile. Not over Rodolfo's problems, but because Hector knew so much about them. "What I need from you is the name of the man who fathered Juan."

She hoped the silence on the other end indicated Hector was thinking.

"He was a drifter, if I remember, since I only heard Rodolfo refer to him once when he told me what he'd done to him, but I believe his name was Ortega. Yes, that's it, Armando Ortega."

Cain moved her finger from check to check until she reached the eighth one on the list. Juan Armando Ortega had used his passport to enter the United States the day Rick had been killed. Gracelia and Juan might have been unstable, but that didn't equal stupid. That Juan was able to get a passport with that name meant Gracelia Luis had kept her lover alive in her memory, no matter how hard Rodolfo had tried to erase it.

"One more thing, Hector. How did Armando die?"

"That is one story that makes me cross my legs whenever I tell it," he said with a chuckle. He gave her the details Rodolfo had shared with him about how he'd tied Armando to a tree and coated his genitals in honey before agitating the large red-ant hill at the base. "Rodolfo told me the ants devoured his manhood before he died, but they didn't leave him alive very long."

"Thank you for answering my questions and for taking my call," Cain said as she circled Juan's given name.

"I'll be in New Orleans soon. Perhaps while I'm there we can share a meal."

"I'll be happy to treat for all your help. Good night."

"What'd he say?" Muriel asked as soon as Cain hung up.

"Our rat has another name and he's here." Cain handed over the page with Juan's name on it. "Katlin's back, right?"

"She's in the pool house."

"Get her up here first thing in the morning before you two head off to finish the Anthony business. If Juan's returned, and he is according to this, I want him found."

"Are you still planning to meet with Rodolfo?"

"As soon as I'm done with you all in the morning." Cain put her papers in the desk and locked it, slipping the key into her pocket.

"Do you want me to do anything else with the casino deal?" Muriel asked. She stopped at the head of the hallway that led to the rear of the house. "With everything that's happened we've almost forgotten it."

"Postponed, Cousin, not forgotten. Nunzio's a hard guy to put out of your head for long, so there's no way I've forgotten him. He'll have to wait until I've squared Juan away." A door opened upstairs, the quiet house making it easy to hear, and Cain expected to see Emma at any minute. "After Nunzio hired someone to kill Remi, it's best to let Ramon deal with him."

"With no input from us?"

"Of course not. I've been considering how best to dispense with this problem."

"You want me to handle our end of things?" Muriel asked.

Just then, Emma came downstairs, put her arms around Cain's waist, and said, "You better take a night to think about asking something that important, Muriel."

"You think I can't handle it?" Muriel asked, not yet sounding insulted but at the cusp of her patience, from what Cain could tell.

"I've got no doubt about that," Emma said as Cain kissed her cheek.

"Then what's to think about?"

"She's talking about points of no return," Cain said. "Up to now you haven't had to answer a challenge like the one Nunzio issued by hiring Jorge. He tried to draw first blood and we've got to answer him."

"Blood demands blood, I understand that perfectly. Don't forget I grew up in this family too, and I did it without blinders on."

"Take the night Emma's suggested, and before you ask me again, remember one thing. To deal with the devil is easy, but the debt you incur weighs heavily on your soul. Not everyone's made to carry the load."

"More wise advice from Uncle Dalton?"

"My father agreed with the words, but your father told me that. Jarvis served Da like you have me for as long as Da was alive, and he never asked to change his lot in life."

Muriel's nose flared as if Cain had finally lit her ire. "Why do you have such a problem with me doing it? I thought we were beyond that."

"I've tried to give you what you asked for, haven't I? But I have a problem with you trying to prove something, not to yourself, but to a woman who you tell me is of no consequence." Cain knew her words were stern, but she needed to say them as much as Muriel needed to hear them. "You don't have to prove to me you deserve your name, but you've got to start thinking like a Casey."

"What do you think I've been doing?"

"If you want the truth, putting yourself in situations to prove to Shelby you're no one's fool. It's time to pick what your debt will be, but be damn sure you're in shape to carry it. I can't do that for you."

Cain tensed when Muriel moved toward her, but just as quickly relaxed into the embrace Muriel initiated. "I don't need time to think. Where you lead I'll follow. It's that simple, and thanks for always watching out for me."

"That's my privilege," Cain said as she kissed her forehead.

"Just remember that I'll follow, but like Emma, I don't want to be left behind."

"That's a deal I can live with."

CHAPTER FORTY-NINE

The house was quiet when Remi got back, and she slowly walked up the stairs, telling Emil good night as he kept going toward the guest room Dallas had pointed out to him earlier. Dallas was in the other bedroom, and Remi hesitated in the hall. What she'd done that night had set Dallas free of everything and everyone that had been a part of her life. And standing there she realized that included herself.

"Are you all right?" Dallas asked as she put her hand around Remi's elbow and led her into the master bedroom. "Do you need me to help you?"

"I'm fine, just thinking."

"If you got a chance to talk to Bob, I'm sure he gave you plenty to think about." In front of the bed she let Remi go and stepped back. "If you want me to go downstairs and sleep on the couch, that won't be a problem for me."

"What I want is to get in that bed and hold you. I'm not in great shape, but I can manage that if you're up for it."

They left the door to the balcony open to let the cool night air in and enjoyed the feel of each other with no barriers between them. Dallas had draped herself over Remi's uninjured side with her head resting on her shoulder and ran her fingers softly over her skin, not wanting to press down on the bruise that dominated Remi's chest.

They didn't start talking right away, so Dallas was content to watch the rise and fall of Remi's chest as she breathed. It was like a miracle.

"Where'd you run off to?" Remi asked as she scratched Dallas's back.

"Just wishing silly things."

"I find that hard to believe. Since we've met you've never asked me for anything, so tell me what you're hoping for and I'll do my best to give it to you."

"I want you, Remington," Dallas whispered so softly she figured Remi hadn't heard her.

"You have me."

"No, I want—" Remi pressed two of her fingers against her lips.

"You have me, Dallas, and not just here." She fanned her arm around the bed. Remi sat up a bit to lean against the carved headboard of the bed, taking Dallas with her. She settled Dallas across her legs.

"I want you to understand something. I've never allowed anyone but my family and close friends to know me this well. No woman has ever come close to owning my heart, but you're the difference I've been waiting for, and I want nothing more than to stand up for you."

"I can't ask you to do that."

"You can't force someone to do that, just like you can't force someone to love you. You're more than my bed-warmer. If you decide to stay with me, I'll keep you safe and give you room to grow into the incredible woman I know you can be, and that doesn't apply only to your career. I'll hold you up so you can achieve your dreams and be there to catch you when you fail. I want nothing from you in return."

"Is that all you want?" Dallas asked. She'd moved so she could see Remi's face as she spoke.

"You're free now, Dallas, maybe for the first time in your life. No one's waiting in the wings to make you do something you don't choose. If you want to explore that freedom, don't feel you're bound to me."

Dallas moved so she straddled Remi's legs and was close enough to see those unique eyes. She placed her hands on Remi's cheeks and spoke from her heart. "If I *am* truly free, then nothing's stopping me from loving you. Nothing's stopping me from wanting to be the last woman in your life."

"I love you," Remi said softly but with meaning.

Dallas leaned her forehead against Remi's. She didn't want to say anything yet, so the echo of Remi's declaration could resonate in her head until it sunk in.

She moved back enough to kiss Remi. "I love you and for once I'm feeling selfish. I don't want to share you with anyone. I want to be free to take care of you and to expect certain things from you. I want you, Remi, but I won't settle for anything but your all. Do you understand what I'm trying to tell you?"

"That's what you have," Remi said as she moved to kiss Dallas's palms.

"No more models?"

"No more women of any kind."

The kiss that followed erased any reservations Dallas had. "Can I ask you one more thing? If you can't answer, then don't."

"Just ask."

"Remember, if you don't want to tell me, you don't have to."

"If you don't ask me I'll have a hard time answering."

"Did you kill Bob?" Dallas's good sense was telling her she shouldn't ask the question, but she had to know.

"No, I didn't, but I won't lie and tell you I made it easy for him to survive. It's a wait-and-see situation," Remi answered truthfully.

"What do you mean?"

"I hurt him pretty badly. Let's just say I broke him of his smug attitude, and then I dropped him somewhere. It's up to him, with some divine intervention, to swim back without something eating him. Maybe that's not what you wanted, but when he talked about you and showed no remorse, I snapped."

"Can I confess a deep, dark secret and not have you think any less of me?"

"Nothing you tell me will change how I feel about you."

"From the time Bob came into my life I've had a list of ways I'd like to see him die. The day you and I met I was well into five thousand, and all mine included lots of suffering."

"That should be incentive for me to behave."

"I'm sorry if I put you in a position you didn't want to be in."

"Bob is one of those people you'd like to kill more than once." Remi ran her fingers along Dallas's hips, obviously being careful because of the pain. "I'm glad I was the one who helped you get this idiot out of your life."

Remi's words made Dallas cry. "I know why you love those adventure books. You're like a knight defending my honor—not that I have much left, if any at all." Dallas wiped away her angry tears.

"Listen to me. Everyone makes mistakes, but sometimes it's because of circumstance, not free will. You had a sister to care for, and you could've taken the easy way out, but you didn't."

"It's good to know that if you keep praying, eventually someone hears you. I'm not sure what I finally did right to be this well rewarded, and at this point I don't care. You're here and you're mine." Dallas kissed Remi and massaged the skin behind her neck. "If we went slowly, do you think we could make love?"

Before Dallas could change her mind and take the question back, Remi put her right hand between her legs, keeping the other one on Dallas's hip. She went slow, using tender, soft touches that made Dallas let her head fall back and close her eyes. Perhaps the world didn't associate tenderness with Remi, but Dallas knew no other kind of touch from her.

Remi's touch branded her heart with a totally new sense of love and permanence. As long as Dallas lived, Remi would be the only one to move her to such heights. Salvation sometimes had nothing to do with churches and religious faith, but rather someone willing to find what was left in you worth saving.

Any other thought had to wait as Dallas gave in to her orgasm. Tomorrow she'd tell Remi the rest of her secrets. For years she wouldn't have readily shared them with anyone except Kristen, but her days of hiding were over. In Remi she'd found someone not only to love, but to help carry the weight of her past.

"When I took Kristen and ran, most nights before I went to sleep, I prayed to my mom to send me something to make things better," Dallas said as soon as she caught her breath. "Maybe it wouldn't have taken so long if I'd prayed for a someone instead. I love you."

"I love you too." Remi scooted down and kissed the top of Dallas's head when she reclaimed her spot on her shoulder. "It's a good thing you're no stranger to prayer," Remi said in a teasing voice. "Once you've met my mother, she'll tell you that to love us is to learn to pray for patience."

"I can't wait to meet your mother, but right now I'd like to talk about something else." Dallas touched her and smiled when she found the abundant wetness. "Let's start right here." She moved down so she could use her mouth and be mindful of Remi's injuries. Dallas knew they should've waited, but for her this was more than just making love. It was a celebration of life and living it in the warmth of the sun out of the shadows.

❖

"Is it time?" Kim Stegal asked Nunzio. They were back in New Orleans to attend Remi's funeral.

"Not until Remi's in the ground. I'm not completely heartless. Let Ramon and his family have their time to mourn, then we'll move to close the deal."

"Your father called again last night while you were on the casino floor."

Nunzio put his menu down and his fists on the table. "Why'd he call you?"

The waiter arrived with the orange juice they'd ordered, and Kim took a sip before answering. "You're either going to trust me or I'm walking. I've been with you too long for you to put me through this shit every time I talk to your father."

"You aren't about to walk away from me."

Kim stared at his hand on her wrist in a test of will. "Let's get something else straight. I work for you. A paycheck doesn't constitute owning me. Try and remember that."

"Last night when I was deep inside you, it sure felt like I owned you." He laughed but let her go when Kim didn't join him. "I'm playing with you, so relax. What did my father want?"

"He's stonewalled Rodolfo as long as he can, but Rodolfo's demanded his money or his product back. Junior wants us to meet with him while we're here and see if we can reason with him."

The waiter brought out a basket of biscuits next, and Nunzio took his time slathering butter on one. "How does he expect us to reason with him?"

"Do you want to play twenty questions or have you forgotten how your father operates?"

"He wants me to lean on Rodolfo?" Nunzio laughed but his question sounded sarcastic to Kim. Half the biscuit disappeared into his mouth. "Does he want to just throw away our plans?"

"Maybe it's time to assert yourself a little more and tell him that, because you're right. If Rodolfo cuts you off, you won't have a chance with the Delarosas." Kim felt as if she were dealing with a skittish deer. Nunzio was usually aggressive, but acted like a perpetual five-year-old when it came to Junior.

"Let's call Rodolfo but we'll go easy on him."

"Whatever you want," Kim said, lifting her coffee cup in an effort to hide her smirk.

"You think I'm weak when it comes to Junior, don't you?"

"I wouldn't be with you if I thought that," Kim said. She reached across the table and took his hand, but she didn't plan to console him like this forever. "You want me to call Rodolfo?" After that she'd move on. Maybe something in Florida, as long as it was away from Nunzio and his family.

"Whatever you want," Nunzio said, pushing his plate away, his appetite apparently gone.

❖

Carlos Santiago stood silently watching the numbers on the elevator go down. Standing next to him, Rodolfo could almost feel the bad mood rolling off Carlos as they left the sanctuary of the Piquant suite to go someplace where Carlos felt he couldn't protect him. Not that Rodolfo had gotten where he had by being a trusting man, but he didn't think twice about accepting Cain's invitation.

"When you were a boy, you pouted the same way when I didn't bring back the caramels you loved so much," Rodolfo said, trying to cajole Carlos out of his bad mood.

"This is different than when I was helping my mother in your kitchen. I'm only trying to do my job."

As much as Rodolfo had invested in Juan, a special bond existed between him and Carlos. He'd watched him grow up, and the attention he'd lavished on him as a child had cemented Carlos's loyalty to him, so much so that Rodolfo had built a house for Carlos and his mother to share in her retirement. She had been one of Rodolfo's many mistresses, but he'd lost interest in her sexually as she grew older. It had been Carlos who had kept her in Rodolfo's life.

"You do your job well enough that no matter what the day holds, we'll be fine," Rodolfo said and put his hand on Carlos's back. "If this were a meeting with someone like Hector or Nunzio Luca, we'd be downstairs in the outdoor restaurant, no matter who was listening in or watching."

"But because it's Casey you go in alone?"

"I'll have you there," Rodolfo reminded him. "Cain isn't interested in us or our business. If she wanted me dead, I'd be lying next to my parents in the small cemetery in the yard by now. She wants something else entirely."

"If she's not interested in doing business with you, why do you care?"

"Because of all the idiots we've dealt with up to now, Casey stands alone."

Carlos held the door for him and pressed the *down* button on the next set of elevators that would take them to street level. "So you do think she's an idiot?"

"Just the opposite. Cain is one of that rare breed of people for whom the world hides very little."

A car was waiting at the Piquant, and Carlos opened the back door and got in behind Rodolfo. "I don't understand."

"She's a good strategist, which I understand was something of a passion for her father, but you can teach only so much. With Juan I tried to do the same thing, but without the same results. Cain took what her father gave her and added that vicious twist, that makes her someone we have to study carefully." Rodolfo watched the buildings they were passing, as he often did when he was in New Orleans.

He'd bet his future on the city because of what he saw the first time he visited. New Orleans was full of history and not like any other American city he'd ever visited, but mixed in with the spice of what made it unique was an edgy side that allowed people like him and Cain a chance to prosper.

"I can accept that she doesn't want to do business with me, but I won't allow her to interfere again. Up to now I've been lenient, but one more move against me for whatever reason, and I'll come after her with everything we have here." Rodolfo spoke softly and placed his hand on Carlos's knee. "People may consider Cain harsh, but we can teach her the meaning of pain, if she desires."

They turned at the warehouse where Cain's offices were located, and Rodolfo closed his mouth and focused his attention, in case knowing the layout would come in handy in the future. They didn't stop at the front but drove straight into the building, and when Cain opened the car door from the outside, Rodolfo tried to keep his face blank.

"Thanks for coming," Cain said, holding her hand out in greeting.

"Cain," Rodolfo accepted her hand, "I've been looking forward to talking with you."

"Come inside." Cain slammed the car door closed and waved Lou off when he went to pat Carlos down. "This shouldn't take long. Sit down."

"It perhaps will take longer than you think. We will never be friends, but we will have to find a way to exist together."

Cain didn't move to sit behind her desk but rather sat on the front edge. Right behind her were the two things that made this conversation necessary. "What I want is for you to stop talking." This time, when Carlos started to reach for his weapon, Cain did nothing as Lou brought Carlos to his knees by twisting his arm up harshly.

"Your word means nothing then?" Rodolfo moved to the edge of his chair.

"It's your word that doesn't mean shit to me," Cain said as she stood straight. "Call off your dog or I'll put him down. I guaranteed your safety here, but he doesn't get the same deal." She pointed to Carlos.

"Carlos, give him your gun," Rodolfo said, but he kept his eyes on Cain. "Why am I here other than for you to insult me? I never took you for someone so crude."

"You want to know what it takes to make me crude? What drives me to want to skin you slowly and with as much pain as I can inflict before I let you die?" Cain didn't raise her voice as she crossed her arms over her chest. "Those aren't hypothetical questions, Rodolfo."

"Like you said, I don't give a shit about you or your questions."

"Being that uncurious is like being a two-legged dog in heavy traffic." Cain reached behind her and picked up Jesus Vega's wallet, holding it up like she thought it smelled bad. "What upsets me is an idiot in a nice suit who plays at being macho, but the only thing he really controls is his bladder."

"What?" Rodolfo yelled. "Fuck you."

Cain had been waiting for that. The control Rodolfo seemed to pride himself on had cracked like a pecan in her fist. "I see you're no stranger to crude, Señor Luis."

Her laugh appeared to make him angrier. "That can't be helped if you brought me here to play games and waste my time."

With a quick flick of her wrist she threw the wallet at him and it hit him in the middle of his chest before dropping to his lap. "I believe that belongs to you."

"What the hell is this?" Rodolfo asked, not touching the wallet.

"An example of how you have no control over your people. What I want to know before I take you back safe and sound, realizing as soon as you make it to the hotel you're at war with me, is what the hell you were thinking when you gave out the orders against my family."

"I've done nothing to make you move against me."

"Open the wallet," Cain said, her voice icy. "Jesus belonged to you, so I assume when he killed one of my men he was acting on your orders. I don't know how you handle this situation in Mexico, but here to kill without provocation invites me to kick your ass."

Rodolfo looked back at Carlos, who shook his head. "This man was not acting on my behalf."

"I believe that's your first admission that you're just an old man who plays at being the head of his family."

"I'm willing to put up with only so many insults before you *will* get the war you want." Rodolfo sat straighter in his chair and pulled his jacket down. "No woman speaks to me like this."

"That's right. You've got a unique way of dealing with people who go against you. You tie them to trees and let ants do the dirty work for you. That sounds manly to me. What about you, Lou?"

"Sounds more like chicken shit, Boss."

"How do you know anything about my business?"

Cain smiled and Rodolfo's eyes dropped to his lap. "I'm a woman who controls what happens in my family and what's done in my name. Unlike you, when I take care of a problem, it doesn't come back to haunt me."

"I have no ghosts to worry about," Rodolfo said, flicking his fingers at her as though to dismiss her. "And I still don't know why I'm here. Is it to listen to you spin tales?"

"You're here because Jesus Vega and Oscar Cardone, along with a few others, went to the airport recently and killed one of my men. Your men killed mine for no reason other than to hide your so-called ghost."

"Enough riddles." Rodolfo's voice rose higher than Cain found acceptable. "You dare—"

"Do you remember Armando Ortega?"

"Armando Ortega is dead," Carlos said. "Just like you will be for showing Señor Luis such disrespect."

"What does Ortega have to do with this?" Rodolfo asked.

"His son is here. What do you think he wants?" Cain finally got the reaction she was hoping for when Rodolfo paled.

"Impossible. I sent him home, and he knows nothing of Ortega." Rodolfo laughed and Carlos joined him. The wallet Cain had given him dropped to the floor when she handed him the passenger manifest. The circled name was hard to miss. "Hijo de puta," Rodolfo whispered as he crumpled the page in his hand.

"Juan Armando Ortega doesn't sound familiar to you?" Cain asked this time, watching Carlos's reaction to the name. "You're right, he's not a ghost, but he's yours nonetheless. I want to know where he is, because if he harms my family you're going to pay."

"I don't know where he is."

"Are you sure?" Cain asked, her eyes cut to Lou which made him wrap his hands around Cain's bargaining chip.

Rodolfo stood up when Carlos grunted as Lou tightened his grip around his neck. "No," Rodolfo said. "If I knew where he was I'd tell you, but Carlos isn't at fault here."

He almost sounded anguished and Cain nodded to Lou, who let go but kept his hands on Carlos's shoulders. "You owe me a debt," Cain said.

"What do you want?"

"Oscar Cardone and anyone he was with that day. Jesus didn't strike me as the kind of man who acted alone."

Rodolfo sat down again, the ball of paper still in his hand. "Done, but I am sure this is not all."

"I want Juan. It's time to completely put your ghosts to rest."

"I'll deal with my nephew."

"Unless you plan to bring me Juan's head in a box, I'll take care of him. You've proven to me that you can't be trusted to take care of anything."

"If I give you what you want, will you consider my debt paid?"

"In full."

Their meeting had ended and Rodolfo stood as Carlos got to his feet. Rodolfo put his hand on Carlos's arm when he reached for the gun Lou had returned to him, then they found their way back to the car alone.

"Think he can find the little shit?" Lou asked when they were by themselves.

"No, but Rodolfo's going to use whatever means he can to look for him. He had no idea Juan's here, and the fact he made it back without detection is scaring the shit out of him." Cain picked up her jacket and walked with Lou to the car they'd left out back. This meeting had been early so she could make it back home before Emma got up. "Losing control of his men doesn't scare him as much as losing control of Juan."

"Both scenarios should scare him." Lou started the car and followed the wharf as far as he could before turning onto the street.

"His men will fall in line with the right incentive, but Juan's a whole other animal, and he's permanently off his leash."

"What makes you think so?"

It took the tail car a while to catch up, but it was about a half a block behind them. Cain was sure they thought Lou was purposely trying to lose them, but he was playing a game. False conditioning, he called it. Make the feds think they were trying to lose them so they learned the evasion tactics Lou taught them to look for. Then when they were really trying to get away, the feds never saw it coming.

"Because the name on his passport tells me that Gracelia Luis might've accepted Rodolfo's help, but she's held a grudge for a very long time, and she shared it with her son. Rodolfo might've given Juan his name and groomed him to be his heir, but Juan knows he's also the man who painted his father's dick in honey and gifted him to the ants." Cain lost interest in trying to see who was driving the car behind them and put her hand on Lou's forearm. "Think about what you'd feel like if someone had done that to Lou Sr. Would that desire for revenge ever cool?"

"You're right, Rodolfo should be scared. If his sister is as good a talker as my mama, I see a big vat of honey in Rodolfo's future."

"I'll be in with Emma for the rest of the day, Lou," Cain said when he stopped by the front door.

She made it inside in time to visit with the kids during breakfast before they headed out to school. Usually Emma was with them, but only Carmen and Mook were sitting there.

"Miss Emma still sleeping," Carmen said. "I left her after you say she don't feel well."

"Be good, guys." Cain kissed the kids and headed upstairs. When she opened the door she saw the empty bed and heard the sound of retching coming from the bathroom. Before Emma could heave again, Cain was on her knees next to her holding her and keeping her hair out of the way.

"Sorry, honey," Emma said, her head falling against Cain's chest. "This isn't a sexy way to spend the morning."

"We're actually going to spend a sexy day at the doctor's office." Cain brought her closer and grunted as she made it off the floor with Emma in her arms. "If this is a bug, it should've passed by now."

"I already called." Emma sat still as Cain stripped her pajamas off. "We have an appointment in an hour."

As soon as Emma was naked, Cain made quick work of her clothes and carried Emma back to the bathroom and into the shower. Cain knew a warm shower was a good way to make Emma feel better.

"Want me to have Carmen bring you something up to eat?" Cain asked as she washed Emma's hair. She had no choice but to laugh when Emma threw up on her chest at the suggestion. "I'll take that as a no."

Emma laughed along with her, and the sound made Rodolfo and his family disappear from her thoughts. Instead, she concentrated on what was causing Emma's sudden stomach discomfort.

"Are you sure you're ready for this, mobster?" Emma asked after she'd rinsed her mouth in the spray. "We're not in our twenties anymore."

"My Da always said that babies keep you young."

"Babies?" Emma asked, then bit down on Cain's nipple. "I've always known you're an over-achiever, but one at a time, please."

Cain lifted her off her feet and kissed her, trying to put every bit of how she felt about Emma into it. When they parted, Emma smiled and wiped Cain's tears away. "It could be a bug, so don't be too disappointed if that's all it is."

"If it's not, we just try again," Cain said and kissed her again.

When they parted, it was Emma who was crying.

"However long it takes, lass. We'll try together until we get everything we want."

CHAPTER FIFTY

"Papi," Mano called Ramon from the foyer.

"Something wrong?" Ramon asked, holding on to the doorjamb that led outside to the large patio.

"Somebody tried to firebomb the club, and two of the day crew are at the hospital with burns."

"*Merda*," Ramon said, but he felt weak with relief it wasn't about Remi. "Cain wanted to wait for Nunzio's next move. I think he's made it."

"You want me to handle it?"

"Not before we talk to Cain and your sister, but this bastard gets no more free shots."

Mano held the door of the study for him, then sat in his usual spot. "I talked with Cain already, and she asked for us to wait until this afternoon. She also asked for one thing."

"What?"

"She wants Richard Bowen at the meeting."

Ramon was about to reach for a cigar but stopped halfway to the humidor. "Richard, for what?"

"She said she didn't feel comfortable discussing it on the phone because she was on a cell, but that's what she wants."

"Take the plane and get him here." Ramon retrieved his cigar and cocked his chair back. "I'll stay and see how the search for that bastard Jorge is going. Until we find him, I don't feel comfortable having Remi or you exposed."

"Don't tell Remi until it's time to meet. If she knows anything's going on, she'll leave Dallas's because she'll think she's not doing her share."

"Be careful, and put Richard in a safe spot until we're ready for him."

❖

Dr. Ellie Eschete knocked before entering the exam room at the end of the hallway. In Emma's chart were the results of the various blood and urine tests they'd run and Cain had insisted on waiting for.

"Well?" Cain asked when the door opened. She was sitting on a stool next to Emma, who was on the exam table. But she looked so nervous any thought of teasing her seemed like a bad idea.

"You don't have the flu," Ellie told Emma.

"Well?" Cain asked again.

"Honey," Emma put her palm against Cain's cheek, "calm down and she'll tell us."

"I'd plan to have another guest for Thanksgiving this year," Ellie said, staying in the doorway to keep clear of Cain's reaction. "It's not a stomach bug, sweetie, it's morning sickness. And if you're lucky it won't last as long as mine."

"She's pregnant?" Cain asked, sounding disoriented.

"She is, and I can even tell you when you got her that way," Ellie said, holding the chart up to hide that she was laughing. "Congratulations, and don't forget to make an appointment before you leave. See you then."

Cain lifted Emma off the table as if she weighed nothing and let out a whoop so loud the guys in the waiting room could probably hear it. They kissed and cried again.

"I'm so happy it's almost as if the time we were apart doesn't exist anymore," Emma said after she dressed. "That feeling is the best gift you could've given me."

"It doesn't exist because it'll never happen again." Cain held Emma's hand as they walked out. "We need to celebrate tonight."

Emma stopped to make her appointment and nodded. "I'll get this. Go share our news with Lou and the others before holding it in kills you."

Lou had his arms around Cain when Emma stepped out but let her go to give her a hug as well. "I'm happy for you, Emma."

"Another one for you to watch over," Emma said. "That'll keep you all busy enough, so it's time to finish what you started."

"You heard the lady," Merrick said. "Let's get to it."

❖

"Señor Luis." Oscar sat in the seat Carlos had put his hands on the back of and puffed his chest out as if preening. "Thank you for your invitation." He accepted the espresso Carlos handed him. "My compadres are jealous they weren't called."

"It's you I want, Oscar." Rodolfo took a sip of his own coffee and tried to even his breathing. "Can I get you anything else?"

"No, Señor, the coffee's fine. What would you like me to do for you?"

"I want you to tell me where Jesus is." Rodolfo put his cup down and folded his hands in his lap. "I haven't seen him, and he didn't say where he was going."

Oscar leaned forward to put his cup down as well but couldn't keep it from rattling before it reached the table.

"Do you think he's with my nephew?"

Oscar let out a nervous-sounding laugh as he turned around and looked at Carlos. "In Mexico? I don't know."

"Don't worry, Oscar." Rodolfo spoke in a soothing voice he'd used on Juan many times when he was a boy afraid of the dark after Gracelia had read him a bedtime story. After seeing the paper Cain had given him, he knew what Gracelia had been feeding him before he went to bed. "I already know where Jesus is."

"Where? I've been worried."

"That's a waste of your time. Jesus is no one's worry anymore."

"Where is he?"

"If I know Cain Casey, he's probably rotting in a dark hole somewhere." He delivered the news in the same soothing voice. "Jesus was first on her list, but she wants me to hand over someone else."

"She killed Jesus?"

"What you should be asking is who she wants next and why. Or do you already have an idea?"

Oscar tried to stand but Carlos put his hands on his shoulders and pushed him back down. "Don't worry. I'm not about to hand you over to be killed for taking out some guy that worked for Casey, but I do need something from you."

"Whatever you want." Oscar put his hands together like he was praying.

"Where's Juan?" As Rodolfo asked, Carlos pressed a knife to his throat and grabbed a handful of hair.

"At the hotel at the end of Esplanade, and he got back the day Jesus killed Casey's man. I didn't want any part of that, but Jesus said you knew about it." Oscar's hands were bobbing from his chest to his lap as he cried. "Then Juan ordered me not to tell you."

"Who's with him?"

"That guy from the FBI. A few of our men come and go, but Juan seldom goes out." As Oscar explained in a begging manner, he glanced back at Carlos occasionally.

"Take him downstairs," Rodolfo told Carlos," but before you cut him loose, I want to know who else was at the airport that day."

"Señor Rodolfo, please, I didn't want to be there."

"Get him out of my sight."

"Like we talked about?" Carlos asked.

Rodolfo stood, walked to the window, and merely lifted his hand in response. When he did, Oscar let out a moan that sounded as if someone had shot him. Perhaps that's what would happen to him, Rodolfo thought, but he wasn't concerned what Cain did to Oscar once Carlos handed him over. All he cared about was defusing the fire keg Juan had lit.

❖

The street in front of Ramon's club was lined with work trucks that morning when Cain and her group arrived. Whoever had thrown the incendiary device had managed to damage only the very front space, but unfortunately two employees had been standing there. From the number of workmen, Ramon didn't plan to stay closed long.

Mano was waiting for them by the bar, and before he led them to Ramon's office on the third floor he embraced Cain and kissed both her cheeks. "Thank you for saving my sister."

"You'd do the same for me." The guards hung back until they finished their talk, and Cain took her time with Mano because she, better than anyone, understood what an emotional wringer he'd been through. "I failed when it came to Marie and Billy, but I'm glad you were able to avoid that pain."

"After seeing how much you care, I can't believe you failed at all. I can't replace the loss of your family, but I want you to accept that you're part of mine. Whatever you need, call me and I'll treat you no different than if Remi was asking."

"Thanks, that means a lot to me."

"Good. Now if you're ready to go up, I got the package you asked for."

Richard looked like he was in shock when Cain entered and saw him standing in the corner, his back against the wall. His eyes were on Remi, and he kept blinking like maybe he could clear Remi from his sight if he tried hard enough.

"Good morning, Richard," Cain said to snap him out of his trance. "Sit down and close your mouth."

"Why am I here?"

"You're here so we can offer you the deal of your life."

"Ramon, what's this about?" Richard asked.

"Cain speaks for me and my family, so ask her. I just brought my checkbook," Ramon said with a laugh.

"The reality of our situation is that you own a casino in someone else's name. You're Junior and Nunzio Luca's front man, but in the eyes of the law you, and you alone, own the Capri," Muriel explained. Ross, Steve, and Dwayne sat next to her merely listening to what was going on. "Understand me so far?"

"If this has to do with the casino deal, you need to call Nunzio," Richard said, his breathing speeding up noticeably.

"We don't need to call Nunzio," Cain said, "when we have the true owner right here."

"Cain, no matter what you do, you're not going to make me sign anything. Whatever you threaten me with, Nunzio's only going to do worse, and you know it."

"Why not listen to what Muriel has to say before you turn us down?" Cain held her hands up. "But before you decide to walk away no matter what, consider this. Today is the last day any of us will talk about this deal, much less consider it. A decision you made without Nunzio's permission brought us to this point. Do you think he's forgotten that?"

"What do you want?"

"We want the casino, and we want to buy it from you."

Richard was laughing so hard he slapped his knees. "That's hilarious. Really, what do you want?"

"I'm not a huge fan of repeating myself, just so you know." Richard's merriment died at Cain's words and the room fell silent again. "But I'll explain again since it seems over your head. You can turn me and the Jatibons down and face Nunzio. Or you can accept our offer and retire to a palm tree somewhere with the money we're going to pay you for signing your name."

Richard sat up straighter and put his hands over his mouth. While he thought about it, Cain made a bet with herself how long he would hold out before he took the money.

"How much?"

Cain accepted a slip of paper from Ramon and handed it over. "That amount in a Cayman account in your name. You can enjoy the beach for awhile if you want, or you can transfer it wherever you like."

"Who's going to protect me from Nunzio?"

"That check has enough zeros to buy all the protection you'll need."

Richard closed his hand over the paper and took a deep breath. "If you tell me why, I'll give you what you want."

"You should know the answer to that," Cain said, "but I'll let Remi explain."

"Nunzio took his shot at me, and this is our response. Hiring someone to kill me doesn't come without consequences. The casino is his consequence."

"I sign it over and you give me the money—it's that simple?"

"You got it," Cain said.

"But it's worth so much more," Richard said as he glanced at the amount again.

"Do you remember how well your negotiations went the last time you tried?" Cain shot back.

"You have the papers ready?"

Cain and Ramon nodded.

"And you'll help me get out of here?"

"I'll have our plane take you wherever you want to go after the transaction is done," Ramon said.

"Let me know when and I'll be there," Richard said, putting the paper in his coat pocket.

"Steve, Dwayne, and Ross will escort you to the Mississippi Gaming Board Office today," Cain said. "The application's complete and waiting for you to sign." Richard stood after Cain did and shook her hand, then Ramon's. "Only your signature, Richard, nothing more that'll delay this."

"When did you set up the meeting with the gaming board?"

"Yesterday afternoon," Cain said, smiling when he appeared surprised. "I'm buying a casino, but I never gamble unless it's a sure bet. You struck me as a sure bet."

"I'd tell you to kiss my ass, but with all that money I don't care what you think of me."

Simon and Muriel left with Dwayne and Steve, but Cain stopped Ross. "Are you sure about this? It's not too late to change your mind if you don't want the added scrutiny in your life."

"You're my family, and I don't mind helping you out when I can. Besides, you don't have to ever question your trust in me. What happened with Richard today will never cross my mind, and it's got nothing to do with Emma or the kids."

"Then we'll have plenty to celebrate when you get back."

Once the group had left, the guards did too, so Cain and the Jatibons were alone. They needed to discuss the rest of their plans, and after considering all the options Cain thought it best to strike back fast.

"Our people are in place at the casino's hotel waiting for our call," Mano said as he handed everyone a folder. "Muriel and I worked up a list of immediate firings. She has the pink slips with her so she can distribute them when she hears from our new owners."

"When are we telling Nunzio?" Remi asked. Her time with Dallas had been productive as far as their relationship, but Cain and her father had given her some time off from her responsibilities to heal.

"His house is a block from the place. He should see the signs coming down," Mano said.

"If he doesn't, I want you to call him," Ramon said.

"I agree. It's only right that it comes from you, so you can tell him we're willing to see him here," Cain said. "From what I hear he's still in town, and it shouldn't be too hard to arrange a meeting since he dropped the ball with Richard."

"Then what?" Remi asked.

"That's up to you," Cain said. "None of us has a bruise on their chest from a bullet impact, but I've got a suggestion."

"Let's hear it."

"I brought you a get-well present, but before you let your anger overrule your emotions, consider how we can best use it." Cain would accept whatever Remi wanted because of what had happened to her, but if she listened, Cain's plan could be the beginning of the end for most of their problems.

"What happened to me wasn't personal, I know that. Nunzio just saw it as the quickest way to get us to come back to the table. I may not understand that logic, but that's all it was and I have to accept it." Remi stood with her hand on her chest. She was moving better, Cain noticed, but from the way her mouth pulled when she had to sit or stand, she still felt pain.

"Lou," Cain said into the intercom to the second floor, "could you come back in with our new friend." It didn't take long for Lou to walk in with a much shorter man at his side. The guy was almost delicate looking, from the slim nose down to his long willowy fingers. "It was a bitch trying to find this guy, but I thought you'd like to meet him."

"Should I know who this is?" Remi asked.

"You may not know him, but you're familiar with his work. Jorge is the one who gave you that bruise and broke your rib."

Remi grunted as she got out of the chair, but she moved quickly to Jorge and punched him in the face hard enough to knock him off his feet. "You're not going to live long enough to regret that shot."

"I hit you," Jorge said, rubbing his jaw. "There's no way you walked away from that."

The complaint made Remi hit him again. "I walked away, and that doesn't make your future worth investing in."

"Remi, if you want to kill him I wouldn't blame you," Cain said.

"What else do you think I should do with him?"

"Jorge, what's your price?" Cain asked him.

"Five hundred thousand a job. It sounds like a lot, but I guarantee success, and until now that's what everyone's got for their money."

"For this job you'll get a much better payoff," Cain said as she pointed him to a chair.

"You want to hire me?"

"I more than anyone here understand business, Mr. Cristo. What you did was your job and nothing personal against Remi." Cain cut her eyes to Remi, who looked like she wanted to squeeze the life out of Jorge. "But you got caught with your hand in the cookie jar, and it's time to make things right."

"What's the job?"

"I want you to take out Junior Luca, and I want you to vary from your usual style and shoot him through the eyes. I don't give a shit what his body looks like after you're done, but I do want to know he's dead." Cain watched him as she spoke and noticed he petted the beard on the left side of his mouth, as if he were trying to get something out of it.

Everyone had a tell when it came to their fear, and she had a feeling this was his. Tells were the body's way of letting out fear and nerves, but they were also a good way to pick up on what a person wanted to keep hidden from the world. In poker they cost you the big pots, and right now Jorge's fear was driving the movements, cluing Cain in to how easy it would be to get what she wanted.

"My price is no different for that."

"You're going to do it and you're going to get only one thing in return, and my offer's only good while you're in this room."

"What's your price?" Jorge said. He pulled his hand away from his face and stared at it as if it had betrayed him by moving to his beard.

"Your life, Mr. Cristo," Cain said with an air of finality.

"You call that fair?" Jorge's hand returned to his face.

"You have the right to turn me down, that's up to you. Turn me down, though, and I'm through with you and it's Remi's turn."

"If you want Junior dead, then he's dead," he told Cain, and turned to Remi. "She's right, this was only business. I have nothing against you or your family, but if you let me go you have my word you and your family have nothing to fear from me."

"Do you swear it on your mother's head?"

"I swear it."

"Cain had her price and her reasons, but I won't forgive what you did that easily, so I want one more thing from you."

"You've got the right to ask me anything."

"Are you right- or left-handed when it comes to your toys?" Remi asked.

"Right-handed."

"Junior Luca's part of the deal, but you have to carry a reminder for you not to come near us again. Maybe with enough time you'll learn to be as accurate with your left hand as the people who hire you expect you to be." When Remi got close to him he wrapped his hands around the arms of the chair. "Your right hand."

Jorge held out his right index finger, his trigger finger. He made no sound as it hit the floor and accepted the handkerchief that she offered him to stop the bleeding.

"You have until tomorrow to do this, and you won't be going alone," Cain said as she waved one of her men over. "Once you finish, you're free to go. Renege, and the guy I'm sending with you will pull his own trigger, and I promise he'll be close enough there's no chance in hell he'll miss."

CHAPTER FIFTY-ONE

Anthony opened his eyes and shut them just as quickly when the brightness of the room felt like it was burning holes in his retinas. He'd spent another late night with Juan's men sitting outside the Casey place watching, but trying to stay out of sight of the other watchers. It was like his old job, only the pay was better. Then there was the new bonus Juan was sharing with him.

The blankets had tangled around his legs, and he glanced down to study the heap of material. His senses were heightened, like the way the sheets felt rough against his naked skin. As he concentrated on that feeling, someone banged on his door.

He took his time, finding it humorous when the banging got louder. With a flick of his wrist he wrenched the door open, making Joe lose his balance and stumble a step forward. "Are you here to make sure I don't oversleep?"

"We need to talk to you so go put on some pants," Joe said. Shelby walked in behind him and studied the front room.

"Should I remind you that I'm not working after Annabel threw me out?" He took a seat on the sofa and put his feet on the coffee table. The position made his white briefs pull tautly against his groin. "Besides, maybe Shelby wants to see what she's missing by sniffing around the Caseys."

Joe advanced on him with his fists clenched, but Shelby stopped him before he got too close. "Agent Hicks asked us to drop by and invite you in for questioning."

"If Annabel wants to talk to me then tell her to get her fat ass down here. I'm through with her and her fumblings. Once my suspension's over, I'm putting in for a transfer, but not before I report her for incompetence."

"Why don't you get your head out of your ass and accept why Agent Hicks suspended you? It had nothing to do with your warped view of the world," Joe said. With the tip of his shoe he pushed a stack of magazines to the floor so he could sit.

Anthony looked from the mess on the floor to Joe and smiled. "I'd love to come in and chat, but my dance card's so full that I simply don't have time."

"You can do it voluntarily or we can come back in a more official capacity," Shelby added. She took a seat at the desk. "If you want to go that route, it'll haunt you at work for a long time."

"You think I care about that?" Anthony wanted to scream but his head was starting to pound. "When I'm done I won't have to worry about any performance reviews, but people like you will."

"I don't know, Joe," Shelby said, her head turned more toward the top of the desk than to her friend. "When you go in for your next review do you think you'll have to explain why you were seen leaving the airport with a known drug dealer?"

"Not to mention that dead guy in the bathroom. It would take quite a story to convince people you were nowhere near." Joe took up where she left off.

"I don't know what the hell you're talking about." Anthony sat up, trying to see what Shelby was so interested in. He'd heeded Annabel's warning about money, and the cash Juan had paid him was stashed in a strongbox in the bedroom closet. "Who got killed at the airport?"

"Shelby and I both know you're a complete ass, but don't compound it by trying to act stupider than you are," Joe said. "You know damn well what we're talking about, and it's time to tell us what you know on the record, so get dressed."

"I'm not coming in without a subpoena, so fuck off."

"That should take about twenty minutes. Why not take a shower and be waiting on us when we get back, because I can promise you, if you're still in your tighty whities, that's how I'm taking you in," Joe said as he got up and brushed off his pants.

The two agents left and Anthony immediately got off the couch and stripped to shower. If Joe and Shelby mentioned the airport, the questioning Annabel wanted to engage in wouldn't be friendly. There was most likely a collage of pictures of him and Juan leaving the airport and essentially the scene of a crime that'd play well to a jury.

He was dripping on the carpet in the bedroom a few minutes later, not caring if the phone was bugged. "Get ready to move," he told Juan.

"The net's in place and the feds are getting ready to close it."

Shelby snapped her fingers in the van and rearranged their surveillance to make sure Anthony didn't spot them. "Are you calling Agent Hicks?" Joe asked.

"Eventually, but right now we're going to stick to Anthony and see where he leads us. Make sure the guys know he's one of ours and, though he's been out of his mind lately, he's been trained to spot us."

"You think he'll trip up enough to give you something?" Joe asked. They were halfway to his car, but Shelby stopped at the corner where their second team was parked.

"Call it a hunch, but yeah. Cain and her crew are still important, but Anthony's playing a dangerous game with an unstable partner." She leaned against the panel van and crossed her arms over her chest. Staying here would also keep her from having to stare at Muriel all day, but she wasn't about to admit that to Joe or anyone. "You stay with the Caseys and we'll meet up later."

"I'll send Lionel back to help you," Joe said, "and don't take any chances. Like you said, Juan's not stable, and unlike our friend Cain across town, he's not going to respect that you're an agent."

"Don't worry. I'll keep my head down. Call me when your shift's done and we'll touch base."

Joe started walking but turned before Shelby could open the door to the van. "Remember to be careful, Shelby. Juan's one part of this, but something's really off about Anthony. Getting the bad guys is important, but it's not worth getting hurt over."

"That goes for you too, Joe. Now get out of here before our boy starts his day." Shelby was getting comfortable in her seat when Anthony strode out and headed for his car. The van parked close to his car was Shelby's decoy, and she laughed when he flipped them off. He peeled out of his parking spot, obviously in a hurry to get to wherever Juan was.

Shelby sat back and closed her eyes as they started at a much slower pace, confident that the three cars she had following Anthony wouldn't lose him. He was up to something that could only help their investigation, but she figured Anthony wasn't aware it would trigger his downfall. You didn't cross a certain line unless it was the FBI's idea, and he'd done it. Now there was no going back.

❖

Cain sat at one end of the table with her family stretched out between her and Ross. When he got back, they'd picked Vincent Carlotti's place to celebrate and were waiting for the main courses.

"Daddy, I think the tycoon persona looks good on you," Emma said of his suit and tie. "The cows won't recognize you."

"I'm having so much fun I might leave the cows to Jerry and his guys."

"Then our brilliant plan worked," Cain said, lifting her glass of iced tea in his direction. "I'm sure if we give these guys a vote, they'd tell you they want their grandpa to stay," Cain said about the kids. "Then there's the other reason."

"The first one's pretty good, Cain," Muriel said. "I'm not sure there's a better reason than grandkids. At least that's what Da keeps telling me."

"Two grandchildren are a great reason," Emma said, "but three might be the clincher."

"You're having a baby?" Hayden asked. "You are, aren't you?" He slid his chair back and sprang to his feet and wrapped his arms around Emma before she could do the same. When he turned to Cain he slapped hands with her before giving her a bear hug. "Hannah, we're getting a brother or a sister."

"I want both," Hannah said as she stood on Muriel's legs.

The doors to the private room opened and Vincent carried in a bottle of champagne and the right number of flutes. "Are you going to tell me now why I've had this on ice all day?" he asked Cain.

Cain popped the cork and poured while Vincent did the same with a bottle of sparkling grape juice. "To my beautiful wife," Cain raised her glass to Emma, "to our children and our family. Those who've come before us, those here with us, and those yet to come."

"Cheers," the group said before they drank. The rest of the night was filled with laughter that Nunzio didn't ruin when he arrived and tried to muscle his way in to see her. The celebration started again when Lou and the others drove them home. Ross had worked hard with a handful of Cain's men and repaired the damage to the walls.

The place was spotless and contained only a fraction of their personal belongings, but Cain had wanted it to be a surprise. They'd worry about their clothes and other things in the morning. All Cain wanted was to make love to Emma in their bed.

"Do you want a boy or a girl?" Emma asked as she lay in Cain's arms trying to catch her breath.

"We've got one of each now, so this one, whatever it is, is lagniappe. What matters is that it'll belong to us, a part of our little clan."

"Was it the clan chieftain who Nunzio Luca wanted to do business with tonight? He was pretty adamant about wanting to talk to you."

"Nunzio's a shit who needs to learn some manners, and tomorrow's going to be his first lesson." Cain yawned and Emma rubbed her hand in a circle on Cain's stomach, trying to get her to fall asleep.

"While you're dealing with him, I'll get us moved back in here and get Hayden's party squared away." She kept up her soft touch and felt Cain's breathing even out as she fell asleep. Once she was sure, Emma dropped her hand and kissed Cain's shoulder.

Emma remembered their first night in this room, but that timid girl who wasn't sure of her place was gone. This time around, the woman she'd become accepted and welcomed how Cain had dealt with the killers who had destroyed their home.

Again she whispered a quick prayer to keep her family safe and to protect the life she carried. As long as God granted her that, she'd bear the rest the best she could, no matter what sacrifice she had to make personally.

❖

"The bastard's gone too far this time," Juan said as he paced the new hotel room Anthony had checked them into on Airline Highway, right outside the city limits. It was one of the only places that didn't rent by the hour to the dozens of hookers walking the strip made famous when televangelist Jimmy Swaggart was caught in a sex-for-hire sting.

The ranting was starting to get old, and Anthony contented himself with another small taste from Juan's box. It still surprised him that he'd stumbled on to the one thing in his life that had triggered the addictive part of his brain. He was convinced he was still in control, but he felt so good nothing much bothered him.

"It was lucky for me you called when you did and I got out before Carlos saw me," Juan continued.

"What was he doing at the hotel and how'd he locate you?"

"My uncle sent him, and I don't know how the old bastard found out I'm back. But if he sent Carlos—he wants me dead."

Anthony unbuttoned his shirt and lay back on the bed. "I saw how he was with you at Ramon's place the night he first met with Casey. Rodolfo doesn't want you dead. You're like a son to him."

"You don't know how Rodolfo Luis works. He isn't a forgiving man, even if it's his family, when someone goes against him." Juan checked the parking lot again before he took the other bed. "I need to get out of here until I can put my own network together, but I want you to do something first."

"Are you keeping it to yourself, or are you going to share?" Anthony asked, fighting to keep the eagerness out of his voice.

"You're the only one I trust," Juan said, and told Anthony his plan. After Anthony gave him some ideas, Juan opened up and became more animated.

"Get some sleep then, because what you want is possible, but it won't be easy."

CHAPTER FIFTY-TWO

The next morning Cain took time to have breakfast with Emma and the kids, then walked Emma to the car Merrick was driving. "Remember, you just point and direct," Cain said. "No lifting of any kind."

"That's the fourth time you've said that in the last ten minutes."

"I'd say it again but I told your father, so I think I'm covered," Cain said as she opened the back door to the car. "Take care, and call me if you need me."

"Please be careful today. I don't like this guy, and I don't trust him to keep his word about anything."

The cameras across the street, Cain was sure, captured how she felt about her partner as she kissed Emma as passionately as if they'd been alone. More than anything she wanted to forget about business and spend her time holding Emma's hand. The pregnancy caused the over-protectiveness, she guessed, but whatever it was, her heart was screaming much louder than her head for Emma to stay home.

"I love you,' Cain said, her lips close to Emma's ear. There was only so much she was willing to share with the world. "And I'm having a hard time letting you go."

"See, when you say things like that you make me think you're a fraud, mobster." Emma put her hand just inside Cain's shirt against her skin. "I love that you show that side only to me, and tonight I'll prove to you how much. Right now, though, I need you to be the devil I know. No mercy, love, because I'm selfish and want you home more."

"Merrick," Cain said as she still had Emma in her arms. "Make sure the guys keep their eyes open today."

"Is there something you're not telling me?"

"I feel like we're standing in the eye of a hurricane, and the stillness makes me antsy."

"We're moving, Boss, what could happen?"

"Whatever does, make sure you get out of it free and clear." Cain kissed Emma again and watched the car until it disappeared down the street.

The feeling of unease didn't leave Cain as she arrived at the office. She stood outside longer than usual, staring at the row of windows across the street. "Here I am," she said softly, barely moving her lips. When she walked in she kept heading toward the back. Lou and Katlin followed her as they walked close to the buildings for more than a mile. Unless Shelby had thought to cover the river, which from their own surveillance she hadn't, they were free to leave.

They weren't going too far, though. Simon was waiting at the door of another small warehouse that belonged to another dead man, but Cain paid the bills.

"Did you have any problems?" Cain asked.

"Nunzio's bitched about what he called the cloak-and-dagger shit, but he's here. Everyone's waiting inside."

"Let's not keep them waiting then." Cain entered and quickly made it through the building and into the next one. As they entered the empty space, Nunzio walked over to Cain with his finger up and came close to poking her in the chest. He stopped when Lou grabbed his wrist.

"Call this fucker off, Cain," Nunzio said, his voice loud enough to echo against the metal walls. "I came here at your invitation and I'm not going to put up with being treated like this."

"What you're going to do is shut up before I cut your tongue out," Ramon said as he crossed his legs. "Did your father really give you the go-ahead to kill my child? I'm curious to know if you're just stupid or if it runs in your family?"

"I don't know what you're talking about." Nunzio stepped away from Lou and stood closer to Kim. "I'm here to offer my support and help you through this, Ramon. What happened to Remi is tragic, but we had nothing to do with it."

"You know that's true, Cain," Kim said. "None of our people touched Remi."

"I didn't realize we were on a first-name basis, but I believe you." The way Kim exhaled made Cain take a seat next to Ramon and touch his hand briefly. "None of your people took that shot because I'm sure the only one who could've pulled it off was you, and you didn't do it. Did you?"

"I didn't have anything to do with it," Kim said, sounding like someone trying to distance herself from Nunzio.

"I believe you too," Remi said, stepping out of the shadows. "Nunzio kept his hands clean by hiring outside talent."

"What's going on?" Nunzio asked, slumping against Kim at the sight of Remi standing there. "I saw you die."

"You saw me get shot, there's a difference."

Cain watched as Kim started to draw her gun. "Simon didn't disarm you, but if your hand goes up any higher I'll have Lou cut it off."

"Cain…Ramon, come on," Nunzio said, his palms up. "You touch me and my father's going to come after you, and that should scare you. Our business has increased his power."

"He has the bigger dick, huh?" Cain asked, making Remi and the others laugh. "You took your shot, Nunzio, and now it's Remi's turn."

"I came here in good faith," Nunzio said.

Remi got close to him as Simon moved behind them. "You think we lured you here to kill you?" She laughed and shook her head. "No, I want the answer to the question my father asked you. Who ordered the hit on me?"

"How can I tell you something we had nothing to do with?"

"Nunzio, have you met Jorge Cristo? Or have you just talked to him on the phone?" Cain asked. "If you haven't, you were missing out. We talked to Jorge and he was very forthcoming about who gave him his latest half-million-dollar deposit."

"It was business, Remi. I've got nothing against you, but me and my father needed Cain and Ramon to come back to the table." He backed up some more and ran into Simon. "You and Ramon would've done the same thing."

"That's true, Nunzio, we would've done the same, but ask yourself this. If we'd missed, what would've it cost us?" Remi asked, but Cain wasn't watching Nunzio. Her eyes were on Kim as she again tried to reach for her gun, only to have Katlin stop her. Cain knew why she was starting to get nervous.

Cain had known that kind of fear only one time—when she was on the floor of her warehouse after Kyle shot her. Death was something they were familiar with, but Cain would never consider it a friend. Watching Emma's face fade from her consciousness had terrified her. Even though on that night they were still estranged, what she felt for

Emma and her children was what had made her fight back. Did Kim have that kind of motivating force in her life?

The phone in Remi's hand rang and only Nunzio glanced down, looking as if the thing was about to blow up.

Remi put it on speaker. "Hello."

"It's done, and my debt's paid," Jorge said.

"Just remember the rest of our deal," Remi said, putting the phone to her ear. "There'll be no forgiveness next time."

"What's he talking about?" Nunzio asked.

"Jorge did a job for you, and now he did one for us," Remi said. "He paid your father a visit, only I asked him to make the shot through the head. Junior's dead."

"You're dead," Nunzio screamed and lunged toward Remi. "You're fucking dead," he said again from Lou's arms.

"Actually it's my turn to hit back," Remi said.

Nunzio stopped struggling and watched as Simon took a blade from her belt and sunk it into Kim's chest as if she stabbed soft butter. Kim let out a small gurgle and coughed, which sprayed her white shirt with blood.

She dropped to her knees and Simon took her knife back before Kim fell forward, dead before her head hit the ground. Simon wiped the blade on Kim's back before putting it back in her sheath.

"It might be hard to hear this, Nunzio, but it's important for you to understand," Cain said, making Lou tap Nunzio's face to make him stop staring at Kim's limp body. "The casino is ours. We're letting you go, but if you return to Mississippi with thoughts of causing problems, that's where you'll end up." She pointed to Kim. "You tried and it didn't work out."

"The casino's mine," Nunzio said, his voice despondent.

"Richard was who we needed," Remi said. "That was your last strike."

"If it takes me the rest of my life you aren't getting away with this," Nunzio said. "Why Kim?"

"Why Remi?" Cain asked in return. "We all have our reasons and we have to live with the results of our decisions."

"This has you written all over it, so I'm coming for you first," Nunzio said to Cain. "When I'm done, you'll lose people you—"

Katlin's phone rang and Nunzio shut up. "What? Slow down," she told whoever was calling.

Cain's phone rang next, followed by Lou's. "Cain, hurry, it's Emma," Carmen said when Cain answered. "They took her."

Cain felt like Simon had stabbed her through the heart. The panic rose so fast she came close to throwing up. Lou stopped her from running out the front door, but they sprinted the entire way back to the office where Nick already had the car running.

"What the hell happened?" Cain asked, part of her afraid to hear, and she didn't expect answers—not yet.

❖

"Do we have enough escorts for the movers?" Emma asked Merrick. They were in the den at Jarvis's house and Emma had her date book out. "I made that mistake already and I don't want a repeat."

"I took care of it. Since we're only moving small stuff, we didn't need to hire that many guys."

"If that's the case, let's go pick up Hayden's gift."

"The gunsmith called about that already?" Merrick asked, sounding surprised as she pulled her jacket on to cover her double holster. "He must've put in some time to finish so quick."

"One of his assistants called this morning after Cain left and said he worked late last night to get it done. I would've thought all that engraving would take more time too, but I guess he wanted to make Cain happy."

Emma followed a foot behind Merrick as they walked around the workmen, her hand on her stomach the entire time. The morning sickness hadn't kicked in until she'd actually eaten something, making her regret she'd chosen waffles.

"It's Hayden who's going to be thrilled."

Emma laughed. "I think my boy's thrilled most days just with the fact that he's Hayden Casey. The shotgun's an added bonus—lagniappe, as Cain likes to say."

The hunting trip Cain was taking him on was only part of Hayden's gift for his thirteenth birthday. They had ordered a twelve-gauge shotgun identical to the one Cain owned, with a vine of Irish roses engraved along the barrel and the Casey family crest carved into the stock. Cain's had been a gift from her father on her fifteenth birthday.

"True, but it's nice that it's ready a few days early," Merrick said.

They turned right out of the drive, and Merrick glanced in the rearview mirror.

"Why do you suppose these guys are always so interested in our little shopping trips?" Emma asked when she saw Merrick's attention still behind them.

"Shit," Merrick said, speeding up.

"What?" Emma asked, squeezing the armrest to brace herself. The car rammed them from behind, making Merrick sideswipe a parked car. She righted them and punched the accelerator, but the car hit them again as they crossed an intersection.

In the more open space they were rammed hard enough that the car Merrick was driving turned sideways. The attacker then slammed his brakes on and threw it in reverse to give him more room to speed up and hit them again. This blow to the driver's side pinned Merrick behind the wheel and broke her left arm.

Even though she was hurt, Merrick tried to get to her phone as Emma lay unconscious beside her. The last impact must've slammed Emma's head into the window, because Merrick could see her blond hair was dripping with blood.

"Emma," she yelled, trying to revive her. "Open your eyes," was all she was able to say as her window shattered beside her from the force of Juan Luis's gun butt.

"She'll be easier to move if she's out, bitch," he said as he placed the gun correctly in his hand.

Merrick forgot about the phone and went for her weapon instead, as someone flung the passenger-side door open.

Anthony Curtis unbuckled Emma and jerked her from her seat and over his shoulder. Merrick framed the word "No" on her lips, but Juan pulled the trigger before she could get it out.

All Juan could do was laugh and stare at Emma in the backseat as they sped away. Anthony's plan had gone off flawlessly, and he had what he'd most wanted from Cain.

"I'm going to enjoy this," he said to Emma, even though he knew she couldn't hear him. "And I promise it'll be slow and long."

"This is the beginning of Cain's end," Anthony said and laughed. "If that bitch had a weak spot, it's ours now to do with as we please."

"Are you sure you know where we're going?" Juan asked.

"I got the address from the file before I quit. It's the last place Casey will look, which will only prove she's not the big shit everyone thinks she is."

"Let's go have some fun then."

CHAPTER FIFTY-THREE

The police had barricaded the intersection where Merrick's car sat mangled. An ambulance was screeching away, and the police had to hold Cain back to keep her from chasing it down.

"It's not Miss Emma," Carmen told her over and over. They were only a block from the house so most of the staff was outside waiting on news. "It's Merrick, she's been shot." Katlin shut her eyes and brought her fist to her mouth.

"Katlin, go," Cain ordered. "You'll be of no use to me here."

"You don't need to—" Katlin said, looking at her as if Cain had punched her.

"If you love her, go. Some things are more important than anything or anyone else. If you have to concentrate on something let it be Merrick—she deserves it."

"Boss," Lou said. "The cops said Emma wasn't here when they arrived, and the people who called it in said only Merrick was in the car."

"Miss Emma left with Merrick, I saw her," Carmen said.

"Somebody rammed them and took her," Lou said, as if Cain hadn't figured it out. "Emma's gone."

Cain roared like a lion that had lost its mate. "No one saw anything?"

"Our boys said a black Tahoe followed the car out but they figured it for feds," one of Cain's men said.

"The feds," Cain said, as she scanned the crowd and found Joe and Claire looking on. "Who was it?" Cain asked Joe. "You vultures are always watching, there's no way you missed this. Tell me who."

"We tried, Cain, but our people didn't get here in time, even if that isn't their job."

"Your job is to protect the innocent. My wife's done nothing to deserve this, so your job was to protect her." Cain grabbed Joe by the lapels and shook him. "Tell me who, you son of a bitch."

"It was Juan Luis," Claire said, "and we've put out an APB on the car."

"Well, if you did that I can go home and put my feet up and wait for Emma to come home. Your job's done and I'll buy you a drink later," Cain said sarcastically. "Was your fellow agent with him? Because we all know Juan couldn't find his ass by himself if someone put a gun to his head and said go."

"If you want us to work with you, you need to calm down," Joe said. When Cain couldn't hold her anger anymore and reared back and coldcocked him, he bumped into three other cops standing around. His nose was oozing blood when he straightened up, and he was in an attack stance. "I know you're upset, but if you try that again I'm taking you in and you can do your worrying in a cell."

"You can kiss my—" Cain was about to completely lose control when her phone rang. "What?" she screamed. Just as quickly she calmed as she held the phone to her ear and said nothing. "Which house is it?" She hung up and strode around the accident scene, not trading any more conversation with Lou or Claire.

"Where's she going?" Joe asked.

"It's got to be the house or someplace close, because she's walking," Claire said. "All we have to do is wait and do what she thinks we do best—watch."

Cain started toward Jarvis's but met Muriel halfway there. The house Cain stopped at belonged to an elderly woman who'd been watering her plants and witnessed the black SUV slam into the car they were chasing, and what came after. Joe and Claire stood a good distance away as Cain talked to her, obviously asking questions. Then she shook hands with the woman and walked to the house.

"Think she's going to stay in and not do anything?" Claire asked.

"I don't see that happening, not unless she has a crystal ball in there that gives her all the answers. I'm not sure where we start searching. What I do know is that Agent Hicks will probably have a warrant out for Anthony and Juan before the hour's up."

"Let's head to the van just in case." Claire glanced back at the car Merrick had been driving one last time and shivered. The agents they'd left watching the house had tried to get to Emma before the two men had taken her, but Anthony had left Merrick's car blocking the intersection from both directions.

"Wait a minute," Joe said and started running down the street. "Shelby," he said when he was inside and struggling to get his phone out.

"She stayed to sit on Anthony, but none of the guys said they saw her when this went down."

"If I know Shelby, she wasn't too far away," Joe said and pressed the call button on his phone.

❖

"Muriel," Shelby said, "please don't hang up."

"This isn't a good time, Shelby." Muriel said her name since Cain was looking straight at her.

"I was tailing Anthony when it happened."

"Where is he now?" Muriel asked, making Cain stand up. "You lost them? How in the hell did that happen?"

"I'd love to tell you that since I'm in the FBI I'm perfect, but I'm not. Once he made it into the neighborhood, Lionel and I didn't have a lot of places to hide, so we had to hang back. Then the bastard left that car in the perfect place on the street, and we had to go around a few blocks and pray we could catch up, but we lost him." Shelby sounded genuine in wanting to help.

"Ask her which way he was headed," Cain said.

Muriel talked for a minute more, then hung up. "She lost them when they stopped at the house. From what she said, someone called the house and talked to Emma, pretending to be the gunsmith's assistant, and told her the gun you guys ordered was finished. Before Shelby had a chance to figure out what he was up to and make it over here, Emma and Merrick had left and fallen into Anthony's trap. It was Anthony who lured her out of the house, and with the moving going on, Merrick and Emma left by themselves."

"Which way was he going when she last saw him?" Cain asked.

"Toward St. Charles, but then he must have doubled back down some of the side streets because there was no sign of him when she got to the avenue."

ALI VALI

Cain sat down and buried her fingers in her hair, wanting more than anything to cry. New Orleans might not be New York in size or population, but right now it could be Podunk USA and she wouldn't have time to find Emma before Juan did something unspeakable to her.

"You can't give up, think," Muriel said.

"They could be anywhere by now, and no amount of thinking will make me pull the answer out of my ass." Cain came close to hitting Muriel as well, but knew she was only trying to help. "It's like Marie all over again. I travel with all this muscle and then leave the most vulnerable of my family unprotected. I should be fucking shot for letting this happen again." She was on a roll as the weight of her failures started to pile on her shoulders, the weight of them threatening to swamp her. Then it came to her. Her greatest failures and how someone would use them to stick it to her and make it hurt as much as humanly possible.

"What?" Muriel said as Cain grabbed her and yanked her toward the back door.

"There's no way he has the balls for that, but then it's Anthony with his hand up Juan's ass making his lips move," Cain said. "Lou, get the men ready to roll and I want every cop out there covered, because we're leaving and I don't want an audience."

Muriel's phone rang again. "Yes?" she asked, and talked for a minute before disconnecting. "Shelby found the Tahoe, but there's no sign of Anthony or Juan."

"Give her a while and she'll come up with the right answer, but I don't have time to drop breadcrumbs for her."

Five cars pulled out ahead of them and blocked the street from sidewalk to sidewalk as Lou turned in the opposite direction, the FBI vehicles hemmed in. Despite the blowing horns and sirens, the cars didn't move until Lou and his passengers were out of sight.

"Where to, boss?" Lou asked.

"The house where we taught Danny the lesson on how to kill a goat. Get there fast but don't get pulled over."

"There's no way he picked that house," Muriel said. "How would he even know about it?"

"Juan wouldn't, but Anthony had access to all the files that pertained to us and our business, including the dark, bloody chapters. He didn't go with Juan because he had a burning desire to lead a life of crime—he did it because of me. Kyle's a dead subject, but he wasn't the only one working for the Bureau who hates me enough to bend the rules when it comes to dealing with me."

Cain couldn't control the bounce in her legs as she willed the car to go faster. "I had other plans for Anthony but that's changed. When I find him I'm going to string him up and shove a cattle prod up his ass and turn it on. He wanted to watch me twitch for him when he brought me down, but he doesn't know the meaning of the concept."

Lou slammed his brakes on in front of the old abandoned shotgun house that now belonged to Cain. She'd bought it before she'd taken Danny there, wanting to watch the place fall in on itself eventually. It was, like she'd said, the site of her greatest failure, and as long as it stood it reminded her not to let her guard down.

In front, parked haphazardly on the grass, was a beat-up car whose hood was still warm to the touch. Lou ran slightly ahead of them with his gun drawn and kicked open the front door, and Cain saw Lionel standing in the first room. On the table where Marie had met her end, Emma was tied spread-eagle and gagged as Shelby tried to work the knots free on her hands.

"Emma," Cain said, and slid next to the table. From her pocket she took Dalton's switchblade and cut her hands free and pulled the gag away from her mouth. "Are you okay?" Her face was caked in blood and the wound on her head was still seeping. Lou finished cutting away her bindings so Cain could hold her.

"I'm okay, honey," Emma said, but clutched Cain as if she'd disappear if she let go. "He didn't get a chance…" her voice faded away, and Cain didn't want to hear the end to that statement as much as Emma seemed not to want to say it. "I need to get out of here."

"I have to get you to a doctor, lass, so calm down." Cain held her as tight as she dared and exhaled into her hair as she shut her eyes to try to keep the tears from coming. But she couldn't deny the swell of emotion that actually having Emma in her arms brought from her heart.

"I'm sorry I left the house and let this happen," Emma said, as if trying to comfort her. "He told me as he was tying me up that he'd killed Merrick. Please tell me that's a lie."

"She's hurt but she's alive," Cain said, hoping it was still true. In all the excitement she hadn't had a chance to call and check on Merrick's condition. "Lou, give me your gun and bring the car closer."

"Cain," Shelby said from the next room, "they're gone. They ran out the back the moment Lionel and I arrived, and didn't have time to take Emma with them. If you want, we'll escort you to the emergency room."

"I don't want to go to the emergency room," Emma said, but as she stood up a sudden gush of blood ran down her legs. "No," she said as she doubled over.

Cain picked her up and cradled her in her arms and headed for the door. "Muriel, call ahead and see if Sam or Ellie will meet us at the hospital." As they headed away from the house, Cain promised herself to come back and burn the damn thing down. She needed no more monuments to the past, and the walls of that horror house had seen the last of its share of cruelty aimed at her family.

"Hang in there, lass," she whispered to a whimpering Emma, "we're almost there."

"Please, don't let us lose this baby," Emma said as she breathed hard. "Not now, we were so close."

"Just relax and I'll take care of you." Cain kissed her forehead and pressed the square of gauze Lou had handed her out of the first-aid kit to the side of Emma's head. "We'll be fine as long as you're okay."

"I don't want to lose—" Emma didn't finish the sentence and screamed before passing out again.

"Lou," Cain screamed in turn, "step on it. Emma." She held her so she could see her face, but the green eyes were closed and her features had softened. "Don't you dare give up on me," she told her as she lifted Emma into her lap. "Please, lass, don't give up on me."

Sam Casey was waiting outside as they drove up, and her partner Ellie was inside getting a room ready for Emma's arrival. "We'll take it from here, Cain," she said as Cain laid Emma on a stretcher. "Go have a seat in the waiting room, and I promise either Ellie or I will be out in a little while and tell you what's going on." It was the only explanation Cain got as they ran into the hospital with Emma.

The wait was excruciating, and as Cain sat and watched the clock, she vaguely realized those with her were watching her. They had a lot to discuss about what had happened today and what they needed to do about it, but right now none of it mattered. She willed Ellie or Sam to walk through the door, and when it opened she pulled her back away from the seat cushion only to see Shelby standing there. But Shelby approached Muriel instead of her, and her cousin didn't push her away when she sat next to her and took her hand.

"Cain," Ellie said from the door a short time later. "I need to talk to you before you go in to see her."

Ellie and Sam talked softly to Cain, neither of them smiling through the exchange. When Ellie stopped, Cain dropped to her knees and sobbed, Sam following her down and held her throughout her rare show of emotion. As she cried, Sam continued to talk.

"Let's get you cleaned up before you go in there and scare her, okay?" Ellie said to her when Cain stood up. She took her to the bathroom and gently wiped Cain's face with a towel. "Emma's a lucky woman," Ellie told her as she rinsed the towel in cold water again. "It's not often that a woman knows she's loved this much, but you've never kept it from her. That's what saved her today, and what will sustain her as she deals with the aftermath."

"Thanks," Cain said, feeling so tired she wanted to curl up beside Emma and sleep for a week. She stepped into the room and locked eyes with Emma. To Cain she appeared lost.

"I'll leave you two alone for a minute, then I'll come in and talk to you together," Ellie said and stepped out.

"I'm so sorry, lass," Cain said, going to the bed and taking Emma's hands in hers. "I'm sorry that the darkness of my life touched you like this."

"I knew you'd find me. Juan and Anthony kept taunting me and telling me you'd never figure it out in time, but I knew. Just like that day with Danny, you made it before I could get hurt."

"Shelby found you before I did."

"She didn't tell you where she was, though, did she?" Emma brought their hands up and kissed the back of Cain's. "You figured it out and you came for me. There's nothing else that means anything to me but that."

"Did Ellie talk to you?"

"If this one's a boy, I want to name him William, and I have a feeling it's going to be a boy." Emma kissed her hand again and tugged her forward to lie with her on the bed.

"What makes you so sure?" Cain asked, feeling the same relief as she had in the hall when Ellie had told her that Emma would be all right and so would the baby, with plenty of bed rest and peace.

Emma stayed on her back and smiled at Cain as she propped her head in her hand and placed the other one on her hip. "Because I've given birth to two Casey children, and this one strikes me as a William, but we'll only call him that when he's in trouble. The rest of the time he'll go by the name Billy Cain Casey, a charmer who'll skip through a blessed life because of what happened today. Sort of like two other Casey siblings I know and love."

"What happened today is something that won't be repeated, if I can help it."

"I know that, and he knows that." Emma took Cain's hand and placed it on her middle. "He's a Casey through and through, which means he's a fighter. He can't help it—he's ours."

"I love you, and you're no slouch in the fighter department." Cain kissed both cheeks and gently tweaked the tip of her nose. "And your number-one son is going to think you're the coolest with two black eyes." She tried to joke it off, but the sight of Emma so banged up was tearing at her heart.

"Can you do something for me?" Emma whispered.

"Anything you want is yours."

"Find him," she said with authority. "Find Juan and kill him. I don't care how you do it, or when you do it, but I do want you to tell me that it's done. I want him dead."

"That's my promise to you." Cain stayed until Ellie and Sam came by again and talked to them about Emma staying in the hospital for a few days, as a precaution. After that, Cain posted a man outside the door and Nick inside, in the chair she'd been using, so she could go check on Merrick.

Katlin was asleep in the chair next to the bed holding her lover's hand, but Merrick's eyes were open. "I owe you my life," Cain whispered to her after she kissed her forehead. "Thank you for taking care of what's most precious to me."

Merrick shook her head, not able to talk yet. From her expression Cain could tell she didn't believe her. "When you get out of here, you're coming to stay with us until you're back on your feet. The day that happens, Emma will expect you at eight as usual with that surly attitude in place. She wanted me to make sure and mention that last part to you." Merrick finally smiled and nodded. "You take care and I'll be by tomorrow to check on you. You bear no blame for what happened today." Cain shook her head and placed her hand against Merrick's cheek. "You did your job, got her out alive, and took a bullet for her. I owe you whatever you ask."

"We just want to do our jobs and be happy together." Katlin voiced what Merrick could not.

"And you'll have that, with every blessing I can give you." Cain kissed them both before going down to stay with Emma for the night. The kids and Ross came for a visit, and he asked for what Emma had requested, adding that he wanted Juan's head on a spike for what he'd almost done to his daughter.

"What are you thinking about, mobster?" Emma asked in the middle of the night. The hospital was quiet and Cain had taken her up on her invitation to hold her. "I promise you won't hurt me if you fall asleep."

"I was thinking about my mother, and I was enjoying watching you sleep."

"What about your mother?"

"That day you came for dinner and met my family for the first time, she told me something that stuck with me." Cain pulled the covers back and placed their hands over Emma's heart. "She told me she wished my Da had lived longer so he could've met you. I'd dated plenty before you, and she'd never said that about any of them before, not that she'd met of any of them at Sunday lunch. No one was ever in the same category as you."

"Why she'd say it about me?" Emma asked, turning on her side slightly.

"My mother wasn't what most would call an educated woman, but she was smarter than most people I've known. She figured something out that day, and because of it she said you two had a lot in common."

"You've never told me that."

"With everything we've been through in the years we've been together, it slipped my mind," Cain teased her. "She said you both had brains and a love for her child. You loved me and I'd never be able to live without what you brought to my life. She said you made me chase you until you caught me, like she'd done to one formidable Dalton Casey years before."

"She thinks I trapped you?" Emma laughed.

"Traps are things most want to get out of, my love, and that couldn't be further from the truth. No, I think she meant you showed me a life full of the possibilities that comes only when you accept that your other half has found you. She wanted me to embrace the chance you were giving me, and that way she could rest in peace."

"You did, and your mom would be proud of the life you've built. I love you and I'm looking forward to years of late-night talks with you."

Cain held Emma as she drifted off to sleep again and left her for a while in the morning as Lou returned with the news she'd asked for.

"They've disappeared like mist in a strong wind. The feds have warrants out on both Juan and Anthony, and Rodolfo asked for a sit-down at your earliest convenience. And to show you he's working in good faith, he promised to deliver Juan to you if he finds him first. Juan acted without his permission, and he said if he can do anything for Emma, just call."

Cain nodded and massaged the back of her neck. "And the rest?"

"In the excitement of yesterday, Remi and Ramon let Nunzio go, after a quick call to Hector Delarosa to tell him Nunzio didn't have the capital to pull off whatever his father had talked to him about." Lou pressed his back to the cinderblock wall and sighed. "The last they saw of Nunzio he was boarding a plane for New York, probably for his father's funeral."

"That's where he is," Remi said as she walked up. "I would've been here sooner, but I didn't want to get in your way. How's Emma?"

"We've been worried sick," Dallas added.

Cain told her, "I'm sure she's awake and wondering where I am, so go on in."

Remi followed Cain to the waiting room down the hall next to the window where visitors could see the new babies. "We've got a lot of loose ends," Remi said.

"We do, and I'm not going to stop until I find Juan Luis and rip his balls off with my bare hands, before I gut him and strangle him with his entrails. No matter what it takes or what it costs, I'm going to find him and kill him."

"Remember we're partners now, and you won't be searching alone. I'm here to help you, as are my father and brother. The load's not all on you anymore, Cain."

"My priority right now is Emma, and the baby she's carrying. The rest of it won't mean shit if anything happens to her."

"We'll take care of business or anything else you need from us."

"I'm only going to take the time I need to make sure Emma's fine at home, then we'll work together to make sure our problems aren't so troublesome in the future." Cain stood and walked her back to the room. When they opened the door, Emma was talking and laughing with Dallas.

Wherever Juan had run, Cain hoped he didn't stay hidden for long, and he wouldn't. Men like Juan were dangerous but they were predictable. They couldn't help but try again, whether they were able to succeed or not, and that was always their downfall. She watched Emma and smiled when she winked at her but was just as engrossed in whatever Dallas was telling her.

Juan would try again, but this time when the snake poked his head from his hole, Cain would be waiting to cut it off. No matter how long it took, she'd be ready, but for now she intended to enjoy her friends, her children, and most importantly the woman whom she chased until she'd been caught. "Mum, you were right about that," she whispered to the heavens. "Emma was my fate, but more importantly, she's the whole of what's good in my life."

Emma held her hand up, motioning her to come closer. "I'll let no one take from me what's mine. That's a lesson you and Da started teaching me, but Emma's completed my education." Happiness was something you accepted like a gift, and after Cain took Emma's hand and sat on the edge of the bed, she leaned forward and kissed her.

"I love when you do that," Emma said to her with a relaxed smile.

"Sometimes I need to show you what's in here." Cain tapped over her heart. "I'm just glad you're inclined to see."

Right at that moment it's all that mattered. Cain would gladly face the rest when she had to, but right now the ones she loved were safe. She had a lot to celebrate, but she wouldn't give in to the complete joy of it until the black cloud looming on the horizon was gone.

♣

About the Author

Ali Vali - Ali lives right outside New Orleans with her partner of many years. As a writer, she couldn't ask for a better, more beautiful place, so full of real-life characters to fuel the imagination. When she isn't writing, working in the yard, cheering for the LSU Tigers, or riding her bicycle, Ali makes a living in the nonprofit sector.

Ali has written *The Devil Inside, Carly's Sound, The Devil Unleashed, Second Season, Deal With The Devil,* and the soon to be published, *Calling The Dead,* all from Bold Strokes Books.

Books Available From Bold Strokes Books

Deal with the Devil by Ali Vali. New Orleans crime boss Cain Casey brings her fury down on the men who threatened her family, and blood and bullets fly. (978-1-60282-012-8)

Naked Heart by Jennifer Fulton. When a sexy ex-CIA agent sets out to seduce and entrap a powerful CEO, there's more to this plan than meets the eye...or the flogger. (978-1-60282-011-1)

Heart of the Matter by KI Thompson. TV newscaster Kate Foster is Professor Ellen Webster's dream girl, but Kate doesn't know Ellen exists...until an accident changes everything. (978-1-60282-010-4)

Heartland by Julie Cannon. When political strategist Rachel Stanton and dude ranch owner Shivley McCoy collide on an empty country road, fate intervenes. (978-1-60282-009-8)

Shadow of the Knife by Jane Fletcher. Militia Rookie Ellen Mittal has no idea of just how complex and dangerous her life is about to become. A Celaeno series adventure romance. (978-1-60282-008-1)

To Protect and Serve by VK Powell. Lieutenant Alex Troy is caught in the paradox of her life—to hold steadfast to her professional oath or to protect the woman she loves. (978-1-60282-007-4)

Deeper by Ronica Black. Former homicide detective Erin McKenzie and her fiancée Elizabeth Adams couldn't be any happier—until the not so distant past comes knocking at the door. (978-1-60282-006-7)

The Lonely Hearts Club by Radclyffe. Take three friends, add two ex-lovers and several new ones, and the result is a recipe for explosive rivalries and incendiary romance. (978-1-60282-005-0)

Venus Besieged by Andrews & Austin. Teague Richfield heads for Sedona and the sensual arms of psychic astrologer Callie Rivers for a much needed romantic reunion. (978-1-60282-004-3)

Branded Ann by Merry Shannon. Pirate Branded Ann raids a merchant vessel to obtain a treasure map and gets more than she bargained for with the widow Violet. (978-1-60282-003-6)

American Goth by JD Glass. Trapped by an unsuspected inheritance and guided only by the guardian who holds the secret to her future, Samantha Cray fights to fulfill her destiny. (978-1-60282-002-9)

Learning Curve by Rachel Spangler. Ashton Clarke is perfectly content with her life until she meets the intriguing Professor Carrie Fletcher, who isn't looking for a relationship with anyone. (978-1-60282-001-2)

Place of Exile by Rose Beecham. Sheriff's detective Jude Devine struggles with ghosts of her past and an ex-lover who still haunts her dreams. (978-1-933110-98-1)

Fully Involved by Erin Dutton. A love that has smoldered for years ignites when two women and one little boy come together in the aftermath of tragedy. (978-1-933110-99-8)

Heart 2 Heart by Julie Cannon. Suffering from a devastating personal loss, Kyle Bain meets Lane Connor, and the chance for happiness suddenly seems possible. (978-1-60282-000-5)

Queens of Tristaine: Tristaine Book Four by Cate Culpepper. When a deadly plague stalks the Amazons of Tristaine, two warrior lovers must return to the place of their nightmares to find a cure. (978-1-933110-97-4)

The Crown of Valencia by Catherine Friend. Ex-lovers can really mess up your life…even, as Kate discovers, if they've traveled back to the 11th century! (978-1-933110-96-7)

Mine by Georgia Beers. What happens when you've already given your heart and love finds you again? Courtney McAllister is about to find out. (978-1-933110-95-0)

House of Clouds by KI Thompson. A sweeping saga of an impassioned romance between a Northern spy and a Southern sympathizer, set amidst the upheaval of a nation under siege. (978-1-933110-94-3)

Winds of Fortune by Radclyffe. Provincetown local Deo Camara agrees to rehab Dr. Nita Burgoyne's historic home, but she never said anything about mending her heart. (978-1-933110-93-6)

Focus of Desire by Kim Baldwin. Isabel Sterling is surprised when she wins a photography contest, but no more than photographer Natasha Kashnikova. Their promo tour becomes a ticket to romance. (978-1-933110-92-9)

Blind Leap by Diane and Jacob Anderson-Minshall. A Golden Gate Bridge suicide becomes suspect when a filmmaker's camera shows a different story. Yoshi Yakamota and the Blind Eye Detective Agency uncover evidence that could be worth killing for. (978-1-933110-91-2)

Wall of Silence, 2nd ed. by Gabrielle Goldsby. Life takes a dangerous turn when jaded police detective Foster Everett meets Riley Medeiros, a woman who isn't afraid to discover the truth no matter the cost. (978-1-933110-90-5)

Mistress of the Runes by Andrews & Austin. Passion ignites between two women with ties to ancient secrets, contemporary mysteries, and a shared quest for the meaning of life. (978-1-933110-89-9)

Sheridan's Fate by Gun Brooke. A dynamic, erotic romance between physical therapist Lark Mitchell and businesswoman Sheridan Ward set in the scorching hot days and humid, steamy nights of San Antonio. (978-1-933110-88-2)

Vulture's Kiss by Justine Saracen. Archeologist Valerie Foret, heir to a terrifying task, returns in a powerful desert adventure set in Egypt and Jerusalem. (978-1-933110-87-5)

Rising Storm by JLee Meyer. The sequel to First Instinct takes our heroines on a dangerous journey instead of the honeymoon they'd planned. (978-1-933110-86-8)

Not Single Enough by Grace Lennox. A funny, sexy modern romance about two lonely women who bond over the unexpected and fall in love along the way. (978-1-933110-85-1)

Second Season by Ali Vali. A romance set in New Orleans amidst betrayal, Hurricane Katrina, and the new beginnings hardship and heartbreak sometimes make possible. (978-1-933110-83-7)

Such a Pretty Face by Gabrielle Goldsby. A sexy, sometimes humorous, sometimes biting contemporary romance that gently exposes the damage to heart and soul when we fail to look beneath the surface for what truly matters. (978-1-933110-84-4)

Hearts Aflame by Ronica Black. A poignant, erotic romance between a hard-driving businesswoman and a solitary vet. Packed with adventure and set in the harsh beauty of the Arizona countryside. (978-1-933110-82-0)

Red Light by JD Glass. Tori forges her path as an EMT in the New York City 911 system while discovering what matters most to herself and the woman she loves. (978-1-933110-81-3)

Honor Under Siege by Radclyffe. Secret Service agent Cameron Roberts struggles to protect her lover while searching for a traitor who just may be another woman with a claim on her heart. (978-1-933110-80-6)

Dark Valentine by Jennifer Fulton. Danger and desire fuel a high stakes cat-and-mouse game when an attorney and an endangered witness team up to thwart a killer. (978-1-933110-79-0)

The Devil Inside by Ali Vali. The head of a New Orleans crime organization falls for a woman who turns her world upside down. (978-1-933110-30-1)

The Devil Unleashed by Ali Vali. As the heat of violence rises, so does the passion. A Casey Family crime saga. (978-1-933110-61-5)